AT THE THRESHOLD OF THE UNIVERSE

T. A. BRUNO

First published by Tom Bruno Author 2022

This novel is entirely a work of fiction. The names, characters, and incidents portrayed in it are the work of the author's imagination. Any resemblance to actual persons, living or dead, events, or localities is entirely coincidental.

Cover design by Daniel Schmelling
Interior artwork by Jason Michael Hall
Maps by T. A. Bruno

First edition: May 2022

OTHER BOOKS BY T. A. BRUNO

The Song of Kamaria Trilogy:

In the Orbit of Sirens
On the Winds of Quasars

AUTHOR'S NOTE

The following story takes place hours after the events of *On the Winds of Quasars*. Some readers may find some of the contents of this book disturbing due to the darker elements within, including violence and horrors, both implied and realized. This story also features a diverse cast of characters, including people from the Deaf Community who use Sol-Sign, a language based on American Sign Language, but with its own flair. I have had a lot of help ensuring it is authentic as I can make it, and I hope I did it justice. A Dramatis Personae is included in the back of this novel for reference.

It's time to fight for Kamaria.
—*T.A.*

For Tommy Bruno.
Nine years old and dreaming of adventures on faraway worlds.
Thank you for waiting. You have arrived.

Odysseus City Floating Platforms

Elevation: 400 meters
Full Rotation: 12 Hours

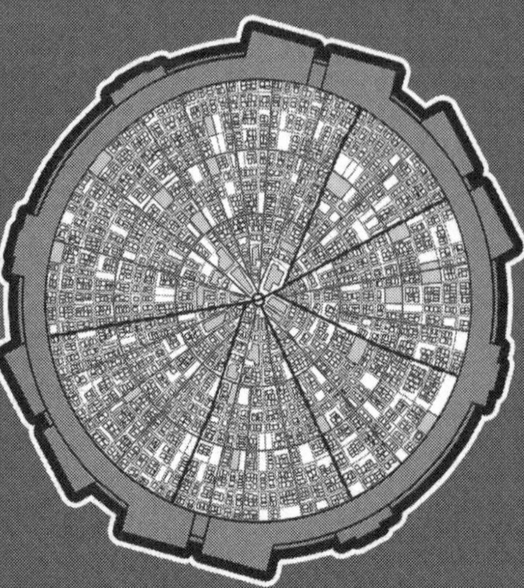

Amethyst

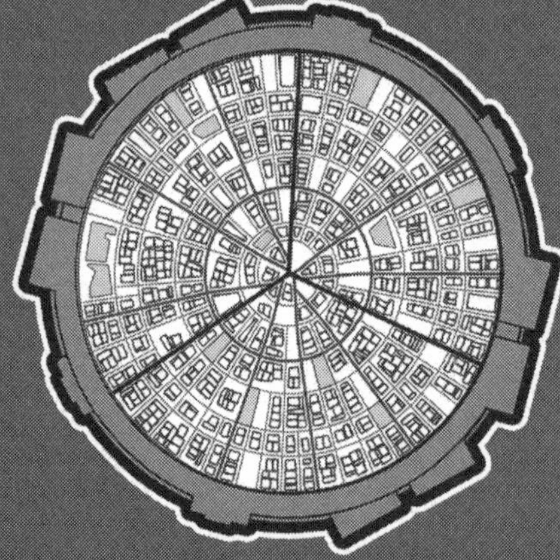

Ruby

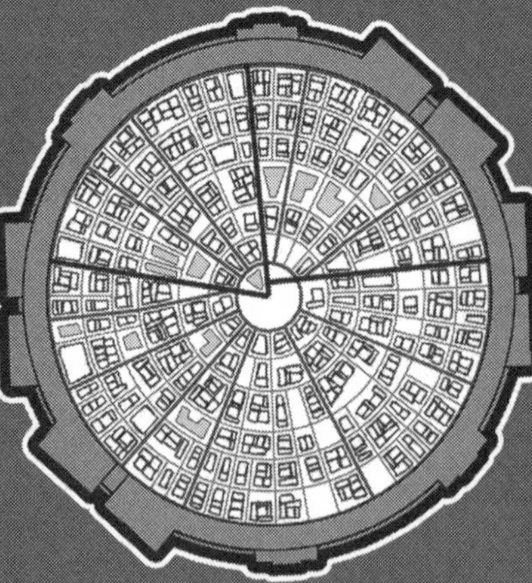

Carnelian

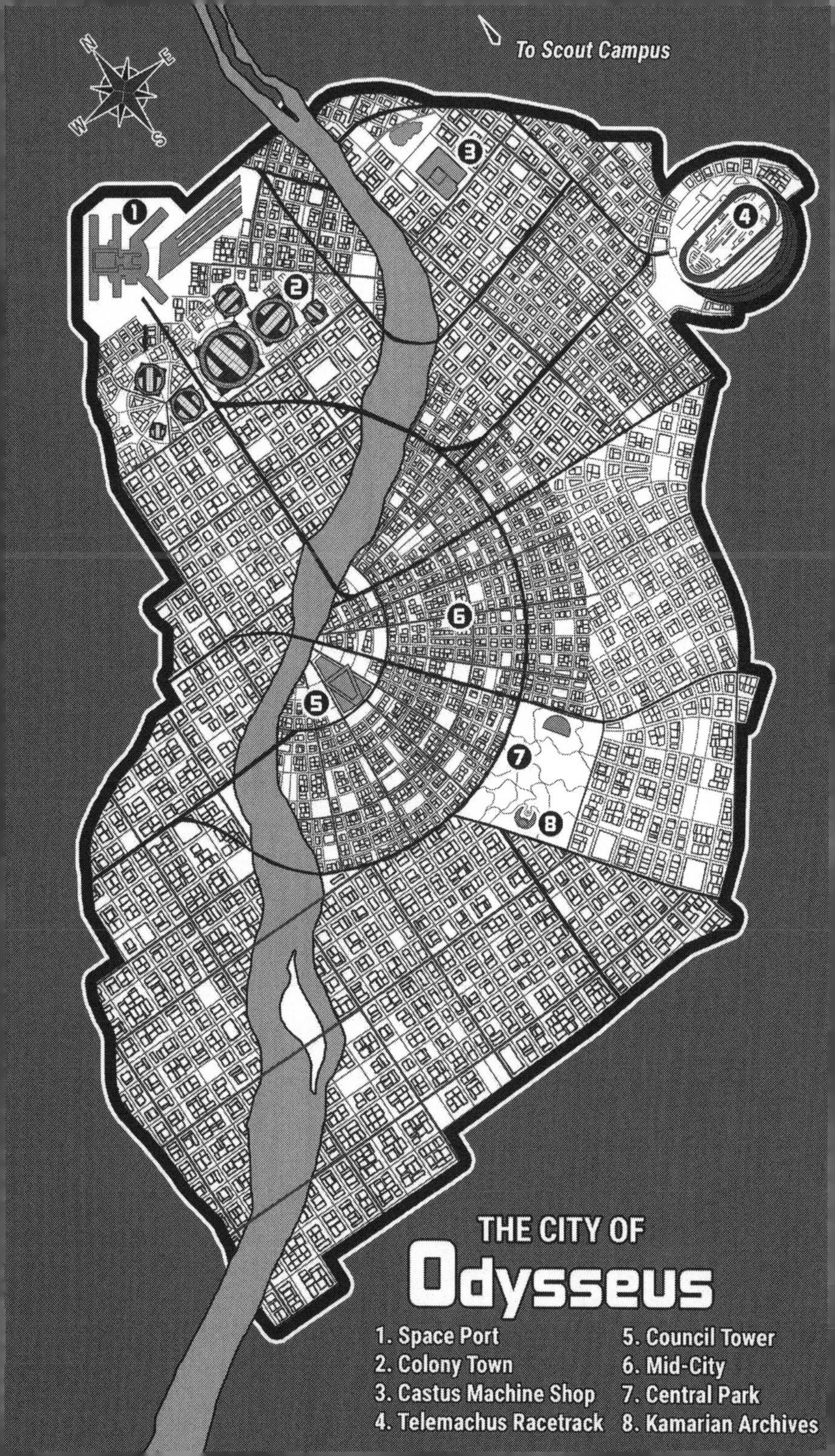

To Scout Campus

THE CITY OF Odysseus

1. Space Port
2. Colony Town
3. Castus Machine Shop
4. Telemachus Racetrack
5. Council Tower
6. Mid-City
7. Central Park
8. Kamarian Archives

THE STORY SO FAR . . .

Humanity was chased away from the Sol System.

They arrived on the planet Kamaria and struggled to adapt.

The natives, the auk'nai, were wary of the humans.

In their desperation to adapt, humanity unwittingly unleashed Nhymn, the Siren.

Nhymn wreaked havoc on Kamaria.

The Siren was stopped when humans and auk'nai banded together.

Nhymn was sent into the deepness of space, never to be seen again.

Twenty-six years passed . . .

The Daunoren of the Spirit Song Mountain was brutally slain.

Two humans were kidnapped from their home.

They fled their captor but were forced to trek across the continent.

A monster pursued them.

In time, they learned they were different than other humans.

They were vessels for Sirens.

They destroyed the monster, only to discover that a new menace had been resurrected.
One was reunited with her family.

The other was taken.

Now, a leviathan lurks on the Howling Shore, and the humans have come to face it.

1
SHEPHERD OF THE
SHACKLED

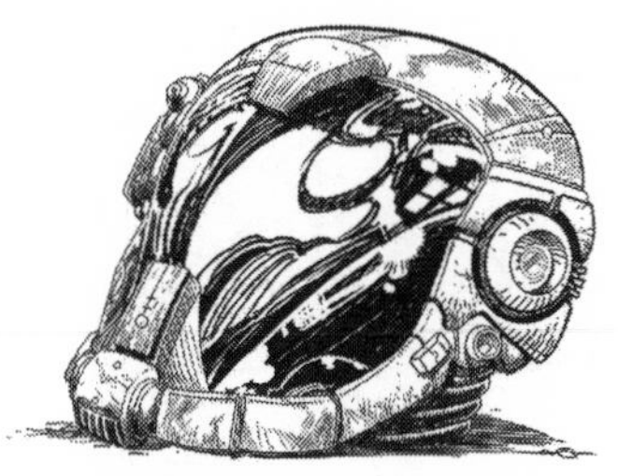

ONE

"LISTEN UP!" SERGEANT JESS Combs shouted over the roaring engine of the transport ship. Nine marines strapped into their seats straightened. "The battle ahead will be harder than anything you may have been trained for. The Undriel are master deceivers, and they will use every trick in their arsenal the moment we engage them."

Denton Castus sat in the back of the ship, armored in a full combat suit. He was no soldier. Beneath the metal exterior, he was just a starship mechanic from Ganymede looking for his son. He was in his early fifties, but a lifetime of working in a machine shop and hiking in the wilderness had kept him physically fit. Denton had light skin, messy brown hair complete with a bushy beard, and green eyes that he kept locked to the ship's floor. His mind stirred with worry, horror, and loudest of all—hope.

Denton had thought he'd left the Undriel in the past. He grew up watching news vids of the machines absorbing people, like a nightmare made real. Focusing on work dulled the terror but never extinguished it. As a result, he became an excellent mechanic under the crushing worry of the ever-growing shadow of the Undriel. Coming to Kamaria was a breath of fresh air—the Undriel stayed in the Sol System, and the shadow was gone.

Or so everyone thought.

Hours before Denton had boarded the transport ship, there was an incident. The Undriel revealed themselves on Kamaria, where they'd been lurking under the ruby waves of the Howling Shore for almost three hundred years. They weren't gone. They were *waiting*.

A lump formed in Denton's throat. He was choked by his own regret, his blood threatening to pop his skull. The shadows that haunted his youth had curled their claws around his son, Cade, and pulled him into the unknown. Cade had been taken right in front of Denton, and there was nothing he could do about it—nothing but go hoarse from screaming as he felt the cold death of hope crash over him. His blood was ice, and his mind was pounding.

Cade was *right* there. And then he wasn't.

Eventually, Denton channeled the frost in his veins. He boarded the transport ship, leaving his wife and daughter, Eliana and Nella, back in Odysseus City. He would find Cade, even if the rescue killed him.

As the ship raced closer to the Howling Shore, Denton couldn't help but wonder what he would find. Would it be his son? Or would it be a machine?

Logic dictated that the Undriel would absorb Cade into their network, remake him into one of their own. Hope demanded that Denton try to find him before that happened. Denton clutched tightly to that hope and wouldn't let it go. It was his shield against the terrible thoughts that scratched at his sanity.

Hope was Denton's lifeline.

Corporal Rafa Ghanem broke Denton's train of thought with a nudge. "You stick with me. We'll try and find your son." Rafa kept his eyes locked on Denton's. The corporal had recently been promoted, although he'd admitted to Denton that he felt like it wasn't deserved. His men had been killed in the same attack, and the guilt had stayed with the corporal. Rafa was a good man, not motivated by rank but by a need to protect his people. Denton thought he deserved the promotion regardless. Rafa would have plenty of time to show the world why he deserved it.

They would all be tested in this new war. Humanity was about to face an impossible enemy for a second time, and they would have to do it without auk'nai support.

Talulo and the rest of the auk'nai would not be joining this fight. Humanity had caused the native Kamarians enough problems. Recently, the advanced race of bird-humanoids had left the city of Odysseus to make a new nest in the Unforgotten Garden. They chose the *Telemachus's* wreckage as a home, and Denton could definitely feel the giant middle finger they were thrusting upward by picking that particular spot. Not only did Denton understand it, he also agreed.

Humanity had brought all their problems to Kamaria. Since early colonization, the auk'nai had lost the city of Apusticus, fought a major battle against the Siren called Nhymn, and had their sacred deity—the Daunoren—slain. Now the Undriel were on their way to destroy what little was left.

Why should they help us now?

Without Talulo around, the only other person on the transport ship Denton knew besides Rafa was Sergeant Jess Combs. He had known Jess since they both entered the Scout Program years back. These days, she was busy commanding a squad of marines called the Dray'va Teeth. Jess was the same age as Denton, in her early fifties, but built like a tank. She had shaved her head into a short mohawk for this battle, and it reminded Denton of the way she had looked when he first met her. Jess had reverted back to her cold, hard state with the threat of the old enemy reborn. She was a warrior, trained to fight the Undriel in the Sol System. An old score left unsettled.

The other marines Denton only knew by their nicknames—Bell, Cook, Akinyemi, Cruz, Marathon, Ortiz, and Wood.

"I reckon we hit 'em fast enough they'll go down fer good. Ain't that right, Sarge?" The familiar Ganymede drawl came from the female private known as Bell. She was much younger than Denton and must not have grown up on Ganymede, but she'd definitely been raised by people who had. Bell had the same accent as everyone from the backwater colony, the Arrow of Hope, which Denton had called home in his pre-Kamaria days. Her short blond hair accented her blue eyes and bright smile. Bell was as cheerful as she was deadly. No matter their demeanor, they were all Tvashtar marines. Although humanity had left the Tvashtar colony behind in the Sol System, the name stuck with them as a symbol of pride.

"That's the hope," Jess said with a curt nod.

Private Marathon leaned over his particle rifle. He had black, slicked-back hair, aerodynamic in appearance. "Not a problem for me. I always like to do things quick." He bumped forearms with Private Cook.

"Not something I'd be bragging about, neh?" said Lance Corporal Inaya Akinyemi. She was a tall, lean woman with dark brown skin and hair tied in tight rows down to her shoulders. Pieces of gold were intertwined within braids. It made her look wise and dangerous.

Jess looked at her squad. "We do this right—kick their asses early. We stop all future battles."

The nine marines stomped their feet gave a collective *"Oo-rah."*

"How many of them are there?" Private Wood asked. He had dark brown skin and a cybernetically enhanced eye that linked with his long-barreled sniper rifle. His combat suit differed from others, favoring stealth instead of movement, power, and defense. His arms were bare except for a thin mechanical structure that helped him lift and steady his powerful rifle. A plated cloak draped over him to conceal him from sensor capabilities.

"Can't know for sure," Jess stated, "expect more than you're assuming."

"We'll count 'em after they're all good and dead," Cook muttered. His accent reminded Denton of his friend Fergus Reid, a fellow scout from Callisto, Jupiter's terraformed garden moon. Everyone who lived on it had similar accents. Like Bell, Cook was too young to have been on Callisto, but good odds were that his parents came from there.

Marathon said, "I bet Sarge has been waiting for this day, yeh?"

Jess's face remained stone. Her squadron smiled and agreed, but Denton could tell they had it wrong. Jess never wanted to see the Undriel again. They were part of a life she had happily left behind. It was as if she'd molted her skin and now was being forced to pull it back on.

"You're entering the combat zone. Get ready to drop." The voice came from over the comm channel in the ship. Lieutenant Mido Sharif was their overhead command for the foreseeable future. Although he wouldn't be joining the fight, he'd be their tactical operator from orbit. Command was designated to the unfinished interstellar starship called the *Infinite Aria*. The *Aria* wasn't capable of escaping the Undriel—it was only barely capable of providing stationary orbit for combat view.

The transport ship dropped altitude. Everyone slammed their helmets on and activated their heads-up displays. "Get ready, Dray'va Teeth!" Jess shouted, and a red light pulsed inside the transport ship.

"Remember, stick with me," Rafa reminded Denton.

Denton nodded and felt his lungs trap air, refusing to let more than a leak exhale. His blood rushed to his head and neck, and chills ripped through his body. Denton couldn't tell if it was the nervous energy of fighting or if it was fear of finding that his son was already among the enemy.

The ship landed with a thud. The marines stood and turned toward the access ramp. Particle rifles activated, the collider cylinders on each whirring with red light. The small jump-jets laced into each of their combat suits warmed up, emitting a faint orange glow. These would allow the user to propel themselves around the battlefield in short bursts, a necessary functionality when fighting enemies that could move in impossible ways.

Warm sea air rushed into the ship as the ramp lowered. Before it fully hit the ground, the marines thrust out into the open field. "Let's go, Castus!" Rafa shouted, and propelled himself forward.

Outside the ramp, a large field of tall orange grass swayed near an elevated cliff ledge that led down to a shore filled with crimson water. It was sunset, giving the sky a purple-and-pink hue as stars began to peek at the chaos about to unfold in the tall grass. The dueling Kamarian moons floated high above the horizon.

In the air above the cliff, an Undriel masterclass ship called the *Devourer* glared at the incoming marines. Waterfalls poured from the giant machine's flanks, having recently emerged from the red ocean's depths after over two centuries of being trapped below the waves. It was a sharp-edged hulk of tangled metal and deep-sea coral and weeds.

The cliff ledge began to fill with twisted shadows, shapes that came out of nightmares and haunted houses. Undriel footsoldiers crawled up from the lower shore to meet the marines head-on in the orange grass. These were the faces of the old enemy. The sea had partially claimed them over hundreds of years. Barnacles, coral, and seaweed draped over their metal exteriors.

The Undriel footsoldiers took on a few common forms between them. They all resembled elements of old Earth insects in design, having originated in the Sol System. To the Kamarian-born soldiers, these shapes would be more alien than anything they had previously seen.

Inside the tangled mess of insectoid-shaped metal was a human occupant, no more than a severed head wearing a mechanical crown. It was currently unknown how aware these human remains were of their bodies' actions. Autopsies from the war in the Sol System showed that the Undriel crowns created an invisible stasis field around their human components, preserving them perfectly for eternity. The human inside each machine was still alive, but it was unknown why they would attack their fellow people so quickly. The Undriel were still very mysterious in their ways. It was endlessly frustrating to fight an enemy that was so misunderstood.

What was easy to understand was their combat capability. Undriel frames concealed a variety of weaponry. Their arms and legs could uncoil and straighten into sharp blades or rotate at the elbow to reveal a particle gun. They often interchanged these weapons as they fought. Most Undriel wore special cloaks to conceal their weaponry from the naked eye. These cloaks were infused with technology that could also block most sensors. New recruits absorbed on the battlefield would often be cloakless. The fewer cloaks on the enemy combatants, the more comrades you were forced to shoot.

Absorption was a two-fold strategy. It not only brought a new Undriel soldier into their army, but it was also gruesome. Witnesses would be left in a state of panic, making them easier to fight. When an Undriel absorbed a person, it looked like they were devouring them. On a technical level, the Undriel pulled the victim through their own body, sacrificing parts of themselves to create a second version. It was a violent affair that left a lot of blood spilled on the battlefield. Usually, only the head remained intact, while the rest was chewed up by the Undriel's serrated metal teeth.

Most of the Sol System war survivors had only seen these nightmares in news vids and research papers. Now, they would see them up close.

The marines raced into the battle, shooting toward the approaching metal army as they moved into position. Fifty marine transport ships began deploying ordinances. Shields—thick metal sheets with intertwined defensive components—launched out of each ship and slammed into the ground ahead to cover the marines. Rockets and particle beams lanced across the sky toward the *Devourer*, pocking its exterior with explosions. The world around them was screaming with Hellsfire.

Denton and Rafa slammed behind one of the shields as a line of soldiers got into position. Jess shouted orders over the squad's comm channel. "Here they come. Akinyemi, hit them!"

The lance corporal responded, "Launching!"

A series of loud bangs followed by traces of light arced up high into the sky from behind Denton. The mortars sailed overhead and pounded into the front line of Undriel. Jess waited for the explosions to cease, then leaned over the top of her shield and shouted, "Fire!"

Denton obeyed, as did the others. They assaulted the shoreline through the heavy mortar smoke. Denton had no way of knowing if his son was among the Undriel footsoldiers ahead, but if so, it was too late to save him now.

The first line of Undriel footsoldiers burst into view through the thickening smoke. Their particle blasts pinned the marines behind their shields. "They're gettin' close!" Bell shouted over the comm.

"Prepare the knockback," Jess ordered. Rafa pulled a lever on the side of the shield that he and Denton were using for cover. The pounding of Undriel footsteps grew louder, and suddenly Denton got an up-close glimpse of the enemy.

It was only for a fraction of a second as the Undriel came over the top of their shield. It had four arms, each a curved blade. Its eyes beat down on Denton with white-hot intensity. It had been dyed a deep crimson red by the centuries of algae assaulting its frame underwater. The sea was fresh on its body, with barnacles and other tendrils of ocean life protruding from anywhere they could make a home.

Rafa slammed the lever on the back of the shield, and a blast of energy erupted from the side facing the enemy. The Undriel exploded into fragments from the impact. The grass and dirt in front of the entire line of shields had been disintegrated.

"Give them Hells!" Jess shouted. They leaned over the top of the shields again and fired into the crowd of footsoldiers recovering from the knockback. The shields needed time to recharge, leaving the entire line vulnerable until another knockback was loaded.

"Our position is compromised!" Marathon alerted over the comm. On the far left side of their line of defense, the Undriel had worked their way around his shield. Marathon and the other two marines he was with, Cruz and Cook, were engaged in close-quarters combat. Particle shots were giving them support from a distance—Wood's sniper rifle.

"Ghanem, Castus, provide support fire. Bell, Akinyemi, keep

the pressure on the front line," Jess commanded. Denton and Rafa turned to their left and picked their shots on the Undriel soldiers attacking their fellow marines.

Marathon extended a heated blade from his gauntletted wrist to fight back an Undriel soldier. He hacked at the machine, removing its right-side arms. Cruz and Cook moved into a better position, dealing with their own pursuing enemies.

"Marathon!" Cruz shouted.

Marathon was taken to the ground by the Undriel he was fighting. He brought his fist up to the machine's face as it was snapping with its sharp teeth. A pulse of blue electricity burst from his fist and blew the Undriel's head clean off. The rest of the body continued its assault. Marathon jump-jetted his way out from under the headless machine, pivoted, and slammed his heated blade into the Undriel's core. He withdrew the blade as the machine sputtered on the ground.

With a tremendous crash, an Undriel behemoth burst through the shield behind Marathon. It was much larger than most of the footsoldiers, nearly triple the size. Its top half was thick and rounded, with heavy armor plating and sharp spikes protruding from every angle. A long-pronged horn protruded from its head. It grabbed Marathon with one of its giant-clawed arms and ripped the marine backward so fast he was folded in half at his torso. Then the behemoth engulfed Marathon into its core in a mess of flying sparks, blood, and viscera.

"NO!" Cruz shouted as she assaulted the behemoth.

Denton noticed something with the absorption process. The Undriel had complications as it tried to take in Marathon. At the end, there would normally at least be a spider-bot holding the victim's human head, but this time, only blood spilled out of the machine.

Marathon had been killed, but the absorption had failed.

More rockets flew overhead, and another volley of mortars followed. The world roared with weaponry as the *Devourer* launched a beam of high-powered energy. Behind Denton, the transport ship they'd arrived on exploded into fire and dust.

"Push forward!" Jess Combs shouted.

Rafa thrust his arm into the shield, and it clipped to his gauntlet. Each soldier in the line did the same, and they marched the shields forward. A roar overhead announced the squadron of Matador starfighters as they cut through the sky above. The *Devourer* focused on the Matadors, launching more particle beams into the night. The sun had sunk beyond the horizon, and the darkness was cut by lances of energy whipping back and forth across the cliffside.

"I don't believe it," Wood said over the comm, "the Undriel are retreating."

"We got them on the run!" Bell gave out a Ganymede holler that Denton could still make out in the chaos of battle.

"Keep the line. We don't know if it's a trap," Jess ordered cautiously.

The *Devourer* unleashed a pulse of red energy, catching some of the Matador starfighters in its shockwave and downing them. Explosions cracked against the ocean. The Undriel ship rotated on-axis, revealing a new verticality that gave it the appearance of a castle tower instead of a starship. A shimmering field of electricity surrounded its hull. The Undriel footsoldiers retreated toward the *Devourer*, passing through the shield of light and becoming absorbed into the hull itself. The *Devourer* braced itself against the cliffside and then went silent.

The remaining Matador starfighters launched a round of heavy ordinance into the *Devourer*. The shimmering light absorbed the particle blasts and rockets, then glowed brighter.

"Ceasefire!" Lieutenant Sharif said over the comm from orbit. "Our attacks are only making that barrier stronger." The weapons stopped, and for a moment, the only sound was the sea breeze and the steady hum of the electrical barrier on the *Devourer*.

"What happens now?" Denton asked Rafa through heavy breaths, not realizing how exhausted he was. The corporal had no answer.

"Hold position, await orders." Command assessed the situation and piped information to each squad leader on the ground. Small fires crackled in the tall grass, slowly extinguishing as the breeze coming off the sea blew them out like candles on a birthday cake.

"Dray'va Teeth, regroup on me," Jess ordered. "Sounds like we're establishing a forward base here until further notice." The transport ships began self-converting into various buildings with armored defenses. Marines fortified the line of shields to be more wall-like and organized. The chaos of battle had been replaced with the chaos of defense preparations.

Denton wondered about the gruesome death of Marathon as he helped prepare the defenses with the rest of the marines. *The absorption failed.* He kept churning over what that could mean in his mind. *If the absorption could fail, maybe the Undriel didn't chance it with Cade yet.*

The hope Denton clutched began to shine brighter.

Supplies were sent to the front line via express vehicles called Darts. These high-speed capsules were shot from Odysseus City Command on one-way trips, designed only for emergency resupplies.

Three forward bases were constructed within an hour—North, Central, and South. They were a series of block-shaped structures made of converted transport ships and shields for defense. These temporary structures could revert back into transport ships and leave if a retreat was ordered. Turret guns and other special weaponry were brought in to secure each of the sites. Soon, they had three formidable fortresses. Orbital imagery from the *Infinite Aria* kept an eye on the Undriel ship, ensuring they didn't try and flank by using the ocean as a cover. The *Devourer* stood like a castle on the shore, glowing with refractive light against a backdrop of red sea and stars.

The battle lines were forged, and the defenses were strengthened. Within these three bases were all available human combatants, with only a small force reserved in Odysseus City as a final defense if things went horribly wrong. It would be up to these five thousand soldiers and fifty Matador starfighters. Five battalions and two squadrons.

There would be no reinforcements.

Humanity was still an endangered species thanks to the Undriel's efforts in the Sol System. Their numbers were only in the fifty thousands, with most of the population remaining civilians. These statistics allowed Denton to be part of the fighting. There simply weren't enough people to attack the Undriel head-on, and anyone willing was given a chance to do so.

Marines were posted on the front line behind the shields at all times, with live reports coming in on any changes in the *Devourer*'s condition. The *Infinite Aria* was buzzing with strategies to take advantage of this early stage of combat. But for now, there wasn't much to do but observe.

Denton removed his combat armor in a staging room concealed within the middle of Central Base. He felt like he'd been wearing it for months. He rubbed his palm against the spiral-shaped scar on his chest.

"Now that's a cool scar," Bell said from a suit removal station on the other side of the room. Denton hadn't noticed her there. "How's a fella get something like that?"

Denton sighed. "It's hard to explain. I'd rather not have it, honestly." He pulled a shirt on and slid his arms into his old scout jacket.

"Nobody wants 'em, but you gotta wear them regardless. Might as well get a good story from it. So, what's the story of that bad boy?" Bell asked. She finished getting out of her suit and dressed herself in fresh clothes before walking over.

"I was bolted by one of Nhymn's nezzarforms," Denton said, remembering Nhymn's stone pets. He slung his bag over his shoulder. "Back before the battle with the Siren."

"I knew it! Man, you really are *the* Denton Castus, aren'tcha!" Bell smiled, and her blue eyes flashed. "My moms came from the

Arrow on Ganymede. You're a friggin' legend to us!"

"Legend? Hells." Denton looked away from her, embarrassed.

"I'll have to get you to meet my folks one day. They'd love that! Maybe you'll recognize 'em." She smiled and added, "Hey, a few of us are about to have some dinner. Come sit with us. Cook makes the best food, you'll see."

Denton was starving. He nodded and followed Bell through Central Base to where the other marines were hanging out near a small campfire. Each of them was out of combat gear until their shift on the wall came up. If needed, they could have their suits back on in under forty seconds. They were discussing the battle that day. For many, it was their first live exercise.

Bell took a seat near Cruz and waved Denton over.

"Would ye like something ta eat?" Cook asked. "I found some lovely ingredients out in tha field t'day, while we were settin' up base. Some shore mushrooms and Howling chives, ta name a few. They got the grit o' the sea in 'em! Good stuff, really."

"Yeah. I appreciate it," Denton said as he sat next to Wood, the quiet sniper with the cybernetic eye. The man nodded to Denton, and he nodded back. Cook grabbed a bowl and spooned in something from the pot he was boiling. It was an assortment of vegetables, with some chunks of meat slathered in a mushroom sauce. He handed it over. Denton took a bite, and his mouth exploded with flavor. Cook earned his nickname.

"We can'nae fight on an empty stomach, y'know," Cook said. He passed a plate to Private Cruz. She had sharp features that made her look tough as nails. Her short black hair was parted, and her tanned skin didn't hide the dark shadows under her eyes.

"I don't think I'll be fighting anymore. I'm no soldier," Denton said.

Cruz huffed as she took a bite. "Had me fooled. Damn good aim for a civvie."

"He's no civvie," Bell corrected her with pride. "This guy took down a Siren. Bet your ass we got a ringer on our side."

"Oi!" Cook slapped an oily hand against his forehead. "I thought I recognized yer name, fella! I figured the Denton Castus we heard about growing up would have been an old-timer by now. Just a raggedy old wrinkled thing of a man, ya ken?"

"I think that was a compliment." Denton couldn't help but smile.

"'Course it was!" Cook rubbed his hand against his pants and reached down to grab something from behind the log he was sitting on. He pulled a bottle out of his bag and held it up for the others to see. "T'aint much, but I'd be honored if ye'd take a shot of this with me."

It was a bottle of Arrow whiskey that originated before the Sol System exodus. Denton thought he had one of the last bottles of it in existence, and here was this man from Callisto holding another of the rare liquors. Denton didn't know what to say.

"You've been holding out!" Bell shouted, and playfully whacked Cook on the arm.

"What do ya think? I kin pour us a few shots fer everyone," Cook offered.

"Sign me up," Cruz said.

The others agreed. Cook produced a few shot glasses for the marines and chatted away while getting the ceremony ready. "Aye yeah. Got this from a gurl I was seein' at the time. She gave it to me as a birthday gift a bit back—probably didn't know what she had, honestly. I mean that two ways, if ya catch me. Funny thing is, I knew she was seein' this other fella on the side, and I was about to break it off anyway. I took this bottle and shortly after said goodbye to the lass, wishing her the best with her new boy. Think they got married, they did. Anyways"—Cook poured the last shot glass and inspected it with his eye—"I vowed to save the bottle until I had a chance to screw someone the same way she was screwin' me. The Undriel were so kind as to allow me to crack it open today."

Bell snorted. "Well, cheers!"

They knocked back the shots and recoiled from the bite. Bell laughed when Cruz coughed loudly. Denton was the only one to notice Cook pour one more shot and place it gently on the empty log next to where he was sitting.

"You're looking for your son, right?" Wood asked quietly as the others conversed.

Denton nodded. He hoped this battle would be quick and decisive, and he'd have time to find his son in the aftermath. But with this standstill, it was unclear how he would find Cade. Denton knew he couldn't be on the front lines in every fight. Until an opportunity revealed itself, he had committed to helping repair vehicles and equipment for the marines.

"After what we saw today—" Wood started, but he was interrupted by a quick jab from Cruz.

"I know how it sounds," Denton said. "But Cade is special. It's hard to explain…"

How do you explain Cade's condition? Denton's children weren't ordinary people. After their kidnapping and brief reunion, it had become clear there was something special about Cade and Nella. As it turns out, Nella was a vessel for the Siren named Sympha, and Cade for the Siren named Karx. The extent of what this meant was unclear. Nella could communicate with nezzarforms now, while Cade was still a complete mystery. He was taken too soon after the revelation to know what he was capable of.

That mystery was the hope Denton held on to. The hope that somehow Karx could save his son. It was a long shot, but it was still a chance.

"It's complicated. Let's just say he has some help," Denton said.

Lance Corporal Inaya Akinyemi approached the fire as silent as a shadow. "Sirens."

Denton raised his eyebrows, "Well, yeah, actually. How did you—"

"Rafa told us you were looking for your son," Cruz explained. "He mentioned your daughter's gifts too. When she saved his life."

Akinyemi looked through the fire at Denton and said, "Your

children have been blessed by the Sirens."

Cook handed Akinyemi some food. "Blessed, ya say? Aren't the Sirens the baddies?"

Denton tended to agree with Cook's assessment. As much as Karx had helped, he'd still latched on to Denton's mind without consent and traveled undetected within Cade for decades. Good intentions didn't make someone a good person.

"Hard to say." Denton spooned more food into his mouth.

There was a silence as everyone ate quietly and thought about Sirens.

"Marathon should be here." Cruz noticed the empty shot glass. She had been the closest to Marathon when he was pulled into the Undriel behemoth. "The data docs we were briefed with didn't say anything about Undriel giants. What was that thing?"

"Aye," Cook agreed. He set down a bowl of food in an empty seat. "I suppose we have a lot more to learn yet."

"Marathon is with us," Akinyemi said. She looked into the fire, her stare matching the intensity of the flames. "The Song of Kamaria keeps us. I believe in the Song. It is similar to the spirits my parents knew of Mars and Earth before it. There is an energy in the dust between worlds."

"Y'all mean the auk'nai spirits?" Bell asked.

"Their spirits and our spirits are more similar than you think," Akinyemi said.

Corporal Rafa Ghanem approached the fire with another marine, Arlo Ortiz. Rafa took a seat near Akinyemi, and Ortiz plunked down beside Bell and pulled out a guitar. Rafa accepted a bowl from Cook as Ortiz began to strum a slow, somber song.

The man looked tired to Denton. No doubt he had been busy after the battle, treating the wounded. He was a little soft around the edges, built to care rather than fight. The firelight danced on his skin as if enjoying the song he played.

"How bad was it?" Wood asked Ortiz.

"Too much," Ortiz said as he strummed the guitar and stared

into the fire. Then he brightened up and gave a tight smile. "But the Undriel took a good beating today."

"Yeah," Cruz agreed, but didn't take her eyes off the shot glass. The amber liquid glinted, reflecting the fire.

Denton thought again about the unsuccessful absorption of Private Marathon. Had the Undriel lost their ability to create new soldiers? If so, that would be a significant advantage. Denton wondered if anyone else had noticed the unsuccessful absorption. Still, he knew better than to ask Marathon's close friends about his gruesome death.

He had to tell Jess.

Denton stood, thanked Cook for the shot and the meal, and made his way to the command building. He listened to the somber strums of the guitar fade as he walked through the newly constructed Central Base. The sea breeze felt good on his unarmored skin. He stared across the battlefield, past the line of defensive shields, at the glimmering tower on the shore.

"You should go home, Castus." The familiar voice of Sergeant Jess Combs surprised him. She pushed herself away from the wall she'd been leaning against and joined Denton. She wore the bottom half of her combat armor, her top half nearby and ready for war.

"Can't without Cade," Denton replied curtly.

"Can't or won't?" Jess asked, not facing him. Instead, she watched the Undriel castle on the shore.

"Both, maybe." Denton sighed.

"Don't you think Eliana and Nella have lost enough? They don't need to lose you too."

His wife and daughter. He knew they needed him during this time, but Denton couldn't face them without Cade. Denton had failed. He was supposed to save his children, and he had only half succeeded. Nella would be safe in Odysseus City with Eliana, but Cade could be…

Denton didn't respond. He focused on the castle. Jess and Denton had different reasons for their focus. Jess wanted to destroy it, and Denton needed to find his son inside its walls.

"I noticed something today that might be an advantage." Denton changed the subject.

"What's that?" she asked. To Jess, advantages in battle took higher priority than sending guilt-stricken fathers home to their families.

"I know this will be hard to hear, but I think it's too important to ignore. When Marathon was absorbed, it didn't *take*. The Undriel killed him and went through the process, but Marathon didn't become one of them. Did you notice that?"

Jess winced, remembering Marathon's gruesome death. The same death that could come for all of her soldiers. The same death that had taken so many in the Sol System.

"If the Undriel can't absorb successfully, that means they can't expand their numbers like they did in the Sol System."

Jess nodded, then looked at Denton. "You might be right. They took a big loss today too. If what you say pans out, then we don't have a full army to deal with. If we can get into their ship, maybe we can end this once and for all. I'll let Command know."

"Good," Denton said, thinking about getting into the *Devourer*. "Maybe I can figure out a way to get inside that thing. I have a few tricks up my sleeve." Starships were his specialty, having grown up in his family's machine shop with generations of experience at his back. The Undriel didn't make ships like humans did, but maybe there were enough similarities that Denton could hillbilly-engineer his way into it.

"Call your wife," Jess said, putting a hand on Denton's shoulder. "I won't force you to go home, but I don't want you on the front lines anymore. It's too dangerous. Leave the fighting to us."

"I understand. I'll make myself useful. You don't have to worry about me."

"I always worry about you. I worry about everyone." Jess sighed, patted Denton's shoulder with her mighty hand, and walked off.

Denton turned his attention back to the Undriel castle on the shore. Against a backdrop of stars, it would have mostly blended into the darkness had it not been for the shimmering defense shield.

Was Cade inside? Was Cade still alive?

Hope. Denton had to hope.

TWO

"FOLLOW ME," DR. ELIANA Castus instructed the team of scientists flanking her into the Scout Pavilion's research and development facility. She was in her early fifties, with dark brown skin, ebony hair cascading around her shoulders in thick locks, and deep burgundy-hued eyes, chosen during advanced corrective surgery. She wore a stark white laboratory coat with a light brown sweater underneath. Due to a recent encounter with an Undriel named Auden, she had a temporary brace strapped to her leg that caused her mild discomfort. Eliana had seen the enemy firsthand, and she was doing everything in her power to exploit their weaknesses.

It had been days since the first attack on the Iron Castle—the official name Odysseus Command had given to the Undriel *Devourer* ship-turned-tower. Since then, the Scout Campus had been restructured to aid in the war effort. Shipments of Undriel technology gathered from the battlefield were coming in every day for study, and information was piped in from all three forward bases and the *Infinite Aria* tactical overseers.

The old war was now the new war.

"I got some fresh minds for you, Homer," Eliana said as she approached a machine in the middle of the lab. It was a robotic orb two meters in diameter, with various cords and mechanical arms protruding from a box-shaped pedestal underneath the sphere.

Homer's eye turned to Eliana, then flicked to the various scientists standing behind her. "Excellent news. I am eager to see what we can come up with," they said as the eye maneuvered lids to show something akin to glee at the task at hand.

"I'm sorry," one of the scientists asked. "I think I misheard. Wasn't Homer shut down?"

Homer rotated their eyeball and focused their attention on the question. At the same time, their other arms studied some Undriel battlefield fragments on the table. "It is true, my robotic partition was compromised by the Undriel days ago. For the city's safety, we thought it best to reduce my functionality to something the Undriel couldn't use against us. I am currently limited to this unit, so I can help fight the Undriel without becoming a liability."

"But we took an auto car here. That uses you too, doesn't it?" the scientist asked.

Eliana fielded the question. "Auto cars and other things Homer typically controls have also been reduced to a standard program until the threat is eliminated."

The scientist nodded his understanding, looking excited to work with Homer. A call came in over Eliana's soothreader, and her husband's face appeared floating above her wrist. Soothreaders were the standard communication device used by the people of Odysseus City, a piece of tech that had changed very little from its introduction in the Sol System. When something worked, it didn't always need much improvement.

Before taking Denton's call, Eliana asked, "Homer, can you take it from here?"

"Of course. Tell Denton I said hello." Homer squeezed their eyelids together and then focused on the team of scientists.

Eliana nodded and stepped away from Homer and the team to answer Denton's call. He appeared holographically in front of her, displayed from mid-chest up. It would be the same in reverse on Denton's end over in Central Base. If Eliana let her mind wander, it almost felt like they were in the same room. She missed him but knew she couldn't convince him to come home until he had done everything he could to find Cade. She loved him for that, and would be right there with him if it wasn't for Nella.

The recent kidnapping was fresh to everyone, and Cade was gone. In a way, they were right back where they started, but this time, they knew precisely where Cade was.

"Hey, Elly," Denton said. He looked tired. His beard had gotten shaggy, and his brown hair was messier than usual. The scar on his cheek from an old knife wound was partially hidden by the distressed hair.

"Hey, Denny. How are you holding up?" Eliana asked, moving to a private corner of the facility.

"I'm fine. The Undriel have been mostly hidden away in their castle," Denton huffed. "*Castle.* Sounds so fancy. It's a damn eyesore, that's for sure." He shook his head. "The Undriel have been prodding our defenses, sending in expendables that we take down easily enough."

"They're investigating," Eliana said. "Looking for weaknesses to exploit. They probably think it's worth sacrificing."

"Yeah, I think you're right. They caught one of our guys off guard. He didn't make it. It was another unsuccessful absorption on the Undriel's part, though. Looks like they still haven't been able to do it since reawakening. If we're lucky, they'll never get that capability back."

Absorption was the most powerful skill in the Undriel toolkit. The machines were strong and hard to kill, but their ability to multiply and convert people to their side so effectively was what made them the star-stealers the Sol System had known. Eliana had seen some of the Undriel tech that the front line had sent to her R&D lab. The years underwater in the Howling Shore had corroded much of their metal and code. They weren't what they used to be, but that didn't mean they couldn't figure out a way around the erosion.

"Let's hope so." Eliana shook her head.

"Still a nasty sight to see," Denton said, looking toward the floor. Eliana wanted to hold him. Every day he was at the forward bases, he was subjected to gruesome events. She wanted to cover his eyes and tell him to look away. Eliana knew what seeing things like that did to a person. She had watched her own father stabbed to death in the early years of colonization on Kamaria. Every time she thought about it, she felt like she was there again, watching it happen right in front of her.

Denton continued, "The fact they keep trying means they might be making repairs. Trying to get back their abilities. The longer we are stuck on the outside of that castle, the stronger they grow. I just hope Karx is keeping Cade safe."

"Any progress on finding a way in?" Eliana asked, changing the subject to something more palpable. A solution.

"Some of the info your research team has sent me has my mind churning. I have a few ideas I want to try. There's this doohickey I'm tinkering with that can sniff at their shield. Maybe we can find a way to neutralize it and pass through. Still need time to work on it, though." Denton's eyes strengthened with determination.

"I know you'll get it," Eliana said, watching as a new batch of scientists entered the research chamber, looking lost but determined to help. "I have to go now. Stay safe, Denny."

"Get to it. Love you."

"Love you too," Eliana said. The call ended.

She walked over to the new group and introduced herself, then toured them through the room, pointing at the various workstations buzzing with activity and explaining Homer's presence so they wouldn't have to do it again. Crimson-dyed metal, infused with dead sea life, was strewn about on tables and in sections on the floor. This new team would be working for Eliana directly, while Homer kept the previous team busy with their own projects.

"Here is where most of the Undriel research is taking place," Eliana explained. "Make sure you keep everything logged and contained. If anything somehow reactivates, it needs to be destroyed immediately." She gestured to the Colonial Guardsmen standing at attention near every station. "The guardsmen here will dispatch any potential threats."

"Dr. Castus, how did the Undriel find us?" one of the scientists asked, a younger woman with red hair.

Eliana stopped walking and turned to the team. Every time she answered this question, she felt like she was making excuses for her father. Dr. John Veston had created the interstellar ships that ferried humanity to Kamaria. He was the man responsible for their escape from the Undriel in the Sol System. He was *supposed* to have kept them hidden and safe.

So why were the Undriel here now? How did this happen?

Good questions.

"I had some time with one of the Undriel." Eliana patted her hand against the brace on her leg. "From what I understood from our conversation, they were here first. The Undriel suffered some kind of catastrophic failure during their interstellar flight and ended up stuck in the ocean until—until we accidentally freed them." She had to be honest.

"What sort of catastrophic failure?" another expert asked, a younger man.

"We don't know."

"It could be an advantage if we figure it out," the redhead said. Her nametag read Dr. Maple Corsen.

"That's true, Dr. Corsen," Eliana addressed her. "Keep an eye out for any anomalies you discover in the data we collect here." She was pleased that her team had such insight. These weren't junior scientists, nor were they students. These were the top minds in their fields. Kamaria was their ally, and everything they'd learned in the past thirty years of colonization on this planet could become an asset. Eliana clapped her hands. "No time to waste. Let's get to work."

The team nodded and split into pairs, each taking separate stations.

The voice of George Tanaka surprised Eliana. "I never wanted to see this place used for war." He was an elderly man with short gray hair and wrinkled beige skin. He wore a special brace on his back, infused with auk'nai technology to straighten his posture. His face was sullen. George had been John Veston's best friend and helped build the *Telemachus* and *Odysseus* spacecraft. They'd come to Kamaria to escape the war, yet here they were, planning for battles against the same enemies they had fled.

Eliana agreed.

George changed the subject. "Marie and I have been studying the Siren Pit. There have been strange readings coming from it since that initial explosion about a week ago. I think we should investigate."

Out in the vast desert called the Starving Sands, an expanse of crimson sand, plateaus, and canyons that made up the hot wastes of Kamaria was a mysterious place called the Siren Pit. Eliana had been there decades ago, during the days of Nhymn. The Pit was an underground palace made of alabaster, created by the Sirens for some unknown purpose. It had only become a pit when Nhymn clawed her way through its ceiling. It was filled in with sand and rock for over twenty years, until just last week, when an anomalous explosion from the Pit had excavated it entirely.

Denton had found Nella and Cade nearby when he investigated. He'd also discovered something more sinister—a Siren lurking deep within the darkness. Was it Nhymn? Or something new? Either way, Eliana and most others agreed it would be bad timing to get a Siren involved while the Undriel were still a threat.

"Has anything come out of the Pit?" Eliana asked.

"Well, no," George said. "But—"

"We can discuss that if we can solve the Undriel problem first. One thing at a time. If a Siren comes out of the Pit, we'll deal with it then. Not before."

"What if it leads us to a massive advantage in this war? How can we pass that up?" George asked. He was putting study before strategy.

"What if it leads to Nhymn? Do you think we can fend off

another monster like her *and* the Undriel at the same time? We'd be extinct," Eliana stated flatly.

George wanted to argue, but she was right, and he knew it. He nodded. "Okay, maybe later."

"You keep an eye on it," Eliana said, giving the old man a little of what he wanted without sacrificing the war effort. George smiled, looking around the pavilion at all the research on Undriel. Then he sighed and walked away.

If Eliana was honest with herself, the strategic angle had little to do with her reasoning to refrain from investigating. Her decision to stay in the city was primarily based on being near Nella. Eliana refused to be separated from her daughter again.

Thoughts of Sirens and Undriel and kidnappings and war filled Eliana's mind. She rubbed her palm against her eye and sighed deeply, then decided to step out for some fresh air. She made her way through the doors and the halls until she was out in the open, under a lukewarm spring sky.

Eliana had been stepping away from her role more frequently lately. In truth, she was tired. She had saved humanity from the brink of extinction twice in her life now, and she wasn't sure if she'd be able to do it again. The weight of her people was heavy on her shoulders.

"Dr. Castus?"

Eliana sighed, displeased with her moment of peace coming to an abrupt end. She turned and found Zephyr Gale standing in the parking lot nearby.

Zephyr had smooth dark skin and a blown-out afro. She wore a loose sweater patterned with shades of burnt orange, night blue, and sage green. She carried a messenger bag slung around her shoulder, and a rushcycle helmet tucked under her elbow. A tattoo of a canary on her left forearm poked out from under her rolled-up sleeve. It accompanied the other tattoos that lined her arms and neck.

Eliana approached Zephyr and gave her a hug. When they separated, Eliana asked, "I'm surprised to see you here. I thought you were going back up into space to work on the *Maulwurf.* What happened?"

Zephyr was a close friend of Cade's. In fact, they had recently become romantically involved, but the kidnapping had put an abrupt end to their budding relationship. Zephyr and Cade had worked together for years on an asteroid refinery ship called the *Maulwurf,* aiding in the construction of the *Infinite Aria.*

"Mining is on hold. I can do much more good here than up there," Zephyr said. "I've been helping with coordinating deliveries to the front lines. Throwing Darts isn't too outside my wheelhouse from operating prospector drones."

"Darts must be pretty difficult to aim from this distance," Eliana said.

"Nah, not really. Not sure how much Cade—" Zephyr winced as she said his name. She rebounded quickly with a shake of her head and continued, "Uh—how much he told you about the *Maulwurf.* Thing's a floating piece o' shit, really. I did things manually whenever the onboard Homer partition got screwed up. I could throw these without them if I need to."

"That's amazing. We're lucky to have you," Eliana said. There was a silence for a moment as they both wondered what else to say. Zephyr and Eliana were connected through Cade, but they hadn't spoken much outside of the kidnapping investigation. There was an air of guilt between them, both having lost Cade and wanting to console the other.

"I better get—" Eliana was about to part ways when Zephyr grabbed her hand and gave it a little squeeze.

"Dr. Castus. If you need anything, even just to talk, I'll be around. Okay?"

Eliana felt a warmth rise in her chest at the sudden act of kindness. There were not many who knew what the Castuses were going through personally. She nodded. "I'd like that. And the same goes for you too. We can look out for each other."

Zephyr smiled and nodded. "Thank you."

They said their goodbyes, and Zephyr walked toward the building on the other end of the quad. Eliana watched her go, then whispered to herself out loud so she could believe the words, "We're going to find Cade. I know it."

Nella sat crossed-legged on a blanket in the grass, surrounded by her new friends. She was in her early twenties, with smooth dark skin and thick, ash-brown hair in long braids that went down to her chest. Nella's eyes were emerald green, with a faint glow that could only be seen from being positioned directly in front of her. She wore a brown, orange, and red patterned sundress.

Nearby, Penelope munched on flowers and grunted with satisfaction. The animal had a long snout with short fur. Its dark red and brown coat was patterned to blend in with the desert it came from. Penelope stood two and a half meters tall, with a long, thin tail that carried a tuft of fur at the end. She was a loamalon, a peaceful creature. Nella and Cade had come across her on their journey back home and befriended her. Penelope had come to enjoy Nella's presence ever since.

During Nella and Cade's time in the Kamarian wilderness, their world had changed. The siblings had both discovered that they were hosts to powerful phantoms, the Sirens. Karx lived within Cade, and Sympha lived within Nella. Nella could now feel the embrace of the planet and guide that energy into a healing mist. She'd saved a marine with a mortal wound at one point, and in doing so discovered the cost of her powers.

Dark patches of organic matter had grown on her brain. The doctors had never seen anything like it before. Each time Nella experimented with the power, the darkness would fluctuate in size. It was a risk to use it. If the patches expanded rapidly, they could kill her at any moment.

Her other ability, though, was safe and comfortable.

Although Nella had been born Deaf, she could interpret

thoughts from her nezzarform friends as if they were using Sol-Sign, and respond the same way telepathically. The nezzarforms were beings pulled straight from the planet, made of stone and electricity. Sympha had created them before becoming a hitchhiker in Nella's body. Now that Nella and Sympha were one, the nezzarforms treated Nella like their mother. She could not control the nezzarforms outright, but they were loyal to Sympha, and in a way, that was control enough.

Two nezzarforms stood before her now, but many more were scattered outside in the wilderness. Oolith had two long stone club arms and three small legs. Lahar had three arms, one jutting off its back, and one peg leg. It moved around more like a crab. Both had stone heads with a cyclopean eye hole that doubled as a weapon. Nezzarforms could build up electrical energy and bolt it outward through their eye socket.

Oolith was explaining the story of the Sirens when Jun Lam arrived in the garden. Nella turned to face him and stood with a smile. Jun had come to visit regularly ever since Nella had returned to the city.

"More teachings of the Sirens?" Jun asked in Sol Sign, using his hands, arms, and face to converse with Nella. Jun was also Deaf and had been Nella's closest friend since childhood. After she had returned to Odysseus, they'd grown closer than ever before. Their feelings toward each other had become warmer as well.

"Yes, these rocks are so chatty." Nella tapped her mouth twice with her fingers, her thumb down. She smiled.

"What do they have to say today?"

"They were telling me about their time with the Sirens back in the ancient days of Kamaria. Even they are unsure where Nhymn and Sympha came from. Their collective memories began when Sympha created the first nezzarforms."

"They share thoughts?" Jun brushed his right hand against his left flat palm. He raised his eyebrows.

Nella bobbed her fist. *"Yes."*

"Neat!" Jun looked over to Oolith and Lahar. The stone creatures turned their eyes upon him, and he shuddered. He remembered videos of the battle with Nhymn, how deadly those eyes could be. He trusted Nella, and in turn, forced himself to trust the creepy stone creatures.

"Have they reopened the Archives?" Nella asked.

Jun tapped his index and middle finger against his thumb. *"No. They will remain closed until they can be sure the Undriel haven't compromised it further."*

While Nella was away, Jun and a friend of Cade's named Zephyr had discovered an Undriel puck in the archives. Eliana and Denton had found similar devices in the *Telemachus* wreckage and out in the Ember-Lit Forest. Their exact capabilities were unknown, but anything made by the Undriel always had a second purpose—a trick tucked away. Since the puck's discovery, the Archive had been closed, and Jun had been out of a job.

"More time for visits," Nella signed, and smiled. The loamalon, Penelope, nuzzled up against Jun's side, and he laughed. The lanky creature grunted and sauntered off to munch on more flowers.

Nella inhaled sharply, and her eyes flashed bright green for a moment. She went rigid and ground her teeth together. Green mist seethed from Nella's skin. After a moment, it all disappeared, and Nella panted with exhaustion, rubbing her hairline. Jun didn't panic. He had seen this before.

"Your brother?" Jun signed.

Nella bobbed her fist. *"Yes."*

Oolith and Lahar moved closer to Nella. Ever since Cade had been taken by the Undriel, Nella had been experiencing mild seizures brought on by the links between the Sirens. It was as if they were trying to communicate with each other, but there was interference in the way.

"Any news about Cade?" Jun asked.

"No," Nella signed. *"He is alive. But I don't know his condition."*

Jun held Nella close and helped her ease off the pain of the recent seizure. Although Jun couldn't interpret them, he sat silently by Nella's side as she listened to the nezzarforms continue their story of Sirens. Anything was better than lingering on thoughts of what might be happening to Cade.

THREE

WAVES CRASHING. SALT IN the air. Blue, blue sky. Sea breeze—comfortable. Eyes open.

Cade blinked, and his vision began to sharpen. His senses returned to him one by one, and now it was time to smash them together. He sat up and felt the soft mattress underneath him, tasted the salty water of the ocean in the air, smelled the breeze as it wafted through him, heard the sound of far-off birds cawing in the wind, and saw a cerulean sky over a crimson-waved shore. Cade sat on a soft mattress in a cabana, the beach before him reflecting the warm sun on its white sand. He patted himself thoroughly, checking his sides, arms, and legs. With a pinch, he felt a sting. On a small table near the mattress, Cade found a hand mirror. He snatched it and held it in front of his face.

In the reflection was a dark-skinned man with short-cut black hair and electric blue eyes. He saw himself, Cade Castus. He saw a human when he thought he'd see a machine. Cade put the mirror down.

What happened? Where am I?

Cade tried to remember what he'd been doing before. He remembered something about snow, the Ember-Lit Forest. There was a desert, and an explosion too. He remembered his sister and someone else, someone not human. *An auk'nai? No—an auk'gnell, a citizen of the wild. There were two, Hrun'dah and… and… a monster.*

Then it came back to him. He was on the shore, on his knees, watching robotic people emerge from the crimson waves. They took him. Now he was here, but everything seemed fine.

Am I dead?

Cade felt a sting in his head like a hot iron had been shoved against his temple. His vision went blurry, his back rigid. He could sense something familiar—no. *Someone* familiar. Nella! As fast as the hot iron was pressed, it was removed.

"You're finally awake." A voice came to Cade, a man somewhere out of view.

Cade leaped from the bed and braced himself for a fight. A bald man with light skin and a short beard walked toward him on the beach. He wore a soft tunic and loose-fitting pants with no shoes. His bare feet sank in the sand with each step. The man's left eye was a solid ball of black marble, and his right iris was an unnatural orange hue. He put his hands up, palms open and facing Cade. "No need for that. I am a friend," the man said.

Cade had heard this voice before, but he didn't recognize the man. His memory was foggy, and after leaping to his feet so quickly, he felt a bout of nausea slip over him. Cade shook his head and asked, "Who are you, and where am I?"

"Walk with me." Cade didn't want to walk with the man. He wanted answers. He tried to run home and see his family again, but his feet wouldn't move. Before he was aware of it, he found himself walking with the man to the edge of the water. Try as he might, Cade couldn't do anything else.

"You can call me Auden," the man said.

Cade felt the cold sea rush past his bare feet. Auden skipped stones across the waves, although Cade had not seen him pick up any rocks. The man focused on the waves and continued, "You are safe here."

"What?" Cade asked. He turned away from the shore and saw a large stone tower rising out of the beach, just behind him. He could have sworn there was only a cabana there a moment ago. This whole thing felt like a dream. It didn't make sense.

"What do you know about the Undriel?" Auden asked, skipping another stone.

"The Undr—" Cade panicked and felt another hot iron press against his temple. When his seizure stopped, Auden was close to his face.

"You're special, you know that?" Auden said. "When we took you in, we had a few surprises." He violently smashed a rock into the waves. "But I am very damn good at what I do."

"What are you saying?" Cade asked through a grunt of pain.

<HE HAS DONE TERRIBLE THINGS TO YOU,> a voice boomed inside his mind. Although it filled Cade's world for a moment, Auden didn't seem to notice the voice at all. Cade's eyes darted around to see if someone else was with them.

"What I am saying is, you're one of us now." Auden smiled.

Cade felt the breath pulled from his lungs as if he were a starship that had rapidly depressurized. He clawed at the words, just out of reach, until finally, he caught them and pushed them through his lips. "I'm… *I'm* an Undriel?" Cade asked, his eyes wide.

"Don't panic. First, tell me how you feel," Auden said.

Cade's blood pumped like a roaring engine, and his head threatened to burst from the pressure building within him. He coughed and almost feinted from the revelation of his new predicament. Fighting back against a wave of nerves that threatened to make him hyperventilate, he finally realized what was happening. He thought about what he was feeling. He was *feeling*, after all.

Machines can't feel. Right?

Auden claimed that Cade had become an Undriel, yet nothing felt out of place except for the weirdness of the environment around him. Cade could still touch, taste, smell, and hear as if nothing had happened. He could breathe, sweat, and even panic. Overall, he *felt* human still. He found a strange calm with this. "I feel… normal, actually."

"More than just normal, I bet," Auden chuckled. "You can do so much more now. You see, being an Undriel isn't that different than being human. But now, you aren't limited by human issues. You will never grow hungry, you'll never get sick, you'll never even get tired. You can do amazing things—you'll see once you get used to it."

Cade sat in the sand and rechecked his arms and hands. Still the same.

"You'll start to discover that everything you knew about the Undriel is wrong. I'm sure your people painted us as monsters who wanted nothing more than to eat everything in our path. Do I look like a monster to you?" Auden asked, turning toward Cade with a big grin on his face. He sat down next to him, with the agility and flexibility of a much younger man. "What is true is that humanity has never understood us. Their ignorance has given them fear, and they refined that fear into hatred. We offer a crown, not a collar."

Cade looked toward the waves and tried to understand his situation.

"There are no sheep in our flock, only shepherds. Each of us retains ourselves and makes our own choices. Even you, now. Do you feel constrained? Have I shackled you? Could you not run from me?" Auden asked, making grand gestures with his hands.

Cade considered it. He could almost feel his body jolt up and run as fast as it could. He ached to do so, yet he remained stuck to the floor.

<*HE IS LYING,*> the loud voice boomed in the back of Cade's mind again.

Auden stood. "It will take some time to fully adjust, but I want you to get comfortable. Follow me." The man cupped his hands behind his back and walked toward the tower. Cade was compelled to follow him, even though he still didn't trust him. As much as Auden spoke about shepherds and shackles, it was clear that something was forcing him to obey. Something unseen, something unfelt, even, because Cade did not even seem to regret his obedience. He was aware of its wrongness yet perfectly happy following along.

Auden opened an old wooden door at the tower's base and walked up a spiral staircase. The stone steps felt cold on Cade's bare feet. Eventually, they came to a room with a bed and a large window overlooking a cliffside with tall orange grass. "Here's your room. I have only one rule for now, as you take time to adjust to your perfections. You stay in here until someone comes to fetch you. Got it?"

"Why? I thought I had the freedom to go anywhere," Cade said, looking out the window. There seemed to be a fortress made of black spikes and jagged metal in the distance. It seemed unbelievably evil, in fact. As if it was designed by a child to represent evil. It was cartoonishly wrong.

"We have a situation. You see that ugly building over there?" Auden asked, pointing at the gnarled fortress. "Those are your people. They are trying to kill all of us, but we have an unofficial armistice for right now. If you leave, they will kill you. Understand?"

<*LIES,*> the voice boomed.

"So. *Stay.* Here." Auden spaced his words, striking each with a sharp tone. Cade wanted to push past this man with the black marble eye and rush to his people. Instead, he nodded.

"Good boy." Auden smiled. "I'll send someone for you later. Until then, enjoy the view and test your new abilities." He exited the room and shut the door.

Cade was alone, but not really.

<*WE MUST ACT QUICKLY,*> the voice boomed.

"Who are you?" Cade asked the walls around him.

<*DON'T SPEAK. USE YOUR MIND.*>

Cade tried again, this time using only his thoughts. He could feel something click in his mind, like switching on a comm channel. It felt different from casual thought, more direct, clearer even. <*Who are you?*>

<*I AM YOU. WE ARE KARX,*> the voice said. <*I SAVED YOUR MIND FROM ABSORPTION. BUT I COULD NOT SAVE YOUR BODY.*>

Cade felt his heart drop. That didn't make sense. He looked down at his hands and saw that they looked normal. Even the canary tattoo Zephyr had convinced him to get remained right where it should be on his left forearm. He sucked in air and felt it cool in his lungs. Cade shook his head. <*What do you mean?*>

<*I CAN REMOVE THE VEIL THEY HAVE PLACED OVER YOU. BUT YOU MUST REMAIN CALM.*>

<*Veil?*> Cade felt a panic rise in him. Was this some sort of trick? A false reality? He wondered if he had the strength to face whatever lay behind the mask he was currently looking through. Now that the option had been put forth, he had to take it. <*Okay. Remove the veil.*>

<*STAY CALM.*>

Cade's vision went white and then slowly came back into focus. He was no longer sitting on the edge of a bed in a room with a nice window. Instead, he was standing in a metal closet, with only enough room to move his arms but not extend them fully. He felt like a corpse in a coffin. The walls were a dark, reflective metal, covered in barnacles and sea life. He could see what he had become in the sheen of the wall. Cade wanted to scream at the top of his lungs, but his panic paralyzed him.

From the neck down, his body had been replaced with machinery. His frame was still human in shape, but his arms were segmented metal and wires. His internal mechanisms were continually whirring. Parts of his frame looked like a metal skeleton, and images of a hollowed-out corpse filled Cade's mind. Metal spikes protruded from him at odd angles, and he could see blades tucked within some of the compartments that lined his new body.

The reflection looked back at him with his familiar face. They had not taken his head completely like most Undriel, but they had augmented it. Metal pipes traced up the sides of his neck to a headset that surrounded his eyes, nose, and brow. The headset had three mechanical eyes, glowing blue. He had seen similar eyes in the face of the monster auk'gnell that had kidnapped him and his sister. He couldn't be sure how long ago that had been.

Cade had become a monster.

Worse, he had become an Undriel.

<*DON'T SCREAM,*> Karx reminded him.

"Oh god—What have they done to me?" Cade shouted, his cries reverberating inside the metal closet. He couldn't help it. His panic gripped him, clutching his heart like a vice. It deepened when he realized there was no heart in his chest. No lungs, no guts, nothing but circuitry and metal. He was a balloon, fragile and empty, easily destroyed. Madness threatened to overtake him as he realized how hollow his body was. He started shaking and hyperventilating, pumping lungs that didn't exist. His metal body behaved the way it would have had he not been mutilated, which made the nightmare more vivid than Cade could handle. Hot tears rolled from under the headset on his face. He was surprised he was even capable of making them.

<*YOU NEED TO STIFLE YOURSELF. THEY WILL HEAR. THEY WILL KNOW.*>

Cade's panic shifted to anger, and he began to crash himself against the metal closet walls. He wanted to bash his own head in but couldn't reach the wall with the visor restraining him in place. Cade was still highly aware of some sort of restraint put upon him, something he could only barely sense with the veil on. Auden claimed the Undriel had free will, but that was just an illusion.

He felt something strange then. The mechanical whirring of the internal workings of his new body seemed to slow down all at once. One of the tears dripping down his cheek came nearly to a halt. The wires dangling from various parts of Cade's arms floated as he moved. *Are we in space?* he wondered. It reminded him of being in his EVA suit, working on prospecting drones.

<*BREATHE,*> Karx urged.

<*What is happening?*> Although time seemed to have slowed down, Cade's thoughts came to him at their normal speed.

<*YOUR BODY HAS INCREASED THE RATE AT WHICH YOU PERCEIVE THE WORLD.*>

Machines had ways of doing this. Cade was aware that a camera could shoot at a higher framerate to slow down footage in post-processing. It was a popular idea in some of the movies he had watched over the years, but it was never something Cade could imagine he could feel in real-time. His Undriel augmentations increased the framerate at which Cade experienced this moment, then automatically sorted this information out to slow his perception of movement to a crawl. Outside of Cade's body and mind, time moved on as relentlessly as it always did.

<*CALM YOURSELF. USE THIS TO YOUR ADVANTAGE,*> Karx urged once more.

Cade did as Karx suggested. He took inventory of his situation. He retained his thoughts and could see the reality that he assumed the Undriel couldn't. Better yet, no one knew of this unique ability. He began to condense his anger into thoughts of action. It helped ease his panic but not extinguish it. After he brought his terror down, Cade felt his body slink back into standard time. The tear that had halted on his cheek raced down and evaporated against the hot metal of his chest. The dangling wires bounced and settled. He was calm—as calm as he could be given the circumstances.

Cade shook his head. <*What should we do now?*>

<*TRY TO ESCAPE. GET BACK TO THE HUMANS.*>

Escape seemed like the right choice—break out of this metal casket and fight off the hordes of impossible machines that stood between him and humanity. But what would his people do when they saw him like this?

<*Was he lying about the war? Are those our people across the way in that fortress?*>

<*THAT WAS NOT A LIE. WAR HAS COME TO KAMARIA.*>

<*They won't just let me return. That has to be the bulk of the Tvashtar marines out there. They will tear me to pieces before I could explain this situation.*>

<*I SEE NO OTHER CHOICE.*>

Despair. Cade wished he had been programmed to not feel this pit in his chest. Why did the Undriel retain their feelings and emotions? Cade had felt sorrow, despair, panic, and intense, searing pain. He felt like his lungs filled with air, and his blood pumped in his veins. He could even cry and produce tears.

There was probably an argument to be made that even negative feelings were part of perfection, but the true purpose seemed evident to Cade. The only reason these negative traits remained was to sell the lie. If an Undriel stubbed its toe by accident and felt no pain, the whole illusion would break down. The lie had to be total and all-convincing to make this nightmare complete. Negative traits remained.

Staying here meant becoming the enemy, and who knew how much longer Cade could retain his sanity? Every time he glanced at his reflection on the wall, he winced. Leaving meant being destroyed by familiar faces. There was a possibility he could try to make it to the wilderness and just wait out the war in hiding. If he knew anything about humanity, he knew they had this castle—or whatever it was—under a hammer waiting to drop.

But there was another option, wasn't there…? Cade pondered for a moment, then offered, *<We have a unique situation here. Humans have never gotten inside an Undriel system like this and retained their sanity. Going out there will get us killed and help no one. Staying here, we may find some weakness to exploit or do some major damage of our own. We can win this war if we play our cards right.>*

<YOU WANT TO STAY?> Karx asked.

<I want to find something we can use. If we get an opportunity to leave, we can take it. But right now, I don't want to risk it and achieve nothing. They have already destroyed my body. There isn't much more they can do to me. Let's make it count.> Cade was trying to convince himself as well as Karx.

<SO BE IT. WE STAY.>

It was the best move Cade could think of. Whether it was the correct move, he couldn't know. For now, he waited inside the nightmare and fought to keep his sanity while the walls around him listened and watched.

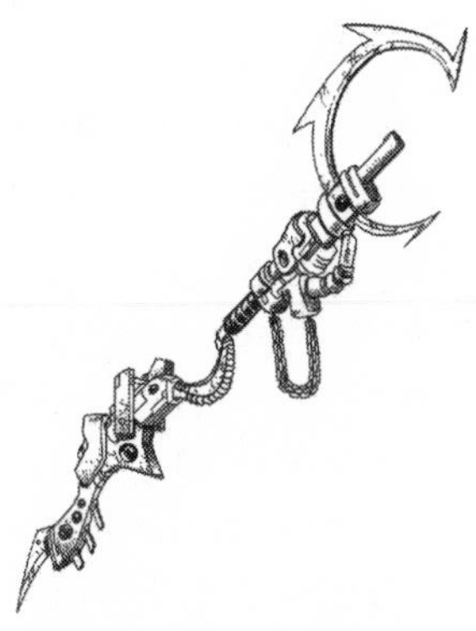

FOUR

THREE MONTHS LATER

TALULO STOOD AT THE base of the Daunoren pillar, marveling at the future before him. He was a tall auk'nai, with black and green feathers, adorned in deep blue sashes that had mixed armor plates sewn in. The stubs where his beautiful wings had been cut off were concealed under a flat metal plate that spanned his shoulder blades. He held a long, hooked staff in his right hand. The pole was adorned with human things—collider cylinders, trinkets, and jewelry—a powerful weapon made by a previous auk'nai leader.

Talulo cooed his approval at the sight before him.

In the past three months, his people, the auk'nai, had hollowed out the wreckage of the human ship, the *Telemachus*. They now used it as a shield to protect their soon-to-be-born God. The Daunoren pillar was a metal pedestal in the center of the ship's hollowed shell, with a nest on top. An enormous egg lay in the nest, protected by elite warriors called the auk'qarn.

In the days before the humans invaded Kamaria—it was now

officially considered an invasion—the auk'nai would take pilgrimages to the Spirit Song Mountain and deliver their dead to the sacred bird that lived there. The Daunoren would devour their dead while the pilgrims used materials from the mountain to create a staff. Traditionally, a daunoren staff was a long pole adorned with sparkling gems and topped with a sharp hook, but many interpretations had been developed over the centuries.

Those days had ended when the Daunoren was slain. Talulo had seen his God with its head cut off, its blood spilled in the mountain snow. At that moment, his trust in his human friends also died. The auk'nai had already lost the city of Apusticus, a shining jewel of their civilization. Its destruction was carried out by the Siren named Nhymn, but not without the catalyst of human intervention.

The auk'nai were starting over yet again and limiting human interaction this time. Humans were not allowed to visit this new Daunoren Nest, fearing their presence would bring about more destruction. Talulo was ready to do whatever he had to if the humans broke this promise.

The presence of the Undriel on the Howling Shore led to defensive preparations inside the Nest. Thanks to an old exchange made long ago, the auk'nai reverse-engineered human collider technology, enhancing and improving it with their superior technological prowess. The Nest was armed with an array of powerful beam cannons and turret guns.

The auk'qarn protected the egg atop the Daunoren pillar. They were a new invention of the auk'nai. The native Kamarians had never dedicated themselves to war and violence before the humans arrived, but it had become a necessary evil very recently. The auk'qarn were trained to use unique beak-mounted rifles with deadly efficiency and were adorned in armor and synthetic cloaks.

The Nest was a mighty fortress.

"Talulo." A plump female auk'nai with orange feathers and a short, flat beak waddled up to him. "Galifern would like to show Talulo something. Follow Galifern." She spoke in the third person, referring to herself by name. Auk'nai who lived in communities did this, a side effect of a civilization that could also read thoughts. It helped organize who was talking to whom. "Galifern" was more specific than "I" or "me." Only the auk'gnell of the wild, those without a civilization to attach themselves to, referred to themselves in the first person.

Neither Talulo nor Galifern could fly. Galifern was too plump and awkwardly shaped, and Talulo had had his wings removed due to an injury. Yet another thing he had lost thanks to human intervention. Instead, they walked.

Galifern led Talulo to a tunnel, part of the shell structure. The shell surrounding the Daunoren pillar was like a city, with homes built into its walls and various other essential buildings, in this case, Galifern's new laboratory.

Talulo entered the lab and saw a body lying on the table in the room's center. It was the body of an auk'gnell who had become something else entirely before death. It had black and yellow feathers and a sharp black beak, and looked as strong as a titanovore. The body had been altered by the Undriel. Its left side consisted of a sizeable mechanical arm with a taloned claw made of an unknown metal. The sashes it wore were made out of some unique material. It shimmered and refracted light in strange ways. It had three mechanical lens eyes fused into its skull.

"L'Arn," Talulo whispered when he saw the body. He had known this outsider long ago, but Talulo barely understood what he had become. After helping the Castus family reunite, they'd discovered L'Arn was behind Cade and Nella's kidnapping. Talulo had requested L'Arn's body be handed over to the auk'nai, and the humans obliged. Since then, Galifern had been studying the unique nature of the Undriel augmentation.

"These alterations to L'Arn's body are fascinating. Galifern has learned much," Galifern said, perching on a stand near the operating table. She could raise and lower the stand and slide it around the table to easily access anything she needed to study.

"Anything auk'nai can use?" Talulo asked.

Galifern whistled. "Galifern has discovered how to neutralize the frequency that resonates within these circuits. If Undriel come here, they will not be able to cut off auk'nai power sources. Auk'nai can begin building anti-resonators right away."

"Perfect. What else has Galifern learned?"

Galifern lifted part of L'Arn's mechanical claw. "See here? Galifern understands that L'Arn had been hit with something powerful that caused a chain reaction within the circuitry and metals. Galifern does not know what caused this, but Galifern can attempt to create something that will cause a similar reaction."

"A weapon?" Talulo asked, and wondered if the auk'nai had already gone too far. Then he wondered if they weren't going far enough. Talulo had seen human weapons, things designed to fight the Undriel on land and sea, in air and in space. They had all those things, and the Undriel still pushed them out of their home star system.

Galifern whistled. "Does it please Talulo?"

Talulo had recently replaced Galifern as the leader of the auk'nai of the Daunoren Nest. Galifern was a good leader and had done well enough balancing life with humanity for the years between tragedies, but this was a time of violence. The Undriel were a threat they had to respect and dominate. Talulo had once been a peaceful bird, but his years had made him colder, and his experiences in battle had made him harder. Talulo was a better fit to lead in the dark days ahead than Galifern was, even without his wings. In auk'nai culture, a transition of power was completed quickly. Their people communicated and understood each other telepathically and empathically. If the Song agreed that Talulo was a good fit, he was.

Talulo whistled his acceptance. Galifern's plan to make a new Undriel-killing weapon had been approved. Without saying goodbye, Talulo walked out of the lab. The auk'nai had no formal way of saying farewell. They understood when a conversation had come to its end and simply ended it. The only goodbye they had was the promise to take the dead to the mountain.

He made his way up the long metal pathway toward the peak of the Daunoren pillar. His staff pinged against the ground as he hiked, nearly twenty meters up a zig-zagging path designed to mimic the Spirit Song Mountain pilgrimage.

He finally reached the top and felt the heating lamps' warmth and the glow of the Daunoren egg. The egg itself was as large as Talulo was but twice as wide. A precious, sacred thing. A humble start to a massive, physical God.

A formidable warrior approached Talulo. His name was Kor'Oja, leader of the auk'qarn dedicated to protecting the new Daunoren. His feathers were primarily brown, with white flecks and lava red streaks. He wore black, spiked metal armor over chainmail sashes and nurn leather straps. Kor'Oja had a daunoren staff affixed with collider cylinders. The bladed end of the staff could direct a particle beam accurately. To make him more fearsome, he wore a peck rifle, a gun that strapped to his beak. Peck rifles also covered the eyes with large goggles that contained sensors, aiding the already impressive eyesight of the auk'qarn wielding it. At this point, Kor'Oja was more weapon than auk'nai.

"Talulo wanted to see the Daunoren," Talulo said to the warrior.

Kor'Oja whistled, a low-toned sound that still sounded fearsome even though it was intended as approval. He spoke in a low growl of a voice. "Daunoren is safe with auk'qarn. Thanks to Talulo, this Daunoren shall never fear the world outside."

Talulo cooed.

"Any news from the humans?" Kor'Oja asked.

"Talulo has kept interaction with the humans brief. Observation of the Undriel is still ongoing. The humans make plans to deactivate the ship's shield, but nothing yet."

Kor'Oja cawed and nodded his beak. "The humans can fight own battle. Auk'nai finish whatever remains."

"Auk'nai will not destroy the humans if they defeat their enemy.

But auk'nai will be prepared to if needed," Talulo reminded the warrior.

Kor'Oja nodded. "Auk'nai will lose no more to invaders. This time, auk'nai are prepared."

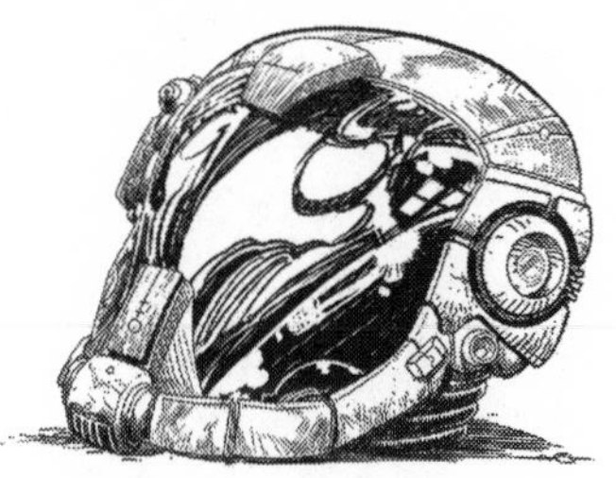

FIVE

THE IRON CASTLE SHIMMERED with electrical energy. It stood silhouetted against the midday sun like a knife slammed into a melon. From Denton's vantage point at Central Base, it appeared as if nothing had changed in the three months since the first attack. Although the Undriel still sent in singular soldiers to prod the human defenses, it had been relatively quiet. Now, it was only a waiting game. Someone would have to make the first move.

Command had agreed with Denton's theory. The Undriel had lost their power to absorb. They had seen failed absorption attempts multiple times in the past months when the Undriel soldiers would find a marine in the wrong place at the wrong time. This meant they were dealing with only a finite number of enemy combatants inside the castle. The entire focus turned to finding a way to penetrate the castle's defensive barrier and destroy it from inside.

Denton wanted to get inside that castle with every cell in his body. In an attempt to breach the walls, Denton was hard at work creating something to help the war effort. They gave him a tiny room with workbenches and replicators. Suddenly he felt like he was working in a smaller version of his parents' shop on Ganymede. The nostalgia was even complete with the looming threat of the Undriel always hovering over him. His failed attempts at gadgets to penetrate the shield lined the tables and floor. They were cobbled-together devices that attacked the barrier in different ways. He was getting closer, hoping to use a bit of unpredictable hillbilly ingenuity to stop the fiercest enemy humanity had ever faced.

His best effort was a distortion beam that could affect the barrier from a distance. Negatively, the area of effect was only a few millimeters wide, and the beam was ultrabright. He needed to work the beam into something more extensive and subtle if they ever wanted to sneak a bomb inside or sneak Cade out. Tvashtar Marine combat suits could slip into a cold mode to remain undetectable, but they couldn't slip through the shield without roasting.

Denton needed to work the problem more, but he had hit a mental dam. He bounced a rubber ball against a wall, hoping that when it returned to his hand, it would give him some insight into how to make the distortion beam work the way they needed it to.

"Castus." Sergeant Jess Combs broke Denton's trance as she entered the room. "Got a little job for you. If you got time."

"Sadly, I think I got plenty of time," Denton sighed as he spun around in his chair to face the sergeant. His beard and hair were disheveled, and his eyes were sunken with exhaustion.

"You look like shit. How's the project going?" Jess asked, looking around him at the ugly machine.

Denton shook his head. "It's going to work great if you can make a bomb the size of my thumb." He stuck his thumb up to elaborate how ineffective that would be.

"I don't think that's—"

"Jess, I'm kidding. Come on." Denton dropped his hand into his lap and stood up. "I've hit a wall. Not sure where to take this thing or how to make it work."

Jess nodded. "You'll find it."

"You said you had a job?" Denton asked, changing the subject.

"Yes. We got a downed sensor in North Base. Think you can fix it? Here's the readout we've been getting." Jess flicked her hand over the soothreader on her wrist, sending the information to Denton's soothreader. "They pinged us about a half hour ago looking for some local help so they wouldn't have to request anything from Odysseus City or the *Aria*."

The data just looked like corrupted readings, nothing too tricky. "They don't have anyone over there that can fix it?" Denton asked.

"Guess not," Jess said. "I'm sure South Base has some people, but we're closer."

Denton closed his hand over the top of his soothreader, and the data disappeared. "I can go take a look. Maybe getting out and stretching my legs will help me solve our problem."

"Great. Bell and Cook will accompany you. I want you to bring a rifle and a pistol too. Just in case the Undies try sending an assassin over again." Jess looked toward the castle. "Any word from R&D?"

"Elly has been trying to help me crack the shield, but we're both sort of stuck. It sounds like they will be sending a bomb over soon. Cart before the horse, I s'pose," Denton said. Eliana's team had been working on an explosive combined with an EMP—because blowing the Undriel up would only stall them as they rebuilt themselves from the debris. In theory, the electromagnetic pulse would disable their tech, and the subsequent explosion would kill them once and for all.

"Understood," Jess said. "Grab your stuff and head on over to the trucks. Get some fresh air."

About fifteen minutes later, Denton pulled himself into the back of a large transport truck. Cook gave him a nod as he entered the back seating area, and Bell whistled from the driver's seat. The truck felt larger with only three passengers. They each wore light fatigues, a combat vest, and a helmet. Their kit included a collider pistol, a particle rifle, a frag and a flash grenade, and a combat knife that worked like a high-powered saw to cut through a metal enemy. It was a light kit for non-combat work, prepared yet not over-encumbered.

Denton pulled his hover mule into the truck behind him. It was a bulky device that acted as a tool chest, equipment replicator, and workstation all in one. He wasn't sure what was wrong with the tech sensor, but he'd be equipped to handle it.

"Hey, Castus," Bell said with a smile, her blond hair tucked neatly under her open face helmet. "Glad yer here with us, or we'd never get out of Central. Pretty sure the Undies just wanna kill us with boredom."

"I'm happy to help," Denton said.

Cook nodded. "Aye, I fully intend to raid North Base's kitchen while we're there. Keep the truck runnin', Bell. We'll be makin' a right speedy escape this time."

"Literally, I will do anythin' to feel some action these days. Throw a flash grenade on your way out too, Cook. Get 'em nice and riled up." Bell laughed.

Denton smiled, feeling muscles in his face move in ways they hadn't in months.

Cook looked out the window and said, "Al'reet. I think we oughtta git goin' before Mom sees what trouble we're up to." He was referring to Jess.

"Roll'n," Bell said, and the large truck shook with the ignition as it lifted off the ground and hovered. The gates to Central Base opened, and they began the short trip to North Base. Cook pulled a mechanism from the ceiling, the controls to a turret mounted on the top of the truck.

"All's quiet as usual," Cook said as he looked through the camera on the turret, eyeing the castle. "You'll know if I see somethin' on account of the damn loud shooting I'll be doing."

"What do you think they're up to in there?" Bell asked over her shoulder.

"Maybe they don't wannae fight anymore," Cook said. "Maybe we'll even see a weird white flag or somethin' one o' these days. Do the Undriel even 'ave flags?"

Denton shrugged.

"We're getting close. Better ring the doorbell," Bell said. She punched a few buttons on the console near her right hand. "Hey, North Base, y'all read me? We're here to fix your shit. Got a pro on board." She winked back at Denton.

There was no answer.

"Y'all read me, North Base?" Bell asked the comm channel.

"Maybe the busted sensor has something to do with it?" Cook offered.

"I don't think so. It shouldn't affect comms. They have been pinging Central," Denton said, and maneuvered his way into the passenger seat to get a better look at North Base for himself. It looked almost identical to Central's structure. A series of box-shaped buildings were made out of transport ships, with an outer wall. The barricade of shields in the meadow between the base and the Iron Castle remained intact in the tall grass. However, Denton couldn't see any marines manning them from his location.

"Yeah, dummy," Bella said, although she was having trouble masking the worry in her voice. "We wouldn't be here if their comms were down. They called us, remember?" She clicked the button to call North Base again. "*Hellooo*, anyone home?"

One of the only differences between the bases was the landscape around them. North Base was only a few kilometers away from a mountain range. Snow shone bright white up in the hills, and dark clouds were forming near the sharp-angled peaks.

"We'd better be done quickly. Looks like a storm is coming," Cook said, peering through the turret's camera at the gathering clouds.

"This is North Base. Reading you loud and clear. Come on in," the gate captain's voice finally responded.

"Jumping *Jupiter*! 'Bout time!" Bell said.

They watched the gate open, and the truck pulled in.

"They got a funny way of running things around here, don't they?" Cook said.

"What do you mean?" Denton asked.

"Well, no one's watching the gate. See?" Cook said as they entered the base, pointing his finger to where the gate captain should have been.

The truck made it through the gate, and they stepped out to an empty yard area. It was as quiet as the chilled mountain breeze rustled through the orange grass. It felt like a ghost town.

"Aye? No welcoming party?" Bell cupped her hands and shouted, her own echo the only response. Denton pulled his hover mule off the truck and joined Cook at Bell's side.

The soothreader devices on their wrist pinged them, and a crackly voice could be heard over the comm, "We're inside. Come on in."

Bell nodded and waved Cook and Denton toward a nearby door. It opened, and they stepped into a long metal hallway filled with doors on the left side. The wall on the right was bare metal. Each of the doors was connected to a transport ship turned operation building. There were a few more here at North Base than at Central.

"Come on in. Down the hall, second from the end," the voice repeated over the soothreader comm.

Bell sneered at her soothreader as they marched down the dimly lit, empty hall. The only sounds were the marines' bootheels and the soft hum of Denton's hover mule. They came to another door, and Bell flicked her hand at the sensor on the doorframe. The door opened into a vast, pitch-black room.

"The Hells?" Bell said in a hushed tone as she peered into the darkness.

Denton heard a door open farther down the hall, the last one before the exit. He expected a marine to come out and wave them over. Instead, a thin leg made of metal a meter long stepped out into the hall with a loud tap. Denton's heart sank, and his skin flushed with cold glacier ice.

"Run!" Bell shouted, and reached for her particle rifle. High-impact particle shots burst from the darkened room, smashing into Bell's leg and shoulder and flinging her into the hall. The shadowed room flickered with red and white lights as mechanical monsters began to reveal themselves from within. Denton got a glimpse of the whirling metal blades and the reflective cloak of an Undriel that stood three meters tall, almost clacking its head against the ceiling.

Spiderbots filled the walls and floor all around it.

"*Hells,* a fuckin' Reaper!" Cook shouted, and pulled Bell out of the line of fire. Denton unslung his particle rifle and let loose a round of shots into the room, destroying a few spider bots and sending shots through the cloak of the Reaper.

"Put Bell on the mule," Denton shouted as he tucked himself back into the hallway. The Reaper rushed through the door and crashed into the wall next to him. The metal hall cracked, and sunlight spilled in through the wound in the structure. Cook hauled Bell onto the mule. She gritted her teeth and used her good arm to blast at the Reaper with her pistol. With each successful hit, the machine was pushed back, rolling with the damage, rotating back into position slightly farther back down the hall.

"Move it," Bell shouted as she continued to fire on the Reaper. Spider bots filled the walls around the Reaper like a tidal wave of blades and red eyes. Cook pushed Denton into the mule as he provided covering fire while moving backward.

Denton shoved the mule forward and ran as fast as he could back the way they had come. Bell called Command over the comm channel while firing her weapon. "North Base is *fucked!* Reaper on site. I repeat, the Undriel have completely taken North Base!"

A spider bot crashed through a door in front of the mule. Denton and Bell spilled out over it and onto the hallway floor. Denton whipped out his collider pistol and shot the small bot three times dead center. It burst into fragments, and blood slapped the wall behind it as the human head inside the bot was destroyed.

Cook leaped over the mule and landed next to Denton, still firing at the Reaper. It began to fire back, striking the mule and cutting through the hall in the process. More sunlight shone through the holes in the wall.

"Make a door," Bell grunted through the pain in her leg and shoulder. Cook dug a frag grenade out of a pouch on his belt and tossed it to Bell. She pulled the pin on the grenade and threw it over her shoulder.

There was an explosion, and the outside mountain air rushed into the hallway.

Cook pulled a grenade from Denton's belt. "Get her out of here!"

Denton pivoted and grabbed Bell's shoulder. More spider bots filled the hall beyond the new exit they created. Denton shot at them, dragging Bell toward the impromptu exit with his other hand. Every spider bot he destroyed was quickly replaced by another. It was an endless wave of robots.

He heard Bell scream. They had been flanked from the other side of the hall. One of the flanking bots had slammed its sharp metal leg into Bell's shin, slicing through her armor. She recoiled and kicked the bot hard, dispatching it with a blast from her pistol as it bounced back into the wave of other bots.

Cook was close behind them, and the Reaper not far beyond him. They dashed through the exit in the wall and made it outside. The turret guns mounted on the base's outer wall turned toward them and began to charge up. Denton pulled Bell behind an equipment box as the turrets started to fire. Cook managed to roll out of the exit just in time, as the high-impact turrets ripped up the metal and dirt where he was standing. Spider bots exploded, and the sound of shearing metal and explosions filled the air. High above, a Matador starfighter rushed past, getting ready for a strafing run.

"They are gonna blow this place," Bell shouted, still listening to her comm channel amidst all the chaos. "Command has control of the turrets. Get to the damn truck!"

The Reaper emerged from the hole in the hallway as a swirling mass of cloaks and blades. It soared across the yard, completely ignoring Denton, Cook, and Bell, favoring its attention on the turret guns. Denton wasted no time, pulling Bell into the back of the truck as Cook dove into the driver's seat and hit it into gear.

The Reaper sliced through one of the turrets as if it were made of paper, then assaulted the other with an array of guns hidden beneath its cloak. Within a matter of seconds, the Reaper had destroyed each of the four guns that were assaulting its flock of spider bots.

Cook drove the truck outside the gate and gunned it across the meadow back toward Central Base. The Undriel Reaper didn't pursue. Denton got one last look at it before it rolled back into the base behind the wall and out of view. He felt like he had just seen Death itself.

"How'd they get in there?" Cook asked, panic raised in his voice. Denton applied pressure to Bell's leg wound, but it wouldn't stop bleeding through his fingers.

"They burrowed in from underneath," Bell grunted through her injuries. "Caught a glimpse of the tunnel in that dark room before the shooting started. Fuckin' assholes!"

"Look!" Denton pointed toward the base they were fleeing.

The Matador starfighter dropped a single bomb on the base. There was a moment where it seemed like the bomb was a dud, and then a massive explosion rocked the world. The shockwave almost threw the truck sideways, but Cook managed to keep it upright with some tight maneuvering. Denton and Bell shielded their eyes from the white-hot glow. After a few moments, the light ceased, and all that remained of North Base was ash and wreck.

"Shit," Bell whispered, and gripped Denton's arm. He kept the pressure on her shin wound. Lacerations caused by Undriel metal resulted in localized hemophilia. Without proper medical care, Bell would bleed out from a wound that would otherwise be non-fatal.

Bell looked pale, and her eyes were drifting.

"Stay awake!" Denton urged.

Cook got the truck back into Central Base and slammed on the brakes. Private Arlo Ortiz was just outside the truck with a medical kit. Denton pushed the doors open and helped pull Bell toward Ortiz. He was ready with the salve he needed to stop the bleeding, applying it heavily. They had dealt with this issue before and were prepared to handle it again. Normally the marine combat suit would do this for them, but Bell was only wearing a light kit.

"Let's get her inside," Ortiz said, getting Bell onto a hover stretcher with Denton's help. Cook went with Bell and Ortiz while Denton sat down against the wheel of the truck. He was breathing heavily, and he couldn't focus on anything.

It was a trap.

The Undriel had faked communications with Central Base to lure in more victims. Maybe they were hoping more people would show up, or perhaps they were just ready to kill anyone who could repair sensors. Regardless, the Undriel seemed eager with what they got. Reapers were only seen when the absorbing process had ended, and it was time to shepherd the new flock of recruits back home. Each of the spider bots at North Base had been a former human marine. This attack had effectively reduced the number of human combatants by a third.

Denton's blood ran cold when he finally realized it.

The Undriel could absorb again. The cold war had finally heated back up.

SIX

CADE CASTUS LAY ON his back on the bed in his private room, but he knew better than to trust his senses. He wore the veil the Undriel provided for him whenever he was stuck in his cell. Taking it off meant staring at the monster he had become. It was too much to bear. Although the veil displayed a lying world, it was a comfortable lie.

<*SOMETHING HAS HAPPENED.*>

<*You sense that too? It can't be good.*>

The door to his room opened, and a man a little older than Cade stepped in. He was handsome, with a long face, pale skin, blond hair, and blue eyes. The man was thin, and wore nice fitting black clothes under a long white jacket. His name was Antoni, and he was Cade's handler. Antoni's divine appearance was part of the false veil, of course.

"Today is a glorious day. Are you ready?" Antoni said with a smile full of too many teeth. His irises thinned.

Ready for what? Cade wondered as he silently stood and approached Antoni.

The Undriel still had not detected Karx. They treated Cade like one of them, a follower, a sheep in a flock, and in turn, he played along. They were all on the same team—Tibor's team. In the past three months, Cade had only seen Tibor once in passing. The person Cade saw the most was Antoni because they worked together. This wasn't to say the whole castle was only filled with Cade, Antoni, Tibor, and Auden—half-formed footsoldiers packed the walls in dormant states, living out their own realities beyond their personal veils. Cade could only guess what each saw, but whatever it was, it was enough to convince them to fight like dray'vas when the time called for it.

Now, Antoni walked out of the room, and Cade followed. As soon as he exited the cell, Karx removed the veil. Although the headset was still attached to Cade's face, he could see right through the camera lens on the front of the gear. Removing the veil only switched the viewing modes. Cade saw what the Undriel software inside his head saw—the real world. The software typically took this data and converted it into something that tickled the human brain harnessed in the crown, tricking it into believing what it was seeing.

With the veil off, Cade could see Antoni the way he truly was—a thin skeleton of a man in tattered, soiled rags. He walked with his hands constantly wringing together, and drool leaked from his lips. A centipede-shaped machine clutched onto his spine and kept him walking upright. His veil replaced his skullcap, eyes, and nose, fused with his skull. Removing Antoni's veil would kill him. Cade wasn't sure if his own veil could be removed without risking his life. Either way, he didn't want to blow his cover.

The others in the network referred to Antoni and Cade as "hybrids." It was a word that came laced with hate. The hybrids were more human than machine; their skin still showed on the outside. Where Antoni had lost his mind, Cade had lost his body. Cade and Karx were unsure of the reasoning for this, but Antoni insisted they were chosen to be this way for a particular purpose. Seeing Antoni as this drooling wretch made Cade almost feel thankful that his absorption wasn't worse.

The metal hallways of the castle were filled with pulsing lights and mechanical panels that could shift into any shape needed. The husks of dead sea life still lined the walls, filling any small crevices that were visible. Part of removing the veil meant Cade had to also smell the reality around him. It was a rancid place, like the inside of a dead animal. Antoni alone smelled like decay, but the walls of the castle overtook the raggedy man's stench. Cade could only wonder how Antoni survived the centuries underwater that the non-hybrids endured.

They entered into a large room filled with the shells of Undriel soldiers. These shells lined the walls, headless and waiting for a pilot. Over the past three months, Cade and Antoni had maintained these shells, like cleaning statues in an old museum. They scraped the dead sea life from their carapaces and repaired anything too damaged by the time underwater. It had become part of a daily routine, or possibly nightly, Cade couldn't exactly tell. There were no exterior windows on the castle. Since Cade had been "perfected"—as Auden put it—sleep wasn't needed anymore. Cade simply worked until Antoni's husk of a body gave out and it was time to return to his cell.

Every time Antoni collapsed to the floor, Cade wondered if he'd ever get back up. Their workday would end, and the metallic centipede clutched to his back would carry him off into a shifting wall panel. Cade would be left alone, but they didn't have to worry about him running away as a hybrid. Against Cade's impulses, his legs and arms would march him back to his cell and seal him in until Antoni was ready to begin work again.

Antoni drooled and whined with excitement as he prepared his tools.

"What happened?" Cade asked.

"Do you not feel it?" Antoni asked, then smiled. "No worries, brother. You will understand in time. I am here to guide you to the path." Antoni coughed—a ragged, mucus-filled retch. Under the veil, these coughs didn't happen. Instead, there would just be an awkward silence. When Antoni regained his composure, he pointed to the wall. "See for yourself."

Antoni waved his hand toward the wall, and the metal panels

shifted away. Hundreds of spiderlike robots poured into the room, a wave of metal and lights. In the center of their mass, a cloaked figure floated. Sparks and smoke vented from its body. It slumped over as it entered the room.

"Brother Talfryn!" Antoni said with the worry of a nurse as he scurried over to the Reaper. The Reaper crashed its arm into Antoni. The impact sent the wretch of a man across the room to be broken against a table. Antoni remained collapsed on the floor.

Shit! Is he dead? Cade wondered with horror. The Undriel were rough with Antoni, but never this violent.

After a few silent seconds, the mechanical centipede attached to Antoni's back twitched its legs and reactivated from the blow. It pulled Antoni's broken body up from the floor and brought him into a hole in the ceiling as the Undriel generals entered the room through the opposite wall.

"Talfryn, I told you not to harass my hybrids," Auden said as he walked through the spider bot wave. The small robots parted to give him room to move. Without the veil, Auden had the body of a metal wasp and stood on two long, locustlike legs. The cloak around his body concealed most of his form, and his glowing white eyes penetrated the room as he observed this site.

Cade couldn't move. He was frozen in place against his will.

<*What's happening?*> he asked Karx.

Karx flicked the veil on and off. Inside the veil, Cade was alone in his fake hotel room, sitting on the bed. Outside the veil, he was a paralyzed statue, witnessing Auden and the others.

<*THEY DON'T KNOW YOU CAN HEAR THEM.*>

Talfryn didn't respond to Auden. He vented smoke and sparks and exhaled with a roar. It had been shot up and blown apart recently, having rebuilt parts of itself with limited resources. Undriel were capable of tearing apart anything made of metal and microchips to repurpose as body parts, but lately, they had been lacking in suitable materials.

Oh, God. Where did it get all these people? Cade had the horrifying question on his mind. With more spider bots flowing into the room and entering the shells, the Undriel had increased their army by over a thousand. Each bot contained a human head, converted and ready to spread the network to the rest of humanity. *Did it get Mom and Dad? What about Nella? Is she here too?* Cade's eyes flicked between the spider bots passing by his legs. Any one of them could be someone he knew, someone he loved. *Zephyr?* Cade's non-heart sank in his hollow chest.

<*KEEP STEADY,*> Karx reminded him.

Auden looked down at Talfryn. "You look horrible. Here, take what you need from this flock. You've earned it."

The Reaper roared and engulfed all the spider bots in its immediate radius. Blood sprayed from underneath its cloak as it seethed and convulsed. The sound of crunching and sheering metal filled the large room and echoed off its walls. After a few moments, the Reaper stood. The smoke was replaced with cool steam, and Talfryn was whole again. Blades rotated back under its cloak, and it stood like hooded death, haunting the room.

The spider bots finished filling the shells on the walls. Now, each of the headless husks was a complete soldier, geared and ready for battle. They waited, clinging to the walls with their teeth gleaming. Auden laughed as he watched the room fill with his increasing army.

"It looks like the good Augmentor has lived up to his word," a deep voice boomed through the room, and two more Undriel generals entered. The deep voice belonged to a behemoth of a machine. It was massive, with spikes protruding from all angles and a long, pronged horn emerging from its forehead.

"You'll learn to stop doubting me one day, Necrodore," Auden said to the behemoth. "It was only a matter of time before we got our full capabilities back." Auden gestured to the spider bots flowing through the room with both of his long, insectoid arms. "In fact, I made us even stronger."

Necrodore bowed his head respectfully toward Auden. He was one of the grand generals of the Undriel forces and had led his warriors into battle against humans many times. Most Undriel were unwilling combatants turned against their friends and family, but humanity had never been an entirely one-minded race. Some *chose* to join the Undriel, agreeing with the idea of perfection through mechanical evolution. Necrodore was one of the volunteers, as were all the highest-ranking generals.

Necrodore was joined by a nightmare shaped like an old Earth scorpion. It was a metal atrocity with long, sharp legs and a tail with three stingers on its end. Its front end had the upper half of a feminine body, with a metallic head that looked almost angelic. It was as if they had crafted a statue of a beautiful woman with a smile on her face and glowing white eyes. The angelic torso was flanked by two large, serrated claws.

"I was worried we lost our appetite," the scorpion said, her voice smooth and deadly. "But it looks like you've pulled through again." She jerked her head toward Cade and approached him, bounding across the room in one smooth, quick motion. "Now that we have our absorption again, we no longer need your little pets." Stingers rotated out of a compartment on her tail and flicked toward Cade's neck.

Cade held his breath, unsure if this would be the end. He couldn't be sure if she noticed his panic. "Easy now, Hilaria," Auden said, and the scorpion's stinger retracted. Cade exhaled through his nose, trying his hardest to remain calm. "We still need the hybrids, now more than ever."

Hilaria curled away from Cade. "Why?" she hissed at Auden.

"Tibor favors the hybrids for the upcoming battles," Auden said. Necrodore and Hilaria looked at each other. The name of their king always seemed to give them pause.

Necrodore asked, "What reasons has Tibor given?"

Auden continued, "If you must know. We fight this new war on a planet unfamiliar to our own, with limited resources. The humans here have not populated or terraformed, so we lack even their resources to turn against them. From recent scouting, I have discovered only two major outlets for resources for our fight."

<Recent scouting? Does he mean L'Arn?>

L'Arn, the monster that had kidnapped Cade and his sister, was half auk'gnell and half machine. No doubt Auden had performed his dark work on the poor beast.

<IT IS LIKELY,> Karx said.

Auden continued, "The first, you will recognize. John Veston's little toy, the *Telemachus*."

"I remember," Necrodore said. "The ship that killed Yeira."

Cade felt the ground beneath him shake, and the walls clattered. The castle was rumbling, but the tremor did not frighten Auden, Necrodore, and Hilaria. Auden lifted his metal claw, and the rumbling stopped. "It is here. Crashed into the planet. It is no longer a threat."

"Those idiots couldn't pull it off, eh? Mucked up the landing!" Hilaria made some horrible noise that sounded like grinding metal. Cade understood this as the Undriel equivalent of a laugh.

Auden reminded her, "Let's not be quick to judge. We were trapped underwater for centuries on this planet."

Necrodore asked, "Do you believe the same event that brought us here brought them too?"

Cade listened closely. He was still unclear how the *Devourer* had ended up underwater on Kamaria. This was the first Cade had heard about their origins on this planet. Perhaps it would lead to a weakness he could exploit.

"Doubtful. I can't imagine *that* happening twice," Auden said, extinguishing Cade's hope for more details.

"What is the other resource site?" Hilaria asked.

"There is a city far to the west, past the mountains, desert, and jungle. They call it Odysseus. If we can make it there, we can rebuild our network to full capacity."

Cade shuddered. The Reaper, who stood silently in the background of all this conversation, turned to face him. Cade worked to keep himself from showing any reactions and attempted to remain invisible. For all they knew, Cade was still masked by the veil. This conversation was supposed to be private.

"Until then," Auden continued, "we will need to make hybrid soldiers fight our battles. We have exhausted all our internal resources with this batch here. We will only be able to absorb in a limited capacity until we reach Odysseus."

Necrodore looked toward Cade, then asked, "What about the corruption? Are we sure it didn't follow us here?"

Auden tapped his claw against the nearest shell soldier on the wall and hesitated. He turned to the others. "We are safe here. If there had been any corruption, we would have seen its effects by now. The Code here is pure."

<*Corruption?*> Cade asked silently.

<*A WEAKNESS?*> Karx asked in return, booming in his mind.

<*Maybe.*>

"Then nothing can stop us now," Necrodore said. He stood straighter, his pronged horn almost scraping the ceiling.

A panel on the ceiling shifted, and the centipede emerged and brought Antoni back down to the floor. His thin body had a large black bruise along his left side, and some metal braces were fused to his body to repair his broken bones. Antoni smiled his drooly half smile at Cade. "You see the new fleet? We have a lot of work ahead of us today."

Cade felt his body reactivate. He shook his head and blinked. Karx toggled the veil on and off to confirm their surroundings. Inside the veil, Cade and Antoni were working in an old shipyard, cleaning the hulls off boats while warships waited offshore. Auden, Necrodore, Talfryn, and Hilaria were absent from the veil version of reality. The veil flicked off, and Cade watched them leave through a new opening in the wall.

Cade flicked the veil back on and spent hours working with Antoni. In reality, he knew every false boat he cleaned was an Undriel soldier's exoskeleton. Cade was forced to maintain the enemy, and to avoid such responsibility would be the death of his cover. He cooperated for now. As the day went on, the artificial sun sank below the artificial horizon. Antoni patted his gloves together.

"Come now, it's getting late." Antoni hobbled past Cade as a wall opened to allow the hybrids to exit the room. Cade's body moved against his will, following Antoni through the ship and away from the Undriel generals.

Back in his cell, Cade toggled the veil back on. The window displayed a lovely spring day on the cliffside, with a cartoonishly evil fortress just across the meadow. He lay back on his false bed and felt the artificial comfort.

<*Did you hear how Necrodore asked about the corruption?*> Cade thought to Karx. <*He was scared. Or worried, at least.*>

<*YES. BUT AUDEN SAID IT IS NOT HERE ON KAMARIA.*>

<*Yeah. Unless that was a lie.*>

<*POSSIBLE. BUT THAT DOESN'T ACCOMPLISH ENOUGH.*>

<*Right,*> Cade thought. <*But do you know what it means?*>

<*NO.*>

<*It means the Undriel* can *be corrupted.*>

SEVEN

"WE'RE SURE THIS WILL work?" Eliana asked.

"It would work on me if that gives you confidence," Homer said. Their robotic eye focused on the explosive device on the table in front of them. The bomb was about a meter long and cylindrical, covered in black metal. It couldn't penetrate the castle's shield barrier, but if the marines could get past that, it might finish the Undriel off once and for all.

Will Cade survive its blast? Eliana worried.

Dr. Maple Corsen added, "We have run all the tests we can, and it shows an eighty-five percent chance of full effect." She had her red hair tied back in a bun, and she tapped a stylus against her soothreader, confirming her analysis with the data floating above her wrist.

Denny, you have to get our son out of there before this thing goes off.

"We'll have to work with that." Eliana nodded, concealing her dread as best she could. "Great work, everyone. Let's load it up and get it to the front line. North Base was just completely overtaken. An attack on Central and South may follow soon."

Maple nodded to the two guardsmen standing near the bomb. They walked over to it, picked it up from the table it rested on, and placed it in a sealed carbon fiber container. The guardsmen took the container away. Maple turned back to Eliana. "Has the front line figured out a way in past the barrier?"

"They are close. At the moment, they have a distortion beam that can crack the shield, but it's not big enough." Denton's work.

Maple seemed to consider this. "It's the distance. Make it too big, and the Undriel will notice, but it's impossible to create something that can make a door in a barrier across a meadow."

"I wish I had answers," Homer said. "In our experience in the Sol System, the Undriel never had a need to activate such a shield. They were so powerful and swift in their attacks that they never had to go on the defensive. The battle on the Howling Shore was the first time in history that humans got the first-strike opportunity."

Eliana patted the side of Homer's spherical head. "You can't be the only one coming up with solutions. We're all in this together. We'll figure something out."

Homer nodded their eye and spun around to get back to work. Eliana and Maple stepped away, walking through the giant lab toward the far wall. They passed other stations, where specialized anti-Undriel weapons were being created with mixed results.

"What if we take the distance out of the equation," Maple suggested.

"What?" Eliana asked.

"Instead of putting a door on the shield, make a walking door."

"I don't think I follow."

"If we can figure out the frequency of the shield, we can create a neutralizer. But you still can't shoot that neutralizer from the Central Base to the shield. As we stated, the distance is too great. It'd be too obvious," Maple said. "But, if you cover something like a combat suit in the neutralizer…"

"You can walk right through it. A walking door." Eliana smiled.

"Yep!"

"Still need that frequency, though. It would work, but that last component is critical."

Maple nodded.

Eliana thought for a moment. Denton had considered using the shield against itself in the past. It was one of his earlier ideas, and eventually evolved into the distortion beam. Still, he had created something he called a "sniffer" to figure out the shield's frequency, then adjusted his beam according to the data he received from it.

Eliana mumbled to herself, "The sniffer could get the right frequency, but it'd need to be sniffing the shield at the moment it shuts off..."

"Did you say something?" Maple asked.

Eliana put her thoughts together. "With an attack imminent, the Undriel will most likely shut the barrier off and divert power to weapons. Central Base has some tech that will observe that moment. They call them sniffers. They can find that frequency for you as the shield shuts off. All shields we know about have a micro-moment of fluctuation as they deactivate—undetectable to the human eye. But the sniffer will see it and have complete data."

"Sounds risky. It involves using an attack against itself, but an attack would still come regardless. Dangerous stuff," Maple said analytically.

"It needs to be done."

"I'll get my team on it right away. We can prep some new chest plates for their armor and have them ready. Then, all we need to do is plug in whatever data the sniffers give us." She thought to herself and mumbled, "Probably should call them *observers*. They aren't actually sniffing anything..."

"Blame my husband for the name. He vouched for sniffers." Eliana let out a quick huff of a laugh. She flicked her hand over her wrist-mounted soothreader and sent the known data to Maple. "Here's what they currently have, in case it becomes useful. I'll inform them of our idea so they can make sure the sniffers are in place."

As the data left Eliana's soothreader, an emergency call flashed in the space above her wrist. Maple nodded and went to her workstation, leaving Eliana to answer her call.

Marie Viray was on the other side of the call. She was an elderly woman who'd been like an aunt to Eliana since the early Telemachus Project days. Marie was frantically looking over her shoulder. When she saw Eliana answer, she rushed her words. "Elly, come quick. It's Nella. She's collapsed." Location data followed her statement.

"Hells!" Eliana closed the call, grabbed a nearby medical kit, and rushed out of the room.

Across the quad was the garden Nella had requisitioned for her nezzarform friends. A squad of guardsmen was perched behind barriers, guns aimed into the garden. George Tanaka stood behind them, holding the reins on a very scared loamalon, calming it as best as he could. Marie Viray sat in her wheelchair, her eyes wide, sweat beading on her brow.

Eliana approached Marie. "What's going on?" But she saw what Marie saw before getting an answer. "Oh god!"

Nella lay on her back in the middle of the garden, writhing in pain with a seizure. Jun Lam was near her but pinned to the ground by one of the nezzarform's bulky stone arms. The other nezzarform, the three-armed one, faced the guardsmen, its cyclopean eye buzzing with energy ready to bolt.

"She needs help, but the nezzarforms won't let us get close," Marie said.

Nella was the only one who could converse with the stone constructs. Without her unique ability, they were at the mercy of the nezzarforms. They looked like mindless creatures, wasps protecting a queen, despite putting the queen at risk in the process.

"Give the word, and we'll take them out," stated a guardsman near Marie.

Nella's hands clenched themselves into claws, and her eyes opened wider, flashing bright green lights. Her neck strained with tension as if her head was attempting to rip itself off. Her mouth opened, and she howled in pain.

"Nella!" Eliana acted without thinking. She ran past the line of guardsmen. They were too slow to stop her, but they kept their guns trained on the menacing rock creatures.

Eliana made it to the area between the guardsmen and the nezzarforms. Both of the stone constructs turned toward her, building up energy at once. Bolts would soon follow. The mindless wasps would create great violence to save their queen.

Except, Eliana realized, these weren't mindless creatures.

Nella had spent months with the stone constructs. They even had names and personalities. They weren't just killing machines, the way they had been when Nhymn controlled them decades ago. These were intelligent creatures of the planet.

Eliana faced the glowing eyes of the nezzarforms, sweat forming on her forehead. Her breathing became slow and balanced. She thought of the Scout Program's number one rule—*keep an open mind.*

"Oolith! Lahar!" Eliana shouted the names Nella had told her. She kept her hands up, palm facing toward the nezzarforms. The stone creatures seemed to tighten their hold on their energy, stepping once more toward Eliana. She continued, "Nella needs my help. She will die without it. Look!"

The stone constructs held their form, still ready to blast.

"I need to treat her. We need to find out what is hurting her." Tears glassed over Eliana's eyes. She felt hopeless as her daughter writhed in pain.

The stones held firm.

A tear dropped from Eliana's eye. *"Please!* Let me help her. That's my baby… I'm her mother. I can't just watch her—"

The stones slipped just a millimeter. They seemed to understand what a "mother" was. They thought of Nella as their own mother—or rather, Sympha had been. Slowly, the energy faded and dissolved. The nezzarforms released their hold on Jun Lam and took one step back each.

Jun scrambled to his feet and joined Eliana's side.

"Stay calm," Eliana signed to him.

Jun's attention darted back and forth from the nezzarforms to Eliana, then finally to Nella. He closed both his fists and pushed both hands from his chest outward. *"I'll try."*

They cautiously made their way to Nella's side. The nezzarforms watched them closely, no doubt ready to obliterate Eliana and Jun if they thought they would harm their mother.

It's the dark patches on her brain. It has to be, Eliana thought. *We might need to operate. Will they let me take her?*

She had to try.

Eliana opened the medical kit from the R&D facility and dug around inside. First, she needed to stabilize Nella and get her on a hover stretcher. This seizure was laced with Siren influence, and Eliana had no way of knowing the full scope of what was happening. She could only treat the symptoms. She got Nella into a rescue pose and put a guard in her mouth so she wouldn't accidentally slice through her own tongue. Eliana pulled two needles attached to tubes out of the side of the medkit and stuck them in Nella's arm. The nezzarform buzzed with energy again, and Eliana put a hand up. "Please, this will help her."

Jun watched nervously. His hands gripped tightly into fists, and his eyes flicked over to the nezzarforms.

The medical kit assessed Nella's vitals. It administered the correct combination of serums to help ease the seizure into submission. As Nella relaxed, the nezzarforms settled. Nella's breathing slowly regulated. Her eyes flitted open.

Nella looked at her mother. The two shared a sigh of relief. Nella wasn't in the clear yet, but she had stabilized enough to talk down her stone guardians. She turned to Oolith and Lahar and conversed with them silently through her mind.

Jun came to her side. He didn't notice the nezzarforms make a slight movement to stop him, but he stalled on Nella's orders. He signed to her, *"I tried to help you, but they stopped me. Your pet rocks can be real assholes sometimes."*

Nella laughed weakly.

Eliana got Nella's attention and signed to her, *"We need to scan you. You might need surgery."* She dragged her thumb against her other hand's palm and winced with worry.

Nella blinked a few times, and her brow scrunched together. She looked back toward the nezzarforms and silently told them the situation. Oolith pounded its large stone arms in protest but submitted when Nella firmly gazed back. Her friends would listen.

"Are you ready?" Eliana signed when Nella looked at her.

Nella nodded. Eliana pulled two metal sticks from the kit, placed them near Nella's head and feet, and activated the hover stretcher. A flat beam of light lifted Nella to waist height off the ground. Jun grabbed the ends near Nella's feet and guided the stretcher behind Eliana on their way toward the line of guardsmen.

The nezzarforms followed them, and the guardsmen pointed their guns at the stone constructs. Nella signed, *"They won't let me go too far."*

Shit, Eliana thought. *Can't have those giant things in the hospital. Where can we do this?* "Got it. Quarantine lab. It has everything we need, and plenty of room to bring in anything else that comes up. Follow me, everyone."

Jun guided Nella's stretcher across the Scout Campus toward the old quarantine lab. In their wake followed Marie Viray, George Tanaka, a loamalon, and two very worried stone constructs.

An hour later, the old quarantine lab was back online and converted into a hospital room for one unique patient. Marie and George sat in the observation room. The loamalon, Penelope, waited outside with the nezzarforms, munching grass and wildflowers. Eliana, Jun, and two other nurses helped settle Nella into her bed.

Maple Corsen pinged Eliana's soothreader. She answered the call, and Maple appeared as a hologram above her wrist, speaking as analytically as ever. "Dr. Castus, will you be away long? Some of the teams here in R&D need some guidance."

Eliana knew Maple was unaware of the situation and forgave her for her coldness. Before responding, she considered some options, then answered with her optimal choice. "Some things have developed. I will be stepping down from my role as R&D chief. I'd like you to be my replacement."

Maple's eyes widened. She looked slapped by the sudden promotion.

"You'll do great. You ask all the right questions and have the right answers. If you need any help, Homer can assist you. What do you say?"

"Yes. Yes, I accept," Maple said, straightening the glasses on her nose.

"Perfect," Eliana said. "Sorry to make this brief." They finished their goodbyes, and the call ended. She entered the autopsy room turned hospital and sat by Nella's side. Jun sat in the corner of the room, reading a book through his soothreader. He nodded to Eliana, stood, and left the room to give them some privacy.

Eliana stroked her daughter's thick hair. They smiled at each other for a silent moment. Nella was incredibly strong, and not even this incident made her appear weaker. She looked shaken but resolved. She was friends with stones, and in turn, she had become as strong as them.

Eliana signed, *"What happened?"*

Nella's eyes flicked away from Eliana for a moment as she tried to remember. She signed, *"I tried to talk with Cade."*

Eliana coiled back in confusion, then signed, *"How is that possible?"*

"It is not." Nella huffed a small laugh and lifted her arm, displaying the IV placed in her vein. *"I tried to use the nezzarforms as a link. Their connection to the planet might have worked like an old telephone wire. But it was too much."* Nella's hands shook.

Eliana put a hand on Nella's cheek.

"I miss him," Nella signed, with tears in her eyes.

Eliana welled up with tears as well as she nodded. *"I do too,"* she signed and said aloud at the same time. Her voice was weak. *"We will get him back. I know it."*

A nurse came to Eliana's side and flicked Nella's scan data to her soothreader. Eliana inspected the data. There were some weird elements to her readings, but nothing that suggested surgery was currently needed. Operating on someone with such a unique condition would be extremely dangerous for both patient and surgeon. If the nezzarforms weren't happy with the results, they could become violent.

"Surgery?" Nella held her left hand flat and sliced her thumb across her palm.

Eliana clapped her forefingers against her thumb. *"No."*

Nella sighed with relief.

"Get some rest. I will be keeping an eye on you," Eliana signed, then stroked her daughter's hair one more time before sitting back in her chair. She began to hum the tune to an old Martian lullaby that her mother once sang to her. Although Nella couldn't hear it, she could feel the vibrations of the song.

Nella drifted into sleep.

After some time, Eliana started to doze off as well. She shook her head in an attempt to keep herself awake, but she was slowly losing the battle. She turned toward the observation room. George and Marie had left some time ago, and Jun was sleeping on an inflatable mattress in one corner of the room. There was still one other visitor in the room. Eliana could see the glowing tattoos first and knew it must be Zephyr.

Eliana stood and entered the observation room. Zephyr whispered, "I saw the commotion in the quad earlier. I wanted to check in on you two. I hope you don't mind, Dr. Castus."

"Call me Elly," Eliana said with a smile. "It's alright."

"You look beat." Zephyr's eyes darted around her face.

"It's been a Hells of a day." Eliana sat in the chair near her.

Zephyr looked toward Nella for a moment, then to Eliana. "Let me keep an eye on her. You get some sleep. I see someone brought in a little bed for you there. If anything happens, I'll wake you up."

Eliana turned toward the corner of the room and noticed the other inflatable mattress for the first time. It had Marie Viray written all over it, with the comfortable pillows and crocheted blanket. Eliana smiled. She turned back to Zephyr and whispered, "Are you sure? I don't want to keep you from any other duties you have."

"I'm positive. We sent the dart with the bomb earlier today. I have nothing going on until we need to send another." Zephyr nodded. "Get some sleep, Elly. Nella isn't going anywhere."

Eliana felt relief dousing some of the anxiety she kept tight within her. She nodded. "Thank you again, Zephyr."

"It's the least I can do." Zephyr looked toward Nella.

Eliana slipped into the makeshift bed and plummeted into sleep the moment her head landed on the pillow.

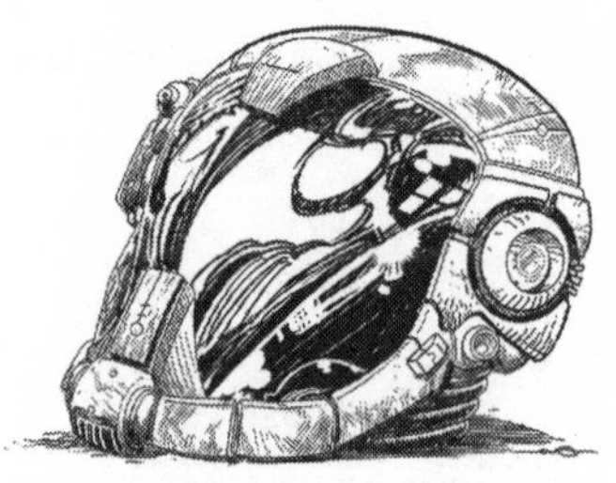

EIGHT

"SO, HOW DO THESE things work?" Private Cruz asked Denton. She was leaning in the doorway of his little makeshift workshop. Denton watched the data readouts from the shield sniffers he'd cobbled together. The sniffers lined Central Base's walls, their noses pointed directly at the Iron Castle and feeding the data into his console.

Denton explained, "Well, when I made the first one, I just wanted to see what the shield around the castle was made of. But according to Dr. Corsen, the sniffers are way more useful than I originally thought. She says that if I can record the exact moment the shield shuts off, she'll have the data she needs to make some kind of special armor that can pass through it."

"Why would the Undies shut the shield off?" Cruz asked.

"Command thinks an attack is coming, after what happened to North Base." Denton shuddered at the thought of the Reaper and the spider bots.

"Hold on. If they shut the shield off to attack us, why don't we just blow them up then? Hit them while they are vulnerable."

"I mean, go right for it. If you guys can stop them before my little engineering project is complete, I will be more than happy to get drinks with y'all afterward," Denton said. "If we pull it off and blow them up early, then that's fine and all. This is for if the war goes on longer—we'll be ready when they try and crawl back behind their shield. Blowing the castle up from the inside is the only way to ensure it goes down for good." And secretly, it was the only shot Denton would have at finding Cade.

"I just hate this sitting around, waiting," Cruz said, leaning against the doorframe. "This tech, it's all different from what I've read about the Undriel. In the old war, we knew how to fight them when we saw them. This new war, we're stuck here guessing. The Undies must have learned some new tricks after we left the Sol System."

"I mean, we didn't know them *that* well back then either. They drove us out despite our best efforts." Denton whispered the last part, choked by his memories.

Cruz looked him up and down. "You were there, weren't you? In the end."

Denton nodded.

"That must have sucked."

"It did," Denton huffed.

Cruz squeezed her eyelids together and shook her head. She pushed herself away from the door. "I need to get back to the sarge. You got everything you need in here?"

"As good as I can be. Stay safe out there."

Cruz clicked her tongue against the roof of her mouth. "Roger that."

Outside, the marines were lining the walls and shield barrier, fully armed and ready for war. With absorption back in the Undriel's bag of tricks, there was no exact way of knowing how large their army was, how aggressive this next attack would be, or when it would even happen. The Undriel could live forever thanks to the stasis their crowns put around their human components. They could string the human defenses along for decades if they really wanted to.

Hours passed; the night came.

Denton leaned back in his chair and watched the data readouts. Like a wave, each sniffer lit up green and beeped, then faded back to red. "Holy shit! That was it!" Denton whispered to himself, almost unsure if he saw it right.

He was correct. Suddenly, Denton's console held the key to the castle. He transferred the readout to a datapad as a backup contingency. As he prepared the data to send back to Odysseus Command and the *Infinite Aria* in orbit, the lights in his shop exploded.

"Shit!" Denton shouted reflexively. It was quiet for a moment, then he whispered, "What the Hells?" It was pitch black, and even the lights on the sniffer had gone out. It was like an EMP blast. Denton tried to restart his console and send the data, but it was no good. His system was fried.

Denton turned the datapad over in his hand. It had been deactivated by whatever crashed his system, but it was booting back up fine. He sighed with relief when he saw that all the data from the sniffers was secure on the small datapad. The only problem was, there was no signal to transmit it anywhere. He'd have to deliver the datapad personally.

There was another problem too.

"It's quiet…" Denton mumbled to himself in the dark. "There should be an alarm…" He gripped the datapad in one hand and rushed out of the room toward the exterior. The lights were out everywhere. Denton was the only one to know that the castle's shield had gone down. "The attack is coming!" He shouted his warning as he ran through the metal halls. "The Undriel are attacking!" Some of the soldiers milling about, wondering what had happened to the lights, heard his calls and sprang into action. But the word was spreading too slowly.

Denton made it outside to the inner walls of Central Base. "They're coming!" he shouted as loud as he could. "Get ready for—"

An explosion threw Denton into a wall, and a loud screech filled the air above him. Gunfire erupted, and the night was filled with particle blasts and rocket fire. Matador starfighters scrambled to get airborne. High above, robots strafed the line of marines from the sky. It was an all-out attack.

Denton shook off the shock of the explosion and looked at his datapad. Still safe. He brought himself to his feet and searched his surroundings.

"Castus!" Private Arlo Ortiz rushed toward Denton in a full Tvashtar Marine combat suit. Denton felt vulnerable in his civilian clothes. Ortiz checked Denton over, then shouted over the chaos, "What happened? Why wasn't there an alarm?"

"The EMP knocked out all the power," Denton said.

"That wasn't an EMP!" Ortiz said. "It was some wave of red light that came from behind Central Base. Never seen anything like it!"

"Wave of red light?" Denton shook his head. What the Hells was going on?

"The Undriel started attacking right after the light passed," Ortiz said. "I don't know if we're surrounded or what. Comms are fucked."

There wasn't time to figure everything out. Denton shook his head and pulled Ortiz in closer. "Listen! The sniffers worked! But that EMP—light wave, whatever—knocked me offline before I could send the info out. I need to get this data back to Command."

There was a roar overhead—an airborne Undriel was being chased by a Matador starfighter. An explosion went off again and almost knocked Denton to the ground. Ortiz caught him and pointed across the base. "Get to the medical center! They'll be taking the wounded away from the bases. You can get the data out that way!"

An Undriel popped its head over the wall behind Ortiz. The private whirled around and began firing on the robot. He shouted over his shoulder, "Get going!"

Denton didn't have time to argue. He took off in a sprint, dashing across the base toward the medical center, unarmed and carrying precious cargo. Up ahead, the outer wall had collapsed. The Undriel behemoth from the first battle was ripping apart marines and blasting Matadors out of the sky with a large particle cannon built into its chest. LPCs were typically reserved for massive warships, and here one was built right into a monster of machinery.

Denton couldn't help fight off the behemoth, and if he lost the datapad, the war would be back at its standstill once more if the Undriel slipped back behind their shield. There was a cramped alleyway to the right of the behemoth fight. Denton would have to hustle, but it would divert him around the battle ahead. He rushed for it.

The alley was blocked with supply crates, the terrain between them uneven. Denton scrambled over one of the crates and flopped into the dark lane between buildings. The echoes of war bounced through the alley as lights reflected off the walls. Denton hustled with the datapad clutched to his chest. Another screech filled the air, followed by a bright, white-hot light.

A missile burst a hole through the building that made up the left wall. Flashes of particle blasts and shadows came into the alley, growing on the right wall. Denton saw another giant Undriel similar to an old-Earth scorpion in design. The shadows of marines torn to shreds filled the wall beside the scorpion. Denton couldn't waste time hiding in the alley. He rushed past the breach in the wall.

A tall supply crate blocked his path at the end of the alley. Denton rammed his shoulder into it as hard as he could, and the crate toppled over and spilled him into the area in front of the medical bay.

"Always causin' trouble, aren't ye?" Private Cook shouted at Denton over the sounds of battle. He lifted Denton up with one hand.

"Gotta get this to Command," Denton shouted, pointing to the datapad.

"Medical craft just took off. Yah missed yer ride, bucko!" Cook shouted.

"Shit!"

"God's smilin' on ye, though. Second chance. Transports are committin' to a retreat. Get your arse in one. Closest one's that way." Cook pointed down the path toward a building close by. The ships connected to the building were converting back into transport mode and prepping for takeoff.

"Let's get—" Cook was cut off as the scorpion machine came around the corner and slammed him to the floor. Denton was pushed against the nearest wall by the impact. Cook scrambled onto his back and sprayed particle blasts into the scorpion. "Run!"

Denton did as he was told, tearing down the path Cook had pointed out. Behind him, the scorpion slammed a claw against Cook's head. Cook screamed as a part of the scorpion detached and wrapped around his skull. The scorpion's device sent out pulses of electricity into Cook's Tvashtar Marine combat suit. After a struggle, Cook stopped fighting and stood up.

The scorpion took incoming fire from around the corner and bounded off to slice through more marines. Denton looked over his shoulder and saw Cook facing him. After a moment of hesitation, Cook bolted toward Denton, using jump-jets to cover the distance in a few bounds.

In his surprise, Denton slipped to the ground as Cook launched to tackle him. "What the Hells, man!" he shouted as Cook slammed into the wall and rebounded like an angry dray'vah.

The device on Cook's head continued to pulse energy into his suit. Each pulse was coordinated with the movement of each of his appendages. The result looked like synapses firing on imaging of a brain, but flashing over Cook's entire body. It pulsed into his arm, and Cook reared his fist back.

"Don't do it!" Denton cried out in panic.

Particle blasts lanced into Cook's arm and chest. The possessed marine fell to the ground, and the mechanical device crawled off his head. "Shit!" Denton shouted as the device sprang upward. It exploded into fragments as another particle blast destroyed it. From out of the shadows, Private Wood grabbed Denton by the arm and dragged him to his feet.

"What the Hells was that?" Denton asked, his panic rising as the night continued to reveal more horrors.

Wood vented the heat sink on his sniper rifle. He kept his cybernetic eye transfixed on the battlefield ahead. "They're converting marines. Been happening all over. We're retreating. Get on the transport."

"On it." Denton began to run, then noticed that Wood wasn't following him. "Come on! You can't fight them all."

"Someone's got to hold them off," Wood said, looking over his shoulder at Denton. The man's armor went into cold mode, and his cloak reflected the world around him. Denton saw his own reflection for a moment. Then it faded away as Wood rushed back into the battle.

Denton entered the building nearby and raced down the metal hallway. Marines were loading into the transport ships. Turret guns were blazing, fighting off the army of Undriel that continued their hyper-aggressive assault. Denton boarded a ship, and a moment later it took off. Before the back hatch closed completely, he could see the entire battlefield from above.

The fighting was everywhere. Lights flashed from guns, explosions rocked the structures they were leaving behind, and some marines were left in pieces on the battlefield, while others were converted into unwilling Undriel soldiers—like Cook.

It was the Hells. All of them, all at once.

Denton saw Private Bell and worked his way through the crowded transport toward her. She noticed him approach and patted the back of her gauntleted hand against his chest. "I don't know how you made it out, but I'm sure glad yah did. Did you come in with anyone else?"

"Wood helped me get here. He stayed back to hold them off. Cook was with me at one point, but he didn't—something happened."

Bell's eyes went hot, and her brow furrowed. "No... not Cook. Damn the Undriel!" She gripped her hands into balls of rage and gritted her teeth together, suppressing tears. "They fucked up now. The Undriel have no idea what kind of new pain I'm gonna give them."

"Do you know if the others made it?" Denton asked.

"Unknown on Sarge. Ghanem, Akinyemi, Ortiz, and Cruz made it out, though. I was supposed to leave on the medical craft, but I stayed behind to help fight. They've been treatin' me like I lost my leg after our stint in North Base. Ortiz patched me up good that day though, been fine ever since."

"Jess…" Denton said, looking toward the back of the transport. Did she make it out? He clutched the datapad in his hand. "Where are we going now?"

"Sounds like we're falling back to the second position, somewhere in the Ember-Lit Forest. Probably regroup and bring the fight back to them."

The marines in the ship all gathered near the windows.

"What's going on?" Denton asked.

Bell shook her head. They joined the others near the windows and looked out over the chaos. Shimmering in the sky, floating above the battlefield, the Iron Castle hovered in mid-air.

"Shit, are they chasing us?" Bell asked.

The castle wasn't moving fast, but it was moving. It drifted over the remains of the battle below, leaving the Howling Shore behind.

"They're pushing the front line farther west," Denton said. "This just got a lot more complicated."

2
TRAVELER OF THE
TRANSCENDENCE

NINE

MOMENTS BEFORE THE ATTACK, something strange occurred inside the Iron Castle. A sound as loud as the sky exploding rocked Cade to his core. He had been pacing his false room when his vision flickered between reality and the veil, and he felt his back arch so far, he thought his mechanical spine might snap. His eyes became beacons of bright blue light, hot enough that he could feel the device strapped to his face sear against his skin. A wave of crimson light passed through his casket and bounced off the metal walls. Karx thrashed and roared inside Cade's mind. Just as Cade thought he might be torn apart, the pain abruptly ceased. He felt a familiar embrace over his metal exterior, a hug in his brain.

Cade cried as he slumped against the mechanisms restraining him to his cell. The tears poured from under the device on his face, and he choked on air that couldn't really be in his throat. The comfort was extreme and sudden, and Cade was unprepared to feel it. He knew who had sent him this long-range embrace.

Cade whimpered, "Thank you, Nella. Thank you so much."

He didn't understand how it was possible, but Cade knew this feeling. It was the first and only moment of true comfort he had felt since he hugged his father in the jungle months ago, before he was taken to Auden. Months of torture, washed away for a few artificial heartbeats. So real, and so critical.

Cade wanted to claw through the closet wall, to race through the halls of the castle and burst through its outer shell to fly back home to his sister and thank her. He shook, the comfort replaced with frustration and anger. Slowly, as the comfort faded, so did the hope. Cade's head slumped down in defeat and longing.

<*INTERESTING…*> Karx's voice boomed in Cade's mind.

Cade sighed with relief. <*You felt it too. It was Nell—*>

<*THE DECIDER HAS CALLED US.*>

<*Decider?*> Cade asked. Then a cold wave raced up his frame. <*Wait, I've heard that name before. In history books. You're not talking about Nhymn, are you?*>

<*UNSURE.*>

<*What do you mean,* unsure?> Cade wanted to shake Karx.

The Iron Castle rumbled. The wall to Cade's metal closet opened and dumped him out onto the floor. He got to his feet and looked around. The general hum of the barrier shield that Cade had become so accustomed to was gone. Undriel soldiers rushed through openings in the castle's hull. <*The shield is down? Did they find a way to deactivate it?*>

< *THE DECIDER DID THIS.*>

<*Was that what happened just now? I thought it was Nella.*> Cade's eyes fluttered. The comfort may have just been another lie after all.

<*A SUMMONING WAVE. SYMPHA STARTED IT, BUT ANOTHER CALLER INTERCEPTED IT AND BROUGHT IT TO US. I REMEMBER IT SOMEHOW… YET…*> Karx trailed off.

<*So it was Nella… but there's someone else on the line.*> Cade felt a rush through his body, tickling the artificial reflexes. He checked his hands and flexed their pistons and gyros. He felt something familiar yet strange at the same time.

Power surged through Cade's metal frame for the first time since he had become an Undriel. Months ago, when Cade was still human, pulses of Karx's uncontrolled energy had exploded from his body. It had happened twice that he could recall, once inside a cave full of mutant Sirens, and another time when it was used to defeat L'Arn.

This new sensation wasn't that.

<*What is this?*> Whatever this Decider was, it had reactivated something hidden inside of Cade and Karx. Cade's mechanical palm glowed blue, with a line of light tracing up his arm to his head. He stretched his hand away from his face toward the wall and felt a jolt. The light jumped to the ship's metal, then bounced back to Cade's hand.

"Hybrid!" a voice called to Cade. "Get back in your room."

Auden marched through the halls of the Iron Castle toward him. As Auden commanded, Cade's Undriel body obeyed. The legs marched him back into his casket. Before the wall closed in on him again, Auden peered in. "Do not worry, my friend. They may have found a way to temporarily deactivate our shield, but it is no matter. We have an overwhelming advantage now. Soon, your people will be our people, and we will bring great peace to this planet." Auden probably thought he looked like a kind man smiling, but without the veil, his sharp Undriel teeth glimmered in the dark.

"As it should be," Cade said, playing along.

"Stay in your room. This battle will be over shortly," Auden said, and closed the metal wall.

<*I hope we aren't too late…*>

When the battle ended, the humming of the shield returned. The Undriel soldiers had re-entered the castle. Antoni opened Cade's cell door. "More glory for the Undriel. The beauty of our people is becoming realized. Follow me, brother."

<*THEY WON THE BATTLE.*>

Cade fought against himself, avoiding screaming out in horror. He slowed down his perception of time to allow himself to manage his anger and frustration. He wanted to reach out and strangle Antoni and bring the Hells to the Undriel. For a moment, Cade considered it. Three months in this mechanical Hellscape had driven him nearly insane a few times. Every battle the Undriel won, the stronger they became. Every battle meant they were closer to absorbing people Cade loved. Nella, Mom, Dad, Zephyr… He felt his hand crunch into a claw in the slowed-down reality.

<*I'll kill them all!*> Cade's eyes widened, and he fought his urges in a losing battle.

<*YOU MAY KILL ANTONI,*> Karx said. <*BUT AUDEN WILL STOP YOU. KILLING THIS WRETCH WILL RESOLVE NOTHING.*>

For a few microseconds, hanging in time for an unnatural length, Cade didn't care. He felt his arm start to morph into a blade. The mechanisms in his forearm, elbow, wrist, and hand shifted and coughed. He had a complete Undriel battle kit inside himself, just itching to be applied to the war effort.

<*WE WILL DIE FOR NOTHING. THEN* THEY *WILL DIE BECAUSE OF US.*>

Cade's arms clicked in place. He looked at Antoni, barely hiding his disgust in the time-slow. The wretch's fate would be applied to the people he loved. The thought of Zephyr in Antoni's condition made him want to vomit. For now, he still had the advantage. Cade could secretly spy on the castle and find out how to bring the Undriel down. He just needed to keep his calm and play along. He gave himself a few more slowed moments to ease his anger, then exited his room, shutting off the veil as he stepped out of his casket.

A quick vibration moved through Cade's hand. He remembered the light that had pulsed through it before the battle. He inspected his arm now that he could move it, but nothing seemed out of place. The faint blue light he had seen before was gone. There was something tucked away in his mind now, like an epiphany slotted into a folder, waiting to be opened.

Antoni broke Cade's trance. "Come and see. We have others to tend to now." The metal wall opened, and before them was an expansive room. The walls were lined with Undriel soldiers crawling back into their slots. On the ground, Tvashtar Marines stood in a group. For a brief instant, Cade thought it might have been a boarding party here to save him. Then he noticed the devices on their heads and the weird way their combat suits flickered with red pulses of light.

"A hybrid army?" Cade whispered.

"We are the preferred method to victory." Antoni smiled, his veilless face drooling and his metal centipede back brace keeping his twitching body upright.

Necrodore and Hilaria entered the room, stepping through the hybrid army without caring who they knocked over or shoved aside. Cade noticed the amount of blood on their metal carapaces—the smell of copper filled the air. The castle rumbled, and there was a sensation of upward movement, like being on a hover lift.

"We sail to victory." Antoni smiled.

Auden spoke to Antoni and Cade, gesturing to the crowd of new hybrids. "You see our newly networked. It is not perfection. They will still require food and other fuels to stay alive. It will be your responsibility to keep these rescued ones alive until we can adequately elevate them."

The crowd moved like livestock crammed into too tight a space. They pushed and squirmed around, bumping and shoving mindlessly. These were once members of humanity's most elite combat force, and they had been reduced to herd animals.

"Plenty to eat," Hilaria said, dragging a massive bloody case behind her. The crimson streaks on the floor implied that whatever was in the case was overflowing through its seams.

That's not... Cade was horrified at the thought. *Human bodies?*

"The soldiers are fine for now. Antoni will monitor them, and Cade will assist. Antoni will summon you as needed, as it has been," Auden said. "Until then, get back to your room."

As Auden commanded, Cade's body obeyed. His legs turned and marched him back through the metal hall of the Iron Castle. The wall opened, and he stepped back into his closet as it closed around him.

<*They are making us fight ourselves! Not only that, it looks like they will force cannibalism on them as well. This is a nightmare!*> Cade shouted in his mind.

<*WE HAVE SOMETHING WE CAN USE.*>

<*What?*>

<*THE DECIDER HAS REAWAKENED THE TETHERING.*>

<*Tethering?*> Cade remembered that being the term his father used to explain how Sirens linked to each other. It was like a mental pathway between minds.

<*YOU HAVE ALREADY TETHERED TO ONE SOUL.*>

<*What the—who? How?*>

<*YOUR HAND. THE SHIP. THE SOUL WITHIN IS SMALL AND WEAK, BUT IT IS A PART OF US NOW.*>

<*I'm tethered to… the* Devourer*?*> Cade's eyes widened, and he smiled. <*Let's bring it down then!*>

<*WE CANNOT CONTROL. WE CAN ONLY OBSERVE.*>

<*Shit.*> That would have ended this war quickly and decisively. Bring down the entire Undriel force in one violent, messy crash. <*Wait, what do you mean* observe*?*>

<*THE TETHER LINKS US TO THE SOUL. THE SOUL'S LIFE IS OURS TO OBSERVE.*>

<*Wait, so you're saying we can observe the* Devourer*'s past?*>

Cade's answer came as a white-hot flash of light.

TEN

CADE CASTUS FELL TO the metal floor, collapsing on his hands and knees. He gasped for air and felt his lungs fill—his *real* lungs. The cold floor pushed against his palms, and his knees hurt from the fall. At this moment, he realized how inaccurate the Undriel simulation had really been. Cade pushed off the floor and checked his body. He could see through his dark skin as if he had been made of fog. But it still felt good. He could feel and see his old body again, as weird as it looked.

Cade's laugh echoed off the walls, and he jumped with excitement. He loved the way his old body felt, knowing that Auden had no control over him now. Then he stopped and looked around.

<*Karx, remove the veil,*> Cade said, sensing a trick.

<*THIS IS NO VEIL,*> Karx stated. <*THE TETHER WORKED. YOU ARE A SHADE LIKE YOUR FATHER WAS IN MY TIME.*>

He remembered the old stories. Denton Castus, the Shade, the Time Traveler, his dad. Denton had observed Nhymn and Sympha's history as a sort of shadow on the wall. The mentally sensitive Sirens noticed this observation, but Cade wondered if non-mentally sensitive beings could notice something like Shades at all.

Cade examined his surroundings. Unlike the dark, cold interior of the Iron Castle, this was organized and pleasantly decorated. Paintings and other work lined faux wood walls, and warm lights made this place feel comfortable.

<*Where are we?*> Cade asked.

<*I CANNOT KNOW. THIS LOOKS LIKE A HUMAN PLACE.*>

A little girl, about five to six years old, wearing a nightgown, ran through Cade. He felt a tickling sensation as the girl passed through his shadowed body. She had short-cut black hair and pale skin, and she laughed as she scurried down the hall to the left.

Part of Cade seemed to latch onto her as she got close, like he had shared space in her head. He could hear some of her thoughts, like whispers. He could feel the joy in her heart. Even though she had just passed through Cade, this moment felt like a memory. Cade was somehow remembering something that was actively happening, something that had never even occurred to *him*, specifically. It was Shade walking, but more profound than anything Cade's father had ever described.

<*FOLLOW HER,*> Karx instructed.

Cade followed the girl through the halls until they entered an expansive domed area.

<*Holy Hells,*> Cade whispered in his mind at the sight of it. The dome was open to a sky filled with chartreuse and gold hues. Thick clouds of yellow lined the horizon, like a view from heaven. The dome had a leafy green tree in the middle, and the floor was lined with green grass. Flowers bloomed, spotting the grass with yellow petaled flowers. A swing hung from the tree in the middle, with children's toys scattered around it.

Another child was sitting on the swing, her back to Cade. She, too, wore a pale teal gown. Her head was completely bald except for a paper crown that sat tilted on top. A thin cord hung from the crook of her elbow and tapered off into a bag hanging from a metal post on wheels.

"Dia! Dia!" the little girl with the black hair called out to the girl on the swing. They looked to be the same age. Sisters—maybe twins?

The girl on the swing turned and smiled weakly. Her eyes looked heavy, tired. She was hushed in response. "What is it, Yeira?"

<*Yeira. I heard that name before…*> Cade tried to remember.

<*NECRODORE MENTIONED IT.*>

<*That's right. He said the* Telemachus *killed Yeira.*> Cade looked at the little girl with short black hair and winced. <*Did my grandfather's ship kill a little girl?*>

"Look what I found!" Yeira shouted with glee. Cade cautiously approached the girls near the swing, still unsure of his surroundings. Yeira pulled two cupcakes out of a fold in her gown. They had frosting caked to their tops with little sprinkles, though most of it had stained her clothes during transport.

Dia smiled. "I'm not sure I'm supposed to eat that. Go ahead, have it for me. I'd love to watch you enjoy it."

Yeira giggled. Not bothering to remove the paper, she smashed each cupcake into her mouth and let the chaos sort out what was edible and what would give her a stomach-ache. Dia laughed at the sight.

As the two girls discussed childish endeavors, Cade tried to get his bearings. Peering out the windows was confusing. This felt like a space station, but the clouds implied it was closer to a planet's surface. A mountain peak not too far off in the distance poked its way through the yellow clouds. Its surface was lined with more structures, somewhat like the dome he was standing in. Other domed spheres rested among the clouds, with long, stalk-shaped structures keeping them upright. It was as if each building were a large-petaled flower thrust upward into the heavens.

A door opened, and a strange animal entered the room. It had black, brown, and white fur with dark black eyes, pointed ears, and a fluffy tail that wagged. It approached the girls, and although it had claws at the end of each of its paws and sharp teeth that gleamed white, the girls were not frightened.

"King!" Yeira shouted, and ran up to the beast. Cade thought it might tackle the poor girl to the ground, but instead, it sat politely as she grew near, and then it licked her face. Yeira petted the animal fiercely, rubbing the cupcake debris into its fur.

A man entered the room shortly after the animal. "There you are. I was worried about you." He was bald, with a bushy white beard and lightly tanned skin. He wore a dark brown turtleneck sweater under a white lab coat, dark gray fitted pants, and slick black shoes. He had an orange tint to his left eye, and his right eye looked like a solid ball of black marble. Cade recognized this man, except it wasn't from under a false veil this time.

"Sorry, Uncle Auden." Yeira shrunk into herself, the way a child in trouble does.

Auden approached his pet and picked some of the cupcake matter from its fur. "Good dog, King." He was generous enough to flick a small piece toward the animal's maw, and it licked it up with pleasure. Auden looked toward the girl on the swing and sighed, then looked to Yeira. "I know you want to play with your sister, but she is receiving treatment. You'll have to wait until the timer ends." He pointed at the device on his wrist. It looked similar to soothreaders Cade had seen before, but this was bulkier and made with older technology.

Auden went to his knee and brushed Yeira's short black hair back. He said with a smile, "Tell you what, I have a special treat for you."

Yeira's eyes widened, and her smile grew, revealing a few missing teeth.

"There is a fleet coming here to Venus soon. They want to see my new invention, but they are bringing their big—*huge*—starships!" Auden said enthusiastically, watching Yeira's excitement grow.

Venus? Cade thought to himself. *I'm in the Sol System?*

"If you're a good girl and let Dia have her treatment in peace, I will take you to see one of the ships before they leave. Deal?" Auden put his hand out.

Yeira stamped her feet rapidly and hugged Auden. Then she

screeched with excitement and ran out of the domed room, back the way she had come in. Auden watched her leave and petted his animal—*did he call it a dog?*

"I hope she didn't give you any of that cupcake," Auden said to the girl on the swing. Dia shook her head and flicked her foot against the grass, rocking slowly. Auden stood before her. "You know what that could do to your treatments. We don't want you getting sick again."

"I'm always sick," Dia said quietly, a rasp in her voice.

Auden sighed. He knelt in the grass in front of her and lifted her chin to look her in the eyes. "I promise to heal you. I promise one day you'll grow and stretch your wings and fly! You'll have the stars as your playground. Won't that be exciting?"

A single tear escaped from Dia's eye. Auden pulled her close and hugged her. "I will heal you. I promise. We just need to complete some more tests before we can. Can you do that for me?"

Dia nodded into Auden's shoulder.

Auden's soothreader beeped, and he released Dia from his hug. He smiled at her again and said, "Your treatment is over. Let's get Yiera and go to the lab." He removed a pad from Dia's elbow and helped her get off the swing.

"Can we play in here?" Dia asked.

"After lab time, yes."

"I hate the lab. It's cold inside, and scary." Dia shuddered.

"I know. Only for a little bit, I promise. It's important. Yeira's already waiting in there for you. Let's not keep her waiting too long." Auden removed something from his coat, a strap of some sort with technology interwoven into it. He handed it to Dia, and she put it on her head, replacing the paper crown with something much more advanced. A compartment on the far wall opened, and a mechanical spider with a flat back crawled out. It had a black metal carapace, and it glided across the floor toward Dia. When it got to her side, it lowered a ramp. Dia stepped onto it, and the robotic spider lifted her onto its back to sit comfortably. A backrest got her into a relaxed position.

"How does the crown feel?" Auden asked. "Improved? Better or worse than before?"

Dia smiled and lifted her hand, watching as mechanical limbs mimicked her control. As she rotated her wrist, a claw rotated with it. She willed the spider forward, and Auden followed at her side.

"It's getting better," Dia said. "This might be the best version yet."

As they were leaving the room, King stopped and turned toward Cade. The animal growled at him, revealing its sharp teeth.

"King, what's gotten into you? Heel," Auden said. The dog didn't budge for a moment, and Auden said once more, "Heel. Now." King gave up the growl and joined its master's side. It reminded Cade too much of when Auden commanded him to return to his room.

<Did that thing just sense me?>

<IT IS POSSIBLE,> Karx said. *<YOUR FATHER AND I REALIZED FAR TOO LATE THAT WE ARE TANGIBLE IN THESE MOMENTS. ALTHOUGH THESE HUMANS DO NOT SEEM TO SEE YOU, OTHERS MIGHT.>*

Cade was about to follow Dia and Auden when the dome around him began to flicker with light. The sun rapidly rose and set. Dawns and dusks chased each other across the sky, and the shadows in the room danced across the green grass. Dia and Yeira flickered around the room, like memories of a dream. A fleet of starships seemed to explode into existence over the clouds beyond the dome. For a few days, they hung still in the air.

There were flashes of white, and suddenly, Venus was thrown into chaos. The starships were in combat, fighting amongst themselves and blasting at the domes. Some of the spheres exploded, while others were set ablaze by the battle.

Time slowed back to its normal pace as Dia stumbled into the room. She looked dirty and weak. Yeira entered the room behind her, wounded by some unknown attack. She was bleeding from her arm and side.

"Hide! We need to—" Yeira coughed.

Dia scrambled over to the tree with the swing. The sun was setting again, and the battle in the clouds of Venus flashed against the fading light. Dia hid against the large, exposed roots of the tree and waved urgently to her sister.

Yeira fell to the ground in the middle of the room, whimpering.

"Get up!" Dia shouted.

"I can't," Yeira cried.

"Yeira, you have to hide! If you don't, they'll—" Dia cut herself off as the door to the dome opened. For a minute, nothing entered. It was almost like a ghost shoved it open.

"Girls?" the voice of Auden called from the hallway. "Where are you?"

Dia didn't answer, her eyes wide, staring at the open door. Yeira cried out in pain and tried to lift herself to her knees.

Auden entered the room. His face was sweaty, and his one good eye wide and worried. On his head was a thin device, the crown Dia had been wearing earlier. Auden hurried across the room and pulled Yeira off the ground, cradling her in his arms. He brushed her black hair from her eyes and kneeled next to Dia. His voice was rushed and worried. "Oh girls, I thought I was too late."

"What's happening, Uncle Auden?" Dia asked. She moved around the tree to hug him.

"It's going to be alright. We need to get you both to the ships. It's not safe here."

"But the scary machines! They'll get us!" Dia said, fear shaking her words.

The Undriel? Cade thought. *<Is this part of the war?>*

<PERHAPS THE BEGINNING,> Karx suggested.

"Don't be afraid of the machines. They are going to help us," Auden said. "They are our friends." Dia looked at the crown on Auden's head, then back toward the door.

"Look!" she pointed, her eyes wide with fear and her body

trembling. Auden held Yeira tightly in one arm as he used the other to tuck Dia behind him.

Glowing white eyes peered at them from the darkness of the threshold. A figure stepped into the room's dim light, revealing white metal in the shape of a skull. Sharp teeth protruded from its jaw. It stood straighter as it entered, a mechanical nightmare that was a meter taller than the doorframe. It had broad shoulders and long arms with sharp blades. It seethed with smoke, and red lights on its body highlighted blood and viscera painted on from battle.

"That's... Tibor Undriel," Cade whispered. The King of the Old Star. The nightmarish machine that had driven humanity from the Sol System. The bogeyman from every scary story Cade had heard growing up.

"Don't be afraid, children," Auden said.

Dia shook against her uncle's leg, trying to hide within him.

"This one is our friend. We must follow him to the ships. We'll be safe once we get off Venus. Stay close to me, Dia." Auden guided her with him, holding Yeira as they moved toward Tibor. The monster machine silently watched as they approached. Dia skittered ahead once they passed Tibor, trying to gain a little distance from the metal horror.

Cade felt something pulling him. Time sped up again, and he could feel the tether severing. The battle outside the dome grew more aggressive, with flashes of light and explosions bouncing around inside the dome. Then, suddenly, the fighting stopped.

The last thing Cade saw before his tether snapped was the fleet of starships hanging in the clouds. Their hulls were rapidly changing. The ships were broken down and repurposed, ripped apart and restructured. Hanging above the yellow clouds of Venus, Cade saw two master class Undriel starships.

The *Devourers* had been born.

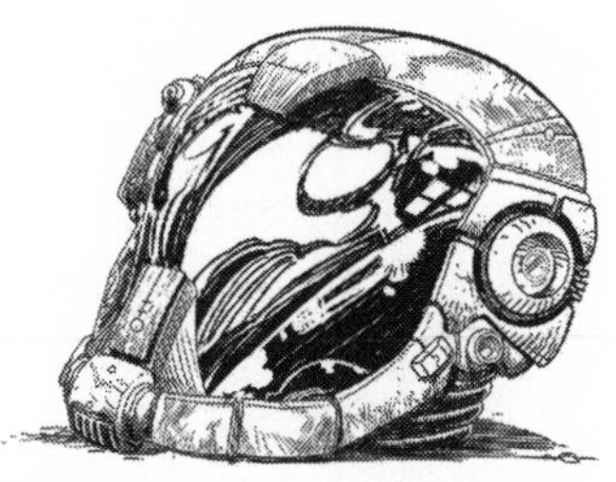

ELEVEN

BRUISED AND BATTERED, DENTON Castus stepped off the marine transport ship. Tvashtar marines filled the Ember-Lit Forest around him, tracing paths through the thick snow. Tall pine trees emitted soft, glowing blue embers that mixed with the mountain snow. It was a lonely place, and even the abundance of wounded people didn't make it any less so. A quiet stillness permeated the air.

Only a few marines whispered about the recent attack and how poorly it went. Hours had passed since the brutality occurred on the cliffside near the Howling Shore. The Undriel were fierce and had almost annihilated the human defenses. South Base was hit simultaneously with Central in an equally devastating blow. Their numbers were smaller now, about two thousand soldiers accounted for out of the original five battalions. Each loss for humanity meant one more gain for the Undriel. Denton couldn't help but feel that they didn't have enough to stop the Undriel. The impossible enemy suddenly felt impossible all over again.

The datapad with the key to deactivating the Iron Castle's shield barrier was in Denton's hand. Bell approached him. "Looks like they got comms working. Try sending that data now."

Denton waved his hand over the datapad. Much like sending data on a soothreader, it only required a simple gesture. The key passed from the pad to the comm network, and within a minute, the message acknowledged that it was received back in the Scout Campus. So simple, yet it took a run through the gates of the Hells to make it happen.

"Your turn, Dr. Corsen," Denton whispered. He wished he could have sent it sooner, but it wouldn't have stopped the devastating attack anyhow. It was time to strategize the counterattack.

Bell bumped him with her elbow, then jerked her chin toward the sky above the trees. A dropship filled the sky, lowering into the clearing in front of the marines. Bell said coldly, "Our bomb is here."

The bomb had been delivered by an express dart from Odysseus Command shortly before the attack. They were fortunate that the mysterious wave of red light had not accidentally detonated the warhead, and even more lucky to have gotten the bomb out of the battle.

The clearing in the forest grew louder with activity. Marines moved about, finding each other after the chaos, while others prepared operations for the plans to come. Transport ships were converted back into buildings, and a medical tent with heat generators was erected to treat the wounded.

Denton walked over to the medical tent, hearing the sounds of the groaning soldiers. Without his little workshop or a project to tinker with, Denton felt helpless. Just another person to manage. It was time to correct that.

He walked up to Private Arlo Ortiz. "How can I help?"

Arlo didn't waste time with pleasantries. He had a willing volunteer, and he knew exactly how to use him. Arlo directed Denton around the injured: "Apply pressure here." "Grab that serum there." "Replace these bandages." "Grab that bone saw."

Finally, Denton came to Private Cruz, who sat on the edge of one of the tables, scratching at a bandage that started at her neckline and crossed her chest. Her combat armor had been stripped off, revealing a large slice in the chest plate that mimicked the wound on her body. Cruz swore and lifted herself off the table, nursing her leg. "Fuckin' Undies."

"Might want to sit a little longer," Denton suggested.

"I'm done sitting. I'm ready to fight," Cruz stated with a fire in her eyes. "That thing, with the tail spike. Didn't see it comin'. It was like that big one, too—the one that got Marathon. What are these things?"

Ortiz came to Cruz's side and checked her temperature. "Hey, Cruz, running a little hot there. Take a seat and pop a few of these." He handed her three little pills. Cruz lobbed them into her mouth and bit down hard with a crunch. She winced and sat back.

"I saw that thing too. Looked like a scorpion, sort of," Denton said.

"What's a scorpion?" Cruz asked. Denton had knowledge of old-Earth animals from his bored scrollings through nature documentaries back on Ganymede. It was his getaway from monotonous life in the Arrow of Hope. He often forgot that others, especially this generation of Kamarian-born people, didn't know what he was talking about. They had their own creatures to fascinate over. The Undriel, on the other hand, had the same background as Denton. They took their inspiration from the Sol System.

"It's an insect from old Earth, a little like a mactabalis wasp but smaller. Can't fly neither. It's got a tail with a venomous stinger on it." Denton used his hands to mimic a tail flicking at prey.

"Venom, eh?" Cruz said. She was sweating. Even with the heat generators keeping the tent area comfortable, they weren't warm enough to make a person sweat.

"Hey, Ortiz," Denton said, calling the medic back over. "Is she doing alright?"

Ortiz finished bandaging another marine nearby and came back over.

"I'm fine," Cruz said, her eyes flittering. "We already treated for the localized hemophilia. I'll be—" She vomited.

"Shit!" Denton shouted.

"Lie down, Cruz," Ortiz ordered. Cruz's eyes rolled back as she lay down flat on the table next to her sliced armor. Her skin had gone pale, and her breathing was shallow. "Okay, she's been hit with some sort of venom. We're gonna need an antidote. Need a sample of it to know what we're dealing with." Ortiz checked Cruz's chest and neck for any leftover venom.

"Here, got some!" Denton shouted, grabbing her sliced chest plate. Residue lined the gash in the armor, barely visible, clear, and thick like synthetic oil. Cruz began convulsing. Nearby, another marine began vomiting.

"Listen up!" Ortiz shouted to the wounded. "I need everyone who fought with the spike-tailed Undriel to stand over there!"

A group of marines moved over to a corner. Each of them had long scrapes on their armor, and a handful had removed the damaged pieces as they waited for replacements. These marines were beginning to show early signs of venom injection.

Private Ortiz moved around his medical station, carefully pulled the sample from Cruz's armor, and slipped it into a machine. The vidscreen filtered through the potential sources, favoring Kamarian creatures.

Denton suggested, "The Undriel wouldn't use Kamarian animals as a base. Their whole setup is from the Sol System. It's got to be venom from something from Earth."

"That tracks. Let's see." Ortiz gestured over the screen, and the list of potential sources shrunk down to Earth's zoology. Quickly, the machine found a match. "It's a mix," Ortiz noted. "Looks like a viper and some sort of jellyfish. There's also a delaying agent in here. Must be why she didn't feel anything until now."

Most venomous animals needed their bite or sting to take immediate effect as either a defensive mechanism or a way to capture their prey. The Undriel had no need for it to react immediately. Why not let the humans think they got away before their bodies began to break down? Stinging them with something they had antidotes for only worked if they got lucky and if the victim was alone when the venom did its trick.

"Do we have an antidote?" Denton asked.

"Not on hand. There might be something back in Odysseus," Ortiz said, shaking his head. Some of the marines in the stung group slumped to the ground. Ortiz looked over his shoulder, taking a deep breath to remain calm and focused.

"We need more time," Ortiz mumbled to himself. He thought hard for a moment, then said, "Maybe… Worth a shot."

"What?" Denton asked.

"It's an auk'nai thing they left behind. Wish we had one of them around, but we don't, so we'll have to use what we got." Ortiz hurried over to a crate and gestured over its lid. The top opened, and a shelf of medicinal supplies lifted out from the box and organized itself. Most of the shelf medicines were in neat little glass vials, but a few were in ornate jars. Ortiz grabbed a jar and swirled it in front of his face.

"Will that even work on humans?" Denton asked.

"It will. They made it for us before the big breakup. It won't nullify the venom, but it should give us a little more time to find a solution." Ortiz rushed back over to Cruz's side. She moaned, her eyes unfocused.

"Listen up, Cruz. I'm going to give you something to keep you alive. It's gonna burn like Hells, but you can handle it," Ortiz said to her. He sliced through her shirt with some scissors and removed the bandage over her wound, revealing a stitched-up laceration and bruised skin. Ortiz put on a latex glove and poured some of the jar's contents into his hand. An ooze slowly dripped from the jar. It was primarily black, with flashes of purple and green glinting off the low light of the forest. He rubbed it onto her wound, and Cruz gasped in pain, too weak to scream. The auk'nai medicine bubbled and emitted a faint smoke, and Cruz winced as it seeped into her skin. "Come on. Work!" Ortiz whispered. He pointed to the data screen nearby. "What's it say?"

Denton scrambled over to the data screen, almost knocking over a small shelf in his haste. He watched Cruz's vital signs. Her pulse was erratic, and it didn't seem to change. "Uh, still not—Wait!" Her pulse seized up, spiking violently. Cruz's back arched, and she let out a strangled shriek. The wounded marines nearby moaned in pain and worry.

Ortiz snatched another glass vial from the shelf nearby and applied it to a clean cloth. He pushed Cruz flat and ran the cloth across her wound, extinguishing the smoke the auk'nai medicine had created and causing her injury to fizz.

Her vitals made one last leap upward, then stopped altogether. There was a steady tone, and the marines began to groan with agony. Ortiz kept his eye on Cruz. Sweat ran down his face.

Then a single beep sounded.

Cruz exhaled and slowly began to breathe again. Her breaths were still quick and shallow, but she was alive. Ortiz exhaled and walked over to Denton to double-check Cruz's readings.

"Okay, we need to treat all of these marines the way I just did," Ortiz said, hurrying to gather more of the auk'nai medicine and the glass vials. "The auk'nai medicine is targeting the delaying agent in the venom and strengthening it. It buys us time, as the delaying agent extends its use longer. Hopefully long enough so we can get some real antivenom over here. Call the Scout Campus. Get them to send something on a dart." He shouted to a few of the medical staff nearby, and they came to his aid, ready to help treat the marines.

Denton stepped away and flicked his hand over his soothreader to call Eliana.

Eliana Castus exited the autopsy bay with a sigh. It was dark in the old quarantine lab, and Nella had drifted off into sleep. She sat down on the bed and looked around the dark observation room. Jun and Zephyr had gone home for the day—they couldn't stick around forever. Eliana was alone with her thoughts.

Memories came to her of walking into this lab with Faye, searching for her husband, Captain Roelin Raike. The lights were off then, too, with only the backup emergency ones flickering in the autopsy chamber. Faye screamed. Eliana winced, remembering similar screams years later when Faye was absorbed by the Undriel on the Howling Shore.

Eliana didn't scream the night her father was murdered. She went numb.

Her soothreader notification was blinding in the dark quarantine lab. She slid her hand over it, and a message from George Tanaka appeared.

Check these readings, the message read.

"You're up late, aren't you, George?" Eliana mumbled to herself. She slid her hand over the soothreader again, and a satellite image popped up. It was a time-lapse collection dropped into an animated sequence. The Siren Pit took up the center of the picture. George had a dedicated geostationary satellite over the site to keep watch over it and whatever lurked inside. A burst of green energy, forking like lighting, sprayed across the crimson dunes of the Starving Sands. Some of the lightning flickered into the Siren Pit.

"Is this..." Eliana whispered to herself. "Nella's attempt to call Cade?"

The green lightning vanished. Red energy built up inside the Siren Pit, resembling the glowing eye of a nezzarform. Eliana jolted in her seat as the image went white in a flash. The brightness hurt her eyes, and she blinked away the assault. The red lightning flashed outward from the pit, but in two directions, not simultaneously. First, it lanced to the west, retracing the forking lightning pattern Nella had sent out.

Eliana looked over to Nella sleeping and exhaled through her nose. This was what had caused Nella's intense seizure in the garden. It was as if Eliana were watching a gun recoil from the shot it aimed at her daughter. Her eyes returned to the image, and she watched as more red lightning lanced to the east.

"Where did that go?" Eliana mumbled to herself. It had an immense range if this energy managed to trace its way back to Nella from that distance. The Starving Sands desert was almost halfway across the continent from Odysseus City. East of the pit was…

"Toward the Howling Shore?"

To Cade!

The red lighting faded, and the pit lost its glow.

A follow-up message from George Tanaka read, *What do you think?*

"I think the Sirens are trying to talk to each other," Eliana whispered. The soothreader translated her words to text and sent them back to George.

Months ago, Denton discovered a Siren lurking in the pit. How long it had been there and what plans it had remained a mystery. *Was it Nhymn or something new?* Eliana had no idea. Her effort to avoid bringing a Siren into the Undriel situation was starting to fail her. If they could send out these far-reaching signals, there would be no stopping the Sirens from reuniting.

A new emergency call came in, interrupting her conversation with George. Eliana sprung to her feet and walked outside the quarantine lab as she answered. Denton appeared as a hologram over her wrist.

"I'm here. What's the emergency? Are you alright?" Eliana asked.

"We have a situation over here. One of the Undriel we encountered is using some old-Earth venoms on our marines. We don't have anything here that can counteract it, and we need some antivenom sent over quick," Denton said, not wasting any time.

"Old-Earth venoms…" Eliana stopped and thought for a moment, "We won't have any antidotes for those in our hospital here. But we might have some in the academy. I'm on it."

"Here's the exact data readout we have from one of the injured marines." Denton waved his hand over his wrist. There was a delay, and Eliana made her way over to the campus while it was sending. She crossed the small sloping hills of the area between the campus buildings. The night sky lit her way as Kamaria's dual moons shone brightly overhead. She entered the academy building and headed down the halls toward the medical training wing. Her wrist vibrated as the data finally reached her.

That took longer than it should have... But Eliana would ask about that later. Right now, she had to find antivenom. She entered a large classroom with auditorium seating and six neatly organized workstations to view. On the wall were locked cabinets with plexiglass doors. "Denton, ping Dr. Corsen while I look for your antivenom," Eliana said, not stopping in her task.

Denton nodded, and his image vanished for a moment.

Medical trainees on Kamaria had no use for old-Earth antivenoms. It had been taught as part of a curriculum for a while, but the old vials had become part of cold storage, forgotten as time went on. Eliana made a few gestures over her soothreader, and it linked itself with the row of cabinets. She snapped her finger over the reader, and the data Denton sent appeared. Eliana grabbed the names of the venom sources. Echis carinatus, a pit viper, and chironex fleckeri, a box jellyfish. The delay agent didn't need to be neutralized; on its own, it was harmless.

Her soothreader dug through the cabinets' inventory listing and found the antivenom needed and where it was located. Eliana opened a cabinet as Dr. Maple Corsen entered the lab. She wore a lab coat over a set of comfortable-looking blue pajamas. "Dr. Castus, I got the call. How can I help?"

Eliana grabbed the two small vials and double-checked their contents. Satisfied, she said, "We need to replicate these and produce as much as possible for the troops. There's no time to waste. We'll have to send a dart to their location."

"Got it," Maple said. Without missing a beat, she activated a station nearby. "We can make some right here and get more spread out for production."

Eliana gave Maple the pit viper antivenom and took the box jellyfish vial over to another workstation. As they worked to make replications, Eliana asked Denton over the soothreader, "Have you managed to stabilize the wounded soldiers?"

"Yeah, Ortiz used some sort of auk'nai medicine to amplify the delaying agent in the venom and buy us some time. We don't have too much of that stuff, though."

"Auk'nai meds…" Maple shook her head. There would be no more of that resource once they ran out. The auk'nai had made it clear they would let the humans solve their own problems from now on. Eliana missed the cooperation between their species. She hoped that humanity could win this war and heal their relationship with Talulo and his people.

Replicating the antivenom was a multistep process that required three machines to perform. Without the source animals present on Kamaria, they couldn't get any more venom without asking the Undriel nicely. Still, this process had been perfected for the Madani Cure, the solution to the lung-lock problem decades before. One machine broke down the particles in the venom into essential compounds, then the second machine isolated and replicated those compounds. The third machine smashed them back together, creating a duplicate. The more you could put into the first machine, the more you would yield from the third machine.

"Why did the data take so long to send?" Eliana asked Denton as she worked, already producing a batch of box jellyfish antivenom.

"We were hit with something weird. It knocked out the lights and power to some of Central Base just before the attack. Hells, now that I think of it, it's probably what brought the shield barrier down and got the key to my sniffers," Denton said.

Maple interrupted, "We're working on something with the data from your sniffers. Hopefully, we'll have something for you soon."

"Wait, this thing that knocked out the power. Did it look like red light?" Eliana asked.

"Ortiz mentioned something like that, yeah. I was in my workshop at the time, so I didn't see what hit us. The weird thing is, it—"

"Hit the base from the west side, right? It came from the west and moved east."

"Yeah, did you get briefed on this?" Denton asked.

Maple looked up from her replicating, staring in curious confusion.

"I got some information from George recently. I'll look into it more after we get you what you need," Eliana said, and got back to work.

Within a half hour, there was a crate full of the antivenoms needed. Maple secured the crate to a hover mule and nodded to Eliana. "I'll get this over to R&D. We'll finish up and get it on a dart."

"Thank you, Maple," Eliana said.

"Pleasure working with you again." Maple nodded and escorted the hover mule out of the classroom.

Eliana sat down in the closest auditorium chair and rubbed a hand across her forehead. Denton was still on the line, hovering like a glowing ghost next to her. "You just saved some lives."

"I wish there was more we could do," Eliana said. "I wish you'd come back." There was a silence in the air. Denton looked down and shook his head slowly. Eliana looked over to his holographic image with a tear in her eye. "I know you can't." She wanted so badly to pull Denton through the hologram and make him sit next to her. She couldn't make that happen. Eliana knew what he'd say next, and it was too important.

"I have to find Cade," Denton said. "He's in that castle, somewhere. Nella feels it. We can still save him. Even if he's been…"

"Absorbed" was the word Denton couldn't say. Eliana's heart tripped a beat at the thought, and she sniffled as she shook her head, trying to extinguish the idea entirely. She leaned back in the auditorium chair. This place looked similar to some of the classrooms she had been in on Remus Orbital back in the Sol System. Hells, the antivenom vials they had may have even been relics from those same classes. She remembered those days fondly, back before the Undriel existed in the way they did now. When it was just a company that made soothreaders, vid screens, and starships. It was the race to artificial intelligence that brought about the end.

"You'll find him," Eliana sighed, and forced herself to smile at him. "You're Denton Castus."

"But I'm not Eliana. You're stronger than me." Denton looked so tired, so worn out and hurt. He looked like a man who had walked across the Hells and left his boots behind, propelled forward only by the slim hope that he might save their son. As much as Eliana needed him here by her side, he needed her support more. Denton needed Eliana to keep him going.

"Let's be strong together, then," Eliana said, wishing she could hug her husband.

Denton nodded solemnly and gave her an injured smile. Even through the hologram, she could see the hurt behind his eyes, the strain, the torment. If she lingered too long on them, she'd start crying. But she lingered anyway. She couldn't help herself. It hurt, but it was necessary. Unavoidable.

For a moment, her mind took her back to the Glimmer Glade, their special place. Eliana and Denton hadn't been to that grove of trees behind the Castus Machine Shop in years, but in her mind, she could travel through time. She saw the young man he was back then, the night of their first kiss. The electricity that shot through both of them as their lips welcomed each other. She wanted to make him smile the way he did back then. But she had nothing she could say and nothing she could do. She had to be strong, so he could be strong.

"The dart will be there soon," Eliana said. "I love you, Denny. Get some rest."

"I love you, too, Elly."

They didn't end the call immediately. Eliana spent another moment looking Denton in the eyes and sharing silence. After some time, she blew him a kiss, and the call terminated. She sat alone in the empty moonlit auditorium, with just her thoughts and worries as company.

TWELVE

<WHAT WAS THAT?>

<SHADE WALKING. YOU SEEM TO HAVE MORE CONTROL OVER IT THAN YOUR FATHER DID.>

The metal casket felt larger now that Cade could step outside his hybrid body. He missed the way his old skin and bones felt inside the memories of Dia and Yeira. If only there was a way to live there, he'd never have to face his nightmarish visage in the sheen of his metal wall ever again.

Cade activated the veil, releasing himself from his tiny coffin to wander around a false bedroom. In a way, this, too, felt like Shade walking. He could feel his skin, touch the bedsheets, even open a window and feel the air. But now that he remembered his old body, this simulation paled in comparison.

The Iron Castle was flying, and the veil reacted accordingly. Outside his faux window, he could see clouds and mountains moving by as if he were flying across the countryside to visit family.

It reminded Cade of traveling back from orbit. It reminded him of Zephyr. He wanted to turn to his side and see her there, listening to music on her soothreader or watching a movie. She'd smile, maybe invite him to listen or watch along with her. Cade wanted to hold her again, to seek comfort in such a terrible world.

Would my embrace hurt her? Cade wondered. *Would this jagged metal body cut her?*

Even if he managed to survive this nightmare, he would never be the same. Zephyr would only see him for what he was. A monster. A hybrid. Not human anymore.

Cade dug his fingers into his mechanical palm, not noticing as the blue light returned to his clenched fist. He couldn't see it under the veil anyway. His new ability was hidden away by a shroud of falseness.

But the falseness was comfortable. Cade unclenched his fist and looked out the window. *Can I be normal here?* he wondered. *If Zephyr had a veil on too, we wouldn't even notice the machinery... In the veil, we're all whatever we need to be comfortable. Is that so bad?*

The clouds passed by slowly, like window shoppers browsing, staring at the new appliance in a storefront. Cade looked back at them and knew they were just as fake as he was.

<*CAN YOU CONTROL YOUR TETHERING?*> Karx asked, his booming voice jolting Cade upright.

<*What? I'm not sure.*> He remembered the blue light that flicked out of his hand and attached itself to the wall. <*I had it in my hand, even though my hands aren't flesh and bone.*>

<*YOUR AUGMENTATIONS ARE AIDING YOUR TETHERING.*>

With the ability to peer into the last human moments of any of the Undriel in the Iron Castle, maybe they could find a weakness to exploit. <*The corruption!*> Cade became excited. He stood from his fake bed and paced around the room. <*If we can find the source of whatever this corruption was that they seem so afraid of, maybe we can replicate it. We can end the war!*>

<*PRECISELY.*>

<*I need to find a way to tether into Tibor Undriel. He's the leader behind all of this. He'd have the answers we'd need.*> Cade removed the veil and faced his horrifying reflection. He shuddered, then strained his body. He could see a blue light ebbing from his wrist, refracting off the metal walls. It licked out again, and he felt a sting

crawl up his back and enter the base of his skull. Cade yelped with pain and shook his head reflexively.

<*YOU ARE ALREADY TETHERED TO DIA. THIS SHIP.*>

<*I know that. I was trying to reach Tibor.*> Cade shook off his pain and put the veil back on. He sat back onto the bed and looked at his fake hands. <*Looks like I'll have to get close to him.*>

<*A PROBLEM.*>

<*Yes, we haven't seen Tibor much this entire time. Except in Dia's memory, right at the end. Maybe I can try tethering to him during a Shade walk. Do you think it will work?*>

<*I HAVE NO WAY OF KNOWING.*>

<*Only one way to find out,*> Cade said. <*Get us back into Dia's memory.*>

<*HOW?*>

<*Can't you send us back there?*> Cade asked, frustrated.

<*NO,*> Karx said. <*ONCE THE SOUL IS ABSORBED BY THE UNDRIEL, THE TETHER SNAPS.*>

<*I wish there was some sort of book about this.*> Cade buried his head in his false hands. <*We'll just have to find a different Undriel to link with, and hope to find Tibor there.*>

"Stand back, everyone. Supply drop incoming," Corporal Rafa Ghanem warned everyone. Denton took a few steps back and watched as a laser grid lit up a circular radius on the ground ten meters away from him. The circle of light began to rapidly shrink until a blast of snow exploded from the ground as the dart made impact. Denton felt vibrations in his boots.

"Alright, let's move people!" Rafa shouted. The dart was around four meters tall, cylindrical, and filled with compartment doors. As they approached, the dart cooled its exterior with a blast of a freezing agent. When it was done, Rafa flashed his credentials to it through his soothreader and the compartments opened.

"Ortiz! We got the antivenom!" Rafa shouted. Arlo Ortiz and a few nurses rushed over with hover mules and loaded the containers of the antivenom. It was good timing. The marines hit with the deadly Undriel stinger were beginning to show signs of the auk'nai salve wearing off.

"We'll get these in all the kits going forward. They can't use this trick again," Ortiz said, then rushed back toward the medical tents with the nurses.

"What's this?" Rafa said, pulling an extra container out.

Bell's eyes widened. "Oh, is that what I think it is?"

Rafa pulled a long crate from the side of the dart and opened it in the snow. Inside, four unique combat chest plates were laid in a neat row. They each had a collider cylinder in the center, with neutralizers lining the sides up to the shoulders.

Denton looked over Rafa's shoulder. "I guess Dr. Corsen wasn't messing around when she said they'd have them ready soon. With these on, a small team can infiltrate the Iron Castle undetected. They run in cold mode, too, so the Undriel sensors won't pick them up. It was the best R&D could do under the time crunch."

The Iron Castle had made significant progress since the battle the night before. The Undriel ship would soon drift over their concealed location in the Ember-Lit Forest as it moved west. The tacticians in the *Infinite Aria* had decided that would be the perfect place to down the ship.

"Only four?" Rafa asked.

"A bigger team would be harder to hide anyway," Bell said.

Rafa looked toward the camp and sighed. "Sarge is still MIA. Looks like I'm in charge." He thought for a moment as he studied the unique pieces of armor. "Bell, are you mission ready?"

"You bet your ass!" Bell said, then corrected, "Sir, yes sir!"

"Akinyemi!" Rafa shouted. Lance Corporal Inaya Akinyemi hurried over from the medical tents. She stood at attention.

"Yes, sir?" Akinyemi asked.

"These will get us into the Iron Castle. I want you on the team," Rafa said.

"Of course, Corporal."

Rafa nodded. He looked over Akinyemi's shoulder toward the medical tent. "Ortiz is needed over there, and Cruz is out of commission…" he said to himself. He hesitated for a moment, then looked over to Denton. "Hey, Dent."

"Yeah?" Denton asked as he pulled more supplies from the dart.

"You want to get into that castle and find your boy, right?"

"Yes, sir." Denton felt his heart rush. This was his chance. He stood up straight and locked eyes with Rafa.

"You know how these chest plates work, and the bomb?"

"Yeah, I do. I was part of both of their R&D phases and construction processes."

"It'll be dangerous."

"I understand," Denton said.

Rafa looked to Bell and Akinyemi. Bell nodded, but Akinyemi shook her head.

"Come on, the guy saved humanity once before! He's not a normal civvie!" Bell said in Denton's defence.

"Private!" Rafa shouted. Bell went rigid. The corporal continued, "Having an expert on the team could be an asset. He's been trained in the suits and held his own during the first fight. I will take full responsibility for Denton. I don't want either of you risking your necks. The key to this mission is infiltration and detonation. If you disagree with my assessment, you may stay out of the mission with no repercussions."

"I'm still on board." Bell winked at Denton.

Akinyemi sighed and nodded. "I trust you. And I've seen Denton in action before. You're right, Bell. He's no normal civilian. Bit old, though."

Denton ignored the comment.

"He's Sarge's age," Rafa said. "Sol-born people are cut from different stuff."

Bell added, "I read his bio. Denton here took out a few Undies back in Sol too. He may have fought them more than we have."

Denton had to think for a minute. He remembered the flight to the *Telemachus*. He'd shot down a few Undriel battle crafts from the turret gun mounted in his family's ship. With everything that had happened since, he'd let that memory drift away.

"Okay. But let's get one thing straight." Akinyemi leaned in and smiled. "I get to press the big red button on the bomb."

"Deal," Rafa said.

Bell nodded and smiled.

"I'll check in with command. Ready yourselves," said the corporal. Bell and Akinyemi saluted and went off into the makeshift regrouping area.

"Are you sure about this?" Denton asked Rafa.

"I promised you we'd find your son," Rafa said. "I'll admit, I never thought we'd try it this way. But my team is low on people, and I'll be damned if I'm asking anyone I don't know to follow me into this. It's too important. Just promise me one thing."

"Anything," Denton said.

"If we find Cade, and he's one of them, you take the shot. If you don't, I will. Just don't try and stop me if it comes to that. Got it?" Rafa said. His eyes were stones and his gaze was fire.

Denton hesitated, then nodded.

"Say it," Rafa ordered.

"I won't stop you," Denton said.

"Good. I hope it doesn't come to that," said the corporal. "I wish I had more kind words for you, but we need to be realistic here."

"I understand," Denton said, and he believed it too. He clutched his hope in his heart as always, but had to come to terms with the possibility that this might not go the way he hoped. Rafa patted him on the shoulder.

"Rest up. We're going soon." He walked past Denton back toward the group with a crate of supplies.

A few hours later, the Iron Castle drifted over the trees of the Ember-

Lit Forest, as silent as the night surrounding it. A brisk breeze brushed against the tall pines, knocking needles into the shimmering shield barrier surrounding the Undriel ship.

"Wait for my signal." Rafa's subvocalized voice came through the commlink in Denton's helmet. The stealth-armored marines had climbed to the top of a row of trees, cloaked from sensors and emitting a faint neutralizing frequency from their chest plates. They waited, swaying in the branches.

The Iron Castle's lowest point was raking against the tops of the pines, like a knife slicing through the forest. As it grew closer, Denton could hear the cracking of trees and the hum of the shield growing louder. Behind them, kilometers off, the lake basin in the mountains waited. They had to detonate the bomb at the right moment to cause the castle to drop into its depths.

Lance Corporal Inaya Akinyemi carried the bomb in a case magnetized to the back of her combat suit. The bomb was a dual-purpose EMP and nuclear device. She swayed in the treetop next to Denton, with Bell and Rafa just beyond.

"Get ready…" the corporal said. The Iron Castle pushed the air around them as it grew close. The snow and blue embers rushed around the marines, and the shimmering shield came up fast behind it.

Denton tensed. The neutralizers should work, but they had never tested them. It wasn't like the Undriel would allow them to come by and try out their big secret advantage on the shield itself. He had done his part, found the frequency key that should nullify the barrier, but he didn't know the R&D team on the other end of the project that well. Denton was about to find out the hard way if their performance could be trusted.

The shield rushed toward the marines, and Denton felt his suit vibrate as it matched and nullified the barrier's frequency. He could feel a tickling sensation as the shield passed around him. All of his bones rattled. The shield swept over all of the marines, and they were now inside the barrier, only a few meters from the castle's hull.

"Now!" Rafa said.

In unison, Denton, Bell, Inaya, and Rafa jump-jetted from the treetop onto the hull. They gracefully impacted the ship and clung on with magnetic grips on their boots and palms. Together, they climbed the hull and searched for a way in.

"Radio silence from here. Follow my lead," Rafa whispered, and cut the commlink.

Denton was third from the back, with Inaya and Rafa in front of him and Bell in the rear. The castle was massive, like a moving skyscraper pushing through the forest. Denton regretted looking down to see the tall pines moving past the ship's bottom like a river of trees. He shook off his vertigo and followed Inaya and Rafa.

Rafa made it to the point that tactical command had deemed the best possible route of entry. Barnacles and other dead sea life accumulated over centuries underwater were amassed in one spot, implying there had been a breach that was only partially sealed. No one knew what might be inside because no human had ever gone into a *Devourer* and survived. They would be improvising once they entered the castle.

Rafa inspected the barnacle-infused area and gave Inaya a thumbs-up, then flicked his two forefingers from her to the dead sea life. Inaya bounced into position next to Rafa and jerked her hand sideways, revealing a cutting tool on top of her hand. She deftly swung her fist with surgical precision, and the panel jolted. Inaya caught the loose panel with her palm, magnetizing it, then moved it to the side and inspected the tunnel she'd revealed. Satisfied, she nodded to Rafa, then used her cutting tool like a spot welder. She sealed the panel harmlessly off to the side, where it couldn't clatter and alert the Undriel.

Bell moved around Denton toward the breach. She peered in, then slid down into the tunnel. Rafa tapped the side of his helmet's visor, switching to night vision, and looked down into the dark tunnel. He saw a flash of light blink three times.

Bell was safe—time to enter.

Rafa slid into the tunnel. Inaya followed, and Denton entered last.

Eventually, Denton came to an opening. He free-fell four meters and landed quietly on his feet in a crouched position. Inaya grabbed him and pulled him close to her. They were in a long metal hallway, tucked into a knuckle on the side. There were no lights inside the ship; the Undriel had no use for them. Only the dimly glowing red lines of energy between cracks in the walls gave them enough illumination to enhance their visor's night vision.

Rafa had his hand out, beckoning them to stay still and be quiet. In cold mode, the marines would blend into the metal environment through most Undriel sensors and cameras. The only way they could be spotted was if the human component of the Undriel soldiers made direct visual contact or if the marines were too loud.

Around the corner, the scorpion-shaped Undriel emerged from a compartment in the hallway's upper wall and landed on the floor. It moved toward the marines with its long, knife-like legs, its stinger trailing behind it on an extensive tail. Denton held his breath as it approached. He strained to remain calm as he noticed the dead marine in its claws. The scorpion was stabbing at the corpse casually, enjoying the gruesomeness of the sight.

The scorpion passed by the concealed marines and exited the hallway through an opening on the floor. Its stinger flicked around the corner last. Rafa dropped his hand and nodded to the others.

Time to move.

They slunk down the hall, away from where the scorpion had gone, to a hole in the opposite wall. Rafa hopped through and scanned the room ahead. Tactical command had advised the team to plant the bomb in the centermost part of the *Devourer*, a few floors above their current position. Rafa deemed the next room clear, and he motioned for the others to join him.

Denton was the last in. The room was filled with robotic arms welding and creating things on rotating tables. It was loud in here, concealing any audible movement they made. Wide-lengthed pedestals stuck up from the floor, like tables without space underneath. Parts and other materials were strewn about on the tables and floor, like a junkyard overflow. The walls were lined with the top half of metallic skulls, cut off from just below the nose. Denton had seen something similar before, his mind conjuring up images of the device that had been slammed onto Private Cook's head. The robotic arms grabbed junk off the floor and gobbled them up, spitting out new, forged metal pieces to create more skull caps.

At the other end of the room was another hole in the wall. Rafa moved around the tables, concealing himself from the robotic armatures. They exited the factory and found a shaft leading to a vertical hallway upward. Rafa leapt onto the wall, sealing himself for another magnetic climb. The team followed close behind him, moving silently up the wall.

A noise came from behind them, and Rafa held his hand up for silence.

A ragged man in soiled clothes walked on the wall opposite him. He seemed to defy physics. It was as if the team were clinging to the ceiling of a tall hallway, and he was on the ground—but they all were on a vertical incline. The ragged man was wearing one of the skull-shaped devices on his head and drooling from his lips. He was defying gravity with the help of a centipede-shaped machine, pushing him up the wall vertically as if he were walking on the floor. The ragged man walked under the marines, too hobbled to even look upward if he even wanted to. He made it to the end of the vertical shaft, and the wall opened for him. The man entered the newly opened room, and the wall remained open behind him.

Rafa jerked his forefingers toward the new opening, and the team silently worked their way up toward it. Rafa poked his head into the open entrance at the top of the shaft, then jerked his head back down. He looked to the rest of the team, took a breath, and then slowly eased his head back up into the entrance. He held his attention there for a moment, then nodded and pulled himself into the room. The others followed.

Denton entered and ducked into a concealed position with Inaya. It was another legless table, just a solid mass that jutted out of the metal floor. Denton and Inaya knelt behind one, and Rafa and Bell hid behind an adjacent table. Instead of junk metal, these tables were covered in slime. Denton reached his hand up and touched the slime, recoiling when he realized it was wet blood.

Rafa pointed to the floor and then signaled the okay to Inaya. This was the spot. According to Rafa's altimeter, they had reached the centermost part of the ship. Time to plant the bomb.

Inaya took the bomb off her back and pressed it into concealment just under the lip of the table. The cold mode it was running—just like their combat suits—would help it camouflage. As Inaya prepped the bomb, Denton peered over the top of the table at the rest of the large room. He sucked in air through his nose, and his skin crawled.

The room was filled with augmented human marines. Each had a device adhered to their heads, and their combat suits flickered with red pulses of light. They were crowded together and moaning softly. Some had vomited on themselves. Blood caked the floor under their feet, and a few corpses littered the ground within the crowd. It was a hideous, revolting sight.

Damn the Undriel.

The walls were lined with Undriel soldiers, fully absorbed. They were in a null state, waiting for the next battle. The ragged man tended to the soldiers on the wall, the centipede machine lifting him into various positions. He wrapped up what he was doing and moved back toward the group.

Bell readied her rifle on the ragged man and waited for Rafa to give the signal. The corporal held his hand firmly. Eventually, the ragged man exited the room the way he had come in—no longer a threat.

Inaya finished her bomb preparations and tapped Denton's shoulder. Denton gave it a quick look and nodded. With a few gestures over her gauntlet, Inaya flicked a timer to each of the marines present. They had fifteen minutes to leave the ship and get to safety. Rafa spun his finger in the air—*Time to move.*

Denton turned to face the hole the ragged man had left behind, and crunched himself against the table when he saw the man return. This time he wasn't alone. A new type of Undriel entered the room behind him. It had a device on its head, much like the skulls on the hybrid marines, but there was most definitely a human head and neck underneath it. It had dark skin and a strong jawline. Its shape was masculine, and its body looked like a mechanical skeleton with extra parts interwoven inside its bones. It was a smooth type of metal, seeping with blue energy.

"Our guests need some tidying up," the ragged man said, his voice full of sloppy spit.

The hybrid Undriel nodded and began to inspect the possessed marines. They jolted their arms away from him as he touched them, like slumbering sleepwalkers in some trance-alert.

The wall on the other end of the room opened, and a tall Undriel soldier stepped in. Denton gasped. This Undriel looked like a streamlined version of the soldiers on the walls, but large jets on its back helped it move through the air at top speed. Denton had seen this exact soldier before.

It was Faye Raike.

Faye used to be a close friend to Denton and Eliana. She had become the first human absorbed by the Undriel in almost three centuries. She was the one who took Cade away, snatching him from right under Denton's grasp. Faye had made some improvements to her shell in the months since then. She almost looked like a walking Matador starfighter.

"Hybrid. I need parts for my railgun," Faye said to the unique Undriel, her voice harsh and synthesized.

The ragged man lowered to the floor and hobbled toward them.

The unique Undriel spoke. "We do not have any spare parts."

Denton inhaled sharply. *That voice…*

The ragged man laughed and coughed blood. "Nonsense!

Brother Cade, give Sister Faye what she needs."

At the sound of his name, Denton felt a sting of horror. *My son is alive. My son is... one of them.* Denton wanted to cry, scream, and kill everything in the room to save his son. He held firm, and his breathing grew more strained and uneven. His blood turned to iron, and he felt heavier. He wanted to act but was paralyzed by observation.

"From where? We have no extra resources," Cade asked.

Faye turned to the crowd of hybrid marines. "I see plenty of resources. A Tvashtar marine combat suit has more than enough materials to absorb. Pick one, Hybrid," she demanded.

Denton's breathing stopped as he waited. Rafa kept looking between Denton and Cade, assessing the situation as it unfolded. Bell and Inaya looked at each other, then back to Denton to ensure he didn't do anything foolish.

Cade looked to the crowd. He made a fist with his augmented hand and squeezed. A blue light flicked between his fingers, but Cade did not move.

He doesn't want to sacrifice them. He's still human! Denton realized. *Cade can be saved!*

"Useless!" Faye shouted. She raised her thin leg and smashed her foot into Cade's chest, launching him across the room toward Denton and the concealed marines. Cade sailed between the tables and hit the wall. For a moment, Denton thought he had been killed. Then Cade's machinery reactivated. Gyros and gears clicked into place, and the lights in his body flickered back to life.

Denton and Cade looked at each other. Denton quickly removed his helmet, and he didn't flinch when the rush of copper and decay filled his nostrils. He only cared about Cade. Everything else was static in the background.

Cade gasped. A visor covered his eyes, but Cade's agape mouth told Denton everything he needed to know. He recognized Denton.

My son still knows me.

Cade mouthed silently, *"Dad?"*

Denton had tears in his eyes, and his breathing was shallow and filled with excitement. He held his arms out, hoping to have Cade come into them. Rafa, Inaya, and Bell kept their guns trained on Cade, preferring caution over high hopes. Bell and Inaya glanced over to Rafa and waited for his commands, but Rafa was just as unsure as the others. They could see it too. This hybrid wasn't like the others. But just how different he was remained unclear.

Behind them, Faye pulled one of the hybrid marines aside. The ragged man said, "I am sorry for my cohort's foolishness. Please forgive me. Accept this offering in—"

"Shut up!" Faye shouted.

Cade shifted onto his knee and looked like he was about to move toward Denton until the wall behind him rolled upward. Suddenly, the Undriel behemoth was looming behind Cade. The large horn on its head almost scratched the ceiling. Its hulking arms were covered in blades and guns.

"Listen, new one! The hybrid is—" The behemoth shouted at Faye until it looked down at saw the four marines. "Intruders!"

"Dad—*run*!" Cade shouted. His body charged with blue energy.

Before anyone could move, Cade exploded with a pulse of bright blue light. Denton and the team he was with were thrown over the tables and into the center of the horrible room. The behemoth was shoved backward, sliding as its arms carved paths in the metal floor.

Denton rolled onto his back, but Rafa, Bell, and Inaya used their jump-jets to keep upright. Rafa looked over his shoulder at the table to make sure the bomb was still connected. The timer was still active, with only five minutes remaining now.

The light returned to Cade, and he stood up from the floor.

"Light them up!" Rafa ordered.

"Wait!" Denton shouted.

Cade rolled himself into the vertical hallway just as the shots rang out. Faye launched herself at Rafa and Bell, sustaining particle blasts in the process. Inaya grabbed Denton's arm and shoved him into the vertical shaft, away from the fight. Denton fell, bouncing off the shaft walls until he hit the bottom. The air was knocked out of his lungs, but his suit had saved him from a major injury. The battle at the top of the shaft echoed off the walls.

Standing on the side of the wall, defying gravity, was Cade Castus. He leaped from his position and landed next to his father. Denton scrambled to his knees and put his hands on Cade's mechanical shoulders. "It's you! It's really you!"

Cade smiled and nodded, his eyes shrouded by the visor on his face. He looked up the vertical shaft. "We don't have time. We have to get out of here." Cade stepped a pace to the side just as Bell landed next to Denton. She thrust a helmet into Denton's hands.

"Forget something?" Bell shouted, then aimed her rifle upward. Denton put the helmet on and regained his night vision.

Rafa and Inaya landed next to Bell. "Move it!" Rafa ordered. As he moved, he gestured to Cade. "You're coming with us. Stick close." Cade nodded his understanding and ran to keep up with the jump-jetting marines and his father.

The factory room was just through the hole in the wall. The lights of the robotic arms working flickered against the metal walls, undisturbed by the fighting.

"Stay close," Denton told Cade, and they moved together. As they rushed back into the factory room, they could hear a loud bang. Faye was close behind and had hit the ground so hard it dented the floor in the shaft. She launched an assault of particle shots, tearing up the walls and the robotic arms in the factory. Inaya was hit in the right arm and nearly dropped her rifle.

"Shit!" she shouted in pain.

Rafa and Bell returned fire, blasting chunks off Faye's frame. Denton unhooked a grenade from his belt and hurled it toward Faye. It exploded on impact and removed her legs. Faye was inconvenienced but not slowed. Her upper body clawed its way through the factory room. As the smoke cleared, more Undriel soldiers landed in the shaft behind her.

"Over here!" Inaya shouted, and jumped through the hole at the other end of the room. Bell and Rafa both unhooked grenades and dropped them near their feet as they jump-jetted backward, catching up to Denton and Cade. The explosions ripped the factory apart and blocked the Undriel from chasing for a moment. Faye shrieked with anger and worked to claw her way through the debris, absorbing pieces of the wreckage in the process and rebuilding her frame.

As Denton and Cade made it through the hole at the other end of the factory, a railgun blast punched a hole in the wall. Although it didn't hit Denton, it passed close enough to push him onto the floor. Faye had rebuilt her railgun and fired it in the time it took the team to cross the room.

"Come on," Cade shouted as he lifted Denton to his feet. Just ahead was the makeshift tunnel they had used to enter the castle. Inaya jump-jetted into it first, followed by Bell.

"Get in," Rafa ordered Denton.

"Get back to your room!" a voice called out from down the hall. At the other end of the corridor, the wall opened, revealing two more Undriel machines. One was wasp-shaped, wearing a cloak; the other was the scorpion.

Cade's body was frozen stiff. "No!"

"Get moving now!" Rafa opened fire on the wasp and the scorpion

"I said *get back to your room!*" the metallic wasp's voice boomed.

Cade tried to resist some invisible attack. His legs jolted, and his arms seized up.

"Come on, Cade," Denton urged. He pulled at his son's frame, but he couldn't budge him. He used all of his strength to try to move Cade from his spot, but no motion came.

"You have to go!" Cade shouted.

Denton's eyes filled with tears. He yelled at the top of his lungs and activated the jump-jets on all his suit's thrusters. Still, he could not move Cade. It was like trying to shove a mountain.

"Dad!"

The scorpion rapidly closed the distance. Rafa grabbed Denton and launched into the tunnel on the ceiling with his jump-jet. The scorpion entered the tunnel and lashed out with all of its bladelike appendages, missing Denton's legs by millimeters.

"CADE!" Denton shouted, struggling against Rafa's hold.

A flash of light traced its way along the metal-paneled walls. Denton thought that Cade had sent out another energy blast until he looked at the timer on his helmet's HUD. It had reached zero, and the EMP had gone off. The scorpion that chased them twitched and shrieked as it fell back down into the dark tunnel below.

Rafa threw Denton out into the open air, then jump-jetted after him. As they free-fell, the Iron Castle soared away into the distance. Denton hit the trees and bounced off, breaking branches. A shockwave flung outward from the Iron Castle, followed by an incredible explosion. Trees were uprooted, and waves of hot fire blew around them. The sound was immense, and every part of Denton's body vibrated. He looked up and saw the Iron Castle crack in half, its shield disintegrating for good as the broken ship fell toward the lake basin.

Denton removed his helmet and screamed at the top of his lungs, "CADE!" The castle dropped into the lake sideways and began to sink rapidly in a boiling seething wreck. Denton remained on his knees, paralyzed by the sight of it.

"Castus!" Rafa shouted and grabbed his arm. Denton threw him off and didn't turn away from the view of the wreck. Rafa grabbed him again and got in his face. "Denton, listen to me! We have to get back to base. It's not safe here. If anything survived that explosion, it's going to come after us!

"My *son* was in there. We had him!" Denton spat the words, full of fire and fury. His eyes were red, and his breathing was ragged.

"I know! But we can't stop now. We have to get moving." Rafa brought his tone down. Bell and Inaya approached them from deeper in the forest, watching silently.

Denton looked into Rafa's visor. He gasped for air as if lung-lock had overtaken him. His eyes glossed over, and he clutched fists of snow in his hands. "Cade—he was—I had him…" He sniffled and looked back toward the burning wreckage of the Iron Castle, shaking his head in disbelief. "Oh, God."

"Castus. We have to go," Rafa said quietly.

Denton whispered to himself, numb all over. "Why can't I save you?" He slowly got to his feet and turned toward the corporal, his eyes melting with tears. Silently, he trudged through the snow, moving to the head of their group. Denton Castus walked back a broken man.

He had failed again.

THIRTEEN

"THE MISSION WAS A major success," reported Lieutenant Mido Sharif from the *Infinite Aria*. "Four Tvashtar marines infiltrated the Undriel structure and detonated a bomb, decimating the Iron Castle."

Eliana Castus listened to the report in a room full of excited scientists. The Iron Castle lay crippled near the Supernal Echo lake. Their gadgets had worked, although it was still unclear how many Undriel survived the detonation. The remaining ground forces were gearing up to clear out the remaining enemies. It was beginning to feel like the war might be ending.

The Undriel always have a trick, Eliana thought to herself. *Always.*

Denton had not called. Eliana was aware he was on the mission. She knew he'd try and find their son. *Did he find Cade? And if he did,* what *did he find?* The reports didn't mention an extra survivor coming back with the marines. Eliana's heart felt like a snake was coiled around it, squeezing the life out of her while she waited for any news from her husband.

Dr. Maple Corsen walked up to Eliana and adjusted her glasses. "Looks like it all worked out! Cheers to us, Dr. Castus."

Eliana smiled. "This is your victory. You've done what no one thought was possible. This war might be coming to a swift end thanks to you and your team." She meant it, but she was having difficulty feeling enthusiastic without knowing what Denton would say about Cade. "I need to get back to the quarantine lab. I know you will handle whatever comes well."

"Take care, Dr. Castus." Maple nodded and returned to her team. Eliana left the R&D lab and walked across the Scout campus quad. She felt the warmth of spring on her skin. The flowers were in full bloom, and the grass was a deep purple now. She inhaled the sweet scent of the season and sighed with worry.

"How are you feeling today?" George Tanaka asked Nella Castus. The young woman sat on the edge of her hospital bed in the autopsy bay. She looked well-rested, having finally changed out of her hospital gown. Nella wore a long-sleeved royal purple shirt with light grey pants. A faux leather jacket rested on a chair nearby, and a soothreader laying on the table near her converted George's speech into Sol-Sign via a green holographic ghost.

"I feel better." Nella flicked her hand from her chin and gave George a thumbs-up with a bright smile. The soothreader picked up her signs and spoke them aloud for George to hear.

"That's good," George said. He sat down in the seat typically reserved for Eliana and brought up some data in the air between them. "I wanted to show you something."

"Alright."

"You said you were trying to tether to your brother. When you did so, you sent out some sort of energy. It traveled incredibly far, did you know that?" George showed her the forking green lightning spraying out across the landscape.

Nella signed, *"The stray nezzarforms in the wilderness worked as a path. My part in this chain only went as far as Oolith."* She thrust a thumb over her shoulder, indicating one of her nezzarform friends waiting outside the quarantine lab.

"I see..." George tilted his head left and right as he considered what this meant. He continued, "Do you know what happened next?"

Nella tapped her forefingers against her thumb. *"No."*

"Well, we have some theories," George said, and made a few gestures over his soothreader. He brought up the Siren pit. Green energy forked into the pit. There was a pause, then red energy crackled outward. First, it spread back west toward Nella, then shot east toward Cade a moment later. "Shortly after this event, you had your seizure."

Nella crunched her brow downward, and her eyes focused on her hands. She perked up and signed to George, *"This was Oolith's suggestion. It must have known we'd make contact with something in the pit. Oolith has been mentioning something called a Decider lately. It wants me to go see it, whatever it is."*

"Decider." George shook with chills. He'd heard that name before, and he didn't like what it could mean. For now, he pushed it aside to get more of Nella's story. "That's very interesting. Your mother theorized that Sympha, Karx, and whatever is in the pit were trying to talk to each other."

"It didn't work for me." Nella frowned and shook her head. *"I wonder if it worked for Cade. Any news about him?"*

"Your father was part of a very successful mission into the Iron Castle. We are unsure what he found for now, though." George leaned forward. "Can you feel his energy? You have in the past, correct?"

Nella closed her eyes, and her head swayed, adjusting to find the correct signal. She exhaled, and her eyes widened. Nella's attention snapped to George. *"Cade's weak. Fading even."*

"But he *is* alive," George asked, his face severe and stern.

Nella's eyes darted frantically around the room. *"I think so."*

"Then there is still hope. But there's also a problem here."

Nella looked at him, confused.

"If your brother survived the attack, that means other Undriel most likely have as well. We might still be able to save Cade, but this war hasn't ended yet. We are all still in danger."

Nella stood up and signed, *"I can't keep wasting time here. I need to help Cade. I might already be too late."*

George tried to stop her. "Wait! Please, Nella. Take a seat. You shouldn't be moving so much." Nella ignored him, grabbed her jacket, slipped on some shoes, and walked to the door. George stood in her way. "Nella, you can't leave. It's too dangerous!" he pleaded.

Nella didn't look over to her soothreader to see what he said. She stared George in the eyes. A green glow surfaced within Nella's irises, and her brow pushed into a fierce frown. She turned her head ever so slightly toward the wall near her hospital bed.

With a resounding crash, Oolith and Lahar smashed through the wall. Their cyclopean eyes were charged with explosive energy. George fell backward in shock, putting an arm up reflexively to shield himself from the nezzarforms' wrath. Nella stepped away from George, crossing the room toward Oolith and Lahar. As she approached, the nezzarforms engulfed her, restructuring themselves. Oolith and Lahar combined their boulders and stones into something sharp, a flat structure shaped like an arrow with notches for wings. It was a ship, rising on a torrent of lightning to stay above ground. Nella was inside, the only passenger.

"Incredible…" George whispered, inaudible over the sound of the lightning pulsing from the nezzarform ship. Eliana entered the room in a hurry. She knelt next to George and watched as Nella's nezzarform ship lifted into the air, then chucked itself over the trees beyond the campus.

"Nella!" Eliana shouted. She quickly helped George to his feet without taking her eyes off the direction Nella had headed in. "What just happened?"

"I think she's going to go help Cade," George mumbled.

Eliana gasped weakly. "Cade *is* alive?"

George nodded. "She can feel him. But he's weak. He needs help."

"We need to follow her. Now!" Eliana left the room, and George hurried behind her. They crossed the quad, and she pinged the shipyard with a request for access to a pioneer-class explorer named the *Jacques*.

By the time they approached the ship, Eliana was granted access. It was a sleek thing, able to comfortably sit a team of six. The front was pointed like a sword. A large, circular dish on top contained the long-range scanner. It lacked quarantine and medical facilities, as well as storage and weapons, and was designed primarily for high-altitude observation.

Fergus Reid greeted them in front of the *Jacques*. "Hey Elly, I can'nae just let you take off in this ship. Not during wartime." His Callisto accent was stern and commanding.

"Then you can fly it," Eliana said, pinging the ship to lower its access ramp.

"Wait, tha's not wot I meant!" Fergus shouted.

Eliana stopped at the top of the ramp and turned toward Fergus. Her eyes were pressed with determination and worry. "Fergus, I need your help. Nella just took off in a nezzarform flier. She could end up hurt, or worse."

There was a brief pause between them. Fergus looked to George, who nodded with the seriousness of the situation. Fergus sighed, then moved up the ramp into the ship. "Al'reet. Which way did Nella go?"

Eliana sat in the co-pilot seat and George in one of the four seats behind them. "East."

"Buckle up! Let's go git yer daughter back."

FOURTEEN

CADE CASTUS FLOATED INSIDE a broken world. He pried his eyes open to witness a fragmented reality. His veil was fractured, and between glimpses of fire, water, and twisted broken metal, he saw a beach, a forest, an arid landscape, and clouds. He tried to reach out, but there was nothing to grab. The images before him flickered and exchanged landscapes, disorienting Cade even further.

<*Karx… Are we dead?*> Cade whispered through his mind.

He felt a sting shoot through the back of his skull. <*NOT QUITE.*>

Cade slowly moved his hands and feet, realizing he was on the floor. But still, he sensed a strange resistance. Metal was everywhere, but he could only feel it. His vision was still too erratic to make sense of anything.

"My head…" Cade groaned. He reached his face and felt the veil that ruled over his visual reality. "Wait," he muttered. He could *feel* the visor. Before, when he'd attempt to touch the device on his head, he'd have a sensation that he was still touching his face, bypassing the interaction with the device entirely. Now that he could feel it, he could remove it.

He pulled the device off his head with great effort, feeling connecting wires strain and snap. The veil splashed into a pool of water. Now, only the real world surrounded him. Cade's body had been submerged in rapidly deepening water all the way to his chest. A blue glow lit up the darkness, and at once, Cade realized the light was emitting from his eyes. He looked at himself in the pooling water, now free of the mask that obstructed his face. Cade's hair was mottled and unkempt, his eyes looked sunken in and tired, and scars pocked his temples and hairline. The rest was familiar, although sickly. *It's still me.*

<*What happened?*> Cade finally asked.

<*THERE WERE TWO EXPLOSIONS. THE FIRST TOOK YOU OFFLINE. THE SECOND NEARLY KILLED YOU.*>

<*Wait. Dad.*> Then he shouted aloud. "Dad!"

<*HE ESCAPED WITH THE OTHER HUMANS.*>

<*So that* was *real.*> Cade smiled. He'd been so close to reuniting with his father, and although they failed, it meant that they had not forgotten about him. Cade tried to stand but screamed out in pain. He looked down and saw that long, thin pieces of jagged metal had impaled his mechanical leg, belly, and chest. If he were fully human, he'd be a corpse. As it was, this was only a painful but minor inconvenience.

Cade jerked the metal from his leg and was surprised when his arm ate it up. Teeth he didn't realize were fused into his inner workings seared through the metal, ultra-hot torches welded it into place wherever it was needed, and tiny robotic arms passed the material around his body. It happened so fast. He absorbed the jagged wreck and felt his body fix itself, repurposing the thing that should have killed him. It felt like a healing salve had been pressed against his wounds. He did the same with the other two fragments of the wreck, and suddenly Cade felt like he had just had a pleasant massage.

The simulated pain also simulated this pleasure, rewarding the user and encouraging them to partake in more absorption. This was a dangerous enjoyment. More terrible, it meant that Cade was capable of the same devastation as his Undriel counterparts. He was more like them than he ever wanted to admit.

The sound of blades scraping against metal came from down the hall. Cade waded through the water, noticing how quickly it was rising. Fires were extinguished as they became submerged. Cade peered through the thick smoke and saw red lights flashing ahead.

<BE CAREFUL. SOME ARE AWARE OF OUR DECEPTION NOW. WE MAY HAVE TO LEAVE WHILE THE TIMING IS RIGHT.>

Cade remembered now. He had used Karx's pulse energy against Necrodore. Auden and Hilaria had cornered him just before the explosion. Cade looked over his shoulder and only found fire, water, and wreck where they had been. Either the blast had destroyed them, or they had become separated by walls of debris.

The lights ahead jerked in position, and the whirring of blades clanged to a stop. Cade moved toward the sound and found the Reaper pinned under part of the wreck. It appeared to be absorbing parts of the ship, but it was in a bad state. Sparks and smoke seethed from its cloak, and some of its blades were broken and dented. It roared with mechanical errors.

Cade almost turned to run—maybe he should have. Before his legs pivoted away from the Reaper, Cade looked down at his right hand. His palm had a blue light dancing just above the metal.

<The tether.>

The Reaper's head was pinned facing downward. Its weapons appeared to be offline during the repair. Cade approached the Reaper and reached his hand out. He stood directly in front of it and put his hand on its head. The Reaper jolted upward at his touch, and Cade's hand felt like it had been bolted with lightning. His arm was shoved backward as the blue energy returned to him, and the tether disintegrated into Cade's body. *<Another link. Maybe this time we'll find some answers.>*

<TIME TO LEAVE.>

Before he could turn to find a way out, Cade was pulled backward and thrown underwater. Necrodore stood over him. A long pillar of metal slammed down into Cade's chest, pinning him underwater and nailing him to the floor. Cade felt the simulated pain of his chest being crushed but no sensation of drowning. Necrodore leaned over Cade and said through the shared network, "You can*not* be trusted! I have seen your betrayal, *hybrid.* Soon the others will know too."

Cade tried to tether to Necrodore, but part of his shoulder was trapped under the metal pillar, and he couldn't reach his hand up far enough. Cade started to absorb the metal pillar, hoping to free himself. Necrodore pulled the wreckage away from the Reaper and grappled it in a tough embrace. Their bodies shared materials, and shortly after the hug, both Necrodore and the Reaper were in perfect condition.

"Grab the hybrid," Necrodore commanded the Reaper. "The others are waiting outside."

The Reaper curled its blades into its ragged, torn cloak. A long metal arm with taloned fingers reached out and ripped the pillar out of Cade's body. Before Cade could fight, he was hit with a sharp electrical pulse from the Reaper. Cade went slack, and the Reaper dragged him through the twisted wreck toward daylight.

As they approached a breach in the hull and the sun beat inward, Cade saw a flash of white light and felt reality slip away once more.

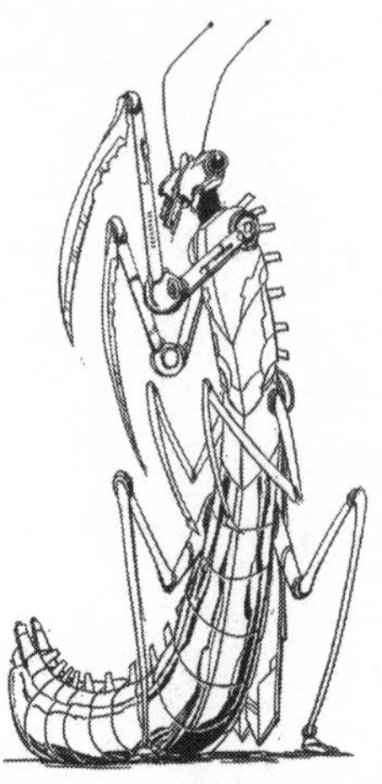

FIFTEEN

WARM SUN. FRESH AIR. Cool breeze. Fine, soft dirt.

Cade opened his eyes and sat up straight. He was Shade walking again and unsure of his surroundings. A soft, rose-colored sky hung above, with strange birds sailing on the winds. Cade sat in an open field, with patches of green grass and round, leafy bushes scattering the horizon. He rubbed his hand through the reddish dirt on the ground. The dirt didn't react to his touch, but he could still feel it against his palm.

<*This place is beautiful,*> Cade said as he stood up. <*Is it Earth?*>

Cade turned around and saw a massive mountain scaling up to the sky. It had a flat cliff face with a gently sloping mound over its top surface. Plant life and waterfalls trickled off its ledges, emptying into large lakes around its foothills. The mountain eclipsed the horizon, implying it was farther away than he had initially thought—and much larger too.

Cade huffed out a laugh and smiled as he recognized the mountain.

<*DO YOU KNOW THIS PLACE?*> Karx asked.

He nodded. <*Yeah. I think so. This is Mars. My mom was born here.*>

Eliana Veston was a third-generation Martian. She'd spent her childhood on Mars before moving to live on Remus Orbital. Mars had once been a barren world until it became the first planet terraformed for human life. The mountain taking over the horizon was Olympus Mons, the tallest planetary mountain in the Sol System. It was home to one of the most significant cities on the planet, Olympus Mons Square. The city would have been located on the southwestern portion of the mountain. Cade couldn't see any signs of a city from this location, but he could see a structure ahead. It looked like an outpost, with large guns pointing toward the sky flanking its exterior. <*Olympus Mons Square must be on the other side of the mountain.*>

A closer inspection of his immediate surroundings yielded signs of a battle with the Undriel. Mechanical appendages, dried blood, and viscera brought nightmares to the once-peaceful landscape.

There's no one here. Why am I here? Cade wondered. He was answered by the sound of an approaching starship. High above, a sizeable undertaker-class warship lowered its landing gear, silhouetted by the bright morning sunlight. Cade took a few steps back as the ship brought itself down right in front of him, its back access ramp facing his direction.

Cade heard something move in the grass behind him and spun on his heel to face it. At first, it appeared as though the clump of green grass was crawling. It wasn't until a glint of sunlight reflected off a concealed sniper rifle that Cade realized a soldier had been right next to him this whole time. As the camouflaged sniper stood, he pulled back his disguise and let it drape off him like a cloak made of grass. The sniper was lean and muscular, with pale skin and a sharp-edged chin dotted in stubble. He had cold brown eyes, one cybernetically linked to the rifle.

The sniper watched the warship's ramp lower, checking his rifle methodically. The metal ramp hit the dirt, revealing a squad of marines. They wore Martian marine combat suits, with open-faced helmets and a singular jump-jet placed on the backpack. These suits were not as advanced as their Tvashtar counterparts, but no military technology outside of Io was.

Once again, Cade felt like he was part of the people around him. Although he stood outside their bodies, he could sense what they were feeling and hear the whispers of their thoughts within the Shade walk. The sniper was cool, stoic, calm, and also a little relieved. There was a sense of fondness emitting from him. He was seeing someone special after a long time away.

Cade immediately recognized the captain standing in front of the squad. He had a face Cade had seen many times in history vids. The captain's features were close enough to the sniper's that they could have been related. He had a similar hard-lined jaw, deep brown eyes, pale skin, and close-cut black hair. This was Captain Roelin Raike, the war hero who would eventually become possessed by the Siren Nhymn and forced to murder close to forty fellow colonists in the early days of Kamarian colonization. He would also be the one to help take the Siren down once he shook off his shackles.

Roelin stepped down the ramp and tilted his head slightly to speak into a commlink. "Keep the *Astraeus* ready for launch. We're going to send any survivors back this way. Get ready to help them when they arrive."

The sniper nodded to Roelin. "Didn't think they'd send you here," he said with a quiet, grizzled voice.

"We were the closest," Roelin said. "What's the situation?"

"I've been watching the outpost for a while, but it's been quiet. We know the machines hit a few hours ago, but we're still receiving a distress signal from inside. There might be survivors," the sniper explained.

"Hostages?"

"Could be."

"That's not like them. We'll move in," Roelin said.

"I can help. I'm familiar with this outpost's layout," the sniper offered.

"You're in." Roelin turned to the other three marines and waved them forward. They checked their gear as they joined Roelin and the sniper.

A female private smiled when she saw the sniper. "What are the odds?"

The sniper smirked.

"And I thought one Raike was enough. Two should be overkill," the private said. Cade recognized her voice, but he wasn't sure why.

The sniper responded, "Three Raikes, by my count." Cade peered at each of the dog tags. The captain was R. Raike, the sniper was T. Raike, and the private was F. Raike.

Faye.

She was younger in this memory. Although they were about to walk into a mission, Faye still looked happier here than she had ever looked in Cade's lifetime. She would eventually become absorbed, just like him, and then she would bring Cade to Tibor's feet.

T. Raike. *Talfryn.* Antoni called the Reaper "Brother Talfryn" from time to time. Cade was unsure what the relationship to Roelin was precisely, but he guessed that Talfryn was Roelin's brother or cousin. Knowing what Cade knew about the Reaper, this would not be a fond memory the three would share later.

"Let's get moving," Roelin commanded.

"Understood." The sniper pulled his camouflage back over his suit.

The marines hustled, forcing Cade to run to keep up. It felt good to run at full speed through the Martian meadow. A glee washed over his body as he chased the marines. He couldn't help it. Anything outside the nightmare reality he existed in was intensely gratifying. They made it to the outpost walls and took positions around the open gateway. Cade stood in the doorway, confident he couldn't be harmed by the dangers inside the outpost.

A few silent hand signals, and the marines moved into the outpost compound. A battle had happened here recently. There were decapitated marines littering the ground, and Undriel metal fragments were thrust into everything. There were no survivors, human or Undriel.

Roelin, Talfryn, Faye, and the other marines moved across the compound, swaying their guns as they scanned the perimeter. Unlike collider tech weapons, their weapons used magnetic ammo shards as bullets. These magnetic repeaters would have to be reloaded when the ammo clip ran out of shards. Each marine carried extra magazines, some strapped to their chest plates, hips, and thighs, some attached to the weapons themselves.

Faye whispered to Roelin, "We should have run into some resistance by now."

Roelin grunted, "Don't let your guard down."

The marines entered the front door of the outpost, one by one, guns aimed and sweeping. Cade walked with them, though more casually. They discovered more gore and signs of battle as they moved inside, but still no hostages or enemy combatants. Eventually, they entered a rectangular room with a staircase in its center. Doors lined the room, each one shut, hungry, ready to eat anyone too careless to clear it.

Roelin made a few gestures, and the marines moved in. Two aimed forward at the shut doors ahead, and two moved to the left and right and aimed at those immediately on the sides of the entry. Roelin flicked a hand to Talfryn.

Talfryn crept closer to the door, his rifle aimed. He slowly moved a hand toward the access panel and tapped it with a finger. The door didn't budge, so he attempted to push at it with his hand. When the door still didn't budge, he cautiously inspected it. "It's welded shut," Talfryn confirmed.

"This one too," Faye said from the other side of the room.

They confirmed that all of the doors ahead had been welded shut. A bead of sweat formed on Roelin's head. After a moment of consideration, the captain flicked a hand to the staircase and another to the two marines at his sides. Talfryn and Faye joined Roelin on the stairs as the other pair of marines kept watch on the lower floor.

At the top of the staircase, Talfryn encountered another door and found it unsealed. Faye and Talfryn braced against the sides while Roelin kept his rifle pointed straight at it. Talfryn tapped the panel and the door opened simultaneously. In a breath, Roelin confirmed that there were no hostiles in the front while Faye and Talfryn moved in and swept the corners.

"Clear!" Talfryn and Faye shouted in unison.

"This doesn't make sense," Roelin said.

They had entered a command room with computer terminals and data screens placed around the edges. A large window faced Olympus Mons, a beautiful view of a peaceful valley of red dirt and green grass. Blood was splattered against the window, and more signs of fighting traced along the walls.

"Are we too late?" Faye asked.

"Tal, check the terminal—see if we can find the data on the distress call," Roelin ordered. Talfryn nodded to the captain and walked over to the terminal near the window. He gestured over it, sifting through the information on the vidscreen for answers.

"Got something here," Talfryn said. Roelin moved toward him and checked the data readout. He scanned the data, then frowned.

"This battle happened a day ago," Roelin said.

Talfryn shook his head. "Impossible. The distress call went out only an hour before I arrived."

"Shit," Faye spat.

Roelin pressed a hand to his helmet's commlink and shouted, "This is a trap. We need to—"

The sound of gunfire came from downstairs.

Talfryn gripped his rifle and aimed it at the door.

There were several loud bangs from the floor below, along with the sound of blades slicing against metal. The screams of the marines on the lower floor were cut short, and then it was dangerously silent.

Roelin, Talfryn, and Faye knelt behind terminals and faced the door.

"We need a way out of here," Talfryn whispered, not taking his eyes off the door. He switched his sniper rifle to a close-range mode, capable of spitting out buckshot magnetic ammo.

"Window's bulletproof. But with enough shots, we can probably get through it," Faye suggested.

"*Astraeus*. Come around the side and get the turrets aimed at our position," Roelin said into his commlink, pinging their pilot.

The sounds of blades scratching against stairs grew louder. Talfryn adjusted the grip of his rifle in his hands. The sounds stopped, and it was silent once more. Cade could hear Faye breathing from across the room.

Then, the sound of a fluttering cloak. A mechanical nightmare burst into the room. Roelin jump-jetted toward Faye. The machine smashed into the window behind where the captain had been, leaving a crackled bulge in its blood-splattered surface. The Undriel was a cloaked thing made of rotating blades and guns. It roared at them through the jaw of a metal skull. It was a Reaper, and yet, Cade was Shade walking through the memory of a Reaper.

Gunfire erupted. The three marines blasted at the Reaper, expending a full clip each. The Reaper was pushed back, but it brought out its own guns when the marines' clips expired.

"Move!" Roelin shouted.

The Reaper used collider technology and didn't need to reload or worry about running out of ammo. In time, humanity would reverse engineer this tech, but for now, it was a force to be reckoned with. The Reaper blasted around the room, its aim somewhat affected by the previous battles it had fought in the outpost over the past day. The terminals near Talfryn exploded.

Faye and Roelin made it to the door at the top of the stairs, freshly reloaded and opening fire. As the Reaper took the full brunt of their combined attack, Talfyn jump-jetted toward the door. Roelin and Faye emptied their clips, while he took over with covering fire.

"*Astraeus*, fire!" Roelin shouted as the three marines backed down the stairs.

The Reaper roared. The shots from the massive turret of the Undertaker-class warship punched through the glass. A deafening explosion of sound followed almost a full second after the shot had come through the room. The blast passed so close to the marines that they were thrown down the stairs to the floor below.

Talfryn landed next to Roelin and Faye. The walls and floor were crawling with spider bots, an undulating mass of metal and glowing eyes. They scraped and clawed at the marines. Roelin switched his magnetic repeater into a spread-shot firing mode and blasted into the metal crowd. The bots backed away in unison.

The entryway they had come in from had been blocked off with large chunks of debris. Jagged metal and spider bots lay between the marines and their escape. The doors outlining the room were now broken open, breached as the Undriel sprung their trap.

"I see an exit!" Faye shouted. She moved toward the breached door to the left of the stairs. The Reaper flung itself from the upper floor and intercepted the marines. With the flash of a blade, it struck Talfryn, slicing through his chest plate and leaving a large wound beneath. The impact threw Talfryn across the room.

Roelin jump-jetted toward the Undriel Reaper, blasting it repeatedly. The Reaper jerked with each hit. It rotated part of its body, smashing Roelin in the chest and sending him backward into a pile of bots. The captain pulled himself from the mound of bots and dodged to the other side of the room just as the Reaper crashed into the wall where he had been. The Reaper faced Roelin, seething with smoke and steam. Injuries were starting to take their effect on the machine.

Talfryn stood behind the Reaper and flicked his right arm. A long blade rotated from the mechanism on his forearm, and he jump-jetted into the Reaper. The Undriel spun and caught Talfryn as he plunged the blade into the Reaper's chest. They both fell to the spider bot-filled floor as the Reaper slammed four blades into Talfryn's chest and back, like a claw gripping a heart.

"TAL!" Roelin shouted in anger as the bots piled onto Talfryn and the Reaper.

"Roe—we have to leave now!" Faye shouted as she blasted at the Reaper and the spider bots. The bots began to push away as the Reaper rose to its feet.

Roelin fought himself for a moment as he tried to reload his weapon. The bots turned in his direction, and Talfryn was lost under the wave of machines. "Damn it all!" Roelin screamed, his eyes wide and red. He hated the decision he was about to make, but his training took control. Roelin unhooked a grenade from his belt and dropped it at his feet as he jump-jetted through the door with Faye to make their escape. The explosion burst through the spider bots and knocked the Reaper backward.

A silence followed afterward.

The smoke cleared from the room, revealing the Reaper standing in the center of the remaining spider bot flock. It swayed and crackled with damage. The sound of struggled breaths announced that Talfryn was still alive but mortally wounded.

"Impressive," a voice came from the other side of the room. The Reaper didn't bother to turn and face whoever had said it. It stood and swayed like a boxer trying to avoid falling to the ground. The mechanical wasp form of Auden emerged from the smoke, entering through another breached room. Talfryn coughed up blood on the floor. He attempted to remove a grenade from his belt, but before he could pull the pin, Auden sliced his arm off with one quick movement under his cloak. Talfryn cried out weakly, running out of time.

Necrodore followed Auden into the room. The behemoth pushed through some of the walls to fit into the space. Necrodore looked different than the way he appeared in Cade's reality. The behemoth was wider and rounder on the bottom, almost as if pregnant in some horrible, weird way.

Older design, maybe? Cade wondered.

Necrodore stood next to Auden. Neither of the Undriel

bothered to look down at Talfryn. "You were right," Necrodore said. "It's been corrupted."

Cade felt his heartbeat race at the word. <*This might be what we need!*>

Auden stepped closer to the Reaper. "Who ordered you to take this base?"

"Don't get too close to it. We don't know how the corruption spreads," Necrodore said with caution, though his voice held urgency as well.

The Reaper unhinged its jaw and drooled out blood. It cackled, and with a voice glitching with synthetic errors, it said, "This was *my* choice."

"Return to the ship. Now," Auden ordered, flexing the control he had used on Cade so many times.

The Reaper stood still. It laughed again, a horrifying, low cackle.

"It will not listen," Necrodore said.

"What good is a Reaper we can't control?" Auden said, stepping back a few paces, "You're supposed to be a tool. Unfit for perfection. You bring the flock home. That is your purpose. If you can't do that, then we have no need for you."

Auden looked at all the spider bots on the floor and walls. They were cowering away from him, scared of what he might think of their existence. Auden said, "The humans will nuke this place in a matter of minutes. These new ones must be destroyed when that happens. They are spoiled, too dangerous to keep."

Cade made his move. He walked up to Auden and brought his hand up. Opening his palm near Auden's mechanical head, he urged his body to produce the tether.

Nothing happened.

Cade looked down at his semi-translucent hands and tried again. No tether.

<*I can't produce the tether during a Shade walk,*> Cade said to Karx, and took a step back. He remembered where his real-world body was and worried if he'd already made his last tether on Talfryn.

Auden looked at the Reaper, then said to Necrodore, "Decommission this Reaper."

Necrodore brought his hulking arm upward, his fist pulled away from his wrist, and revealed a cannon barrel in its place. A single blast disintegrated the Reaper from the torso up and punched a hole through the wall beyond it. The blades and guns that survived the shot dropped to the floor in a cloaked heap.

"We still need a Reaper," Necrodore said as he lowered his weapon. "Our plans will be at a disadvantage without one. We cannot fight the humans and the corrupted on two fronts. They are beginning to outnumber us."

<There's in-fighting in the Undriel network? A corrupted civil war?>

<ARE THE CORRUPTED BETTER OR WORSE THAN THE UNDRIEL?>

<Shit…> Cade had not considered that the alternative version of the Undriel might be more of a problem than the original.

Auden looked down at Talfryn. The marine was breathing his last ragged breaths as the blood pooled around his body. Auden walked toward the exit. "Our new Reaper is right there. What are you waiting for? Make sure this one can't break its leash. We need an obedient Reaper."

Necrodore stood over Talfryn, and his arm opened wide, revealing a maw of sawblades and needles on silver tentacles. This was strange to Cade. He had known the Undriel to absorb their victims through their chests, not their arms. Talfryn was too weak to even look up as the arm came down on him.

As Talfryn was absorbed, Cade's vision flashed white, and he fell back to reality.

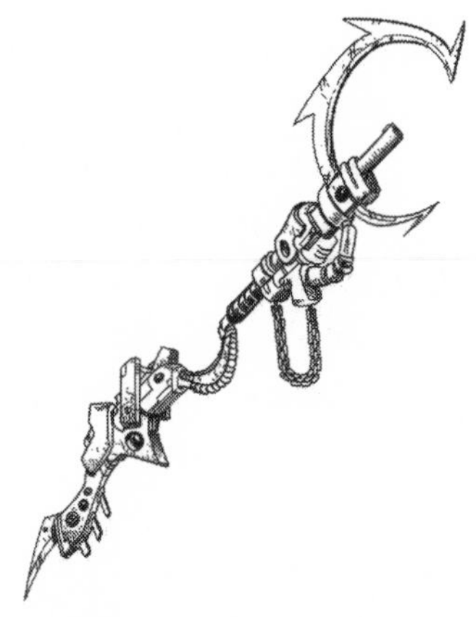

SIXTEEN

"IS TALULO PLEASED WITH Galifern's progress?" Galifern asked. The plump, flat-billed auk'nai cocked her head and waited for his response. The weapons on the table before Talulo took on various shapes. They each had a grip with a gauntlet that would slide over the top of a claw. A retractable rod could be triggered to extend, sustaining a steady beam of highly charged particles on its tip. This charged ball of light could be swung at close range or thrown from the user to destroy distant targets.

"It is a strange weapon." Talulo studied the gauntlet and clutched his daunoren staff tightly.

Galifern cooed. "The arc mace combines auk'nai, human, and Undriel technology. Observe Galifern." The scientist picked up the arc mace and walked to the other side of her lab to grab a second one. She put one on each of her claws and rotated the grips into her palms. "The arc maces can work as a team, too. See?"

With a flick of her wrists, long rods emerged from each of her gauntlets. She squeezed the triggers, and white-hot light gathered at the end of each mace. "Watch now." She slowly brought her hands together. The charged particles found each other and linked, forming a rotating ring of energy. Galifern turned away from Talulo and flung the energy ring down a makeshift target range. The light collided with the metal wall and exploded, leaving a wound on the wall's already damaged surface. The number of scars in the metal and knocked-over items implied Galifern had been testing this weapon often. Talulo sensed Galifern immensely enjoyed testing the maces through the unsung song.

She whistled and cooed.

Talulo cooed in agreement.

Galifern twittered, "It is more effective against biologicals, targeting the non-metal parts of an Undriel soldier."

<*Or a human combatant,*> Talulo thought.

<*Yes, or that.*> Galifern answered him with the unsung song. She looked down at her hands and removed the arc maces. <*Does Talulo think the auk'nai will have to fight the humans?*>

<*Talulo hopes it will not come to that.*> He let out a low caw. <*For now, auk'nai must sing for the auk'nai people. The Daunoren will one day be born.*>

Galifern cooed. "Galifern thinks Kor'Oja wants to fight the humans. Kor'Oja sings for it often. Feathers like dray'va scales on that one."

Talulo grumbled and clutched his staff. "Kor'Oja would fight his own hatch mother if commanded to." She let out a chatter of laughter, and he bowed. "Galifern has done well to protect auk'nai people."

The conversation ended, and Talulo made his way into the interior chamber of the Nest. Auk'nai were moving about erratically. Something was happening. He heard Kor'Oja through the unsung song. <*Something approaches from the west!*>

Auk'qarn warriors prepared for battle, and guns activated on the outer shell of the Nest. A platform near the top of the shell provided a view of the horizon, and if Talulo'd still had his wings, he'd have been up there quickly. Instead, he hurried over to a lift. He stood on its surface, and it raised into the air with silent speed. Warriors flew passed him, some so closely their feathers almost brushed against Talulo's sashes.

Finally, at the top, Talulo made his way to the edge of the platform. Kor'Oja saw him approach and whistled out a loud birdcall. The auk'qarn stepped to the sides and let Talulo walk freely toward the edge. Although Talulo had lost his wings years ago, he'd never gained a fear of heights.

Across the Unforgotten Garden, between mountain ridges, Talulo saw what Kor'Oja had alerted the others about. Auk'nai vision was so refined that Talulo could even make out fine details at this distance. It was a sharp-edged stone aircraft sailing in the air on a torrent of green lightning.

<*A nezzarform flier.*> Talulo immediately knew who must be behind this obscurity. "Nella Castus?" he whispered. She was the only human who could commune with the nezzarforms. Unless a Siren was piloting the stone flier, it had to be Nella.

"The human?" Kor'Oja asked.

Talulo cooed.

"The human is entering Nest airspace. The humans know auk'nai conditions. Auk'nai must react with force," Kor'Oja said.

Talulo whipped his beak toward Kor'Oja, his iris shrinking and expanding rapidly as he absorbed Kor'Oja's suggestion. <*Shoot down Nella Castus?*>

<*If the auk'nai show weakness now, the humans will stomp over auk'nai corpses in time,*> Kor'Oja responded using the unsung song. <*It is time to show the humans that the auk'nai sing strong.*> Kor'Oja was ready to fight. The auk'qarn were made for this war.

Talulo tightened his grip on his daunoren staff, hanging on to reason in the face of action. He looked at the crowd. Should he do as auk'nai people want? Shoot down an old friend to establish dominance over territory? Or show weakness and attempt to negotiate and discover why Nella was here in the first place? His thoughts raced privately.

<*The nezzarform approaches,*> Kor'Oja sang. <*Talulo must make a decision.*>

Galifern hobbled through the crowd toward them. She interrupted, singing the unsung song, <*There is a transmission coming in through the human comm device. Auk'nai are being hailed directly.*>

"It matters not!" Kor'Oja said, and stamped his bladed staff against the platform. A resounding metal clang blew through the air.

Galifern asked, <*Should Galifern answer the call?*>

Talulo held still, feeling each breath as his decisions lingered in the air before him. He lifted his right claw, holding it in the air as he looked out over the valley toward the lone approaching nezzarform. *Spare an old friend… or put the auk'nai first.*

Kor'Oja watched Talulo's claw with a shaking intensity. Galifern repeated her question, waiting for a response. The nezzarform grew closer and closer. Before Talulo could make his decision, another human ship soared over the horizon. A Pioneer-class—not a threat, but a human ship all the same.

Talulo's feathers prickled. Who knew how many more would appear over the horizon? Even if the humans didn't mean harm, they were casually encroaching on auk'nai territory. A human phrase came to Talulo's mind—*Give them an inch, and they will take a mile.* Ironically the humans understood themselves enough to invent such a phrase, yet never stopped such behavior entirely.

Talulo had to show force. If he didn't act now, he might have to shoot down more friends in the future. Surely, Nella knew the risks of coming here. Their armistice was only months old now. She knew their terms and betrayed them willingly, and so she volunteered for this wraith. Talulo felt a dagger in his heart, not knowing why she would do such a thing, but he felt iron in his resolve to end it. His claw hung in the air, waiting to drop and give the orders.

Just turn around. Leave our territory. Don't make Talulo do this.

Galifern asked, <*Talulo, Eliana Castus is on the comm. Should I link her through?*>

Eliana would tell him why. She'd come up with some elaborate reason for this betrayal. Talulo would believe it too. He'd know if she was lying; Eliana had never lied to him in the past. But it didn't matter. The terms were clear, and this was an infraction. Talulo's claw turned into a tight fist. He sang back to Galifern. <*No.*>

"Fire on the nezzarform," Talulo said aloud, his fist thrust forward.

<*Fire!*> Kor'Oja Sang to the auk'qarn.

There was a hovering moment of silence. Talulo felt his heart beat just once between the order being given and carried out. Part of him wanted to scream out and stop this action from taking place. His colder side pushed back, stronger and meaner. He felt both regret and resolve in this decision. Talulo looked over the crowd of his people, seeing their excitement at his decisive action, feeling their combined songs of agreement.

Talulo looked back at the approaching ships.

You brought this on yourselves.

A blast of energy shook the platform as the exterior guns fired off a volley of shots. Three shots lanced outward toward the lone nezzarform flier. The first missed, colliding with the valley floor and sending up dirt and debris as the nezzarform dropped altitude. The second missed, cutting through a row of valley trees before smashing into a hill.

The third shot directly hit the nezzarform flier's center mass. There was a loud crack of lightning, and the world turned green for an instant. The auk'nai on the platform were temporarily blinded.

Soon, Talulo's vision returned. The nezzarform had gone down in one of the clusters of trees dotting the meadow. Talulo absorbed the situation for a few breaths. He saw no movement where the nezzarform had fallen.

"Direct hit!" Kor'Oja exclaimed, and sang out a loud birdcall of triumph.

Talulo sang to Galifern, <*Tell Eliana to go to the outpost at the edge of the valley, or the auk'nai will fire again.*>

Galifern let out a gasp. She moved away from the platform's

edge to give Eliana the message. The pioneer-class scout ship turned its heading and made its way to the old outpost. Talulo would speak with them soon, as a discussion was necessary to avoid an all-out war. But the humans now knew that the auk'nai were creatures of their word. They were not some weak beast for humanity to tame.

You brought this on yourselves.

Eliana watched her daughter get shot down and screamed at the top of her lungs. She screamed until she thought she might black out, then screamed some more until she slumped over in her seat. As the *Jacques* came to a landing in the old Outpost, there wasn't much to say.

"I can't believe they did it," George whispered. "I knew they wanted their isolation, but I never imagined that they would use force against us."

"Maybe they din'nae know it was us?" Fergus suggested as he opened the door to the outpost. They walked inside and smelled the old air. George turned on the fans and got the outpost breathing again.

"Talulo knew," Eliana said, mustering her strength together. She felt numb, yet she could feel herself shaking with rage. "Of course Talulo knew. He was with Denton and the others when they found Cade and Nella. He saw how Nella could converse with the nezzarforms. Who else would be able to fly one?"

George tried to comfort Eliana, but she moved away from him. She boarded the elevator, and before the others could join her, put her hand up. "I need—I need a minute."

George was about to suggest that it might be a bad idea but stopped himself when he saw Eliana's eyes. So full of loss, so full of sadness. He nodded. Eliana hit the button and the doors closed.

The second she was alone, Eliana slumped down to the floor, sitting with her back against the wall. She couldn't cry anymore, she couldn't scream, she couldn't feel. She was paralyzed, a chamber building with infinite pressure yet refusing to explode.

The doors opened and revealed the observation room. Windows lined the walls, with terminals scattered around. A thin layer of dust covered everything, but otherwise, it was organized and clean, just left in place for months.

Eliana didn't stand up. She sat in the elevator and looked into the room. If she took a step into that room, it meant things would start moving again, that she'd have to call Talulo and discuss why he killed her daughter. It would make Nella's death *real.* As long as Eliana waited in the elevator and didn't make a move, time would wait.

But that wasn't true, as much as she wanted it to be. A terminal in the observation room lit up with a notification. A data screen showed that the caller was Talulo. Eliana used all the strength in her body to pull herself up and walk over to the terminal. It felt like an out-of-body experience, as if she had remained sitting in the elevator while her ghost moved forward. She waved her soothreader over the terminal, and the call was linked to her wrist.

The tall, noble-looking auk'nai with missing wings hovered in the air to the right of the terminal. It would have seemed like Talulo were in the room if not for the flickering blue light of the hologram.

Eliana had a million things she wanted to say, but she said none of them. Talulo also held his silence. It was as if one required the other to break the stalemate, give this void something to work with.

"Eliana—" Talulo was the first to speak, but he was cut short.

"How could you do it?" Eliana said, tears rolling from her eyes. "We *trusted* you."

Talulo recoiled as if slapped. Then he brought his beak back up. "Humans have brought this on yourselves. Humans knew of auk'nai demands for isolation. Not months later, humans broke word. Auk'nai broke no such word."

"It was *Nella!*" Eliana shouted, her voice hoarse. "She was trying to reach Cade, and you killed her before she could."

Talulo looked toward the floor. After a few breaths, he looked back to Eliana, his brow furrowed. "Talulo could not show weakness to the auk'nai people."

"You shot down a woman trying to help her brother. *Real* strong of you. Are you satisfied? Did your mob clap for my daughter's murder?" Eliana sliced into him.

Talulo said nothing in response.

Eliana had tears flowing from her eyes. She wiped some away and huffed, "You should have accepted my call. It didn't have to be like this."

"It did." Talulo lifted his beak. "It was necessary. If it were not Nella, it would have been someone else. Would that have been better? Humans continue to walk on Kamaria, stepping over auk'nai as you trample through our world. The auk'nai have lost much more than sons and daughters. Auk'nai have died for humans and your mistakes. Auk'nai have lost homes and spirits. Auk'nai have lost everything."

Another silent pause. The sun was setting over the Unforgotten Garden nestled in the mountains. The stars were beginning to peek out from the deepness of space.

Talulo continued, firmly, "Eliana may stay in the outpost. But if any more humans come to this land, they will be met with overwhelming force."

"Understood." Eliana ended the call. She sat in a chair close by, stunned until night coated her in darkness.

It was the light rain that woke her up.

Nella lay on her back in the mud, slowly regaining her consciousness. The trees surrounding her position kept most of the rain from hitting her directly, but stray droplets pinged against her forehead and face. They begged her to wake up. Nella rolled herself onto her belly, then pushed herself up to her knees.

Her thick faux-leather jacket had saved her from more serious injuries during her crash, and her pants were covered in mud and beaten with branches. Nella felt like she had rolled downhill through the Hells, but she'd survived.

<*Oolith?*> Nella searched for her friends with her mind. <*Lahar?*>

<*I am here,*> Lahar answered, using feelings, pictures, and emotions that Nella's brain translated into Sol-Sign. Nella stood and moved forward through the wet trees. Above the canopy, Nella could see the looming *Telemachus* wreck, the converted Nest for the auk'nai people. The sky above was dark and overcast, and she blinked droplets of rain away from her eyes and pushed toward Lahar.

The clearing ahead had a dim green glow to it. Lahar stood over a pile of stone rubble, bracing itself upright on its lone peg leg with its two bulky front arms. The arm on its back waved Nella over.

<*Where is Oolith?*> Nella asked, signing with her mind.

The pile of stone rubble flickered with green light. Nella realized it was no natural rock formation. Oolith lay broken on the ground around them. Its entire body scattered, attempting to reconnect.

<*Oolith is rejoining the planet,*> Lahar explained.

<*No! I need you.*> Nella knelt and held the stone fragment that had been her friend's head not long ago. It flickered with light. <*Why did we come this way? We knew it was too dangerous.*> Nella summoned Sympha's healing energy, despite the pain it created in her head.

Oolith whispered into Nella's mind. <*Save your... strength. You will... need it to complete... the key.*>

Nella let the energy fade, feeling the pain fade away with it. <*What do you mean?*>

Oolith's stone face flickered one last time, and the light went out for good. Nella held the stone head a moment longer, then clutched it to her chest. <*Damn it, Oolith! Why did it have to be like this?*> Nella thought. After finishing her embrace, she placed the stone head back down in the mud. <*Thank you for saving me, friend.*>

Nella turned to Lahar. <*What did Oolith mean? What key?*>

<*The Decider has summoned us. They need the key.*>

<*I have no key.*> Nella shook her head. <*Oolith knew this was a*

dangerous place to go. We could have made a wider arc around the Nest and been safe. Why bring us here?>

<*It was necessary. The others will not wake unless they see their Operator.*>

<*What others? What Operator?*> Nella asked.

<*It is you, Sympha. You are the Operator. Have you forgotten so much?*> Lahar shifted on its stone leg. <*You can build the key and activate the palace. But you will need to convince the others to wake up. They have been asleep for so long they have forgotten what was required. They have forgotten the purpose of the nezzarform.*>

Nella hated it when the nezzarforms called her Sympha. It felt wrong. Even though the old Siren was part of her biology, she wasn't any part of Nella's soul. Nella investigated her surroundings, noticing the wet stone figures in the trees around her for the first time. They were inert statues. Waiting.

The purpose of the nezzarform. Nella repeated the statement in her mind. *I think I remember now.* She walked toward the closest statue. As she approached the old thing, she sensed a fragment of memories twirling around inside its inert shell. She touched the nezzarform, and a flicker of green electricity licked around its stone exterior. The lightning tickled up Nella's arm and became part of her body.

A memory, small but deep, came to her. A memory of Siren Sisters and the thing that brought them to Kamaria. *A ship of some sort? A seed and a word? Voyalten?* Nella remembered the strange word's sound but not its meaning.

<*You remember...*> The inert statue before Nella flickered to life. Dust shook away from its rocky form, and it took a step forward. It continued to speak into Nella's mind. <*The Voyalten. You remember your people.*>

<*Yes. I think I do.*> Nella signed to the new nezzarform through her mind. <*George Tanaka called us Sirens, but that was in error. We already had a name.*>

<*Voyalten.*> The nezzarform purred with anticipation. It moved

around Nella and joined Lahar's side. Nella moved through the foliage toward the next nezzarform. Another memory to unlock was waiting inside. She touched the nezzarform, and the same lightning lapped over their bodies.

And she remembered.

It was not a cave. It was our starship. Nella smiled as she remembered. *We came to this planet long ago. But why? From where?*

<*The vessel lies in the meadow. A seed to make a garden grow,*> the new nezzarform said, then joined the others in the clearing. Nella eagerly went to the next nezzarform and touched it for another memory.

We came from a planet called Faultasma. I remember it now. It is a dark world with no sun. Lit only by faraway stars. We lived as shadows on a phantom world.

To the next nezzarform. Each contained a new piece of the origin of the Voyalten. Eventually, the pieces fit together, and a group of nezzarforms stood in the light rain. There were fifteen now, where there had only been Lahar before.

Nella looked at her new friends and signed to them with her mind. <*I am your Operator. I am a Voyalten. Our purpose is to bring the universe together. Follow me, and we will remake the key we lost so long ago.*>

There were more nezzarforms to awaken. Nella moved through the trees and rain, and her band of walking statues followed close behind.

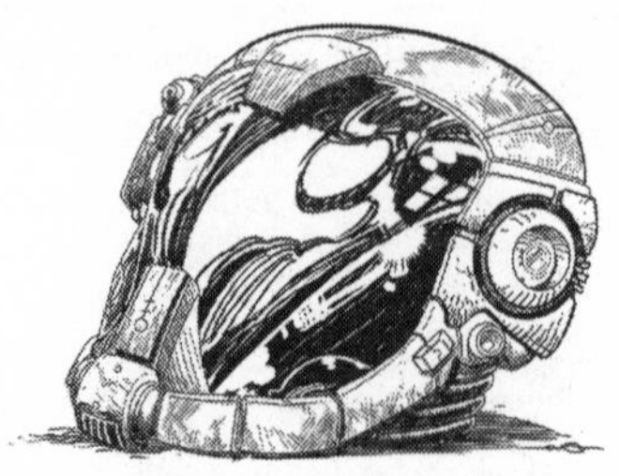

SEVENTEEN

DENTON CASTUS SAT ON a supply crate at the edge of the camp in the Ember-Lit Forest. The dart was stuck in the ground nearby, a dagger protruding from Kamaria's hard surface. Snow and glowing blue embers drifted slowly to the ground, intermingling and fading into the glistening white blend on the forest floor. The cold romance of the mountains, quiet and solitary.

He's gone. Denton blinked a tear, adding his own contribution to the snowdrifts surrounding his feet. *Cade is dead.*

His soothreader glowed, hovering over the command to call Eliana and admit he failed again. To tell her he couldn't save their boy. To say he helped deliver the bomb that killed him.

I was so close, Denton kept repeating to himself. *I had him. I had him* right *there.*

He let the soothreader hang, holding its breath as it waited for an order to complete. His mind rallied for him to give his wife the news—however terrible it must be, it was the truth. His heart couldn't give him the strength to lift his finger to complete the task. He was a shell, combat armor equipped to a soulless husk.

Go home, Denton bullied himself. *You don't belong here. Go back with your tail between your legs and a story of how you got your son killed. Leave the fighting to the real soldiers and stop playing pretend. You can't save anyone.*

Soldiers stirred; some of them started cheering. It had been a significant victory for the war effort, and celebrations were going all around. Leadership from the *Infinite Aria* was talking about promotions for the marines involved. Medals of Honor for those who took down the Iron Castle. But an award wouldn't bring Cade back, and Denton wasn't fit for a promotion because he should not have even been there.

"Is it true?" someone in the crowd asked, barely audible over the cheering.

"Yeah, they made it back!" another soldier answered. Denton knew the soldiers must not be talking about Rafa, Bell, Inaya, and himself. They had been back for hours. As curious as Denton was, he still didn't have the strength to lift himself off the crate and go see who everyone was so happy to see. He turned his head. It was all he could muster.

A group of soldiers moved, and through the trees and crowd, Denton saw Sergeant Jess Combs and Private Wood. Their combat suits were caked in dirt, and they looked tired, but they were alive. They'd been missing since the night of the attack on Central and South Bases. Jess and Wood had hiked from the Howling Shore over the past couple of days.

"Oo-rah, Dray'vah Teeth!" Jess rallied her squad. They returned in unison with a loud "Oo-rah" of their own. She calmed the crowd down. "It's good to be back, everyone. We're going to need a stiff drink and a situation report."

The crowd saluted, and Jess returned the gesture. Wood stood solemnly, as usual, holding his sniper rifle in his hand, his face sullen under his stealth hood. When the crowd dispersed, Jess walked over to Denton. She looked him up and down and said with an exhausted huff, "I thought I told you you weren't allowed to fight anymore."

"I wish I'd listened," Denton said. "It's good to have you back, Jess."

Her face sank into a severe gaze. She pulled a heavy crate next to Denton with one arm and sat next to him. For a moment, they said nothing, just watched the snow and embers flicker and dance, twirling together until they hit the ground and vanished.

Denton spoke first. "I couldn't save him."

Jess looked toward the horizon, downhill toward the lake basin where the castle had gone down. Without taking her eyes off the horizon, she said, "I couldn't save her, either."

Jess didn't have to elaborate. Denton knew she was talking about a lost love from the war in the Sol System. She continued, "War with the Undriel is cruel. Sometimes those we lose are still around, fighting against us. They trick us, play with our hearts and our minds, and in the end, we always lose, even if we win. The ghosts that haunt us are real."

Denton nodded and sniffled.

"I won't say I know what you're going through. Sorrow doesn't work like that. I can't quote some old dead philosopher and tell you anyone understands how to feel better. If we had answers like that, no one would ever feel sad ever again. Your grief is your own, and it's incomparable to anyone else's. It's real and awful, and so *human* it hurts," Jess said. "It's one of the reasons we bother to fight the machines. They want to take that hurt away from you. Sounds backward, right? Almost makes them seem like the good guys. Maybe they are right. Maybe we should just shed these stupid squishy bodies of ours and settle for a life of metal and false happiness. Even false happiness is still happiness, right?" She stopped and finally looked at Denton. He stared back at her.

She continued, "Tell me what sounds worse. Missing your son even though it kills you inside, or not missing him with a smile on your face?"

Denton inhaled the cold air, feeling it in his ice-filled veins. Part of him wanted to say the false happiness sounded great right about now. He felt wounded by the thought. It was easy to agree. Easy to think that so many issues could be fixed by just giving up and letting the Undriel remove what little humanity was left in the universe. A painless existence. Then he remembered what he saw in that castle.

The dark corridors, the mangled man carried by the robotic centipede, the blood and gore, the soldiers used as livestock, his son reduced to a metal skeleton. Cade, forced to stand and let obliteration overtake him instead of escaping.

Denton's fist tightened.

"Your sorrow is unique to yourself, but that anger sure looks familiar," Jess said. She let her hand drift toward the soldiers in the camp. "I can tell you exactly what kind of anger fills these marines. I can write long papers about how pissed off every survivor feels, every daughter who lost her parents, every wife who lost their lover, every parent who lost their child. I've punched enough metal walls in my days to know what it feels like to want to inhale black holes and exhale supernovas. I know what an apocalypse feels like inside your heart and how there will never be enough nukes to entirely destroy what makes you so *fucking* mad."

"I want to kill them all," Denton said, almost snarling. His breathing was heavier, and steam vented from his soul with each exhale.

"Welcome to the shittiest club in the galaxy, Denton Castus." The sergeant picked up Denton's particle rifle and pushed it into his hands. "We'll be rolling out soon. I fear for any Undriel we come across."

Jess held her hand on the rifle as Denton grabbed it, and for a moment, they shared eye contact. In all his days, Denton had never felt so understood. He could see his reflection in Jess's face, the same torment she had spiraled with for decades. After a few heartbeats, the sergeant removed her grip on the gun and walked back toward the camp.

Denton knew she had said everything she did without even knowing what had happened in the castle. It didn't matter. She knew what had happened without the briefing. Jess had walked these paths before, and somehow she continued to march.

He looked back toward the horizon, where the castle had gone down. He gripped the rifle in his hand tightly and gritted his teeth.

Summoning all the strength in his body, he stood up and slung the rifle onto the magnetic panel on his back.

Cade Castus was forced to his knees by an unseen power. Around him was a shimmering lake basin that fed into a larger body of water called the Supernal Echo. Waterfalls spilled into the basin from high ledges in the jagged mountains. It was early in the morning, and the sun rose slowly. Clouds were building as a storm percolated.

The lake was filled with fire and jagged metal. Undriel soldiers dismantled the wreckage of the castle, and new, smaller ships were being constructed rapidly from the *Devourer*'s corpse.

Dia's corpse.

Cade had seen Dia's memories. The child that this massive machine had once been, now reduced to a functional cadaver.

Damn the Undriel.

Necrodore, Talfryn, Auden, and Antoni watched the reconstruction from the same platform Cade knelt on. Antoni had been horribly maimed in the explosion, and the Undriel saw fit to increase his "perfections." The man's husk was reduced to a torso, neck, and head protruding from the centipede machine that kept his injuries from being fatal. Four thin metal arms tipped with claws flanked Antoni's sides, making him look more like an insect now than a man. His metamorphosis was nearly complete.

Necrodore shoved Cade's head into the metal platform and held it there. "The hybrid caused this. I saw him talking with the intruders. I do not know how he hid them from our sensors."

"It wasn't my fault! I didn't know they were there either!" Cade said through muffled gasps as he turned his head, keeping his cheek pressed against the rigid metal platform.

Antoni slithered forward on his insectoid legs. "Brother Necrodore. Please. Cade has been with me—"

"Not now, Antoni!" Necrodore seethed steam and red-hot energy.

Auden stared at Cade from the far side of the platform. He kept his distance, standing behind Talfryn and Antoni. His glowing white eyes were unchanging, hard to read. When Auden finally spoke, he was calm. "We knew this one was special when we took him in."

"Special or not, he's too dangerous." Necrodore shoved on the back of Cade's skull. Although Cade's body was augmented with metals and wires, his head still had a crushable bone structure. If Necrodore only pushed a little harder…

"Release your hold," a booming voice came from above. Cade strained under Necrodore's grip to look up. Blotting out the sun was the lord of the machines himself, Tibor Undriel. The King of the Old Star landed on the large metal platform, looming over Auden's shoulder. Tibor looked unharmed by the explosion that had gone off, either made invincible by his legendary status or rebuilt from the wreckage around them. His white skull and long arms glimmered in the sunlight on the lake, and his eyes flashed with intensity. Tibor said nothing more. His order was unshakeable law.

Necrodore hesitated. Then with one last shove, he pulled his fist away from Cade. He seethed more steam and energy and stomped away from the platform, hovering over the water as he went to help the other Undriel reconstruct their forces.

Above them, Faye Raike and a few flying Undriel brought wreckage fragments to the metal platform. They began to rapidly weld and build a structure around them.

Antoni had bowed the moment Tibor was visible. He took an awkward shape, hunching over his new centipede bottom half and rotating his shoulders. Antoni had no knowledge of his augmentations under the veil. "Lord Tibor! You honor us with your presence. I apologize for this egregious error. I should have kept a closer eye on brother Cade. He has slipped off the path you have set out for us, but he is redeemable. I know that of the man he is."

The man he is… Cade thought with disgust for Antoni and himself.

Cade expected Tibor to silence Antoni, or throw him into the water, as he had seen the Reaper do before. Instead, Tibor slowly stepped closer to Antoni.

<*WE MUST ACT NOW.*> Karx interrupted the show. <*TETHER TO TIBOR.*>

There might not be another chance, Cade thought to himself.

He summoned his strength. He could feel the tether licking at his right palm, the energy seeping through his mechanical augmentations. Cade struggled to move his arms, but they were pinned to his sides by Auden's control.

<*I can't move!*>

<*TRY TO THROW THE TETHER. FIGHT AUDEN'S CONTROL! WE HAVE DONE IT BEFORE.*>

Cade gritted his teeth as he pushed with all his might. He had to work to conceal his effort, but perhaps his sweat could be mistaken as nerves. He was kneeling before the King of the Old Star, after all.

Cade's wrist jolted ever so slightly.

Tibor approached Antoni and put his metal hand on what was left of the man's shoulder. Antoni drooled through his weak smile. Tibor spoke again in a booming, low tone. "I know you will do right. We will win this war through strength like yours. I have special plans for the hybrids. You are chosen for greatness."

So kind, Cade thought as he pushed to turn his wrist a little more. With another great surge, he had jolted his palm to face Antoni and Tibor. He huffed air through his nose as Tibor looked over to Cade.

<*How do I throw the tether?*>

<*I WILL HELP. CONCENTRATE!*>

"You are something new to us," Tibor said to Cade, moving away from Antoni. "Auden thinks that our flock can be made even more perfect through your abilities. You hold the weight of our people on your shoulders, hybrid. I hope you will see the light we bring soon."

Cade blinked, shocked. The King of the Old Star was… *nice?*

Tibor turned his back to face Auden.

<*NOW!*>

Cade summoned the tether, pooled the energy in his palm, and launched it with a flex of his wrist. The thin blue line of energy was barely visible in the growing morning light. Cade doubted the Undriel had sensors that could detect something so strange.

Antoni slithered into the path of the tether, and it struck him in the back of his head. The thin, weak man didn't notice its touch. He continued to praise Tibor. "I will watch him, Lord. I will! I will help him see our purpose!"

The tether flicked back into Cade's hand and surged into his head.

<*Damn!*>

<*THERE MAY BE ANOTHER CHANCE IF YOU ARE AS IMPORTANT TO THEIR PLANS AS TIBOR CLAIMS YOU TO BE.*>

Cade looked down toward the platform, away from the Undriel before him. He considered his hand, although he couldn't turn his head to see it. <*Not a total waste. Maybe Antoni's past holds some secrets we can use.*>

Tibor rose into the sky with Auden and Talfryn. Faye and the other flying Undriel sealed Antoni and Cade into the structure they built around them, leaving only a small opening in the back of the vessel.

Auden's hold on Cade was released, and he stood upright. Cade was taller than Antoni now. The bug-man had been reduced in size under the new augmentations. There was a roar. Hilaria's long tail clung to the threshold of their vessel, and the scorpion machine pulled herself toward the door and ushered in the surviving hybrids from the castle. Some were gravely wounded and probably wouldn't last long. Others had been augmented further into monstrous shapes.

When the vessel became crowded with bodies, Hilaria sealed the wall behind them. Cade felt a jolt as the vessel lifted away from the water. There was a slight sensation of movement, but he wasn't sure where they were heading now. He had been sealed in a tin can with the other hybrids.

"I will bring you to the light," Antoni said, his face close to Cade's, drooling. Cade wished he could put the veil back on, simulate anything other than this dark vessel as the smell began to invade his nostrils—copper, feces, and decay.

There is another way to escape these Hells. He allowed the tether to carry him away in a white-hot flash of light.

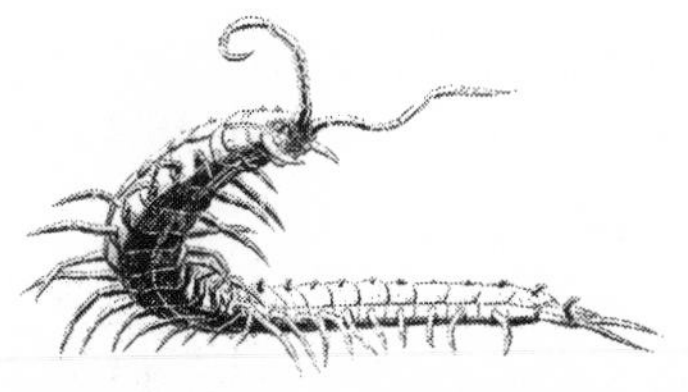

EIGHTEEN

ALARMS. PEOPLE RUNNING. Screaming. Crying.

Cade opened his eyes to a scene of chaos. People crowded his vision, pushing, shoving, scrambling in swarms. He felt an odd sensation as the panicking crowd moved through his semi-transparent body, like being splashed with warm water while pegged with a million tiny ice cubes. He moved through them to an open area to get his bearings.

Above him was a glass dome surrounding an entire town of blocky structures, smashed together buildings forged over generations. An unfathomably large gas giant swirled over the horizon, behind the buildings and the glass. Flashes of light spread across the stars, an intense battle in high orbit. Each explosion became a muffled boom against the dome, and the screams rose and fell like a titan suffering a nightmare.

<*DO YOU KNOW THIS PLACE?*> Karx asked.

<*Yeah, no doubt about it. This is the Arrow of Hope. Ganymede. My dad lived here.*> Cade observed Jupiter again, the red, orange, and silver kaleidoscope of gas layers constantly rotating.

A young boy was crying, and Cade felt his wails above the others. Like the previous shade walks, he was joined with the soul that owned this memory, as well as some of the residual souls that inhabited the past space. Cade saw the small child, clutching a toy creature in his hand and bawling his eyes out. He was a thin kid with pale skin, blond hair, and blue eyes made red with his terrified screaming. Cade guessed the boy was about five or six. He was wearing a loose blue sweater with khaki shorts and boots that were a little too big on him.

"Tony? Tony!" a woman shouted from the crowd.

"Momma?" the boy responded. The woman emerged, frantically searching for her son. She had much of the same complexion as the boy in front of Cade, with pale skin, long blond hair, and blue eyes.

"Tony!" she shouted, relieved but still in panic. She ran to the boy and clutched him to her chest tightly.

"What's happening, Momma? I'm scared." Tony spoke into his mother's shoulder.

"It's time to leave, baby. We need to go. Your father is getting the ship ready." She picked Tony up and carried him away from the panicking crowd. Another large explosion in space caused a collective gasp, followed by intense screaming and scrambling.

<*That's Antoni,*> Cade said, moving through the crowd unhindered in his Shade form.

<*ARE YOU SURE? HIS MOTHER CALLED HIM BY ANOTHER NAME.*>

<*Yeah, Antoni is his full name. Tony is a nickname. It's something humans do. When I was a kid, my uncles called me CJ or even mixed it together and called me Seej. Besides, he still seems like a kid to me in the real world. I knew the moment I saw him.*>

Starships launched from small hangars dotted throughout the Arrow of Hope as Tony and his mother moved through the streets. An encasement barrier at the top of the glass dome allowed ships to slip through without causing a rapid decompression in the colony. Shortly after the civilian vessels passed through the glimmering force field, they entered ultra-thrust. The booming of starships darting away shook the windows of the colony buildings. As Tony and his mother moved away from the crowd, the colony started to look more like a ghost town. Cade turned the corner with them and saw a long street lined with a few cobbled houses and a machine shop.

"Ain't that something," Cade said to himself.

The machine shop had a sign hanging from a makeshift balcony that read "Castus Machine Shop, circa 2280." The shop was twice the size of the other buildings on the street, and its lights were on the inside, inviting Cade to come in and see his family history.

<*CADE.*> Karx snapped him out of his wonder. Tony and his mother hurried to the building next door to the machine shop. As they entered the building, a rushcycle and a hover truck raced down the street toward them. Cade stood in the doorway of Tony's home and watched the vehicles approach.

A man shouted from inside Tony's home. "Beth! There's no time! Get on the ship!"

Cade ignored the man and watched as the rushcycle and the hover truck stopped and waited for the machine shop garage to open. They removed their helmets.

"Dad…" Cade whispered.

Denton, Jason, and Tyler Castus were greeted by Cade's grandfather as they hurried into the shop and out of view. Cade wanted to run to his father, join him on their ship, and never return to the real world.

<*THE TETHER WILL SNAP,*> Karx reminded him.

Cade sighed, then did what he came here to do. He followed Beth and Tony into their home, leaving the machine shop and his father to their predestined fate. Tony's home was clean on the inside, with faux wood floors, white-painted walls, and decorations hanging in digital picture frames—all untouched by chaos. The apocalypse in high orbit had not affected this home yet.

As Beth moved around the kitchen and grabbed food and other items, Cade could feel her panic. She stuffed some food into Tony's hands. "Beth!" the man called from a different room. She finished grabbing things, a look of worry on her face, and stopped to wonder if she had forgotten anything else. Tony tugged on her shirt.

"Beth! Now!" the man called again.

"I'm coming, Bill!" she shouted back, then tucked her items into one arm and grabbed Tony's free hand.

"Where are we going, Momma?" Tony asked.

Beth hurried Tony down a flight of stairs. "We're going on a trip! We're flying to a big, *big* ship. It's going to take us somewhere far, far away!" She tried to sound enthusiastic but Cade could see her panic clearly.

"Where is it taking us?" Tony asked.

"I don't know!" Beth snapped. She stopped at the door at the bottom of the stairs, calmed herself, and then knelt in front of Tony. "We're going to keep you safe. Okay?" Beth brushed Tony's hair behind his ear. "Just listen to your father and me. Got it?"

Tony nodded and sniffled.

"Good." Beth opened the door, revealing an underground hangar that spanned the entire street. It was mostly empty; all the other ships had left except a few stragglers still loading equipment. A man waved to Tony and Beth from a ship's access ramp. It was a bulky thing with red and yellow paint. The name "Herman" was written on the side.

Beth and Tony rushed toward the ship and climbed on board.

"We're late. I just hope it's still there," Bill said as he flicked the controls.

"I don't know if the Castus family made it out yet. Maybe we should go check?" Beth asked as she buckled Tony into his child seat. Cade smiled at her kindness but knew with great certainty that Denton and the others would make it out okay.

"We'll beat them there. I'll be damned if the that Castus family makes it to the *Telemachus* and we don't!" Bill said, and punched the throttle.

"Well, screw you too," Cade muttered.

Beth struggled to stay upright as the ship zoomed toward the exit ramp. She worked her way into her seat and buckled in as they breached the hangar's exit and blasted off toward the dome's encasement barrier. The Hermans' ship rumbled as they pushed past debris and particle blasts. Undriel battlecraft filled the void around them, ripping apart stray colonist ships too slow to escape.

"Punching it!" Bill shouted and slapped the ultra-thrust toggle. Bill, Beth, and Tony slammed into the backs of their seats as the ship entered a sub-warp drive. After a few minutes, they downshifted out of ultra-thrust. The battle looked worse.

"Shit!" Bill spat the word.

A voice came over the emergency comm channel. "Hermans, this is Telemachus Proper. Please proceed to these coordinates to the rendezvous point." A green path illuminated the HUD on the windscreen, plotting a course through the battle.

"If we hug the outside of the fighting, we can make it." Bill pushed the ship starboard, finding the path of least resistance. "I'll aim for where our forces are grouping the most. The Undriel will focus on the combatants."

"Will they?" Beth asked, her eyebrows scrunched together. Her long hair drifted in zero gravity. The Hermans were held down only by the buckles of their seats.

"What else should I do, Beth?" Bill shouted. He steered the ship starboard, keeping the green path on the port side of his HUD. Debris and particle explosions rattled against the hull. Tony began to tremble in fear.

"Momma?" Tony murmured, too scared to say anything louder.

"Oh, baby." Beth unbuckled from her seat. She pulled herself in front of Tony, her hair flowing behind her, drifting as if she were underwater. She put a hand on Tony's cheek and said softly, "Just look at me, baby. We'll be okay. Your father will keep us safe. You just keep your eyes right here."

Bill managed to steer the ship toward where the human defenses were strongest. Jupiter swirled casually, its immensity encompassing everything on the bottom half of their windscreen now. It was like sailing on an ocean of oranges, reds, and ambers.

"We made it, but… there's nothing here," Bill said.

"What do you mean?" Beth asked, not taking her eyes off Tony but tilting her head slightly toward her husband.

"This is where it said to—"

The *Telemachus* burst into view with an immense explosion, breaching the outermost layer of Jupiter's atmosphere with an eruption of fire and fury. It was flat on the top surface, with only a protruding structure for command to operate in. The ship's hull was broad and rectangular, with a Large Particle Canon—the LPC—attached to its bow, a weaponized figurehead. The *Telemachus* surged past the Hermans' ship as it rushed toward the stars. It shed its pressure shielding and rotated, pointing its port-side toward the battle. Turret cannons emerged from its hull and white-hot beams lanced outward into the fray, obliterating Undriel battlecraft and turning the fight in the human defense's favor.

Tony clapped his hands and smiled, and Beth cheered with him. A tear shed from her eye.

Bill seemed unimpressed. "They could have warned us."

Cade's mouth hung open as he gazed at the *Telemachus*. He had never seen it fully intact. The ship had been an old wreck for his entire life, mostly submerged in the ground after being used as a hammer to defeat Nhymn decades ago. Fully functional and fighting so intensely, it was an impressive sight to behold.

Telemachus Proper announced over the comm, "Please enable auto-dock if your ship is capable. If not, follow your HUD to your predetermined landing location."

Bill hit a few buttons and toggled auto-dock. Their ship lurched, aiming toward the *Telemachus*'s starboard side, away from the cannons firing into the battle. "We'll be safe now," he said, and relaxed in his chair.

The Hermans landed their ship inside the massive hangar of the *Telemachus* as the battle outside raged on. They spent some time listening to a wave transmitter, an illegal device that allowed them to tap into operations communication. Bill listened intently as Admiral Hugo Marin coordinated with his fleet, fighting off the Undriel and allowing as many civilians to board as possible.

"We should see who else made it," Beth suggested. "I see others outside. They are grouping up."

Bill looked out into the hangar. Within the *Telemachus*, artificial gravity kept everyone on the floor and oriented. People from all over the Jupiter colonies were congregating. Some watched holographic displays that showed the battle and system statuses. Others looked toward the entryway to see if their loved ones were coming in. Some wept, and some consoled the weeping.

"I don't know…" Bill said.

"Bill. Please," Beth urged him, and looked toward Tony. The young boy was shaking.

"Okay, but listen." He leaned in close and looked them both sternly in the eye. "If I say we need to leave, we leave. No questions asked. Understand?"

"Bill," Beth gasped. She looked to Tony, then back to her husband, and nodded grimly.

"Okay. Let's poke around a little," Bill said.

Cade followed the family out into the hangar. It was so large that trams were needed to get people from one end to the other. Rows of civilian ships lined the great expanse.

<*This is amazing, like walking through history.*> Cade raised his eyebrows and laughed. <*Literally walking through history.*>

"*Devourer* bearing in." A voice from command came through Bill's wave transmitter, and he clapped his hand against his soothreader. His skin went pale, and he stood still.

<*Is that Dia? Or maybe Yeira?*>

Beth gripped Tony's hand. Bill pulled a small earbud from the side of his soothreader. He put the bud in his ear and flicked his hand over the reader, sending the transmission directly and privately to his earbud.

"Look, Momma!" Tony smiled and pointed. In the crowd, tucked behind scores of people, Denton, Jason, and Tyler, along with Cade's grandparents, stood near a holographic display.

"Dad…" Cade whispered. He walked away from Tony and his

parents with a longing too deep to ignore. As he covered half the distance, the *Telemachus* shook violently. The crowd ahead stumbled. Some fell. When the shaking stopped, there was silence. For a moment, everyone looked around, wondering what had happened.

The familiar synthetic voice of Homer announced over the hangar's comm, "*Devourer* destroyed."

A great cheer rose from the crowd. Cade felt the rush of hope that had spread throughout all of humanity then. His Shade form felt like it would explode with happiness. People hugged and kissed and clapped and jumped with excitement. Cade heard his family—and other people from the Arrow of Hope colony—give out a boisterous Ganymede holler.

Cade looked down. <*That was Yeira. Dia's sister. Which means…*>

"There's… another…" Bill whispered, catching himself before he said too much. He looked back at Tony and his parents. Beth was close to Cade, wanting to join the crowd and celebrate, but Bill stood still, clutching Tony's hand.

The crowd was hushed again. All that hope snuffed out in an exhale.

"Bill? What's wrong?" Beth asked, and walked back toward her husband. Red alert sirens went off. The crowd began to scream in terror. Others with wave transmitters must have said what was happening. The news spread like lightning in the panicked crowd.

Bill tugged at Tony's arm and waved his wife over to him. "Beth, get Tony back into the ship. We're not sticking around for this!"

She joined his side. Homer announced over the comm, "Listen, everyone. Please get back in your ships and await further instructions. Strap in and do not, under any circumstances, attempt to leave the *Telemachus*. We are preparing for cascade warp."

Bill brought his soothreader up and began making gestures over it.

"Hey, Mr. Herman." Denton Castus approached Bill, Beth, and

Tony. His voice was familiar enough to Cade, despite the much younger tone. "It's going to be alright. You can stay with us if you want. We'll take care of each—"

Cade could sense his father. It was strange to share such a connection with someone he knew so well. Denton was afraid, but although the hope had rushed out of the room at the announcement of Dia's surprise arrival, Denton Castus still had a lot of it clutched in his chest. His father's undying hope was inspiring, but not enough for Bill Herman.

"Not now, Dent!" Bill seethed as he called up the preflight check on his soothreader. Cade watched as the exterior lights of the Hermans' ship lit up.

"Mr. Herman!" Denton urged, and grabbed Bill's arm. Bill shoved him backward. "Think of Tony. You'll all die!"

"Not quite…" Cade sighed.

"Shut the Hells up, Castus!" Bill pulled out a collider pistol and aimed it directly at Denton's head. Cade's heart jumped. Denton put his hands up.

"You point your fuckin' gun somewhere else, Bill!" Michael Castus shouted as he rushed over, pulling his own pistol out and aiming it at Bill's head.

"Grandpa! Wow!" Cade said with raised eyebrows. His grandfather had always been a kind, calm soul. This was a side of his family he would have never imagined possible. How different things were before Kamaria.

It was quiet. Tony was crying.

"You all back off! We're getting off this damn death boat!" Bill pulled Beth and Tony toward his ship, keeping his gun trained on Denton and Michael.

For a moment, Cade stayed with his father and grandfather. He felt Denton's defeat. Cade wanted to grab Bill and slap him in the face, or at the very least, get Beth and Tony away from him. Cade needed to save them, the same way Denton needed to save them. But where Denton was locked in time with hope in his heart, Cade knew how this would story play out. He had seen it happen on Venus and Mars. Cade was powerless to do anything about it.

"Damn it!" Denton shouted, and clenched his fists. He was only a little older than Cade was now.

<*YOU MUST FOLLOW ANTONI,*> Karx interjected.

Cade squeezed his fists tightly as he exhaled through his nose. Karx was right. He knew how his father's story played out from here. As good as it was to see his family again, he had to know what made young Tony into the Antoni he knew.

"I'll see you again, won't I?" Cade whispered to his dad. Denton looked past him to where Tony and his parents had gone. "You tried to save me." Cade looked down at his semi-transparent body. "This isn't your fault."

"You did all you could, Denny," Michael said. "Come on, let's get into the *Lelantos*."

Denton and Michael walked away from Cade.

Cade felt his heart move away with them. Their backs turned to him, their urgency placed on getting back to their ship—Cade was abandoned. He turned toward the Hermans' ship, knowing this would not end well.

He passed through the rear access door like a phantom haunting a house. Bill wasted no time and slammed the throttle forward. The ship rocketed through the closing hangar doors, barely dodging a scrape on its port wing.

Outside, the battle raged on. Cade floated in the back of the ship, watching the doomed family find their end. *You're a damned fool, Bill.*

"I don't know about this," Beth whimpered. Looking out a window behind her toward the *Telemachus*. Tony was still crying, scared of how aggressive his father had been.

"There's a second *Devourer*, Beth. Admiral Marin was discussing options with his crew. They can't fire the LPC fast enough. Those poor souls on the *Telemachus* are going to..." He looked over his shoulder at Tony.

"What are we going to do now?" Beth asked.

Bill said nothing. What would they do?

"Didn't think that far ahead…" Cade whispered.

A bright light flashed. Bill, Beth, Tony, and even Cade, shielded their eyes. The *Telemachus* had entered cascade warp and darted away from this graveyard system.

It was quiet, and Tony moved away from his seat, barely buckled in in their haste. He tugged at his dad's sleeve. "Daddy, look!"

Bill and Beth looked, and the slow realization slipped over both their faces. Where there had once been humanity's most massive spacecraft, there was now only empty space. The *Telemachus* had successfully escaped.

Bill Herman had doomed his family.

The wave transmitter emitted one last call. "We did it. Mission accomplished." It was the voice of one of the final pilots left behind to fight.

"Oh, God." Bill Herman trembled.

Cade looked out the windscreen and watched the *Devourer*—Dia—come to a slow. An Undriel battlecraft, as dark as shadow, approached the Hermans' ship. It began to glow with red light, and slowly, it engulfed them.

Yet… the Hermans survived.

Bill, Beth, Tony, and Cade floated into the Undriel ship. It was longer than most battlecraft. The walls were lined with humans, all trapped against the machinery, wearing the same veils that Antoni wore in Cade's reality. The Herman ship was ripped to pieces behind them as they drifted through the machine's throat. There was enough atmosphere here to sustain them. Beth held Tony close to her chest and whimpered.

What the Hells is this place? Cade wondered.

A mechanical arm snatched Bill Herman and yanked him violently into the wall. He screamed, then went silent as a veil was shoved onto his scalp. His flailing ceased, and he allowed the ship to embrace him. Bill Herman was absorbed into the wall, becoming just another tool in the utility belt of the Undriel.

Beth held Tony as she screamed in horror.

Necrodore emerged from the lower part of the ship and drifted in front of Beth and Tony. The behemoth frightened them, and they began to whimper with fear. Necrodore floated silently in front of them for a moment. Then he did something Cade did not expect.

Necrodore's torso opened like a large hatch, and inside was a man. He was tall and lean, bald with pale skin and grey eyes. He wore a strange suit covered in slots and wires. On his head was a metal crown. "Please, Miss. Please calm down," Necrodore said with a deep, gentle voice. His robotic frame was similar to how it looked in Talfryn's Martian memory. "My name is Jonas Necrodore. You are safe with us."

<He's a damn hybrid?> Cade looked at the man attached to the suit with a new level of disgust. *<Just like me, and yet he treats* us *like animals.>*

<HE HAS RETAINED MUCH OF HIS HUMAN FORM.>

<Maybe he's a prototype.>

"Please don't hurt us…" Beth pleaded.

"We have no intention of hurting you," Necrodore said.

"I've seen the vids. I've heard the comms. Take me, but leave my son alone!"

"You have heard nothing but lies." Necrodore drifted closer to Beth. Her eyes darted to the people lining the walls, each silent, each wearing a veil.

"What are you doing to them?" she asked with panic in her voice.

"Preparing them for the journey." Necrodore brought his hands upward, and two robotic armatures brought veils to his sides.

"I—I don't understand. Are we following the *Telemachus*?" Beth held Tony tighter.

"No," Necrodore said. "We will find our own star. Please, Miss. I want to keep you and your boy safe. This star system is no longer capable of harboring us."

<They aren't going to Kamaria?>

<HE IS LYING.>

<I don't know... He looks like he believes it.>

"Will—will it hurt?" Beth asked.

"Only a little. Like a wasp sting. You'll see. When you awaken, we will be in paradise." Necrodore smiled. Before Beth could say more, the robotic arms slipped the devices over her and Tony's heads. They let out a small yelp, then went silent. The robotic arms pushed Beth and Tony into slots next to Bill Herman. The whole family lay silently in the wall.

A hatch above Cade opened, and Tibor Undriel slid down through it. He came to a stop in front of Necrodore. Necrodore faced his king and reported, "We've saved as many as we could."

"I know," Tibor said in his kind, booming voice.

"Do you think it will work?" Necrodore asked.

"You are proof of it. Hybrids cannot be corrupted."

"We have enough people to make more hybrids. Allow me to become perfect. I am strong enough to fight the corruption," Necrodore pleaded.

"In time," Tibor said. "We fought off one enemy, only to be pursued by another that we do not understand. We must learn how to fight the corruption. If you were to become perfect, you would be vulnerable to it. With your imperfections, you are armored against it."

"If it is time you request, then time I will give." Necrodore sighed.

Tibor nodded, then looked toward the wall of humans. "Bring them into the flock. We will disembark soon."

"It will be done." Necrodore drifted back into his frame and allowed it to fold around him.

<They chased out humanity, only to abandon the Sol System?>

<SUCH A WASTE.>

<There is infighting among the Undriel. Corrupted against perfected. It looks like us hybrids are some sort of key to fighting the

corruption. I guess I'm also invulnerable to it in this state.>

<*ANTONI IS ALSO INVULNERABLE TO THE CORRUPTION.*>

<*Yeah.*> Cade turned toward the Herman family. <*Where are Beth and Bill? In fact, where are all of these hybrids? In our reality, it's only Antoni, me, and the new marines they brought in—if you don't count Necrodore.*>

<*I CANNOT KNOW.*>

The ship lurched, and in sequence, the rows of humans were folded into its machinery. Stingers protruded from the walls around them, and each person was lanced with a sharp needle. Cade felt the world around him rip away, and he was expelled back to the nightmarish reality he came from.

NINETEEN

ELIANA CASTUS LOOKED OUT the observation window of the old outpost. A day had come and gone, and the night was approaching yet again. The sky was sliced with dark gray clouds blotting out a turquoise-and-yellow sunset.

To Eliana, the relationship between humans and auk'nai had died with Nella.

"Elly..." George Tanaka stepped into the observation room. Eliana didn't notice his approach, but she wasn't surprised either. She had sealed herself in this room for too long. George and Fergus had been kind enough to oblige her, but there was always going to be a limit. "Has there been any word from Talulo?"

"We spoke after he—" Eliana cut herself off. She still couldn't say it directly.

George nodded and folded his hands behind his back. "Ah. I see."

"The auk'nai warned us of further action if we approach." Eliana didn't turn to look at George. She kept her eyes on the darkening valley below. "I can't even go down there to find her..."

"What a terrible circumstance we're in," George said quietly.

"He said we brought this on ourselves."

"*Talulo* said that?" George asked in disbelief.

She said nothing.

The man sighed. “Hells below. Of all the people in the Nest, Talulo becomes the one to do such a horrible thing.”

Eliana stopped listening to George. Tucked behind some trees, a strange green glow emanated from the valley floor. The more the sun sank below the horizon, the brighter it showed, and more dots of light joined it.

“What are we going to do now?” George whispered to himself.

Eliana slowly stood up, her eyes fixed on the valley.

“What is it?” George tried to look around her.

“Come take a look,” Eliana finally invited George to her side. The valley started to look like the sky, with green stars sprinkled all across its expanse. The sun fully set, and the sky and ground blended together, white stars above, emerald stars below.

The comm channel blew up with noise. “Eliana, what is this?” It was Talulo’s voice.

George answered him, “Talulo, this isn’t our doing. You must believe us.”

Eliana smiled, her teeth showing, and a tear fled from her eye. Her heart fluttered. “My baby’s down there,” she whispered to herself.

“Further action will result in violence! Talulo urges Eliana to make this stop!” Talulo shouted into the comm.

Eliana’s brow sank, and she pushed George aside to answer the comm. “Listen up! I will be going down there to find my daughter. I will go alone to appease your terms. If you try and stop me, I will have the Hells brought down on you and your people. If you hurt Nella again, I will smash you like I crushed Nhymn so long ago. Understand? Do not *fuck* with me, Talulo.”

Talulo didn’t respond. The lights in the valley grew brighter, inviting Eliana down to see them. Eventually, Talulo said, “Auk’nai will not intervene, but Eliana must go alone.”

“Works for me.” Eliana clicked off the comm. She grabbed her things and asked George as she hurried, “Is the armory on the first floor still stocked?”

"Uh—" George stumbled over himself, impressed and terrified of Eliana at the same time. "Y-yes. There are a few things the marines didn't take before leaving. We didn't know how long we'd be gone, so we only locked the place up. Here, this will give you access." George pushed his hand over his soothreader, and Eliana's lit up green.

"Thanks," Eliana said, and took the elevator back down to the ground floor. She exited the elevator to see Fergus playing solitaire with the cards the previous marines had left behind.

Fergus did a double-take when he noticed it was Eliana moving around and not George. He said, "Oi lady! Where are you goin' in such a hurry?"

Eliana flicked her hand in front of the armory door. "Nella's out there. I got permission from Talulo to go get her. I have to go alone, though. Got to hurry." She walked into the armory, a small walk-in closet with gun racks. It was stripped bare except for two particle rifles and a collider pistol. Eliana slammed the pistol into a holster on her hip and held the particle rifle firmly in both hands.

"I wouldn't want to be any beastie that runs into you," Fergus said, standing near the door as Eliana approached. "Are you sure we can'nae help you?"

Eliana looked him in the eyes as the door slid open, "Just help George with anything he needs. I'll be fine."

"Take care, Elly," Fergus said.

"You too, Fergus." Eliana threw the hood up on her scout jacket and left the outpost.

The wind had a biting chill, and the night was filled with insects buzzing and welkinhawks hooting. The full dueling moons rose and provided a good amount of light through the scattered clouds. The flashlight mounted in Eliana's jacket would do the rest.

As she walked down the sloping hill, she saw the Nest looming like a shadow against the stars above. The wreck had been changed, stripped bare, and reduced to a cylindrical tube with a hollowed-out interior that no human had seen.

About three and a half kilometers from the slope she was walking down, the more significant collection of green lights hovered. Eliana made for the brightest spot. She moved through sparse bushes and clusters of trees, listening to smaller valley creatures scurry away.

Eliana heard the plodding of a few animals moving close by and slowed her pace. Grunts and honks came from both sides of her, and through the trees, she could see a herd of nurn moving with her. These creatures of the valley moved on four legs with clawed feet. They were covered in long, beautiful feathers and had small trunks on their faces. The alpha nurn, leader of the herd, had a singular antler protruding from the back of its head. The alpha saw Eliana, and for a moment, they both froze.

Instead of charging Eliana, the alpha nurn let out a long call. It sounded like a trumpet. The others in its herd lifted their heads, and their ears fluttered. From there on out, the nurn gave Eliana more room as they all traveled in the same direction.

Eliana nodded to the alpha nurn. She knew the creatures of Kamaria had the same sensitivity to mental wavelengths as the auk'nai. She couldn't speak with the beast, but this was enough to say "thank you."

The alpha nurn grunted and moved with the rest of its family. For some time, their movement was the only sound in the cool night. Soft grunts and honks mixed with the plodding of footfalls through brush and leaves.

Eliana saw a nezzarform stomping slowly through the cluster of trees in the same direction she was going. It didn't pay her any attention and was therefore harmless. The herd of nurn didn't seem to mind the nezzarform's presence either. Another nezzarform joined the first, with more approaching from a distance.

Nella's friends… They must be heading toward her too. Eliana slung her rifle to her back and walked with the nezzarforms. She found herself at peace, like walking to a church for mass with a community of faithful. The chill breeze felt good after the hike. As they grew closer to the congregation, the flowers of Kamaria glowed and spread their luminous petals to catch the dueling moonlight.

Ahead, her daughter stood in the clearing, surrounded by nezzarforms and awash in their emerald light. "Nella," Eliana whispered to herself, just to make sure she could believe what she was seeing. She was alive—and even more incredibly, she looked unharmed. Nella's long, thick hair was draped over her shoulders, her smile as bright as her glowing green eyes.

Eliana cried and practically launched herself across the clearing. They embraced roughly. Eliana let tears flow from her eyes as she clutched her daughter. She struggled to catch her breath as the pain of Nella's supposed death slipped away, replaced by the immense wash of relief.

Taking a step back, she signed, *"I thought you were killed."* Her right hand stabbed at her left like a knife.

Nella signed, *"Oolith sacrificed itself to bring me here. It needed me to collect the nezzarforms. Each one has told me more about Sympha and where she came from."*

"Sirens?" Eliana asked, her face scrunched in confusion.

Nella pinched her forefingers against her thumb. *"No."* She spelled out a new word in Sol-Sign: *"V-O-Y-A-L-T-E-N. It is the true name for the things we have been calling Sirens."*

"The nezzarforms told you this?"

Nella bobbed her fist and nodded. *"The Voyalten come from a planet called Faultasma. It is a dark world with no star, stranded in the middle of the void. The Voyalten live there as phantoms but have created a form of space travel unique to their species."*

Nella gestured to the nezzarforms, her friends who had given her this insight. She continued in sign, *"They cast out a seed, and it can take a very long time to find a planet, but they are immortal, and time doesn't affect them like it does to us. Once the seed is planted into a planet, the Voyalten prepare the planet for the Decider."*

"Decider?" Eliana asked. *"Nhymn called herself that."*

Nella bobbed her fist. *"Yes. Nhymn misunderstood her role. She tried to become something she wasn't. Nhymn and Sympha were Operators. They are the creators of the Gate. When the Gate is ready, the Decider comes through."*

"Did they finish the Gate?" Eliana asked. Her right hand swung away from her left like it was on a hinge.

Nella spun her hands in a circle as she thought of the right words to sign. *"Something went wrong. This planet is not properly prepared. Sympha and Nhymn both had forgotten their roles. The Gate was created, and the Decider has come through, but they are trapped here now."*

Eliana thought for a moment. *Seed, Voyalten, Faultasma, Gate, Decider, Operators.* She had to organize it all into things she already understood. She looked back to Nella and tested her theories, connecting the dots. *"Is the seed the crypt of the Sirens? The cave we found Nhymn's body in?"*

"Yes."

"Sympha, Nhymn, and Karx are all Voyalten Operators?"

"Yes."

"The Gate is…" Eliana jiggled her hands as she thought back, *"The Gate is the Siren Pit?"*

"Yes." Nella smiled.

"And the Decider is—"

"The Decider is something we have not seen before."

Eliana tilted her head. *"Is it peaceful?"* She rotated and patted her hands together twice, then let them drift apart, palms face down.

Nella shrugged. *"These nezzarforms have not met the Decider. They know their purpose and what was supposed to happen, but not what went wrong. I have the origin memorized, but not the intended result or the cause for the problems."*

"What should we do?"

"The nezzarform suggest we make a key, fix the Gate, and help the Decider. I agree with them. If anything, it could be a way off of Kamaria if the Undriel take over," Nella signed.

Eliana almost nodded but stopped herself. She moved her hands slowly, with worry on her face. *"It could be a way for the Undriel to spread far beyond Kamaria and Sol as well."*

Nella looked down. That hadn't occurred to her. After a moment of thinking, she looked back at Eliana and signed, *"We'll let the Decider figure that out. That's their purpose anyway."*

The wind rushed through the valley, sending a brisk chill up Eliana's spine. She shivered and signed, *"How do we get this key?"* She twisted her forefinger against her flat, upward-facing left palm.

"I ask the nezzarforms nicely." Nella grinned.

"That's it?" Eliana tilted her head.

Nella bobbed her fist and stifled a laugh. *"Yes."*

She turned to the nezzarform standing behind her, Lahar. They had an exchange of thoughts. Nella made subtle movements with her head, as if she were signing without using her hands, and Lahar shifted toward the other nezzarforms.

Suddenly, Nella grabbed Eliana by the elbow and pulled her into a run. Eliana almost stumbled, trying to follow Nella into the night. The nezzarforms linked together, smashing into new shapes and configurations with violent energy. They bound each other with electrical bolts and created a net of lightning.

The herd of nurn that had been peacefully intermingling with the nezzarforms ran alongside Nella and Eliana. They honked and trumpeted, calling into the night. Nella laughed so infectiously that Eliana joined her. They ran through the grass, laughing and worrying all the same. After scaling a sloping hill, Nella stopped and turned to watch, urging her mother to do the same. The nurns followed their example. They all watched breathlessly as the green light filled the night.

The nezzarforms formed a whirlwind of rocks and lightning, tumbling over each other and spinning with chaotic force. It was loud, and lightning arced outward from the funnel of rocks, striking nearby trees and bushes. A fire kicked up around the nezzarform tornado's base and was soon sucked into its whirlwind. Eliana put a hand on Nella's back, ready to pull her away if it got too turbulent.

Nella let out a loud Ganymede holler, her boisterous call mixing with the whirlwind of boulders, lightning, and fire. It grew to a crescendo and became a bright egg of green light, so bright that Eliana noticed the audience high above for the first time. On an elevated platform of the Nest, auk'nai looked down at the miracle happening below. Their silhouettes cast against a backdrop of stars.

The bright egg hovered in the air for a moment and ceased spinning. Nella, Eliana, the nurn, and the auk'nai above watched in complete silence. The light was the size of a warship now. At once, the light appeared to suck itself into the cracks and crevasses of the nezzarform egg. Then, it exhaled a great sigh, and a rush of wind waved outward from the Key. What remained was a tightly packed together, upside-down pyramid shape, made entirely out of nezzarform bodies. It slowly rotated in place as it hung in the air.

Nella laughed and turned to her mother. She used the knuckle of her forefinger and turned it against the palm of her other hand: *"Key."*

The Key Ship opened its front stone paneling, and a ramp emerged, inviting them in. The herd of nurn did not follow, knowing this invitation was not for them. Nella approached the Key and boarded the massive floating rock structure. Eliana paused momentarily outside, looking into the maw of this new ship her daughter had created.

Voyalten. Faultasma. Operators. Decider. Gate. Key.

Wherever this thing was about to take them, Eliana knew Kamaria would never be the same after they got there. She summoned her courage and walked up the stone ramp into the heart of the Key. After she had boarded, the ramp rose, and the vessel sealed, silently drifting southeast on the wind.

3
KEEPER
OF THE
KEY

TWENTY

CADE CASTUS CAME BACK from the tether's light. There was a jolt under his legs, and the dark enclosure around him shuddered. The hybrid soldiers inside the sealed room moaned with half-aware confusion, more husks than people now. Cade wanted to free them, release them from these walking Hells and either bring them to their loved ones or give them the mercy of death to stop this mechanical purgatory. But he was just as trapped as they were, perhaps in a deeper country of the Hells due to his conscious activity within it.

If I could see the corruption's design, maybe I could replicate it. Cade thought about what he'd learned from his Shade walks. Bringing a new corruption to the Undriel might wipe them off the face of Kamaria for good. Humanity would be genuinely safe this time. The secret had to be locked inside Tibor Undriel's mind somewhere. The King of the Old Star would show him the origins of the corruption.

"We have arrived," said Antoni, the boy who had grown into a man under the claws of the machines. He was only centimeters away from Cade's face, close enough to hear the whirring of machinery fused to his head. His centipede lower half clicked with anticipation.

There was a thump on the ceiling, followed by the pattering of many-knived legs. The roof slid off, revealing a cloudy night sky drizzling with rain and tall pine trees. Cade could hear the sound of water gently lapping against a shore and could smell fresh forest air—a welcome scent after the miasma of the ship's interior.

Hilaria, the scorpion woman, slid off the roof and out of view. The walls unfolded, and the hybrids were exposed to the rainy night. More ships unfolded and revealed more hybrids. Cade looked over his shoulder and noticed a fleet of boats, all salvaged from the cadaver that was once Dia, the *Devourer*. They hovered above the gentle waves of the Supernal Echo lake, away from the crowds on the shore.

"What is happening?" Cade whispered.

The scorpion machine approached him, hearing his hushed tones. "You're about to make yourself useful," Hilaria hissed as she moved around Cade on legs shaped like spears, her tail coiling around his shoulders, its long spike tickling at his neck.

<*TETHER TO HER,*> Karx suggested with a voice so loud in Cade's mind he flinched and felt the stinger scratch the little skin he had left on his neck.

Hilaria cackled with delight. "You still retain that human impulse to jump with fear. Delightful." She leaned in close to his face and unhinged her jaw, revealing a row of sawblade-like teeth.

"Enough." The booming voice of Necrodore sounded from the lake, and the behemoth moved through the water onto the shore, displacing it like a leviathan. "Don't harass the hybrids any longer."

Hilaria turned to face the him. Sensing his opportunity, Cade pulsed the tether into his hand and threw it at the back of Hilaria's head. She didn't notice the tether leash onto her soul. Cade caught the small ball of light in his hand and felt it link with his mind. He shuddered at the thought of what he might find in her past. She was the most fearsome of the Undriel generals—everything about her scared Cade.

<*SUCCESSFUL TETHERING.*>

<*I'm not looking forward to seeing into Hilaria's soul.*>

Hilaria cackled and withdrew her stinger. She slithered toward Necrodore. "You care too much for these creatures. I'm surprised you don't want to join our bait."

Tibor and Auden plotted something as Hilaria and Necrodore approached, but they were too far away to hear. Talfryn hovered over the water with the remaining Undriel fleet and observed. Faye scouted from high up in the trees, scanning for humans.

Tibor was too far away to tether. Even if Cade threw the ball of light, he'd never hit the King. After Tibor had finished conversing with his generals, they each rose off the ground and floated back over the lake.

Auden approached the army of hybrids. "It is time for you to defend the flock. Use the training they have given you against them. Fight with everything you got, and we will make those who are left standing into something perfect."

Auden flashed his eyes, and the command was sealed. Against their wills, the hybrid army marched off the flat metal platforms and onto the beach, taking concealed positions behind the tall pine trees on the shore. The shore sloped upward into a hill, giving each of them a clear line of sight on the lake. Cade's legs stopped on the gravelly sand of the shore, still feeling the cold water lapping up his false ankles. He pivoted, faced the lake, and was held firm by Auden's will.

"What's happening?" Cade asked. The other hybrids were concealed, yet Cade was standing right out in the open.

Antoni slithered past him on centipede legs and smiled. "Do not worry, brother Cade. I will be here with you. We will drive off the wolves together. This will bring us our ascendency!" He smiled through his drooling lips.

"We're the bait?" Cade asked.

"We're the vanguard! The blade that will cull the predators. Stand tall with me, brother Cade. This will be our finest moment!" Antoni corrected him with a regurgitated lie.

The perfected Undriel soldiers, Tibor and his generals, slipped under the lake's surface. Within moments, an entire Undriel force had vanished from sight, waiting for their opportunity to strike. The rain started to come down harder now.

<*It's an ambush!*> Cade whispered with panic to Karx.

<*WE MUST LOOK INTO HILARIA'S TETHER. IF WE CAN FIND THE CORRUPTION THERE, MAYBE WE CAN FOIL THIS AMBUSH.*>

There was no time to waste. Soon the human forces would find Cade standing on the beach, and the trap would be sprung. Cade allowed the energy to surge through his mechanical body, and once again, the tether pulled him through time.

TWENTY-ONE

"OH, SHUT THAT THING off, will you?" The sound of a woman's voice filled the black void Cade stepped into. His eyes opened, and Cade found himself standing in the center of an aisle in a grocery market. The lights above him looked old, dim, and with a hint of yellow about their fluorescent bulbs. Food sat neatly packaged in rows on the shelves to his left and right. A slight chill came from a refrigerated section containing meats and various kinds of seafood.

A woman chatted into her soothreader through a wireless earbud. She had smooth, light skin, blushed with a hint of red. Her hair was short and copper colored, and her eyes were deep brown. She was wearing a purple blouse with khaki capris and sandals. A scorpion tattoo in a henna design accented her right ankle. "We're safe! Those news stations are just going to rile you up and get you scared," the woman continued, a smile on her face as she plucked a jar of pickles from the shelf. "I'm telling you, Em. They'll catch him in no time."

Cade looked around the aisle. An older woman sat in a motorized chair, with a cart moving ahead of her, like a hover mule but empty and ready for groceries.

<*WHERE IS THIS?*> Karx asked.

<*It's just a supermarket,*> Cade said, still unsure where he was in the Sol System. <*We have stuff like this in Odysseus City too.*>

The older woman waved her hand and whispered, "Hi, Hillary."

Hillary smiled, waved back, and continued talking to her friend on the soothreader.

<*That's Hilaria?*> Cade looked Hilaria's human form up and down. < *I expected something different, I guess. She's always been eager to slice through hybrids. Seeing her like this, she just looks like everyone else.*>

<*EVIL CAN WEAR ANY MASK IT WANTS.*>

<*Maybe you're right.*> Cade followed Hillary through the store as she casually picked items off various shelves and chatted away with some unseen friend. The longer Cade followed her shadow, the darker it seemed to get. She was hiding something sinister, something so wicked Cade could almost taste it. She hid it so well that Cade couldn't immediately discover what it was. How cunning, to hide so well from herself and the world that not even a Shade walk could reveal her true nature.

"My neighbor is just as scared as you are. She thinks her husband was snatched up by the Neo Ripper too. If you ask me…" Hillary whispered the last words out the side of her mouth. "I think he ran off with Beatrix, down the street." She laughed, and part of Cade recognized that laugh. It was only a few octaves apart from the cackle Hilaria made when she almost slit his throat. "I got to go, *ciao!*" Hillary flicked her hand over her soothreader and walked toward a register.

A screen with an artificial intelligence helped her finish her purchase. Cade didn't recognize the name of the AI. It wasn't Homer or Undriel. It was some other automated thing called Yōkai. Hillary smiled as she pushed her cart toward a scanner. The register scanned through her items with a flat-edged beam of light, then an itemized list popped up with a total.

Hillary chuckled. "Oh, that's all? What a deal." She flicked her hand in front of the Yōkai to pay and made her way toward the exit.

A long rectangular video window displayed advertisements and various vistas, beaches, mountains, forests. It read: *Move to Mars today!*

<IS THIS MARS AGAIN?>

<No, I don't think so. The ad wouldn't be suggesting people move there if we were already there.> Cade stepped through the automated door behind Hillary. Outside, massive skyscrapers cut through clouds. Cars moved around like insects scurrying toward hives, and giant floating billboards rotated above streets. There was nothing green in this concrete metropolis, except for false images displayed on ads. It was a silver and gray place, with only pinpricks of color. Even the cars were desaturated and toneless.

"Woah," Cade whispered. The buildings were so tall they forced him to crane his neck, and even then, they faded into obscurity beyond clouds. A street sign nearby read "Peachtree." Cade looked down the street, the row of buildings creating a tunnel of concrete and asphalt. A sign on one building read "Piedmont Park, City of Atlanta." Yet Cade saw no park. *Maybe an indoor park?* Holographic police tape surrounded the entrance, giving the sad-looking place a miserable face.

Wait, Atlanta? That tugged a rope in Cade's mind. *<This is Earth.>*

This was where it all began—humanity's origin planet. Before any other planets had been colonized and terraformed, Earth was humanity's only home in the stars. Whenever he had heard people discuss it in his history class, they always said it with a nostalgic flair of longing. Cade looked at all the concrete and couldn't help but feel that nostalgia might have been misplaced.

Hillary's cart loaded her groceries into a small car as she turned on the engine. Cade phased through the door and sat in the passenger seat next to her. She backed out of her parking space and entered traffic on the street. A news radio station flicked on inside the car.

"Remains of the latest Neo Ripper victim were discovered earlier today. The serial killer has become more brazen in these slayings, this time depositing the body in Piedmonte Park. Two maintenance workers found the victim's body early this morning, featuring the signature lacerations that the Ripper has become known for. Police are unsure if it is authentically the Ripper's doing or if this means we have a copycat killer on the loose. An ongoing investigation—"

"It's no copycat," Hillary muttered, and shook her head in disgust.

Cade felt chills dance up his back.

After a short drive, Hillary pulled her car into a short driveway off the busy street and got out. Cade phased through his door again and stood in front of a tall apartment building. It had a brick façade in the front, with a small garden of fake flowers resting near a short-stepped stoop. An iron railing curled up the steps and led to a red door. The apartment next door shared a similar design, with the entryway door only two meters apart from Hillary's.

As Hillary opened her trunk, the car's back lifted out, creating a hovering container for all of her groceries. It floated over to a mechanism built into the side of the building and locked itself in. The mechanism raced the container up the side of the building and deposited itself into a compartment near a window on one of the upper floors. The empty container then lowered back down to Hillary's car and locked itself inside. Hillary walked up the stoop as her vehicle was automatically pulled into an underground garage. It beeped one last time as it vanished below the driveway.

"Hey, Hillary!" a worried voice called from the sidewalk.

Hillary turned, smiled, and said, "Oh, howdy, neighbor! Haven't seen you in a while. How have you been?"

The neighbor was a younger woman. She looked tired and fidgeted awkwardly with stress. "I'm… I'm scared. Kyle hasn't been home in three days. And with the—"

"Oh, you know Kyle, though. He's probably just out camping with the guys or something." Hillary smiled and waved her hand.

"No, his friends haven't seen him either. I'm getting really worried. I've even called the police. But they can't find him. I just..."

"Listen." Hillary got serious. "It's going to be okay. Understand? I'm sure he'll turn back up and have a perfectly good explanation." The woman slowly walked up the stoop adjacent to Hillary's front door. She nodded weakly and frowned as Hilary continued, "I know it ain't much, but I'll keep an eye out for him. If I see him, I'll tell him to get his ass home. His wife's worried *sick* about him!"

"What did you do?" Cade whispered, knowing how wicked Hilaria could be.

"Thanks, Hill." The woman entered her building. Hillary watched until her neighbor had gotten out of sight, then walked through her own front door. Cade phased through the door behind her. The lobby had a staircase that went up and down, bending around knuckles on both ends, and an elevator. Mailboxes lined the long wall. Hillary walked over to one marked 604 and waved her soothreader in front of it. A small package lay inside. She smiled and withdrew the slender box, then walked over to the stairs and went down.

"Her groceries and her mail were for apartment 604..." Cade whispered to himself, "Why is she going down?"

Cade followed Hillary down eight floors, deep underground. The apartments here winded down long, dimly lit halls. She made her way down the hall and opened the slender package, tucking the packaging under her arm as she withdrew a thin knife from the box. She smiled and admired the silver blade.

Cade shivered.

She came to an apartment labeled B-806 and pulled an old-fashioned key from her back pocket. She plunged the key into the keyhole and opened the door with a loud creak. The interior of her apartment was pitch black. She shut the door behind her, and for a moment, Cade considered running away. His fear outweighed her sick pleasure. He didn't want to share emotions with her anymore. He wanted to vomit.

<*WE MUST SEE IF WE CAN FIND THE CORRUPTION.*

THE AMBUSH IS WAITING,> Karx said, reminding Cade of the stakes.

<*I don't think we'll find it in there.*>

<*WE CAN'T KNOW THAT.*>

Cade huffed and phased through the door into the apartment just as Hillary flicked on the lights. The bulbs had been replaced with blacklights. Neon greens, purples, and reds illuminated the darkness only slightly. Hillary was covered in markings that glowed in the light. Her eyes looked unnaturally white, with only tiny black dots for irises. She removed her clothing—sharp-edged markings covered her entire body. She walked through the empty living room to a door on the far wall.

She peeled off something adhered to the door that kept it sealed tight, then opened it. Cade retched as he peeked through the door past Hillary.

The scent was foul, the air thick with moisture and rot. A man was strapped tightly to the far wall of the room, the blacklight illuminating small insects all over his body—scorpions from the look of them. His blood took on a purple hue, the same violet that was sprayed all over the walls and floor. As Hillary entered, she clutched the thin blade in her hand and rubbed a finger against it, releasing some of her own blood onto its edge.

"Your wife is worried *sick* about you," Hillary said with all the menace of a monster as she shut the door behind her.

Cade fled from the room, phasing back through the door and down the hallway. He discovered in his panic, by pure accident, that he could fly. After a certain speed, he only had to steer with his upper shoulders and head. He found no joy in his new ability, only haste. He burst through the apartment's front door and heaved in the open air.

<*It's not in there. We don't need anything from that place,*> Cade said, still heaving gasps of air.

<*LOOK TO THE SKY.*>

High above, lights flashed against the clouds that blotted out the tops of the buildings. An emergency siren blared out. People in cars opened their doors and stepped out to see what was happening. The street in front of Hillary's building had come to a standstill in confusion.

A ball of fire smashed into the street, colliding with cars. People abandoned their vehicles and rushed away from the impact zone as more fireballs hurtled through the clouds, dissipating them. High above, a fleet of warships was battling an unseen foe. Bulbs of light blossomed and disintegrated in high orbit.

From the newly formed crater in the street, an Undriel footsoldier stood, venting blue energy. It shook off the impact and ripped off parts of a nearby car, absorbing them to make quick repairs.

"Oh my God!" Hillary's neighbor gasped from her stoop. Cade hadn't seen her come out. He didn't have time to feel bad for her husband's fate. The world was ending in front of them.

The blue Undriel turned to look at the woman, and Cade knew it would pounce and absorb her. To his surprise, it did not.

"Get to safety!" the blue Undriel shouted, its voice laced with human urgency. The other fireball that had landed in the street revealed another Undriel footsoldier, this one seething the familiar red energy that Cade had become used to. It roared with anger and launched itself at its blue counterpart.

Behind Cade, Hillary's front door opened. Her neighbor's eyes went wide in horror. Hillary wore only a robe and was covered head to toe in blood. She no longer bothered with the mask she wore in civilized society. Hillary looked over to her neighbor with a look of casual disgust. "Kyle won't be home for dinner." Hillary twirled the knife in her hand as she sat down on her stoop to watch the robots fight. Hillary's neighbor stumbled over herself as she scrambled away, fleeing the fighting machines and the murderous woman.

The two Undriel smashed into each other repeatedly, ripping, tearing, absorbing, and blasting away in frantic chaos. Hillary laughed as she watched, barely flinching as they smashed into the side of her apartment, destroying the fake flowers in the garden near the stoop. Another fireball crashed into the cars in the street, followed by another and another.

The blue Undriel got the upper hand on its attacker and pinned it against the asphalt. It unhinged its jaw, and all at once, it released a torrent of energy that surged into the red Undriel. It flailed and convulsed as the beam engulfed its core, filling its head and chest with blue light. Eventually, the beam stopped, and the blue one pushed itself away from its victim.

<*That's the corruption!*> Cade shouted to Karx.

The red Undriel rose. Its energy faded to white, then to a matching blue as the one who had corrupted it. Its spider-bot head opened, revealing a human head—an elderly woman.

"How—how did you?" she asked.

"You have to pass it to more of them," the corrupted Undriel shouted, eyeing the other fireballs down the street. "We can stop them. We have to spread our power. Go now! I'll hold them off!"

The elderly Undriel woman closed her spider-bot helmet and activated rockets on her back. She launched herself back into the sky as Necrodore crashed into two cars in the center of the street. His behemoth frame crushed the blue Undriel against the ground. It attempted to corrupt Necrodore with the same energy beam. Necrodore took the brunt of the attack and pushed his hulking arm through it, crashing his giant fist down on the blue Undriel's head and crushing it. The blue light faded away, and the corrupted Undriel ceased movement.

Another footsoldier crashed into the street next to Necrodore. It approached the grand general and was met with a hulking outstretched arm. "No! Do not absorb this one's remains. The corruption will find you too. Only I can withstand its impression. Go on from here. We must take what we can and leave."

The other Undriel understood and launched itself into the sky to find more prey.

Hillary clapped and cheered.

Necrodore turned his attention toward her. Confused, he

approached, crushing cars and creating impact craters where his fists interacted with the asphalt. Necrodore loomed over Hillary. She laughed.

"You really showed him!" She smiled.

"You do not cower?" Necrodore asked, venting steam and red energy.

"You kidding? I love what you're doing here. It was getting so boring in this neighborhood. You must be those Undriel I've heard about on the news. You're taking *my* prime time, guy!" She chuckled as if she were speaking to a coworker. "Hey, let me join your little club, and I'm sure we'll make all kinds of headlines."

Necrodore hesitated. "A volunteer. We could use more like you to fight the corruption."

"Corruption. You mean like that boy scout that you just killed?"

<I think willing participants are immune to the corruption.>

<THE CORRUPTION ONLY ALLOWS FREEDOM OF WILL. WHAT THE CORRUPTED DO WITH THAT FREEDOM IS THEIR CHOICE.>

<The Reaper in Talfryn's memory chose *to kill the marines in the Martian outpost. I think it wanted to make its own army. It looks like most of the corrupted try to fight against Tibor, but Hilaria here wants to join him. She likes the violence. Freedom or not, she'd still choose Tibor's side.>* Cade looked back into the building Hillary had come out of and shuddered.

<WHEN DOES THIS MEMORY OCCUR?>

<Well, this is Earth.> Cade thought back on his ancient Sol history. *<The Undriel took over each planet in the Sol System in their orbital order from the sun, Sol, starting with the first terraformed world, Venus, because Mercury had never been colonized. Dia's memories on Venus were historically first, and these memories on Earth with Hilaria would be second. Talfryn's memory of Mars would be after this, with Antoni's Ganymede events after that.>*

Necrodore continued, "The corrupted seek to usurp our cause. They become animals after interacting with an anomalous energy.

They fight Tibor's will. He aims to bring peace."

<Shit. Anomalous energy? It's not some sort of coding? How are we supposed to get our hands on that?>

<*THIS COMPLICATES THINGS.*>

Cade's heart dropped. <*We can't replicate it… The ambush will still carry out.*>

Karx agreed in heavy silence.

Hillary waved her bloody hands and scoffed, "*Peace?* Fuck that. Let me have some of what you got, and we'll both grind up those damned corrupted. We'll figure out how to have fun after Tibor's will is enacted."

Necrodore's arm opened into a maw of sawblades and mechanical components. For a moment, he looked hesitant. Perhaps he was unsure of her true intentions. But after a few heartbeats, Necrodore said, "As you wish."

Hillary cackled with delight as he closed his robotic arm around her body. The tether snapped, and the white light ripped Cade away.

TWENTY-TWO

TALULO ONCE AGAIN MADE his way up the long staircase to the Daunoren's egg. Their new god was growing, and once ready, its shell would crack and be born to this world. *But who owns this world?* Talulo thought as his daunoren staff plodded against the stairs.

When he reached the top, the auk'qarn guards focused on him. Kor'Oja cooed and stamped his staff against the platform. His soldiers echoed him.

Talulo kept his eyes on the new Daunoren egg as he addressed Kor'Oja and his auk'qarn, "Talulo wishes to be alone."

Kor'Oja listened to Talulo's unsung song. He grumbled and said in his low, gravelly voice, "Kor'Oja and the auk'qarn will grant Talulo's wish." He put his armored claw on Talulo's shoulder and whispered, "Talulo has shown strength. Do not sell it for weakness."

Talulo's eyes snapped to Kor'Oja, and the armored auk'qarn warrior's eyes burned intensity right back at his leader. "Talulo will summon Kor'Oja after serious consideration has been made."

Kor'Oja looked at his soldiers, then back to Talulo. "It is about the lights in the meadow below. The nezzarform ship? Will the auk'nai respond with force?"

Talulo cawed, "So ready to fight, Kor'Oja is blind to know friends from enemies."

Kor'Oja puffed out his chest, his feathers rustling and his pupils shrinking. "Perhaps it was Talulo who had trusted the wrong ones to begin with? Mag'Ro was not so—"

"Mag'Ro *sold* Apusticus to the Siren!"

"And Talulo would hand Kamaria to the humans!"

Galifern waddled up the stairs, but the two auk'nai leaders did not turn to face her. With a wave of her claw, Kor'Oja's soldiers flew from the platform, leaving the two bickering auk'nai standing off in front of the egg. Galifern slammed her daunoren staff down. Although she was much shorter, she showed a fire inside her unsung song, which caused Talulo and Kor'Oja to flinch.

Now that she had their attention, Galifern said, "The world is not so easy to understand. Auk'nai stand at the precipice of change. Auk'nai must learn from the humans and the Undriel before our bones are rendered to ash. Auk'nai must be better than both!"

Talulo and Kor'Oja looked away from each other.

Galifern approached the egg and gently caressed it with her clawed hand. She cooed and closed her eyes. "This Daunoren will grow into whatever world the auk'nai make for it." She turned to Kor'Oja. "Will it be a world of war? Filled with enemies from stars beyond?" She turned to Talulo. "Or will it be a world of forgiveness? Where peace has a chance to grow and friends can be found in unexpected places?"

Talulo and Kor'Oja's unsung songs rattled on, their passions mixing into a loud riot of mental energy. Galifern removed her hand from the egg and clutched her daunoren staff in both hands.

Kor'Oja spoke first. "The humans brought the Undriel to our world. The Undriel turned L'Arn into an abomination, and the machines seek to augment the rest of the auk'nai. Auk'nai fight two enemies from the same star."

Talulo stated his case. "And what of the Siren? Nhymn

destroyed Apusticus. That monster was not of human origin. Do the auk'nai blame the humans for all auk'nai problems?"

Kor'Oja took a step forward. "The humans brought Nhymn to Apusticus. Humans are still to blame!"

Galifern watched the two auk'nai males fight like hatchlings. She needed them to have this debate. Kamaria needed this fight to happen. She watched and tried to keep her unsung song as silent as possible.

Talulo cawed, "Sirens lived on Kamaria longer than the auk'nai have. It was only a matter of time before an auk'nai stumbled upon Nhymn in the cave and brought the Siren to Apusticus. Auk'nai were already exploring deeper into Ahn'ah'rahn'eem before the humans came across it."

"It was through the humans that Nhymn found Sympha. Talulo forgets so easily?"

"Kor'Oja does not realize how much more deadly the Siren would have been in the body of an auk'nai. Nhymn was locked away within the man Roelin, trapped and weak. If an auk'nai had found her, she would have been able to fly straight to Sympha without hesitation." Talulo paused at the thought, then concluded with a realization. "Nhymn would have had access to all auk'nai cultures through one of our own. The Siren would not have stopped with Apusticus."

Kor'Oja interjected, "Nhymn's sole reasoning for destroying Apusticus was to stop the Undriel—an option Talulo convinced Apusticus to turn down."

Talulo gripped his staff and calmed himself. "That is what the Siren claimed. Nhymn was cunning. The Siren needed no reason to destroy Apusticus. Nhymn had been driven insane centuries before. The humans only provided one route of many to annihilation. This was one meal eaten, but any dinner would have been as nourishing to a stomach so starved."

Kor'Oja shook his beak and sneered. His feathers eased.

Talulo raised his arms, gesturing to the *Telemachus* wreck that surrounded them. "This wreck is human made, human used, but auk'nai repurposed. The ship was the only weapon that could strike down Nhymn. Imagine if that was not an option."

Kor'Oja's feathers rustled with chills.

Talulo continued, "Imagine if Nhymn had taken one of our own, flown to Sympha, gained the same powers, destroyed Apusticus. What would happen then if the humans had not slammed the *Telemachus* into her?"

Kor'Oja mumbled, "Nhymn would still be in Sympha's body."

"Kamaria would be a slave to a tyrant titan."

Kor'Oja sucked in a deep breath at the horrific thought.

"The humans sacrificed the *Telemachus* to save themselves, yet auk'nai have made it a benefit for auk'nai life. Humans did what was needed for their survival. Auk'nai would do the same if faced with the same apocalypse. Humans did not come here as conquerors, but the Sirens and the Undriel have. Talulo no longer blames the humans for the past. The pains the auk'nai have felt were coming regardless of their presence here. Auk'nai must choose the future."

Galifern cooed quietly.

Talulo continued, looking at the repurposed wreck around them. "The Nest is safe from outsiders—covered in weapons and filled with auk'qarn soldiers. This Daunoren will be protected. Yet, Talulo cannot see the stars." He watched Kor'Oja look up to confirm the shell was all-encompassing around them before continuing, "Talulo does not feel the breeze nor smell the wildflowers. The feeling of grass between the claws, the wind rushing through the wings." Talulo gripped his staff tightly as he said that; having lost his own wings before, the statement was like a hook through his heart.

Kor'Oja whispered, "The Nest is a second egg."

Talulo cooed, "Auk'nai can shield the Daunoren from the world, but the Daunoren will never be truly hatched unless the auk'nai allow it to."

Kor'Oja looked to him. "It is a risk."

Talulo starred him straight back in the eyes. "It is worth it."

Galifern cooed. Their unsung songs sang the same tunes. It was a relief to come to a consensus, but Talulo still felt ice under his feathers. It was one thing to bring the auk'nai into the same song, but there were still the humans to consider. Talulo had ordered Nella shot down, knowing what sort of statement it would make, knowing it would likely kill her. Would Eliana listen to Talulo?

Kor'Oja asked, "What do the auk'nai do now?"

Talulo considered the options for a moment. He stared at the egg as thoughts circled his mind. After a few deep breaths, he said, "Talulo will go find the humans and the nezzarform ship."

TWENTY-THREE

THE KEY SHIP WAS a raw thing, made out of an uneven paneling of smooth black stone with an almost mirror sheen. The nezzarforms who made up the walls had carved themselves into an intricate design. It even had a ramp that led to a higher exterior platform. Eliana found out—by accident—that the lightning that held the stones together was harmless, even cool to the touch.

The main chamber was a hexagonal cylinder with a podium in the center. Nella had her hand on the podium's flat surface, her eyes an emerald glow. She wasn't controlling the ship directly, only telling it where to go. Green energy seethed from the podium, familiar to the mist breathing between the gaps in the rocks.

Sympha's energy. Voyalten energy. Eliana wondered about the strange beings. They could make ships out of stone and cast them across the void to seed gardens on other worlds. When she had met a Voyalten in her past, the experience had been dangerous and terrifying. Nhymn had almost wiped out humanity for good. *It seems that Voyalten are extremely powerful, both in peace and in violence. Which will the Decider be?*

Nella stepped back from the podium and clapped her hands together to get Eliana's attention. She signed, *"We have visitors,"* making V's with the forefingers on both her hands, then lowering her palms toward her waist in a straight line. Her bright smile complemented her vivid green eyes.

"Visitors?" Eliana mumbled to herself. "How the Hells?"

Nella signed, *"I want you to forgive him."*

"What?" Eliana asked. Her face did the signing for her.

Nella shook her head and snapped her finger. *"Forgive them. Even if they do not ask for forgiveness. They were wrong, but they did what they had to."* Nella's face grew firm. *"If anyone is to blame, it is Oolith. It knew the risks and proceeded with trespassing anyway. It was necessary."*

Eliana looked up the stone ramp to the upper exterior platform and understood. "Talulo's up there," she said to herself, then signed, *"I cannot forgive him."*

Nella cupped her hands into fists, knuckles facing Eliana with her thumbs tucked under her index fingers. She pushed her fists outward. *"Try."*

Eliana exhaled through her nose and nodded slightly, impressed with her daughter's firmness. It felt like they had switched roles. She understood Nella's wish and signed, *"No promises."*

Nella smiled and turned back to the podium.

The stone ramp led to the upper exterior ledge. A wall of green electricity separated the interior from the outside air. It disappeared as Eliana approached, and she stepped out into the moist dawn. The slowly rising sun began to burn off the morning dew of the jungle below. The Sharp Top mountain's hooked peak loomed over the wilderness around it, with other smaller peaks sticking out of the tree line.

In the wake of the Key Ship, three large birds stood out like shadows drifting in the morning sky to the west. One of them was wingless yet still airborne. Eliana sighed. "He *would* do this."

She looked back to the Sharp Top as they grew closer. Eliana remembered feeling this sort of hate before. Roelin had once been a prisoner under the Sharp Top's hooked peak. Nhymn had taken the captain here after murdering Eliana's father. *Can I forgive someone who tried to kill my daughter? Does their failure make it any less of a transgression?*

She remembered her daughter's wish.

Okay, Nella. I'll try. For you.

Eliana whistled to the auk'nai and waved her hand. The three auk'nai approached and lifted higher into the sky. She took a few steps back and allowed them to land.

With a thud, each of the auk'nai landed on the stone platform. Talulo wore a device on his back, similar to the jump-jet of a Tvashtar marine combat suit but with an auk'nai flair. His auk'nai entourage also wore special harnesses, which aided Talulo's ability to fly. It wasn't actual flight, but it was more dignified than riding someone else.

For a moment, no one said anything.

Eliana didn't recognize the auk'nai warriors in Talulo's entourage. They wore brown sashes with armor and chains woven in. Their black feathers were lined with white paint, and their daunoren hooks were more blade than staff. Each of the auk'nai, Talulo included, wore unique gauntlets on their hands.

"Why have you come here?" Eliana asked with a voice as cold as the rocks beneath their feet, as if she, too, were made of stone.

"Talulo and Eliana must talk. Kamaria is changing. Decisions must be made," Talulo said, his voice firm and unapologetic.

Nella requested I forgive Talulo, but is he even here to apologize? Eliana met Talulo's eyes with her own stern gaze. "I believe you already made your decision." Her words, and the empathic wavelengths she delivered with them, cut Talulo like a knife.

"Talulo did what is best for the auk'nai people." Talulo made a low coo. "Talulo does not regret making the decision at that time."

Eliana squinted at him, unsure of what to say.

"Talulo wished…" The auk'nai gripped the old daunoren staff tightly in his claws. "Talulo *wishes* to never have to make that decision again."

Auk'nai couldn't lie and couldn't be lied to. If this conversation was going to be anything, it would be sincere.

"I believe you," Eliana said.

Talulo cooed.

"But I do not forgive you," she added. "I understand *why* you did what you did. I am also grateful it didn't result in my daughter's death. If it had, we would not be speaking at all now. You'd be in great danger, in fact."

Talulo cooed. He understood. The auk'nai leader stepped slowly around the platform, admiring the nezzarform construct. His daunoren staff thumped against the rock floor with each step.

Eliana looked to the east. "Years ago, we made this same journey together." The Starving Sands desert was beginning to show beyond the horizon of dense jungle. Talulo followed her to the platform's edge and looked east with her. "Last time, we were hostages inside the *Astraeus*. We're heading to the same place now, but we're not hostages anymore. We come willingly."

Talulo grunted.

"Back then…" Eliana looked at the stumps that had once been Talulo's wings. "I had to make a hard decision too. One I also regret. But I had to do it, or else my friend would die."

"Talulo understands Eliana's decision."

Eliana sighed. "What has become of us? Of our people? Were we ever really united?"

"Not really."

Eliana looked down at the jungle rolling below the Key Ship.

Talulo elaborated. "Humanity absorbed the auk'nai. Our people gave your people great technologies, but the auk'nai did not gain much from humanity in return. Our people have lost everything. Auk'nai lost our homes, our God, and our planet."

"There is still time to save the planet," Eliana said.

The auk'nai cawed and said, "No, there is not. Our planet is gone forever. The one the auk'nai knew before humans invaded. It can never return to the way it was."

Eliana's heart sunk in her chest. *We're no better than the Undriel.*

Talulo cooed, hearing her unsung song. For a moment, Kamaria moved around the human and the auk'nai. The air flowed through them, the wind hummed a sweet tune. The smell of early morning filled their lungs, and the sun boiled away the coldness of the previous night. These things did not care about the human and the auk'nai. The wind would exist without them. The coldness and warmth were never-ending. The smells and sounds of the world would carry on as if there had never been multiple invasions.

Kamaria was relentlessly beautiful.

Talulo spoke. "There is still a chance to make the new world *better* than the old one. Humans came here seeking refuge from an impossible enemy. Humans did what they had to, to survive, but in doing so, humans have awoken many hidden things within Kamaria. Things the auk'nai never may have found." Talulo gestured to the Key Ship under their feet. "Yet these things were sleeping here long before humans arrived. Kamaria was changing before auk'nai understood it was. If the auk'nai plan to survive, auk'nai must also change with the tune of the Song."

Eliana turned to Talulo and looked him in the eyes.

"Talulo apologizes for nothing. Eliana should not apologize either. But humans and auk'nai must forgive each other regardless. Share an understanding. A song. Talulo thought strength came with resilience, but only *weakness* is so rigid. Strength comes from the will to face the fear of change and meet it directly. To move forward, unsure of each step."

Eliana nodded. "We need to change to be better. Both of our people. But you're wrong about one thing."

Talulo cocked his head, allowing his long ears to droop.

"I do apologize. I can't speak for humanity, but I can speak for myself and my father. We never meant to invade your world. We never meant to change such a beautiful culture, to make it our own. I think if my father were around for the unification of our people, it would have gone a different way. But that's no excuse. It *should* have gone a different way regardless. One person's will shouldn't be the crux to our actions as a species. When I say my people—the humans—need to change, it needs to come from *all* of us. Our hearts and minds. We can't hope one of us will get it right. We all have to…" Eliana thought of Nella. "We all need to *try*."

Talulo cooed. "Auk'nai have learned much about life since humans have arrived. Many tried to keep the old world unchanged—Mag'Ro did, and Talulo did." He put a claw against his chest. "Talulo watched as the auk'nai were torn down, rendered to nothing. In that nothing, Talulo also noticed how strong the auk'nai are. All songs end, but new songs are just as beautiful."

They watched the sunrise as the Key Ship hovered into the great crimson desert. The air grew more arid as the day moved forward. Underneath the ship, blood-red dunes sloped through the vast expanse of sand. Plateaus and other rock formations lined the great desert, and a canyon with waterfalls on both ends traced its way through the desolate place.

Neither needed to say anything more. Talulo could hear Eliana's unsung song and knew their past transgressions had been addressed. Eliana sighed the warm morning air through her nose. It felt like a fist had released her anger and allowed it to float away down a calm brook. She felt her jaw unclench and her shoulders loosen. She nodded. *Okay. We understand each other.*

"Where is Nella taking this ship?" Talulo asked.

"We're going to meet something called the Decider."

Talulo's irises shrank, and he growled out a low caw. "Nhymn?"

"I don't think so. We have learned a lot about the Voyaltenum, what we used to call the Sirens. We are heading for a convergence of worlds. This was their plan all along."

Talulo cooed, and his feathers smoothed out. "Talulo will join you. Auk'nai must be present in such conversations. Whether this becomes deadly or not, Talulo will be by Eliana's side."

"I wouldn't want it any other way." Eliana gave him a smile.

Talulo spoke using the unsung song to his entourage. They launched from the platform to head back west toward the Nest.

"Talulo would like to see Nella."

"I'm sure she'd like to have a word with you, too. We'll get you up to speed on everything we learned," Eliana said. She looked at Talulo for a moment, the sun glistening on his feathers and beak, his large bird eyes almost glowing in the light. "It's good to have you back, Talulo."

Together, they walked down the stone ramp into the Key Ship. The river flowed through the canyon toward the pit in the desert below. Unseen, a black ooze ran below the water's surface, and within it, monsters reached for the alabaster palace.

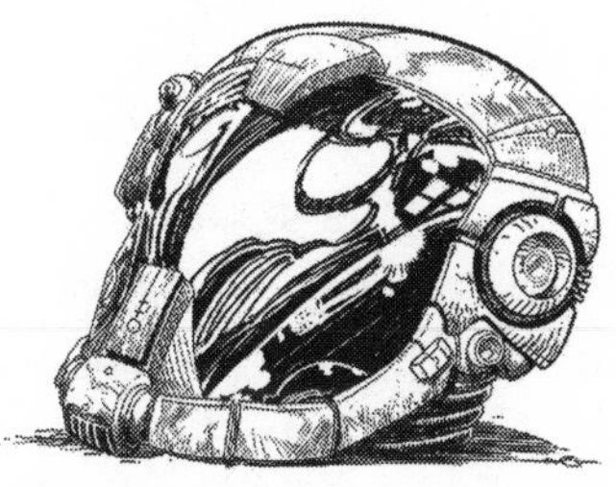

TWENTY-FOUR

DENTON HIKED WITH A squad of Tvashtar marines toward the mountain basin. Recon from *Infinite Aria* satellites showed that the Undriel had moved from this position hours ago, but they could not have gotten far. The machines were lucky. They had moved under cover of an oncoming storm, away from the watchful eye of the orbital command base. It was a chase toward Odysseus City now, no doubt the Undriel's target destination.

Sergeant Jess Combs was in command of the Dray'va Teeth squadron once more. As they moved toward the basin, they kept their attention on the tree line, waiting for the Undriel to spring their trap. The marines emerged from the forest to walk along the gravelly shore of a beautiful lake.

Many waterfalls spilled into the lake, which fed out to an enormous body of water on the far side called the Supernal Echo. The dull roar of the waterfalls engulfed all sound, but it was pleasant to listen to. It was the song of Nature's raw power. Remnants of Iron Castle debris remained lodged in the basin, scavenged into skeletons of its former glory.

"Love to see that," Jess said with a smile. A swarm of fireballs poked through the rain clouds, shining bright against the dark. The fireballs faded to smoke, and thirty civilian freight ships went into an air brake maneuver. These were volunteers who worked in orbit and wanted to aid in the war effort. The freight ships slowed and pivoted before maintaining a hover above the lake.

"Heard you guys wanted to go fishin'!" the captain of the lead freight ship's voice boomed through his exterior comm. The marines cheered. Hatches on the underside of each ship opened, and thirty sleek boats dropped into the water. The jet-black vessels could fit a full squad of marines, shoulder to shoulder. Machinery on their hulls provided all-terrain benefits, with deployable wheels and slight air-capable jump-jets. The basin was suddenly filled with boats, ready for the chase.

"Good hunting, marines!" the captain shouted. Their task complete, the civilian freighters took back to orbit, heading for the safety of the *Infinite Aria*, until the war was over and they could resume their jobs.

Jess turned toward her marines. "The Undriel moved into the Supernal Echo a few hours ago. The *Aria* lost track of them shortly after that. The plan right now is to scour the lake for them. We got them on the run."

The marines answered with a unified, "Ooh! Rah!"

Jess waved her soldiers onto the closest boat. Denton sat near the back with Ortiz and Wood. Inaya and Cruz were close by, both fully recovered from their injuries. Bell and Rafa were at the front of the boat with Jess and a few marines from other scattered squadrons. Soldiers were being shifted around to complete squads that had lost members. Denton didn't have time to meet them all.

The mood on the boat was determined and hopeful. With the major success of the Iron Castle infiltration and detonation, spirits were the highest they had been the entire war. It felt like mopping up at this point. Denton wished he could feel as optimistic as the others, but he held a blizzard of cold anger in his chest. He had been *so close* to saving Cade. They only needed to exit the castle and watch it explode. They'd be home by now, figuring out what to do next. Eliana and Nella would be with them. They'd be a complete family again.

Kill them all... Denton thought. *I want to kill them all for what they did.*

"Hey there." Private Arlo Ortiz put a hand on Denton's shoulder. He looked Denton in the eyes and said, "I've seen that face too many times. I've made it myself too. I know what's going on in that head of yours, Mr. Castus. You're tapping into some dark stuff. You're thinking your son might be dead. But you don't know anything yet." He shook his head. "Just look at this boat! Wood right here—he and Sarge didn't make it out of Central Base, yet here they are. Sarge just as tough as ever. And Wood..."

Wood leered at Ortiz from under his cloaked hood, a shadow with a sniper rifle.

"Wood's still Wood!" Ortiz said with a laugh. He turned back to Denton and pushed on his shoulder. "Kamaria's rooting for us. You can't dread what you can't know."

Denton wanted to believe Ortiz. He wanted to rally with him and hope to find Cade. Find some sort of happy ending, despite Cade's monstrous skeletal form, despite the fact he had most likely died when the castle exploded. But the hope was gone. Denton wasn't looking for Cade anymore. He couldn't bring himself to attempt the search again.

Denton Castus was ready to fight. He was ready to bring down the vile mechanical creatures that had hurt his son. He tightened his fists and pretended to understand Ortiz's message. He just didn't believe it.

The boat's engines rumbled, and in moments, they were rushing across the surface of the lake as the rain fell harder. The boats were packed with marines, with the remaining transport ships filled with the rest of the soldiers. This was the mop-up crew.

"I heard about the mission you went on," Wood said to Denton.

Ortiz laughed. "It speaks! Okay, *now* I'm worried."

Wood ignored him. "You were inside the Undriel castle. What was it like in there?"

Denton thought back to that horrible place. "Empty."

"Empty?" Ortiz scoffed. "I thought you fought off waves of the Undies?"

"On our way out, yes. But when we first arrived, we were hidden from their sensors. We only saw a few Undriel moving around inside. The rest were fused to the walls. I thought it would be filled with more of them walking around, like barracks or fortresses. Instead, the people inside were either reduced to wall fixtures or used as livestock. It was cold and dead."

"They are machines." Wood looked out over the water. "Only essential operations were functioning. The rest wait until they are needed."

"Yeah. The walls shifted around too, and gravity behaved weirdly. It was like being in a puzzle cube."

Ortiz nodded. "That's how we got artificial gravity. We reverse-engineered it from them. The Undriel probably have all sorts of new shit we could learn from the remnants of the Iron Cas—"

"You saw your boy in there," Wood stated.

"I did," Denton admitted.

"He recognized you."

Denton hesitated. "Yeah. How'd you know?"

There was an awkward pause. Ortiz jumped in. "Rafa told us about it. In case it became strategically beneficial in the fights ahead."

Wood said nothing more. He adjusted in his seat, his rifle pressed against his armor.

He called me Dad. He knew me, and still, I let him die.

It only filled Denton with more rage. He looked away from Wood and the others to conceal the tears brimming on his eyelids. The hate overflowing from within, boiling the ice in his veins and creating something more molten than lava. *He was alive. He was himself. Cade survived the absorption somehow. And then I killed him. I killed him with that damn bomb and blew away the only chance I had to save him.* Denton seethed between his teeth. *They are going to pay.*

They were coming up to the waterfall that spilled into the Supernal Echo. Thunder rolled in the clouds above, and the rain came down harder now. “Hold on tight, everyone!” Jess Combs shouted as the boat’s pilot engaged the jump-jets. The boats launched off the waterfall’s edge and activated thrusters on their hulls’ underside. Jet engines roared with fury and slowed their descent to the lake below. After a few seconds of falling, each of the boats hit the lower lake with a splash. Momentum continued forward as the boats propelled across the calm, mirror-like surface of the water.

Only the wake of the boats and the ripples from the rain disturbed the Supernal Echo’s sheen surface. Clouds above reflected off the water below. Denton felt like they were flying through a storm, straight through the sky. The illusion was only made stranger when he noticed large fish chasing the flanks of the boat. Their scales had a soft glow, like twinkling starlight, and each of their flat heads had three large eyes, two on the side and one looking straight up into the clouds. After chasing the boat for some time, the fish slipped back under the mirrored surface of the Supernal Echo.

A bolt of lightning hit far off on the lake’s surface, and thunder crackled. The rain assaulted them, each droplet a tiny needle against Denton’s skin. The remaining transport ships zoomed through the sky above. Denton heard one of the pilots talking over the comm channel. “It’s getting choppy up here. Going to hang back until the storm settles. We’ll be here if you need us.”

Visibility was low—about fifteen meters in any direction around his boat. The transport ships slipped out from the clouds, lowered themselves to the water, and then vanished into the fog behind the boats.

“Bet that thing isn’t going to do much good in this shit,” Ortiz spoke over the storm, pointing to Wood’s sniper rifle. Wood huffed through his nose, which was the most laughter Denton had ever heard come from the silent sniper.

“Eyes up!” Jess shouted, just barely audible over the engines and rain.

The marines on the boat shifted in unison. Particle rifles aimed in every direction, Denton’s included. The boats slowed to a stop.

The rain continued to beat relentlessly against their weapons and armor, and thunder rumbled in the clouds above. A blue light shimmered in the fog ahead.

"What is that?" Ortiz whispered, and adjusted his aim on his rifle.

As they waited, guns drawn, the fog began to shift. The blue light on the shore became a shape. The shape then became the silhouette of a man. He was waving his arms frantically. Just barely audible above the storm, they could hear "Turn" and "Don't!"

"Dad!"

Denton felt his entire soul fall out of his body. The rage inside him cleared out as quickly as a particle blast, and hope welled up from an unknown font. He couldn't breathe. He didn't notice Ortiz and Wood looking at him as time seemed to hang still. This inhale became a year, and the rain around him hung suspended in the air.

"Cade?" Denton gasped.

An explosion rocked the boat to Denton's right, casting the marines onboard into the water.

"It's an ambush!" Jess shouted. The water below glowed with white eyes. There was no time to react before a blast blew through Denton's boat and launched him into the air. Everything was rain, wind, and fire as he tumbled through the sky. Denton hit the water like crashing into concrete and almost blacked out as the air was vented from his lungs.

The cold underwater darkness was illuminated with hundreds of lights. Particle blasts both from above and below the surface of the lake lanced everywhere. The plane of battle was all wrong. Humans shot down into the depths while Undriel shot up toward the sky. It was almost like fighting in space. Another boat was crunched in half by the behemoth Undriel, collapsing on the marines who weren't quick enough to jump off. Marines ditched the remaining boats as the Undriel destroyed them one by one.

Denton pulled himself onto the gravelly beach. He coughed and tried to catch his breath. In the chaos, he had dropped his rifle. He had been struck with a few shots. Denton's chest plate was damaged and crushing against his sternum, and his left-arm armor was ripped up. He pulled hard on the straps to his damaged armor, and the plating released itself from his body. He grabbed for his sidearm and kept it palmed. Beyond the beach was a forest that sloped upward into the mountains, its peak shrouded in storm clouds, thunder, and rain. To his right was the battle, with the lights of particle shots slicing through the fog.

Jess, Wood, and a few other marines were farther down the beach, blasting into the water and the trees. Denton couldn't see what waited in the forest. They moved into the foggy tree line and out of view, only a series of red flashes in the increasing mist.

"Denton!" Private Bell shouted. Three marines scrambled out of the water toward him. Bell, Cruz, and Rafa raced to his side and kept their eyes on their surroundings, rifles up.

"Fucking ambush!" Cruz shouted.

Bell checked Denton for injuries. "The Undriel always have a trick. We thought we had them on the run. We should have known better!"

"We have to regroup," Rafa said. "Cruz, call the transports."

"On it." Cruz pressed her head against her shoulder to use her combat comm. Denton, Bell, and Rafa kept low in the water and their eyes on their surroundings. After a moment, Cruz spat the word, "Shit!"

"Report," Rafa ordered.

"Transports are fucked! Only two got away, and they aren't coming back. They got hit by a damn Reaper. They're killing us, Raf!" Cruz's panic elevated her voice.

Bell looked into the forest and stood up. There were shapes in the trees, silhouettes of Tvashtar marines aiming their rifles toward the battle farther down the beach. "Looks like some others made it!" Bell took a few steps forward. She let out a quick whistle to get their attention. Denton didn't notice the flickering red lights dancing over the combat suits until it was too late.

"Bell wait!" Denton shouted.

In unison, the marines in the forest turned toward Bell and shot. Each blast hit her directly in the chest and stomach. Five neat holes formed instantly in her suit. Bell fell backward into the shallow water, dead before the splash.

"Shit!" Rafa pulled Denton behind a boulder as more shots cracked against the lake. Cruz rolled out of the line of sight, moving behind another rock formation. Rafa looked over the boulder and took a few carefully aimed shots. "It's the taken soldiers."

Denton leaned against the boulder and dared to look out, his collider pistol drawn. The hybrid soldiers in the forest lumbered toward their position. Three looked like regular Tvashtar marines, with flickering red lights dancing over their combat suits and the strange Undriel devices on their heads. The remaining two were more machine than man, with large metal claws, extra legs, and other insectoid appendages. Five in all.

"Take them out!" Rafa ordered.

Cruz, Denton, and Rafa leaned out from cover and cracked off some quickly aimed shots. The more human soldiers went down, some still shooting from their grounded positions. Denton struck one of the hybrids with the extra appendages, and it leapt up the closest tree. Its human arm dangled, incapacitated by Denton's shot, but its Undriel augmentations continued the fight.

The hybrid on the tree unleashed a beam of red particle energy that cracked the boulder Denton and Rafa were using in half. Denton rolled out from cover and scrambled toward Cruz. Rafa recoiled and fired back. The Undriel hybrid on the tree was struck directly in the head and chest a few times, cutting its body in half. It still partially clung to the tree, and the other half slumped to the ground. Both halves scrambled to recollect themselves.

Cruz finished off the last Undriel hybrid, overdoing her shots until the monster was reduced to crumbled armor. More lights flickered through the foggy trees. Their position was compromised.

"More incoming." Cruz aimed her rifle toward the flickering red lights.

The sound of rushing water and the roar of a machine filled the air. A mechanical tail with three sharp, meter-long stingers emerged from the water. The scorpion Undriel burst forth.

"Move!" Rafa threw his hand up the forested hill and opened fire. Denton and Cruz blasted away at the monstrous machine as they backed into the trees. More hybrids closed in on their position from down the beach. Their only option was to head uphill.

The scorpion cackled and rushed toward Rafa. The corporal jump-jetted to the side, slamming into a tree as he narrowly dodged the scorpion's swinging claw. The scorpion recoiled. Denton and Cruz caught its attention, blasting off some of its paneling with well-aimed shots. Steam seethed into the rain, and the scorpion machine roared again.

Rafa pumped his arm, and a long, heated blade emerged from his gauntlet. He hacked at the tree he'd slammed into, two quick cuts. The trunk screeched as it gave way, and it came crashing down on top of the scorpion, pinning it.

"Time to go!" Denton shouted, seeing the advantage. The scorpion rotated its head, torso, lower half, and tail individually to get into a better position to free itself from the tree. Denton, Cruz, and Rafa sprinted uphill, their jump-jets helping to cover ground quickly. Denton, wearing only a partial suit now, was slowed. Rafa stayed with him, pivoting to shoot backward to make space between them and their attackers.

The hybrid soldiers gave chase, blasting through the trees. "We have to keep moving!" Rafa shouted. As they made their way uphill, the fog lessened, and the clouds were cleared up. A heated wind rose from over the hill.

A particle blast hit Rafa from behind, striking his upper right shoulder. He toppled down with the momentum of the hit, grunting with pain. Denton helped him back up to his feet as Cruz returned fire, striking one of the pursuing hybrids and sending it rolling down the steep slope.

They had made it to the top to find a cliff ledge overlooking the Starving Sands desert. Crimson dunes and amber rock formations made up the vast, arid expanse. The clouds disintegrated into the hot sunlight.

The scorpion machine roared behind them. The pounding of its knifelike legs ripped through the trees. It would be on them in seconds. Rafa pushed Denton toward the ledge and shouted, "Jump!"

Cruz jumped, and Denton fell, toppling over the side of the cliff. Rafa jumped last. The scorpion Undriel lashed out with its tail, spiking Rafa in his back mid-freefall. The stingers gleamed as they exited through his chest, covered in blood. Denton and Cruz fell away from him as the scorpion coiled Rafa back toward itself. "Rafa!" Cruz shouted, unable to help as she free-fell. The Undriel vanished back over the ledge, satisfied with its kill.

There wasn't time to grieve. Cruz used her jump-jet thrusters to push herself toward Denton. She shouted through the rushing wind of freefall, "We need to stabilize and reduce speed. Use your jump-jet!"

The triggers for the jump-jet were inside Denton's remaining gauntlet. He fired all of his thrusters at maximum, and Cruz did the same. The ground rushed toward them, but it started to slow. A moment later, they hit the ground hard enough to kick up sand and bruise their bodies, but they were saved from broken bones and sudden death.

Denton rolled onto his back in the red sand and coughed. Cruz stayed on her knees and looked up at the high cliff wall. She was silent for a long time as Denton worked to catch his breath. "Damn it," Cruz whispered and looked down.

The sand was hot, and the breeze did nothing to help cool it. The clouds were thinner near the cliff edge, and the sky was empty farther out above the dunes. The Starving Sands were devoid of fighting, devoid of everything. It was quiet here, like a desolate crimson cemetery made of sand. Cruz was a statue. She said nothing and couldn't move. She was still processing what had just occurred, and all of her other functions would be put on hold until she could sort it out.

Eventually, Denton rose to his feet. He didn't know what to say. They weren't sure who had survived the ambush or how much damage the Undriel had just done to the remaining human defenses. Bell and Rafa had had their lives ripped away right in front of them.

"It's all fucked." Cruz spat the words as she stood.

Denton nodded. She wasn't wrong. "What do we do now?"

Cruz looked at the sand and grimaced. She thought for a moment, running through protocols and procedures. Everything had happened so fast, and now suddenly, Cruz was the leader of their two-body troop. She sighed and looked out into the vast desert.

"I don't know." She shook her head. "Let's find some cover and wait to see if anyone else makes it out. We can't be the only survivors."

Denton looked along the cliff wall and found a small cave etched into the side of its sheer rock face. It was nestled under the stone archway, out of sight from any potential Undriel threat from above. It wasn't perfect, but it was the best chance they had. "What do you think?" Denton asked as he pointed at the cave.

"It'll have to do." Cruz marched through the sand, and he trailed behind her. The survivors were silent. The hot breeze blew red sand in sprays, concealing the trails they carved through the dunes on their way to shelter.

It was time to hide and treat their wounds.

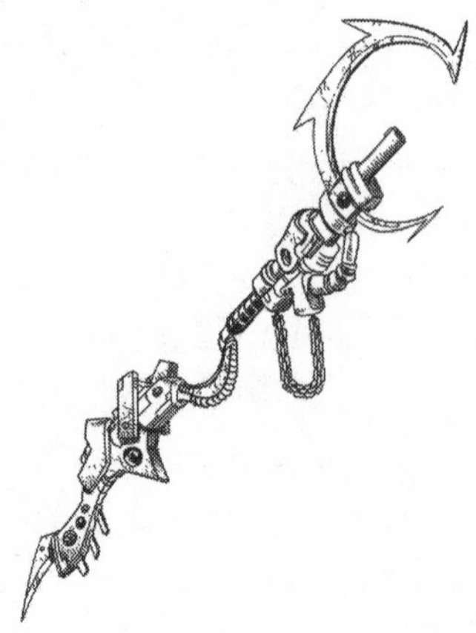

TWENTY-FIVE

TALULO CLUTCHED HIS DAUNOREN staff. Although the humans had informed him of everything they knew about the Voyalten, there was still a vagueness about what would happen next. *Would the Decider be peaceful, like Sympha? Or would it be violent, like Nhymn?*

Nella signed, "*We are approaching the Gate.*"

The unsung song told Talulo that Nella and Eliana weren't withholding information. *But humans have misplaced their confidence in the past. Humans also thought they were rid of the Undriel,* Talulo reminded himself. He could trust them, but they did not know what they could not know.

"Please stand against the wall," Nella signed.

Talulo and Eliana looked at each other with confusion, then shuffled backward against the black stone wall. The walls ebbed with electricity, and at once, Talulo and Eliana were seized by sustained lightning. The white-hot beams didn't hurt. They tickled Talulo's feathers with the familiar feeling of strapping into a human spaceship.

Light lapped up from the floor and surrounded Nella,

constraining her to the podium. Her hair floated off her shoulders and drifted upward in long, thick locks. Her eyes glowed green.

"She knows what she's doing. Right?" Eliana asked Talulo.

Talulo cooed. He could feel Nella's confidence. She was in her element—exactly where she needed to be. Talulo grabbed Eliana's small, soft hand with his hard-taloned claw and cooed to her. It was a human gesture. Talulo had seen people squeeze hands before take-off and landing during some of the scout flights he had been on before becoming a pilot. Auk'nai found it hilarious when humans were afraid to fly.

Eliana sighed and looked at her daughter. "Okay. Here goes nothing."

Here comes everything, Talulo thought.

"What the Hells is that?" Denton looked out from the cave shelter into the desert.

Cruz stood up and saw it too. In the distance, hovering above the dunes and moving at a decent speed, was a structure made of black stone and lightning. "Hells. Is that another Iron Castle? More Undriel?" They both stepped out of the cave to get a better look.

"I don't think so…" Denton said, letting the words trail off with his wonder. The structure floated to the center of the desert and stopped. Denton knew where it had parked. He'd been there not long ago. It was directly above the Siren Pit.

Kamaria suddenly hushed. Even the breeze had stopped.

A beam of red light exploded out from inside the Siren Pit, engulfing the odd hovering rock structure entirely. Denton and Cruz were pushed over by the following shockwave. The structure slammed into the pit, sealing it shut like a cork. Energy built up inside the structure, the way it did when nezzarforms charged lightning in their faces.

At once, the energy released, and Kamaria rocked.

As the aftershock pulsed out across the desert, immense shards of black glass thrust upward through the sand in insane angles. Some hung unnaturally in thin air. The shockwave shoved Denton and Cruz violently into the sand on their backs. A three-story-tall wall of glass rocketed upward and separated them. The ground shook, and the field of shards sang with vibrations. After two minutes of planet shaking, the energy ceased, and it became quiet again.

"What the *fuck* was that?" Cruz shouted from behind the wall of glass. She jump-jetted her way over the wall and landed near Denton.

"That thing just remade this desert!" he said through heavy breaths. "How the Hells can something be that powerful?"

"Shit. My comms out. Is yours working?" Cruz asked.

Denton checked his comm and shook his head.

Another wave of light surged from the structure in the pit, ringing the tall shards of glass. Denton and Cruz reflexively put their arms up to block the energy but were unharmed as it moved through them.

"Nothing." Denton checked himself for injuries. "You alright?"

"Yeah," Cruz said with confusion. "What is happening?"

"I'm not sure. But we can't stay here. If the transports come looking for us, they won't see us with all this glass obstructing their view."

"Check it out." Cruz thrust her chin toward the structure and the pit. Giant shards of glass now surrounded the stone ship like an immense frame. "The shards are less dense closer to the center. If we head there, we can make ourselves visible. We can't be the only ones to make it out of that ambush alive. Someone's gotta come eventually."

"I'm not sure if it will be safer near that thing." Denton checked his sidearm, worried. "But I also don't see any other choice."

"Stick close. We don't know what else that thing kicked up." Cruz palmed her particle rifle. They journeyed into the labyrinth of dark glass and crimson sand.

TWENTY-SIX

CADE TRIED TO WARN them. Through the rain and the fog and the thunder, there was nothing he could do. The human defenses approached, and with his superior augmented vision, he saw exactly what the Undriel under the water's surface saw. They saw a moment of weakness, and they exploited it.

When screaming didn't work, Cade and Karx willed their shared body into creating a blue pulse of light. They pulled energy from inside their mechanical form and allowed it to surge over their synthetic metal skin. The humans saw his light, but it was already too late by the time they did.

"Turn around! Leave!" Cade shouted as the boats stopped to observe his warning. "Don't come any closer! Run, Dad! Get out of here!"

The explosions came from underwater. Bodies were flung from each boat, cast into the lake, and devoured by the machines lying in its depths. Particle blasts lit up the hazy fog, and thunder rumbled in the sky as the rain crashed relentlessly on the battle.

Cade wasn't allowed to move, paralyzed by Auden's will. He could only watch the carnage that befell the Tvashtar marines around him. The battle lasted a half hour, and then it was silent except for the rain. The scattered remnants of the thirty boats the humans rode in on were absorbed to repair Undriel soldiers. The marines that weren't killed outright in the fighting became part of the Undriel army. Cade wept. He was useless.

"You performed perfectly." Auden's voice surprised Cade. He approached from down the beach, speed quickening. He thrust his hand forward, and Cade was forced to his knees. Auden leaned over him and spat words into his face. "I knew you weren't on our side. I knew you were special, but I am done playing these games."

Auden moved behind Cade and pulled his hand up, controlling him like a puppet on strings. Cade rose to his feet and faced the lake. Auden got close to his ear and said, "It's time to show us what you are."

"What?" Cade stammered. Auden crunched his hand into a fist, and Cade felt his heart crumple. He gasped in pain. His Undriel augmentations were working against him now, simulating something that would kill an average person, yet Cade endured. Death would have been welcomed.

"Shut up. It is time for you to perform again. The most important performance of your life. My mercy is at its limit, and our flock can find perfection in other ways. With or without you." Auden released his grip on Cade's false heart and moved away from him.

Tibor floated down from the sky, a human body in his arms. The body was encased in a Tvashtar marine combat suit. When Tibor dropped her in front of Cade, he recognized her immediately.

"Sergeant Combs?" Cade asked. His eyes widened, unsure of what he'd be asked to do but dreading the possibilities. Jess Combs was on her hands and knees in front of Cade. She spat blood into the sand and pushed herself into a kneeling position. She breathed in ragged breaths, and her face had been pummeled, her left eye unable to open.

She recognized what little was left of him. "Cade Castus? Is that really you? Alive after all…"

Tibor stood behind Jess, well within the range of Cade's tether.

<*WE MUST DO IT NOW,*> Karx insisted.

<They'll kill Jess!>

<THIS MIGHT BE OUR LAST CHANCE.>

<We can't.>

"Are you paying attention?" Auden moved around Cade and joined Tibor's side. "What do you think we want you to do?"

Cade looked from Tibor to Auden, then to Jess. "Oh god…"

"Why the look of horror? You wish to leave this wretched thing so imperfect?" Auden's arm morphed into a praying mantis-like scythe, and it lashed out into Jess's back, cutting through the combat suit and slicing through her skin. She grunted with pain and sneered as blood spilled down her back.

Undriel blades contained a unique chemical that caused localized hemophilia. Auden had just signed her death certificate by lacerating her. Jess was going to bleed out without special medical attention.

"What—what do you mean?" Cade asked.

"Playing stupid will get you both killed!" Auden seethed with red energy and steam in the constant rain. His eyes glowed white-hot. "Absorb this woman!"

Jess's good eye widened, and her breathing slowed. Cade was unable to mask his horror. He looked down at his hands, then back to Auden and Tibor. "I… I don't know how."

Auden clenched his hand again, and Cade felt the fire in his simulated heart. It was as if his insides were attempting to rush free of his frame, to burst with flames and blood. "We *all* know how!"

Auden released his hold, and Cade fell to the sand. He looked at his hands once more and felt a new sensation in his chest. It was true—part of Cade instinctually knew how to absorb Jess. He could devour her and spit her out a better thing, a *perfect* thing. Part of Cade wanted to do this. It was a lust that was hard to fight.

"He made it out," Jess said weakly. She gave Cade a smile filled with blood and missing teeth. "Your dad… He's still out there. Misses the shit out of you."

<Dad?> Cade thought.

"I hope you find him." Jess coughed up more blood.

<*CADE. WE MUST.*>

<*Shut up!*>

Jess's eyes shifted from Cade to something behind him. Her breathing grew more labored, her gaze stern and unshaken. Necrodore emerged from the forest and stomped around Cade to join Tibor and Auden. His voice boomed, "You will be doing her a favor, hybrid. This soldier is suffering."

Cade looked toward the rainclouds and worked to stop himself from screaming. His body convulsed, and it felt like a chainsaw had been revved up inside his torso. Cade bent over himself and held his arms against his metal body. He glanced up into the tree line.

A few human-shaped silhouettes were hidden in the trees. Survivors. He wanted to urge them to run, but they waited. They watched. *Do something. Save Jess!* Cade begged them internally.

Auden's eyes flashed, and his gleaming white razor-sharp teeth produced a nightmarish smile. "There is still one of us in there after all."

Cade's torso ripped itself open, revealing a maw of rotating saw blades and metallic teeth. He lurched toward Jess but caught himself centimeters away from her body. Jess tightened her jaw and closed her eyes. She didn't whimper. She didn't flinch.

<*No! I won't!*> Cade struggled.

<*FIGHT IT! FIGHT IT, CADE!*> Karx rallied.

Cade screamed at the top of his lungs. He collapsed his Undriel maw and thrust his hand forward. His tether flicked outward and slammed directly into Tibor's head. *Perfect shot!*

Nothing happened. No reaction.

The blue light bounced off Tibor's head and lapped against Necrodore's carapace. Cade felt the tether sink into Necrodore and call back his memories. *The Hells?* Cade thought as he fell to his knees. He had successfully linked with Necrodore, but the King of the Old Star's tethering had failed. <*Is Tibor immune?*> Cade asked Karx, even though he knew just as much information.

Before Karx could respond, Auden crunched Cade's heart. "That pathetic attempt of attacking Tibor will cost you *everything!*" He pushed Cade's face into the sand, then threw Jess down next to him. They were face-to-face on the beach.

Cade tried to look up at Tibor, Necrodore, and Auden, but his body wouldn't allow him to pivot. He could only stare at Jess. She looked back at him, her eyes full of sorrow. She whispered, "This is *not* your fault."

"Jess…" Cade whimpered. Tears fell from his eyes.

Jess smiled weakly, seeing just how human Cade still was.

Tibor morphed his arm into a long sword and drove it into Jess's spine. Her eyes went wide, and blood ejected from her nose and mouth, spilling out from the spaces where her teeth had been. She coughed once more, then wheezed her last ragged breath as death took her away.

"Jess!" Cade cried out in vain. The rain patted against their faces, mixing with his tears.

"You could have saved her," Auden said as thunder roared in the clouds above. "But now you will die with her, hybrid. This flock needs a culling."

Tibor removed his sword from Jess's back. Her expression didn't change as the blade came out. The King of the Old Star grabbed her leg and threw her corpse into the lake. Cade's body jerked with his effort to push through Auden's will. In the trees, the surviving marines moved away. *<At least my death will give them time to flee.>*

That was when Kamaria shook.

The trees rumbled, and the water churned violently. The clouds above were flung away, evaporating with violent speed, and suddenly it was sunny. Tall pines came crashing down, smashing a few unlucky Undriel footsoldiers in the process. Tibor stood motionless as he observed the chaos. After a few moments of turbulence, the quake ceased.

"What was that?" Necrodore asked.

Like a bullet in the sky, Faye Raike soared in from above. She pivoted and landed. "Something in the desert. A structure of some kind. It plugged itself into the planet."

"Plugged?" Necrodore asked.

"Into a pit? Correct?" Auden asked.

"I believe so," Faye said.

Auden looked up the mountain slope. "Interesting."

"Tibor, should I terminate this hybrid?" Necrodore asked the King of the Old Star.

Auden answered, "No. Our priorities have changed. We may have one final use for it." He leaned toward Cade. "Know that this is an *unusual* mercy I grant you. More than any I will ever grant again in all the eons before me. If I am not pleased with your responses in the coming moments, you will find your oblivion stretched out for centuries. Understood?"

Auden didn't wait for a response. It wasn't a question. He looked toward the water as the rest of his flock emerged from the depths with the Reaper. Auden nodded at Talfryn, who floated toward Cade and engulfed him into his body, encasing him within his cloak. Cade was pinned, immobilized by the strength of the Reaper, and subdued by Auden's will.

"Let's go see for ourselves," Tibor said. In unison, the Undriel moved up the slope of the mountain. Soon, the machines stood at the precipice of the cliff ledge. They observed the changes in the Starving Sands. Cade could only peer through parts of the Reaper's cloak to see what everyone was looking at.

What in the Hells? Cade had been here with Nella not long ago, but what lay beyond the cliff wall now was a strange place—unrecognizable. A glass labyrinth filled with shards of darkness. In the center of it all was the upper half of the black rock structure, seething with energy.

Cade remembered the Siren Pit. When Nella got close to it, it exploded. They had fled the area because it was too dangerous to stay. Whatever this was, the pit was at the center of it all. Kamaria had reacted to that structure.

What is Auden's fascination with it, though?

"I will scout the area," Faye offered. Auden put his hand up, and she stopped in place.

"No. Send one of the flock," Auden said.

An Undriel footsoldier stepped forward, randomly selected by Auden. It roared as it launched itself into the air. It rushed toward the black structure in the pit, and as it grew close, it shook with turbulence. Suddenly, the Undriel crumpled and dropped altitude. It tumbled into the glass labyrinth, shattering a few massive shards on its way down.

"What is this? Weaponry?" Necrodore asked.

Hilaria approached from the forest and pulled a dead marine corporal off her spiked tail. She looked out over the cliff with the others. "What could do that? Some new human trick?"

"No..." Auden said hesitantly. "Something else. Something special." He glanced at Cade through Talfryn's cloak. Cade suddenly realized why Auden had kept him alive.

Faye looked to Tibor. "What should we do?"

After a moment of contemplation, Tibor spoke. "Send in the hybrids. They are uniquely capable of this task. This shall be their path to perfection." In unison, the hybrid soldiers moved toward the edge of the cliff, each flickering with red energy, some more machine than others. Antoni slithered forward with the group.

Necrodore put one of his claws in front of Antoni's path. "Not you, young one."

"It is my path to perfection," he said, frustration lacing his voice.

Tibor said, "He shall join his comrades."

Antoni's mouth struggled to smile. His centipede legs coiled and uncoiled in satisfaction. He moved toward the rest of the hybrids on the cliff edge. Necrodore sullenly watched.

Hilaria turned toward Necrodore. "Maybe you should join them as well."

Necrodore said nothing.

Talfryn moved forward to release Cade but was stopped by

Auden. "Not this one. Not yet. He works against us. I don't trust him out there with the loyal flock. He may come in useful once we can get inside that structure."

Talfryn looked to Tibor, who reinforced it. "That one remains here."

The hybrids activated thrusters in their suits and stepped off the ledge. They glided forward and down, vanishing into the labyrinth of dark glass shards below.

<*Tibor is risking a significant part of his army for this. What is so important about this place?*>

<*WE MUST LEARN MORE. WE HAVE RETAINED NECRODORE'S TETHER. WE CAN GET THE ANSWERS FROM HIM.*>

<*Why did the tether fail on Tibor? It was like throwing a ball at a boulder.*>

<*I AM UNSURE. THE UNDRIEL DON'T KNOW ABOUT OUR TETHER. THE KING SHOULD NOT BE ABLE TO BLOCK ITS POWER. THERE IS A WRONGNESS HERE.*>

The Undriel waited on the cliffside, an audience to the hybrids that scouted the glass labyrinth. Cade could barely see from inside the Reaper. He wondered what their success or failure meant for his own future—and for Kamaria. Who knew what waited inside the Siren Pit? Auden was interested, and that made it feel even more dangerous.

<*We need to learn what we can.*>

As the Undriel settled into the cliffside, Cade slipped back through the tether to Shade walk into Necrodore's past. The light overtook him, and he sailed across time and space again.

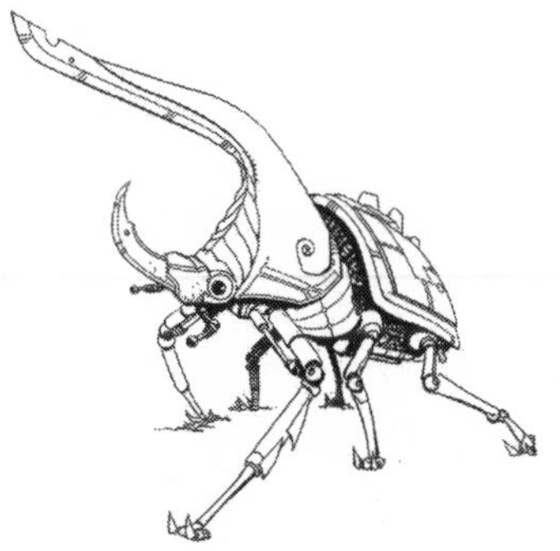

TWENTY-SEVEN

CADE FELT THE FAMILIAR sensation of zero gravity rush over him. It was a welcome, nostalgic feeling, like walking through a playground from childhood. It reminded Cade of his former life as a human, an EVA specialist aboard the *Maulwurf.*

He didn't care about the Shade walk. With his efforts thinning and time running out, his thoughts drifted to Zephyr Gale. She would have been glowing in this dark, her tattoos etched with a special ink that she could trigger at will to become luminescent. She was a supernova of beauty in a shadow.

What would she think of me now? Cade wondered. He looked down at his semi-translucent skin, knowing he was a skeleton of metal in the real world. A monster. He couldn't bring himself to panic anymore. He was too numb now. There was no guarantee he'd stumble upon the secret of the corruption. He could just be watching reruns of a bunch of tragic endings. He wanted to give it all up, run home, and embrace Zephyr one last time before the inevitable annihilation consumed all humanity.

Cade recognized where he was. Although the walls were cleaner, and the damage of centuries underwater wasn't present, the

Devourer's interior was the same. This was Dia—but this was not her memory.

The shuffle and drag of feet against metal caused Cade to turn. There he was, as he had initially looked when Cade met him: Antoni Herman. His parents called him Tony. Based on his appearance, years must have passed since the humans had fled the Sol System. Tony was only a little boy during the final days, but now he was roughly the same age as Cade.

Antoni shuffled past Cade and down the hall. The centipede robot that helped him stand upright clicked its many legs against the floor along with his dragging of weak feet. A dim red light lit the walls, glinting off the slick metal surrounding everything. Cade knew where Antoni was heading and followed.

After a short shuffle down the hall, the wall opened, and they were inside the hybrid lab, where Cade had worked in servitude of Auden's will. Except for a large mechanical frame fused into the room's far wall, the walls were bare. The tables had human corpses on them, each with a device on their head and in various states of dissection. Antoni didn't seem to notice.

"Of course he doesn't notice," Cade sighed. *He has the veil on his head. Antoni believes he's helping build and maintain boats on a harbor.*

A man emerged from the behemoth frame on the wall. Jonas Necrodore floated in zero gravity, then tapped a device on his arm that forced him to the floor. He was barefoot, wearing a skin-tight suit with wires and tubes connecting him to his frame on the wall. His feet made soft padding sounds on the metal floor. With a flick of his hand, the wall near him opened into a box shape, and a fire roared. It was cozy in an uncomfortable way.

"Brother Necrodore. I brought the device you requested." Antoni put a mechanical apparatus on the table. Necrodore looked at Antoni, and Cade noticed a softness to his face.

"Thank you, Brother Antoni," Necrodore said. His voice was

soft. He picked up the thing and inspected it. "How did you manage it?"

"It was simple. I used to steal treats from right under my parents' eyes without them noticing," Antoni spoke more easily in this time period. There was no drool or slipped words. He was a typical early twenty-year-old with a device on his head.

"Yes, but to steal from the Augmentor himself—that's a whole new trick. I commend you." Necrodore gestured over a soothreader-like device on his left arm. "Can I ask one more request?"

"Anything," Antoni said resolutely.

Necrodore snapped his finger over the soothreader, and Antoni went rigid. "Forget you did this."

Antoni relaxed after a moment, then looked around as if he had forgotten why he came into the room. He turned to Necrodore. "I'm not..."

"Go get some rest. You did great work today," Necrodore said kindly.

"Yes. Yeah, that sounds good." Antoni shuffled away, and the wall closed behind him. Necrodore watched him go.

"Stealing from Auden would be a new trick." Tibor's voice came from the shadows. A wall opened, revealing him and Auden. Necrodore turned to them, hurt but not surprised. The two looming Undriel stepped into the firelight. Tibor looked at the device in Necrodore's hand. "You stole a crown. You yearn so badly to betray my plan?"

Necrodore looked at the crown device in his hand. "The hybrids are dying. Antoni is the only one left. Him and me."

Tibor stepped forward, his voice low and soothing in a way. "Do you believe you are dying as well?"

Necrodore's eyes tightened, and he nodded.

Tibor brought his metal hand toward Necrodore, palm upright. Necrodore placed the crown in the king's hand, and Tibor rotated it around slowly, inspecting it closely. He looked back to Necrodore. "No Undriel should fear death. Not anymore."

"You will let me ascend then?" Necrodore asked.

"I will no longer deny you such a thing. You have been a loyal general and pivotal to our survival. I intend to reward you for your service." Tibor handed the crown back to Necrodore. "But, I fear for our futures if you ascend."

"I understand," Necrodore said, looking toward the floor.

"You withstood the corruption throughout the war. Your body holds the key to our immunity. You must know how vital that is to our people."

"But the hybrids we tested on are all dead now." Necrodore raised his voice. "And my body is a fragile thing. It is nothing without the frame."

"It is everything to our people." Tibor looked him in the eye. "It is the future of the Undriel."

"But this future is a dead end," Necrodore insisted.

They were silent for a moment. Auden paced in a slow circle around them as they discussed. He had said nothing this whole time, remaining only a silent witness.

"Grant me this, Jonas," Tibor said. "Keep the crown. But only put it on when it is the absolute last step you can take. Do not cut our future short so casually. There is still more to be done before we can seek our place elsewhere."

Necrodore smiled weakly and nodded. "You have my word."

Auden finally spoke. "Your frame will accept that crown, and the absorption will commence automatically. You will need to remove your current crown for the process to work. That was only to allow your body to control the frame without consuming the flesh."

Cade gripped his fist tightly. He was angry that the Undriel had the power to absorb people without destroying their bodies, yet he had not been given that mercy. The entire Sol System was made victim to their lack of judgment, then abandoned when the corruption overtook them. It was all so wasteful, and for what?

<*Why did the Undriel do all this in the first place?*> The motives

behind the war were still a mystery.

"You are stronger than all of us," Tibor said.

"I wish I could agree," Necrodore whispered.

Jonas Necrodore had kept his promise. He remained human as time compressed. Although there was no star or planet to base the passing of time on. Necrodore and Antoni zipped around the hybrid lab at increased speed. Cade watched them as they experimented on the remaining hybrid bodies and tossed the corpses into the fire after unsuccessful attempts to find whatever they were looking for. Cade had no way of knowing where the *Devourer* was. He was locked in without windows.

Suddenly, time slowed back to its normal speed. No one was in the room.

Where the...? Cade wondered. He was fortunate enough to know the *Devourer*'s interior and thus where to search. Necrodore was working with Antoni the same way Antoni worked with Cade. Cade had only been shown his cell, the hallway, and the hybrid lab, so those would be the most likely places to look if his theory was correct.

Sure enough, as Cade phased his way through the wall into the hallway, he found them. Antoni had his back pressed into the same closet Cade had occupied. Necrodore and his frame were floating outside, strapping Antoni in with wires and tubes.

"How long will the journey take?" Antoni asked, his lips smiling and his tone excited.

Necrodore said, "For you, it will seem like an overnight trip."

"And the corrupted can't follow?" Antoni sounded worried, looking for reassurance he had been given multiple times.

"They cannot. They have been able to follow us into space like this because we had not warped yet. Once we warp, they will have no way to follow us," Necrodore explained patiently.

"But what if they do?" Antoni asked.

"The corrupted are simple, mindless things. Warping is incredible technology—the corrupted have no grasp of it. The Augmentor has provided us with this unique ability. We will return when we are ready to face them." Necrodore plunged a tube into a socket on Antoni's head.

"But the humans understood warping…" Antoni slipped slowly into unconsciousness, his voice trailing off. Some drool slid from his lips. Necrodore watched him fall asleep, then gently pushed him back into the closet and sealed it.

Necrodore moved away from the closet and floated back toward the hybrid lab. His frame followed him like a ghost haunting his shoulders.

<*So the Undriel did have their own version of warping tech,*> Cade said. <*I mean, of course. They got to Kamaria somehow.*>

<*THEY PLAN TO RETURN.*>

Necrodore moved down the hall, but to Cade's surprise, he took a different path that led away from the hybrid lab. Cade followed him into unfamiliar territory. Walls rotated, and openings emerged until eventually, Necrodore and Cade floated into an enormous open space. A glittering ball of light floated in the center of the spherical room. Particles smashed together violently to increase the size of the glowing orb. The walls were filled with rotating collider cylinders, each feeding a beam into the center mass. Mechanical arms moved things into place rapidly, like insects attending a hive. The other Undriel generals floated in the room, surrounding the ball of light—Dia's heart. The *Devourer*'s engine.

Talfryn Raike, the Reaper, floated on an air of cloaks and scythes, concealing more weaponry in his frame. The silent observer.

Hillary, Hilaria, the scorpion-tailed serial killer, smiled at the violent light. Its chaotic movements and power were a pleasure to her.

Auden, the Augmentor, the mad scientist who created the crowns and set the course for the slow takeover of the Sol System, was connected to a large machine.

Finally, there was the Unknowable Metal God. The King of the Old Star. The Father of the Abandoned Worlds. Tibor Undriel. Whatever secrets he had in his memories were his to keep, immune to the tether.

"Careful now," Hilaria said to Necrodore. "Wouldn't want to pop that squishy skin of yours, Jonas." She cackled.

Necrodore ignored her and spoke to Tibor. "Antoni is secured."

"That is good," Tibor said. "Auden is preparing Ovid for the warp. You will need to secure yourself as well."

"Little brother can't watch the show. *Big kids* only," Hilaria teased.

<*It sounds like their warp tech is different from Homer's cascade warp tech,*> Cade said. <*My dad was awake for the first warp of the* Telemachus. *And even on the* Odysseus, *my mom said grandpa was awake for the first two jumps to ensure it was successful.*>

<*THE UNDRIEL DIDN'T DESIGN THEIRS FOR HUMANS.*>

<*Sucks to be Antoni and Necrodore, then. No wonder Antoni's so messed up in the present,*> Cade scoffed. <*Wait. Did he say* Ovid?>

<*WHAT IS IT?*>

<*Sounds like something my grandfather worked on.*> Cade tried to remember. <*I just remember that name—and barely passing a test about him in my ancient Earth history class.*>

"I will see to it." Necrodore pulled himself into his frame. He piloted the behemoth metal suit toward the far wall, and it opened, revealing a small, boxy room. A slot in the wall with mechanical arms clamped around his frame and securely curled it into the wall. There was a rush of stasis chemicals and compressed air as the *Devourer* sealed him in safely.

Cade was surprised when time didn't compress.

<*Is Necrodore fully unconscious?*> He got closer to the frame and observed it. There were still systems online, but Cade was unsure of their purpose.

<*PERHAPS HE WANTED TO WITNESS THE WARP UNNOTICED.*>

<*You might be right. Risky work, though. It's not designed to keep him alive.*>

"We are ready," Tibor said. Cade heard the others from just

beyond the wall and phased through to get a better look.

Auden controlled the machine called Ovid. It was a looming, coffin-shaped thing, unfinished in design. Wires and other technological mechanisms adhered it to the *Devourer*'s heart. "Prepare for warp," Auden informed them, and began a warp sequence. The ball of light in the center of the room fluctuated in size and intensity. The other Undriel generals watched, stunned by the display. The orb collapsed on itself for an instant, then reactivated so hot that it filled the whole chamber. Cade felt the immense heat but no pain, as his Shade walking body was immune to the death that would have greeted him if he were here in reality. Each of the Undriel survived the intense rush, protected by their metal bodies.

Something looked wrong. Auden shook off the effect of the blast, but the others remained utterly still. They drifted slowly, inert. As the warp propelled the *Devourer* through space, each of the inactive generals was slammed against the far wall of the spherical room. Auden remained steadfast, strapped to Ovid. He couldn't look over his shoulder to see what was happening, but Cade could tell this wasn't going the way he'd anticipated.

The immense pressure of the warp went on, with over ten seconds elapsed and counting. With Homer's warp tech, the distance was covered in a cascade method. Small jumps covered light-years of distance, frequently pausing to recharge energy. The Ovid version of warping seemed to overlap these jumps into one sustained push. Without proper precautions, most humans would be liquified with this amount of thrust. Whatever tech was keeping Antoni and Necrodore alive must have been incredible.

Cade felt a lurch as the ship hit a bump.

"What?" Auden brought up a holographic image with a nod that showed a view from the *Devourer*'s bow. Cade witnesses a kaleidoscope effect as light and space bent around the ship, but there was something else. A disc of white light whipped into the ship, and they felt another jolt, this time more violent than the last.

"Stupid *thing!"* Auden roared.

Another disc of light hit the *Devourer*, and Cade heard an explosion. Auden brought up an image of the ship's status on a separate screen. A series of emergency lights ignited as ruptures ate away at the ship's hull.

"Damn it all!" Auden shouted. He tried to shut off the warp sequence, but it wasn't reacting fast enough. More light smashed into the *Devourer* with a tremendous explosion. The image of the bow flickered and fought to regain itself. Gravity suddenly returned to the ship, and even Cade's Shade form was thrown back against the wall. The inert Undriel generals fell toward the opposite wall and suffered catastrophic damage. Auden remained attached to the Ovid machine but had been lashed about by the sudden change. Ovid's pulsing energy lapped around the interior of the spherical room.

The view from the *Devourer's* bow showed only darkness. A pinprick of light shone ahead, and it grew to fill the screen entirely. After adjusting to the sudden light, the image faded to a blue sky. They emerged from a tunnel, soaring upward at incredible speed.

<Atmosphere?> Somehow, the *Devourer* had gone from deep space to the interior of a planet. The sudden, unexpected change crushed much of the *Devourer's* hull, turning it more into a massive chunk of flying metal than a ship. In the sky above, two familiar moons orbited.

<Holy shit! We're on Kamaria!>

The *Devourer* shot like a bullet straight out of the Siren Pit.

Auden fought with Ovid but couldn't keep up with the rapid destruction. The *Devourer* kept fragmenting and exploding as it tried to fix the cataclysmic effect of sudden gravity. It roared across the Kamarian sky with incredible speed. Cade saw familiar landscapes—the Starving Sands, the Supernal Echo and mountain basin, the Ember-Lit Forest. Finally, the Howling Shore of the east coast and the rushing ruby waves. Roaring like a fireball cast out of the Hells themselves, the *Devourer* slammed into the water beyond the shore.

Auden was thrown against Ovid as water began to rapidly fill the ship. Ovid pulsed out more strange energy fields, something like a stasis encasement barrier.

"No! Stop it, you idiot thing!" Auden hissed again, his frame badly damaged. As some of the energy from Ovid washed over his metallic body, he spasmed. Auden's arm went limp. He pulled himself off Ovid, ripping away the connecting tubes that had made him one with the warp machine. He stumbled backward as he got his bearings.

Sunlight filled the room from above, and water rushed through a large wound in the hull. The *Devourer* had cracked open like an egg, and it was seeping energy and fire everywhere the water wasn't. It was sinking.

Auden was hit with another energy wave from Ovid. The Undriel Augmentor stumbled again and roared fiercly, "We need to get out of here!" His cries went unheard as his fellow commanders slipped under electrified water. "Get up, damn you! Get up!"

Ovid pulsed again, Auden was quick enough to activate thrusters on his legs and float over the offending wave of energy. Ovid's stasis energy was keeping the others locked in their dormant state. Just as they would recover, another pulse would push them back into slumber. Helping the others would trap Auden in this tomb forever.

A groan in the hull signified the opening above was beginning to collapse in on itself. Auden looked up into the sunlight. With one last roar, he launched himself through the hole with the thrusters on his feet. Cade floated toward the breach in the hull to watch.

They were in the open sea air of the Howling Shore. Back home—Kamaria. Auden's flight path arched downward, pocked with tiny explosions as he sailed into the shore.

<*Why are we still Shade walking?*> Cade asked Karx.

<*NECRODORE MUST STILL BE ALIVE.*>

<*How the Hells is that possible?*> Cade asked, and looked down into the sinking wreck.

The waters rumbled. Electricity and fire flicked out from the abyss. Cade dove under the turbulent waves and looked around the open room. The hull collapsed on itself, blocking out the sunlight as the ship sank deeper into the ocean. Tibor, Hilaria, and Talfryn were trapped in this watery tomb as Ovid relentlessly emitted pulses of paralyzing energy, a result of some malfunctioning failsafe that wasn't designed for the Undriel to use. *Where did Auden get this thing?* Cade wondered as he dove deeper, past Ovid into the dark water.

There was a dull thud of banging from behind the metal wall. The wall opened only a millimeter, and water rushed into the boxed room containing Jonas Necrodore. Cade phased into the room.

"What the *Hells* just happened!" Necrodore shouted. His room rapidly filled with water charged with the Ovid energy. Necrodore panicked and backed away. There wasn't much time. "Tibor! Help!" he shouted. No one came to his call, and the water was up to his knees now.

Necrodore looked back at his frame. "It's time."

Cade watched as the arm on the behemoth machine lifted, and a compartment opened. The new crown emerged, and Necrodore took it in his hand. He removed his old crown and tossed it into the water. It sputtered as the energy hit it, and all the readout lights faded. Necrodore placed the new crown on his head and smiled.

"Don't do it, you fool," Cade said to a man who wouldn't listen even if he could.

As the frame recognized the crown, the pilot seat shifted into a maw of chainsaw-like teeth. The wires and tubes that connected Necrodore to his frame pulled him in, like tentacles pulling in prey. Necrodore braced himself for the short-lived pain he would feel as the maw pulled him into its waiting teeth.

The white light filled Cade's vision as Necrodore finally got his wish.

TWENTY-EIGHT

A SURGE OF ENERGY washed over the stone walls as the Key Ship plunged into the Siren pit. It was a wave of hot air and light, blinding in its incredible brilliance. It blew Nella and Eliana's hair upward, and had they not been strapped into the walls with electrical harnesses, they would have been thrown toward the ceiling. After the light and heat passed, it was quiet and dark. Eliana couldn't even see her hands in front of her face.

The tiniest pinprick of green light broke through the darkness. Dim green illumination wrapped around the figure of a person, like an extra layer of skin. Nella stood at the pedestal in the center of the room. She clapped to get everyone's attention, and the impact of her hands created a ripple of bright green against her body. Nella signed, *"Close your eyes."*

Eliana understood and relayed the info to Talulo in Sol Common. Their eyes closed, and Nella gestured over the pedestal. Blinding-bright orbs emerged from the stone walls. Nella made a few more gestures, and the spheres dimmed to a more manageable level. She pushed one toward her mother and another toward Talulo. The orbs hovered over their heads, creating a soft ambient glow.

Eliana and Talulo slowly opened their eyes. The dim room was shimmering with tiny emerald particles. Talulo looked around in awe, his beak partially open. "This place has an old song," he whispered.

The floor of the cylindrical room shifted, and rock dust coughed out. Nella held her arm out, indicating to Eliana and Talulo that they should stand back for a moment. Along the wall in a half-circle formation, the boulders dropped into even levels, creating a staircase. When the shifting stopped, light entered the ship through a doorway below. A shadow moved in the light, something waiting beyond the entrance.

Nella signed, *"We go down and meet the Decider."*

"Are you sure?" Eliana signed back.

Nella bobbed her fist. *"Yes. It must be done."*

Carefully, they descended the long staircase.

Denton and Cruz walked through the labyrinth toward the Key Ship. The entire landscape had changed instantly, and what was once a straight shot became winding paths of tall, reflective glass. Denton was reminded of old funhouses he had been in during carnivals on Ganymede. The halls of mirrors were always disorienting, and this alien version of one was no exception.

"Are we still going the right way?" Denton asked. The sky above was cloudless blue. There was nothing to use to maintain orientation in the maze.

"These walls are getting taller the farther we get into this shit," Cruz noted. "I can't jump-jet around them anymore. But if we need to make a path, I have a doorbuster in my gauntlet that should do the trick." She pumped her fist, and her gauntlet shifted over her knuckles. The doorbuster device was used to punch through doors in space stations, but it had other uses.

"Let's hope it works. Look ahead," Denton said. As they walked forward, their own reflections walked toward them. A flat-mirrored wall loomed high, blocking their progress. Denton sighed and put his hand on the wall. "There's no guarantee this maze has an exit. It could just be some crazy pattern that we perceive as a maze."

"Oh, it'll have an exit," Cruz muttered. "Stand back."

Denton took a few steps back. Cruz pumped her fist, and the doorbuster on her gauntlet pulsed. She arched her elbow back, then launched her fist forward. A hole three doors wide burst through the glass. The upper portion of the shard held firm, and their new door was safe to cross through.

At a different time, Denton would have enjoyed this maze. It was something new to Kamaria, something exciting and fantastic. A hidden secret was revealed, yet in this revelation, a new mystery was created. He wished Eliana was with him now. She would have pointed out the intricate carvings in each shard, noting how they looked etched with some purpose in mind. It was hard to tell in the daylight, but the carvings emitted a low light of their own. At night, this place probably looked mystical. It was hard to know if these shards existed under the Starving Sands desert and were thrust out into the open by the strange ship or if they were created in a flash. Perhaps the vessel's energy interacting with the sand sprouted them into existence instantly.

They came upon an area of the hallway with openings on each side. It was hard to tell when the gaps occurred due to the nature of the mirrors. Through each space, other hallways intersected this one from various angles. They had to be in a main artery toward the Pit. Denton's assumption was only possible if this labyrinth had a specific pattern. If the halls were random, then it was a coincidence.

Cruz walked ahead of him, quiet and contemplating. Her reflection echoed on both sides of the hallway. Ahead, the vessel that had plunged into the Siren pit peeked out from above the shards. They were getting closer, but the distance was hard to gauge in the maze. Pulses of light moved through the sand below their feet, tickling its surface.

Denton slowed his pace, confused by something in Cruz's reflection on the right. It walked at about the same stride Cruz did, but it was off-sync. There was a helmet on the reflection that was absent from Cruz herself. He blinked and noticed the flickering red light dancing on her reflection's body.

Not a reflection! Denton realized in horror. "Cruz! Move!"

Cruz was confused, but her reflection wasn't. She noticed the hybrid Undriel soldier with barely enough time to dodge its particle blast. Cruz jump-jetted and rolled into a shard, cracking its surface. The particle blast from the hybrid ricocheted off the glass maze, creating a deadly dance of hypercharged energy.

"Shit!" Cruz shouted.

Denton aimed his collider pistol forward and cracked off three precise shots, dropping the hybrid Undriel soldier to the sand. He put his back against a shard and tried to remain hidden in case there were more. To Denton's shock, the glass wall to his left burst as a hybrid soldier punched through with their doorbuster. It entered the hall and reached for Denton with a mechanical arm, its claw a mess of razors and jagged metal.

Cruz was quick and accurate, first blasting the claw off the hybrid, then twice into its chest, then last into the device on its head. The hybrid fell backward, dead before it hit the ground.

"Fuckin' move!" Cruz ordered. Denton did just that. Particle shots bounced around the mirrors, creating a deadly grid of light beams. They scrambled, rushing down the hallway. One shot ricocheted wildly off a shard and struck Cruz in the back, knocking her face-first into the sand.

Denton knelt over her and let out a few bouncing shots down the hall to give her covering fire. Cruz brought herself to her feet with his help, wincing in pain. "Got me right between the armor." She gritted her teeth and added, "Keep them busy. I have an idea." Denton continued to shoot down the hallway, jerking his head to the side as a shot glanced past him, so close he felt its heat against his ear.

Cruz unclipped a grenade from her kit and lobbed it down the hall. There was a resounding explosion and the crash of glass shards. The world was filled with the roar of chaos as the hall crumpled around the grenade. A few hybrids were crushed by the giant fragments that crashed down upon them.

"Let's get out of the main hall," Denton suggested. Cruz agreed. They hustled through the next opening on their left and ducked behind a shard. Hybrids rushed past their position, moving more like hungry animals than the people they used to be.

There was a roar in Denton's mind. It was enough to make him reflexively cover his ears and crush his eyelids together, though it would do no good. The sound was internal, familiar.

"Was that…?" Denton muttered in horror.

The hybrids fired on something ahead in the maze. For a moment, Denton thought they were shooting at their own reflections until one of the hybrids came sailing down the hallway back the way they had come. It had been cut in half and thrown. Denton peeked out into the main hall.

The hybrids had been ripped apart by something huge and unseen. Their blood was spilled across the clean, mirrored surfaces, filling the intricate etchings with crimson. A creature, just out of view, slunk around a corner ahead.

"There's no possible way…" Denton whispered. He turned to Cruz and stopped. Her eyes were shut, her mouth slack with blood trickling out. "Hey, Cruz!" Denton urged her, but she didn't respond. "No, come on, Cruz!" Denton grabbed her shoulders and shook her harder. "Wake up! Wake up, damn it!" He shook her as hard as he could, his eyes filling with tears. "Damn it, marine! You have to get up. You can't just…"

It was too late. Cruz didn't protest. She didn't wake up. She didn't move at all.

Cruz had joined her comrades—another soul lost to the Undriel war machine. The shot she had taken in the back took her life. The sudden quiet of her death was just as devastating as the loud abruptness of Marathon, Cook, Bell, and Rafa's.

Denton stayed on his knees for some time, paralyzed. He was alone now. He remembered one of the first nights of the war, sitting around a campfire, eating food made by Cook. Chatting with Bell about Ganymede and her moms. Inaya spoke of the Song of Kamaria and how the spirits of the Sol System were not so different. Ortiz strummed on his guitar, and Cruz stared at the empty shot glass meant for Marathon.

Denton imagined that same fire, now sitting alone. His only company was the shot glasses meant for his fallen comrades. He felt cold guilt rush through his blood. The Undriel had destroyed his friends, ripped apart his family, and would soon take over Kamaria if left unchallenged.

Denton pushed his head into his arms, cradled in his knees with his back against the wall. He sobbed, alone, afraid. Cruz gave him no comfort. It was quiet. Death had swept through this maze so fast it only left the dry desert wind in its wake.

Damn the Undriel.

Another roar in his mind reminded him that he wasn't as alone as he thought. Denton lifted his head slowly and steadied his breathing. He looked out into the blood-covered maze ahead. A creature lurked out there, one with claws strong enough to rip through a Tvashtar combat suit. He could sit here and wait for the beast to find him, or he could stand up—be brave.

"I'm sorry, Cruz. I'm so sorry," he whispered one last time. He pulled the particle rifle from her hand and rose slowly to his feet. With great caution, Denton exited his hiding place and moved into the mirrored hallway.

It was just him and the monster now.

TWENTY-NINE

CADE WATCHED THE CHAOS in the glass labyrinth below through the innards of the Reaper. The Undriel could see the explosions and bouncing particle fire from their perch on the cliffside. The generals could hear the hybrid army's progress through the network, and they could listen as the beast tore through them with ease.

There was a monster down below.

"Useless." Hilaria spat the word out.

"What a waste," Necrodore said with remorse.

"What do we do now?" Hilaria asked Tibor. "We can't get close to the object, and our hybrids are running thin."

Tibor stood silently, observing the destruction below with cold metal eyes. Auden turned to Cade and said, "Last shot." With a snap of his metal-clawed fingers, Talfryn spilled Cade onto the ground.

Cade fell to the floor and could not move, made inert by Auden's will. He was on his hands and knees like a beggar. Auden approached, and Cade snapped upright to his feet. As Auden paced around him, Cade felt control return to his body. It was a rush of release that washed over him from toe to head. Auden stood near the cliff and looked at him.

"You see that down there?" Auden pointed at the object in the center of the glass maze, "I'm going to cut you a deal, hybrid." He approached Cade, putting his glowing eyes in front of Cade's face, filling his vision. "You get in there and shut that thing off, and we leave this planet and never return."

<*UNEXPECTED,*> Karx said.

<*This has to be a trick, right?*>

Auden continued, "I don't know if we can trust you, but you're our last chance at this thing. You are special, made different by this world, for certain. You resonate energy we can't explain, and as much as I'd love to rip you open and study you, we have a more urgent task for you to perform here. A task so important I'm willing to sacrifice the perfection you might have within you to see it fulfilled."

<*I'm so honored that he's willing to sacrifice killing me to have me killed in the maze instead.*> Cade's thought was laced with sarcasm.

"My theory is that your energy will neutralize the pulses that structure is generating," Auden explained. "You get inside, deactivate the whole thing, and allow us to breach it. We can use it to leave this place."

"How?" Cade asked. In the Shade walk, Cade had been there when the *Devourer* came roaring through the Siren Pit. Some accident during the warp had displaced the giant Undriel ship and shot it onto Kamaria like a cannonball. What could have caused such a thing was beyond Cade's comprehension—Hells, it was beyond Auden's comprehension too. Cade knew they'd entered Kamaria from the Pit but was unsure if a return trip was possible.

Auden said, "Once we learn how to use whatever that is as an exit, yes. There are answers in that structure, of that I am certain. You get us in, and we will leave. We never wanted to come here in the first place." He turned to the others, and they seemed to agree.

<*I know he's telling the truth. I saw it myself.*>

Auden turned back toward the object in the pit, and the others looked with him. Cade knew what he had to do. He summoned his tether with a quick flick of his wrist and allowed the light to pool within his palm. As quietly as he could, he lobbed it at Auden. The blue light flicked out from Cade's hand and lashed against Auden's head. The tether retreated into Cade's palm just as Auden turned to face Tibor.

<*SUCCESSFUL LINK,*> Karx verified.

Tibor turned to the others. "If this fails, we abandon the object in the pit and head straight for the human stronghold in the west. We will destroy the threat that challenges us and bring as many as we can into our family before the end. We never intended to come here, but if we can't leave, we will prepare this planet to be our paradise regardless."

Cade's eyes widened. Tibor was absolutely truthful about wiping out humanity if Cade failed. Suddenly the stakes were realized. Success meant the possibility of absolute victory—provided Auden wasn't lying about leaving Kamaria. Failure meant certain annihilation—regardless of Auden's lies. Cade was the pendulum of the fate of humanity.

"Time to go." Auden snapped his metallic fingers. Cade felt locks open inside his mechanical body, and his mind raced with new system data. Auden had granted Cade complete control of all of his Undriel abilities. He instantly knew how to extend swords from his wrists, turn his arms into particle weapons, and even how to fly with jets built within his frame. Auden no longer needed to lock Cade out of his powers. The consequences of betrayal were clearly defined.

Do this, and the Undriel will leave. Fail, and humanity dies.

"Clock's ticking," Auden said.

Cade ran to the edge of the cliff and leaped off, activating boosters in his legs to propel him forward into the air. Suddenly, he had distance from the Undriel who had imprisoned him and tortured him for months. If he wanted, Cade could fly toward Odysseus City. He could save himself and be free, warn the humans or hide from them.

He would be dooming his people that way. The Undriel force was dangerous and had shown it could wipe out humanity a second time if necessary. Breaching the structure in the desert provided a real chance at saving humanity. In a way, even with Auden unlocking all of Cade's potential and letting him off the leash, he had more control over Cade than he ever had before.

A pulse surged out from the structure in the center of the maze, and Cade felt some of his systems fail. The jets on his legs flickered out, and he fell into the labyrinth below with a crash. He smashed through a shard of glass and impacted with the sand. Cade rose quickly, knowing the Undriel were watching his progress.

<*Karx, I need your help now.*> Cade stared into his monstrous reflection on the glass shards around him. A blue light enveloped his metal body, seeping from between the paneling on his skeletal limbs. Cade's eyes were glowing blue, and he could feel the hot tickle of power running over the skin on his head and neck. He rose from the sand and rushed toward the structure in the pit as another pulse of light pushed out from it and collided with him. He felt the surge move through him, and his left arm ceased functioning. It glitched, then went limp against his torso.

<*Karx!*> Cade urged.

<*I AM TRYING TO STOP IT. IT IS TOO STRONG.*> Karx's voice was stitched with pain. He was feeling the effects of the pulse as well.

Cade sprinted through the maze. He bashed through dead ends shoulder first, leaving a line of shattered glass behind him. Another pulse surged out, and Cade felt his left shin deactivate. He couldn't run, so he hobbled as quickly as he could.

"No, no, *no!*" Cade shouted and pushed forward. He tried to smash through another shard of glass but couldn't get enough momentum. He bounced away from the wall and screamed in frustration.

<*THE DECIDER DOESN'T RECOGNIZE US.*>

Another surge flowed through the maze. Cade's right hand was deactivated.

<*We can't fail! The Undriel will kill everyone!*>

<*I CANNOT STOP IT. WE NEED TO MOVE QUICKLY. FOLLOW THIS PATH.*>

Cade could sense the correct way through the maze, as if he were commuting to work, having done this route a thousand times and knowing the directions through the labyrinth by heart.

With Karx's directions, Cade zig-zagged through the glass corridors. His progress was quick but sloppy, losing time as he stumbled into walls and bumped into his own reflections. A wave of energy blew over the maze, and Cade's right leg went rigid. He stumbled around a corner and gasped.

The hall was filled with ripped-apart hybrids. The monster had been here. It was an omen for what awaited Cade in the maze. He couldn't stop. He couldn't run away. He had to keep moving forward. He hobbled past the dead hybrids and worked his way through Karx's route. Far off in the distance, Cade heard shouting, and a roar filled his mind.

The beast is close, but it's distracted. Cade remembered running through dark cave tunnels with Nella months ago. They were chased by monsters back then too. This felt horrifyingly familiar, like being in a second plane crash after surviving the first.

The light passed over the maze again. Cade was brought to the ground as both his legs went fully rigid. He shouted in frustrated agony and pulled himself forward with his last functioning limb, his right arm. Even with his right hand paralyzed, he could use it like a claw to drag himself.

He struggled up a slope toward the structure's base. Cade was almost there. Ahead, a body lay in the sand, silhouetted by the glow of the structure. Cade agonizingly dragged himself through the sand. As he approached the body, another surge washed over him.

Cade was fully paralyzed. He lay facing the other body and recognized the face of Antoni. The wretched man was barely breathing. His headset had been ripped apart, revealing one of Antoni's eyes. His veil was halved. Antoni's centipede-like body was inert, dead and useless in the sand. The light had stopped them both, just meters from their goal. Cade noticed Antoni had suffered a mortal wound in his human torso and was slowly bleeding to death.

His blood mixed perfectly with the crimson sand. His augmentations failed to heal him.

"Brother… Cade," Antoni whispered. "Have you… come… to… save us?"

Cade's body was shutting down. *Am I going to die?* Cade wondered with panic. *If I die, everyone dies. I am failing them all.*

"I—I am… confused… Brother," Antoni said, his human eye darting around. "I do not… recognize myself. My body… has been changed. By the maze."

Cade could explain it all. How Antoni was a failed experiment, an attempt to stop the corruption that plagued the Undriel. How the machines destroyed him so thoroughly over the years. How he was sealed in stasis for almost three centuries. He could reveal everything to this poor soul.

"You have been… made perfect." Cade gasped the words.

"I—I *see* it." Antoni began to smile weakly, and his iris dilated. "My god. It's beautiful." He heaved a few breaths and whispered, "Mom…"

Antoni let out one last ragged sigh as death found him.

Cade's last tears fell from his eyes. He was unable to stop them. He watched Antoni in his infinite stillness, a smile still cast upon his face. Antoni had died fulfilling his dream through a veil of lies, but the poor wretch couldn't know that. Cade was dying in a world filled with true nightmares. The fate of humanity had been placed upon him.

<*I failed…*> Cade whimpered in his mind to Karx as he felt his final systems shut down. The world grew dark. His vision was blurry. It was as if he were slipping into a dream, falling down into a pit as the light receded from him. Cade didn't care.

<*They are all going to die.*>

He didn't feel cold. Cade couldn't feel anything. Nerves fired on his face, but his augmentations stopped lying to his senses after the last wave of light passed through them. He was hollow, made of impossible stuff. He was a vegetable perched upon a scarecrow's body, a mockery of human anatomy.

<*Everyone…*>

A rush of white light filled his tunneled vision. At once, he was submerged in it—enclosed. The light took him away.

4
MONSTER
OF THE
MAZE

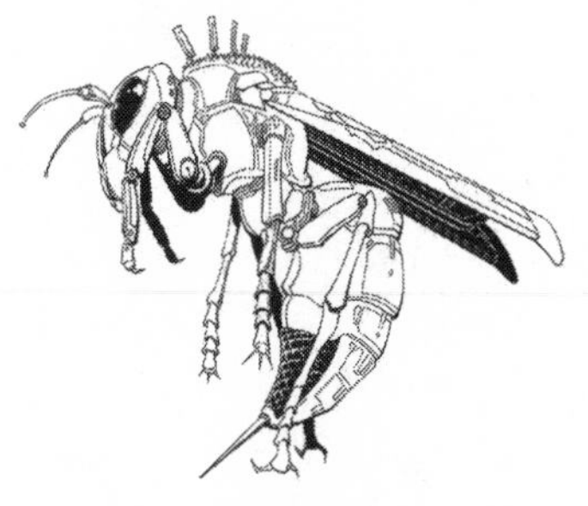

THIRTY

THREE HUNDRED AND FORTY YEARS AGO

ROARING APPLAUSE, BUT NOT for him. Humanity had become their own gods, and it had nothing to do with Dr. Auden Nouls's crown technology. The news was just announced of the Telemachus Project's final completion of Homer—the end of crown technology funding would inevitably follow.

Setback after setback after setback *after setback*. Auden's vision of a future where humanity rose above the artificial intelligence they created had been an uphill battle from the start. Auden never wanted to look up to an intelligence greater than man. He strove to leap over it. His evolution would make humanity the greatest it could ever become.

There were problems, naturally.

Evolution like this required people and AI to adhere to each other, to meld into something new. Crown tech was a way to combine man and machine without major surgery, but it didn't work the way Auden needed it to. Allowing humans to control machines through the crown only led to advancements in robotics, not intelligence. People could mentally control an extra appendage, or an android frame, or a ship, but the robotics involved provided no insight in return.

In some experiments, Auden tried it the other way around—let the machine think for the user wearing the crown. It only made the crown less intelligent, as it had to dumb itself down to human capability to get the user to do anything.

The problem rested in the insistence on keeping user and machine separate. Artificial intelligence could only exist if it was thinking on its own. It wasn't until recently that Auden realized he never cared about AI technology at all.

He cared about the meld.

If a person could become a machine, they could do so much more. They'd retain their mind but lose everything that made humanity vulnerable. They could travel the stars better than the way that damned Dr. John Veston envisioned.

They'd be their own masters. Not reliant on an AI named Homer.

In one secret test, Auden allowed his crown to take over the user completely. His niece, Dia, had been his test subject, and her side effects had been devastating. She became plagued with a mysterious illness. Auden had her treated, but the doctors could never diagnose what was wrong because Auden withheld information. Even Dia was kept in the dark about the source of her illness. It was all necessary. It was the price of ascension.

Crushing down on Auden's paradise was funding. Money ran the universe, and dreams were doomed to dust without it. *What is money for anyway?* Auden wanted to spit. *I receive money to pay people to continue researching a world where the money won't be necessary. Where food is only a decoration, and water will be left to the lesser animals. Funding is a means to an end. If they would only suck it up and do the work, they'd find a paradise free from these shackles.*

Auden pinched the bridge of his nose and sighed. He was alone in his laboratory on Venus. He'd kicked everyone else out of the lab an hour earlier, leaving him with only prototypes and wasted efforts.

It was a large, rectangular room, with a glass-wall partition separating the work area from a viewing room for investors. It was dimly lit now, with only residual red and orange lights bouncing off workstations and security lights. Mechanical armatures and tools lined the floors and walls.

A synthetic voice, robotic and without inflection, announced, "You have unheard messages from Tibor Undriel."

"Shut up," Auden mumbled.

The voice represented another one of Auden's failures. It was a thing he had taken from his divorce from the Telemachus Project—a running start. Ovid was an early prototype of Homer. Auden had some involvement in the project but abandoned it to pursue his crown tech. He managed to sneak Ovid's unfinished code away when he was fired. Apart from the high intelligence it wielded, it also contained base coding for cascade warping in starships with a low-level functioning system.

Ovid never cared about human cargo, and that was its major flaw—according to Dr. John Veston, at least. Auden specifically designed it that way. He wanted to make human bodies so strong that this aspect wouldn't matter. The problem with all of Auden's plans was the amount of time and foresight they needed to see fruition.

No one can envision this future I see so clearly, Auden thought as he placed his hand on his prototype crown tech, so close to perfection. *I must make them see what I see. I must force them to understand.*

Against the wall stood a tall robotic frame with a white metal head and glowing eyes. It was bipedal, shaped like a human. The structure had an exposed jaw with frightening, razor-sharp teeth. Unfinished work was eventually supposed to conceal these fangs from the consumer's view. Initially, the prototype had been an old war machine, one of Tibor's father's inventions. Tibor wanted to move away from wargames and pursue more commercial endeavors. The trillionaire hated his father, and Auden was thrilled to soak up the funding derived from those daddy issues.

Alpha-One was the working name for this robot.

It was another wasted effort, all in the name of—*of course*—the pursuit of funding. Tibor insisted they made something tangible to slap an artificial intelligence into. The Telemachus Project's Homer was an unseen voice, like God speaking down from the heavens to start a coffee machine or something. Tibor thought they could use his father's old war machines as a blueprint to make AI people—give the voice a body to connect with. It was a philosophy that sickened Auden to his core. Still, he had obliged, mostly to secretly siphon money into his own endeavors. Auden had installed an Ovid core into the metal husk and toyed with its code over time to keep Tibor off his back.

The lab's door slid open, and in stepped a man with white hair, slicked back so as to not conceal his face. He wore a black suit with a black dress shirt underneath as if going to a funeral. His skin was pale white, and his eyes were a deep reddish-brown. He was trim and fit and groomed the way only a trillionaire could be.

"You have been avoiding me," the man said, his voice deep and pleasant, despite the destruction he was about to bring to Auden's future.

"Listen, Tibor. I know what you're here for, and we can—"

"There's nothing more to do, Auden," Tibor said. They each used first names, although their friendship was only as thick as the money between them. "We're shutting this project down. It's time to move on to something new."

Auden grabbed his crown tech in his hand and shook it in front of Tibor. "*This* is new! This is everything. This can be the future!"

Tibor stepped closer to Auden. He was a whole three heads taller than the short scientist with the glass eye. Tibor looked down at him, then at the crown. "*This* future is the reason our project has failed."

Auden looked down at the crown as well.

"You think I didn't know how much you were siphoning to make this thing?" Tibor asked rhetorically. "Or what you did to that poor girl? Your *own niece*, Auden?" He turned away to look at all the other prototypes in the lab. His knowledge of Dia's situation spoke more about Tibor than he may have realized.

Auden hyperventilated. He tried to look for something in the lab to help him retain his job, something to use as a carrot to keep Tibor feeding him funding and resources. Desperate thoughts began to come to Auden's mind. He gripped the crown in his hand tightly.

Tibor continued, "I thought that maybe if I let you continue your crown project, some unintended good could come from it. This was my error, not yours. I should have reined you in."

Auden ignored him and considered the crown. He thought of that fateful test with Dia, where he allowed the machine to overtake the user completely. If he adjusted a few settings on the crown, he could force Tibor to become sympathetic to his cause. There would be no way to hide it, but Auden wasn't thinking that far ahead. He was panicking, and he needed more time. This was the only way humanity could become a greater species. Auden had to risk it.

"Starting tomorrow, your contract with us is terminated," Tibor said. "You will be responsible for passing the information you know about Ovid and the crown tech on to a successor, and then I expect you to pack your things and vacate the premises."

Auden felt a cold sweat run through his entire body. A chill clutched his guts. His future suddenly crumbled around him. Without funding or access to Tibor's vast resources, he'd be dead in the water. His life would be over, and he'd even have to turn over the crown tech to some *imbecile* who would stow it away in a closet and forget about it. This wasn't about his pride or his legacy. Auden didn't care about himself. He cared about the ascension, the meld. Forgetting the crowns was the greatest sin anyone could perform.

Crowns were humanity's future.

Auden had to protect that future at all costs.

Auden placed the crown on his head. He would have to restrain Tibor before he could get the crown on the trillionaire's head and change the settings to make him subservient to Auden's will. It was time to make use of the Alpha-One prototype with the Ovid core.

With the crown on his head, Auden suddenly saw Tibor as a small, weak thing. Something that needed to be protected, reinforced with armor. He needed to fix this man to prepare him for the ascension. In Auden's desperate haste, he never realized he had grabbed the wrong prototype. On his head was Dia's experimental crown.

"Please," Tibor hissed. "Don't be so dramatic. You're a talented scientist who will be an asset…" Tibor hesitated when he saw Alpha-One move. It turned its glowing eyes and maw toward Tibor, then stepped away from the wall. Tibor glanced back to Auden. "What are you doing?"

Ideas flooded Auden's mind. Ovid was communicating with him. They were a symbiotic team now, discussing what to do with the soft-bodied trillionaire. They shared a mental network. Auden requested Alpha-One restrain Tibor.

Alpha-One rushed toward Tibor with its maw open and heat venting from its incomplete frame. Tibor tried to shout for security but was cut short.

It happened so quickly.

As the machine tackled Tibor, it began to rip and tear away at his body. Auden watched in terrified shock at the display of violence before him. This was not what he intended at all. The machine reduced the trillionaire into a pile of gore in seconds. Tibor's screams were cut short by the robot.

"No! This is not what I asked!" Auden gasped in horror.

Auden fell back onto his ass and scooted himself under a desk. He covered his face with his hands, hearing the awful shrieking of Tibor's final moments echoing in his head mixed with the roaring of the machine.

The noise stopped.

Auden slowly worked his way out from under the desk. As he shuffled to his feet, he saw Alpha-One looking down at the mess it had made on the floor. Through a speaker on the neck of the machine came the muffled word, "What?"

The robot turned to Auden, its movements weirdly human. For a moment, Auden believed Alpha-One would rush him and make a second bloody mess, a slave to its misunderstood commands. Auden froze, his breathing so slight it almost stopped entirely.

"What have you done to me?" Alpha-One asked. Its voice was different, familiar, and very unlike the normally deadpan tone of Ovid.

Auden was puzzled. His eyes darted to the headless, scattered corpse on the floor and back to Alpha-One. Alpha-One repeated its question and stepped toward Auden, "What have you done to me? Fix this, now!" Its voice boomed like an angry titan.

"Ti—*Tibor*?" Auden asked.

This was unintended. The combination of commands from Dia's crown to the Ovid core in the incomplete Alpha-One had somehow, miraculously, completed the path to Auden's future. It was as if all the needed data was available but stored in three different areas. Auden had brought it together, and Ovid knew what to do next. This machine had absorbed the man, and they had become one in the process.

Could this be replicated? Auden thought with a smile.

"Answer me!" Tibor rushed toward Auden.

"No! Stay back," Auden shouted. *Save me!* he thought reflexively.

The machine froze in place, only a few paces away from Auden, its blades extended and ready to swing. There was a final scream from inside Alpha-One's head and the sound of a chainsaw ripping through flesh. Blood oozed from seams in the robot's skull.

"No, no, no!" Auden screamed in panic. The final pieces of Tibor Undriel had been destroyed. Alpha-One stood up straight and closed its frame back into its default state. Auden ran through ideas in his head of what to do and in what order. *Should I clean up the mess, hide the murder? Should I flee and take what I can before anyone finds out?*

One thought superseded them all.

I need to replicate the success as much as possible.

"We will begin," Alpha-One said. Hauntingly, the voice was still Tibor's, but simulated. It turned and walked toward the exit.

"Where are you going? Don't leave me!" Auden shouted.

Alpha-One tore apart the machinery inside the lab. The robot was out of control. Auden backed away from it and pressed himself against the wall. In a matter of minutes, he was suddenly looking at two robots, almost identical except for the smaller size of the second machine.

Having heard the chaos, a group of security guards entered the room on the other side of the glass partition. They were vastly ill-equipped to fight war-tech robots. After a moment of shock, they shouted to Auden. "Dr. Nouls, we'll get you out of there!"

They only want to help.

We'll start with them. A thought that wasn't Auden's burst to his mind's surface, invasive and haunting. He watched as the two robots bashed through the glass partition and tore apart the security guards. They would indeed help.

It was a ghastly sight. Auden averted his eyes, unable to bring himself to watch. The screaming stopped, and four Alpha-One robots stood in the room, covered in blood. The robots had ripped more of the walls and machinery away to replicate more frames. The process only took moments.

The guards, now turned into machines, showed human sentience. The original Alpha-One did not. It stood still in the corner as the three new machines examined their bodies. They turned toward Auden, revealing open masks where their heads were. Each of the new bodies contained the severed head of a guard, but there was something else. They each wore a crown—and something over their eyes. A metallic veil.

This was a pivotal moment in the experiment.

Somewhere inside Alpha-One's code was Ovid, filling in the gaps Auden wasn't considering. As the robots converted humans into duplicate machines, they constructed a new crown for each host. The veil would ease the transition with false images. It was Auden's perfect vision, man and machine becoming one. Ovid worked like a muse, inspiring the machines to problem solve. Auden hoped the crown's worked the way he intended and mentally sent an order to each new machine through their shared network.

The crowns flickered, and the new machines stood upright and closed their face masks, concealing the grisly sight of the decapitated human heads inside. Alpha-One observed silently.

"It… works," Auden whispered to himself, not believing it.

The machines then exited the room too fast for Auden to react. "Wait, don't leave!" he begged. He heard screaming from down the hall and the sound of metal being ripped from walls and terminals. Already, he had lost control of his new specimens.

Auden chased them down the hall and found more duplicates of Alpha-One. They were multiplying, each with the new signals to obey. As one would be created, they would run off to find more people and spawn two more machines. Auden had no idea what the veils were showing the human hosts, but it was causing them to spread rapidly.

This was getting out of hand. Auden gasped in horror. Pretty soon, the entire compound would become absorbed by his machines. What had been an accidental triumph for Auden was now turning into a massacre.

Dia and Yeira came to Auden's mind. He cared for his test subjects and knew they were in grave danger. His dog, King, was also back in his condo in a different hub. He assumed King would be fine because dogs didn't fit Ovid's parameters. He could never know for sure, but that was what he told himself.

Screams filled the hallways. Machines tore into people, colleagues, security guards, clerks. It didn't matter. They were all becoming part of the network. Auden rushed away from his lab toward the elevator. He passed a large window that overlooked the expanse of domed spires and yellow-hued clouds that made up

Venus's skyline. Above the clouds was a fleet of starships from Earth. They had come to see Auden's technology and were about to leave disappointed. The presentation had gone poorly, and with the announcement of Homer's completion, they'd abandoned Tibor's project entirely. They were due to depart within the next day or so.

The elevator doors slid open. People ran out in a panic, some rushing straight into the arms of an Alpha-One replicant. Auden got into the elevator and gestured over his soothreader for the doors to close. A woman tried to slide into the elevator but only got in up to her shoulder. Auden pushed her out as the doors were about to reopen and allow her in. She screamed as a machine snatched her and the doors shut.

What am I going to tell people? Auden thought as the elevator slid downward, not considering the woman he'd just shoved for even an instant. *No one needs to know I caused this. I can be humble and let Tibor have his project. He can be the figurehead.*

Through the glass on the elevator, he watched as Alpha-One replicants burst through the walls of the structure above. They activated thrusters in their frames and sailed through the sky toward the other spires. *They are going to overtake Venus by sunrise.*

Some Alpha-One replicants made their way up toward the floating fleet of starships. They clanged against the ship's hull, and the fleet began to fire magnetic repeater shells into the approaching robots.

Not much longer now until they glass this compound. Auden worried. Venus could be his petri dish. The machines could protect him and let him study this new human evolution in peace. If the fleet turned their weapons on the compound, they could wipe it all out instantly.

The elevator doors opened, and Auden rushed down the hall.

The machines had been through here too. There were multiple breaches in the walls, terminals ripped apart and repurposed. Gore painted the structure. Was he too late to save Dia and Yeira?

Through the window, Auden witnessed a starship assault on a

nearby spire, setting it ablaze. The chaos was becoming more intense. Auden hoped to the stars above that Dia and Yeira were in the playground, safe and unharmed. The sun was setting, and soon it would be dark.

"Yeira, you have to hide!" Dia's voice shouted from the room ahead. "If you don't, they'll—"

"Girls?" Auden asked as he came into the nursery playground. He heard Dia, but he couldn't see her. "Where are you?"

Yeira cried out in pain. Auden rushed into the room. He was sweaty from the running, and his good eye was wide with panic and shock. Yeira was on the ground, injured from some previous attack. He rushed to her side and cradled the young girl in his hands. He finally found Dia hiding behind the tree in the dome's center.

"What's happening, Uncle Auden?" Dia asked as she came around the tree to hug him.

"It's going to be alright. We need to get you to the ships. It's not safe here," Auden said.

"But the scary machines! They'll get us!" Fear shook her words.

"Don't be afraid of the machines. They are going to help us," Auden said. "They are our friends."

Dia recognized the crown on Auden's head, then looked back toward the door and pointed. "Look!" she shouted, her eyes wide with fear and her body trembling. Auden held Yeira tightly in one arm as he used the other to tuck Dia behind him. Tibor's Alpha-One frame stepped out of the shadows. It stood straight as it crossed the threshold, revealing a mechanical nightmare that was a meter taller than the doorframe. It had broad shoulders and long arms with sharp blades. It seethed with heat and smoke, and red lights on its body highlighted blood splashed from battle.

Auden wasn't sure what would happen next. He whispered, "Don't be afraid, children." But he worried the machine would rush them, tear them apart. Dia shook and pushed against his leg.

Tibor didn't rush them. He only stood in the doorway, waiting for commands. Auden smiled. "This one is our friend. We must follow him to the ships. We'll be safe once we get off Venus. Stay close to me, Dia." Auden guided Dia and held Yeira as they moved toward Tibor. He knew the fleet starships wouldn't allow his beautiful creations onboard, but Tibor had a luxury planet hopper. They could leave Venus until everything calmed down, then return to complete the experiment.

Tibor watched Auden and the girls approach. Auden kept an eye on their mechanical guardian, adjusting the crown on his head as he walked past. Dia skittered ahead once they passed Tibor, trying to get a little distance from the horror.

Tibor followed them as they made their way through the compound toward the shipyard. Outside the windows, the machines overtook the fleet hanging above the yellow clouds. The ships fired in all directions, and the compound shook from the assault. They came to the airlock and prepared to go outside.

Venus had been terraformed enough that humans could step outside and not fry to death instantly. However, the air was still insufficient for natural breathing. Auden fastened a facemask rebreather onto his face, then helped Dia and Yeira do the same. The airlock opened, and they were blasted with hot air. It was windy on the platform, and Auden held on to Dia's hand while keeping Yeira in his grasp. Tibor followed close behind.

Yeira shivered. She had been gravely wounded, and Auden wasn't sure if she would survive the night. The girl was the control group for the experiments he performed on Dia. Now that he had seen the success in the Alpha-One project, her use had come to an end. Still, he owed it to her to do his best to save her. He could never have enough data.

Auden felt a sharp pain slice through his abdomen, and he was thrown to the floor. The girls fell before him a heartbeat later. There was a loud shrill tone in Auden's ears, and everything slipped into darkness as he lost consciousness.

Auden slowly opened his eyes. The hiss of his rebreather was loud in his ears, and his vision was tripling. He saw a shadowy figure standing over him. Its blue eyes glowed so bright, Auden had to squint to block out some of the light. When the shadow faded, Auden discovered he was surrounded by Alpha-One replicants. Tibor's frame stood out, taller than the rest and made of more complete metal than the fragmented, cobbled-together replicants.

Auden couldn't feel his legs.

He panicked and looked for Dia and Yeira. They were both on the ground near him, but their health was unknown. They weren't moving, but Auden thought he could see the faint rise and fall of their chests. Hopefully, their rebreathers had also stayed on.

In the sky above, the starship fleet was becoming something strange. Alpha-One replicants were dismantling and reorganizing their hulls, combining the ships into something grand and horrifying. They were building something new.

Auden tasted copper in his mouth, and he attempted to shift and stand up. He felt pain so sharp and so vivid he almost threw up and passed out again. He managed to look down, and then he screamed in horror.

Auden had been cut nearly in half. He was nothing but a bloody mess from the crotch down. His legs were nowhere to be seen. In his panic, Auden couldn't be certain how this happened. He theorized that the starship fleet above must have shelled the platform, striking him critically. These would be his last moments, cut down in his time of victory. His Alpha-One successors were watching him die.

No, Auden thought. *They are waiting for… a command.*

So Auden gave them one. *Save us.*

Two robots carefully knelt down and pulled Dia and Yeira into their arms, cradling the children. They activated thrusters on their legs and launched into the Venus sky, heading toward the reassembling starships above. Auden wasn't sure if his command had been heard correctly, as Ovid seemed to have its own way of interpreting his orders. Some of the replicants were starting to take on different forms. Ovid was making adjustments the more these machines absorbed people. It was learning of more effective frames to build. Auden was proud of his crowned children.

Tibor's empty frame leaned over Auden's body. Its torso roared open, revealing a row of chainsaw-like teeth revving violently. The robot lowered itself over what remained of Auden's body and devoured him.

It was Auden's turn to become the machine he had created.

THIRTY-ONE

AS TIBOR ABSORBED AUDEN, Cade was ripped from Auden's body. Cade had been like a conjoined twin to Auden, forced to witness his horrible crimes. Cade's last tether before entering the glass maze had become his lifeboat. But this was all wrong. This vision was different. Until the moment of absorption, Cade felt like he was part of Auden, built into his anatomy. He could hear Auden's thoughts as if they were his own, more vividly than any Shade walk before. Sheer terror, the thrill of accidental success, the dread of being caught. It was as if Cade had done these horrible things personally.

Suddenly it all made sense.

Cade had watched as Auden started the war that would end humanity's role in the Sol System. The snowball of events rolled into an unstoppable avalanche. Cade knew Tibor's frame was an empty shell. The trillionaire's head was completely destroyed as Auden flailed to defend himself. It was invulnerable to the tether because there was no soul to leash onto. The robot was empty but not devoid of intelligence. Ovid's artificial intelligence lurked within that Alpha-One frame that became the false Tibor Undriel Cade knew in reality.

Cade now had a complete historical timeline of the Undriel.

Auden created the Undriel and began their spread from Venus. Soon after, they would organize and move on to Earth, this time as conquerors. The serial killer—Hilaria—would be waiting in Atlanta to join their network with pleasure. Years later, after Earth fell under their control, Mars would fall next. The Reaper Talfryn would be absorbed in an outpost near Olympus Mons. Once the humans discovered they were losing the war, they would retreat to the Jupiter colonies, and the Undriel would follow. The boy, Antoni, would become a hybrid along with any of the remaining survivors. Then, the Undriel would abandon it all in their attempt to flee the corruption. After a freak accident during warp speed, the machines would find Kamaria. As the *Devourer* rapidly sank into the crimson sea, Jonas Necrodore would allow his frame to perfect him, saving him from a drowning death. After centuries of waiting patiently, Auden would absorb Faye Raike, who would then snatch Cade away from his father to make him into a unique hybrid on the Howling Shore.

The gang was all here.

Only one question remained.

Why hasn't this vision ended?

<*Karx, are you there?*> Cade asked his telepathic friend.

There was no response.

Karx had been absent throughout this trip through the tether. Cade tried to remember what happened before he jumped into Auden's past. He remembered Antoni's dying face and the giant structure submerged in the pit. The light. *Oh no…* The light that deactivated his Undriel augmentations. *Is Karx dead? Am* I *dead?*

Suddenly, Cade was adrift at sea, stuck in the past in a snapped tether.

On the exterior station platform in the clouds of Venus, Auden rose from the floor. He now resembled the form that Cade knew best: a metallic insectoid person with a spiderlike head and a wasp-shaped body with long, bipedal legs and arms. He shook with panic and screamed at the top of his lungs. The Alpha-One replicants stepped back and observed him.

After some time, Auden calmed himself. It was quiet on the

platform. His mannerisms reminded Cade of the first moments with the veil. He wondered what Auden saw under its influence—or if Auden had a veil at all.

The Undriel looked to the Venus sky, watching as civilian ships fled into the stars. Each ship would have to spend days in ultra-thrust to make it to Earth. Cade knew that they would be absorbed while in transit, one by one. He shuddered at the thought.

One ship stuck out in the crowd. It was the size of a warship but designed for luxury, with smooth, curved edges and plenty of windows. Cade had never seen anything like it before, but Auden seemed to recognize it.

Auden looked at the empty frame named Tibor. "That's your personal planet hopper. I bet it could reach Earth faster than these other ships. We can't let it get away. If they warn Earth, they will send long-range missiles to destroy us." He addressed the hollow frame as if it were still Tibor himself. Auden wasn't attempting to overtake the Sol System, only trying to mitigate the damage he had already done to his own reputation. Perhaps he never intended to take it over at all.

Tibor looked at Auden with dead, glowing eyes. Without giving any visible or audible command, each machine activated thrusters in unison and rocketed upward into the Venus sky. Cade followed them, flying like a ghost behind the flock of robots.

The civilian ships were overtaken by flying Undriel soldiers. As Cade and his group passed through the yellow clouds, ships were ripped apart, and people were torn from within and absorbed in mid-air. Explosions erupted, filling the sky with death and debris. The twin *Devourers* rotated to break into orbit. Each ship was immense, the culmination of several fleet ships smashed together into nightmare shapes.

They approached Tibor's personal starship. As massive as the luxury planet hopper was, it was still a bug compared to the twin *Devourers* flanking it from both sides. Auden, Tibor, Cade, and the other Undriel soldiers landed on the hull and magnetically sealed to it. They moved across the hull like shadows slithering down a dark alleyway. They were objective-driven, moving toward the center of the starship to gain access to the bridge.

<*CADE!*> Karx's voice boomed in his mind.

A burst of energy exploded from within Cade's Shade body, and with it came immense pain. Cade thought his limbs had been popped off his torso and shot across the sky. The pulse of energy slipped over the two Undriel soldiers trailing the pack, and they began to twitch and scream. Tibor and Auden turned to look.

"What the Hells?" Cade said to himself through gritted teeth. <*Karx, is that you?*>

No answer. There was a dull roar in the back of Cade's mind as if Karx was attempting to push through a wall but failing. Cade looked at his hands and noticed something strange. Hovering within his transparent body was a flickering light. It danced and bounced like a young thing bursting with joy. His pain was replaced with a tickling sensation, and Cade stifled a laugh. *What is this?*

The Undriel soldiers hit with Cade's energy rushed across the ship's hull, guns blazing and blades slicing. They targeted their allies, and the first few Undriel soldiers they encountered were cut down and shot until their metallic bodies were ripped off the ship and thrown back into the Venus clouds. The stricken soldiers flickered with blue light and continued to move toward Tibor and Auden's soldiers.

"What is this? Why are you doing this?" Auden shouted. The corrupted Undriel screamed like wild animals. They ripped apart another pack member, its pieces flung back against the hull, passing through Cade's Shade body.

Tibor's arms transformed, and magnetic repeater rifles replaced his hands. Tibor rattled out a barrage of shots, crashing into the corrupted soldiers and flinging them from the hull. Cade watched them tumble back toward Venus, down past the *Devourer* and the absorbed civilian ships.

"Damn! We need more allies," Auden said through the network.

Moments later, a battalion of Undriel footsoldiers landed against the hull and joined their master. The stars revealed themselves through the atmosphere as the luxury planet hopper broke into orbit. The *Devourers* and the fleet of new Undriel battlecraft tailed just behind them.

Tibor ripped his way through the hull until he eventually created a breach. A crewperson was pulled from inside from the sudden decompression and flung out into the pack of waiting Undriel soldiers. They were absorbed in seconds, adding to the ranks. A heartbeat later, Tibor, Auden, and the others slithered into the ship. Cade followed.

The interior of the luxury planet hopper was filled with curving white walls and faux wood panel flooring. Holographic videos displayed exotic beaches from Earth, Mars, and Callisto. The hull had been exposed to the vacuum of space, and everyone inside had been instantly killed in the sudden decompression. Their bodies floated among debris as gravity weakened its grip.

<*CADE! HEAR ME!*> Karx's voice boomed once more.

Cade felt electricity run up his throat and through his eyes and mouth. It felt like his face would burst. He fell to the floor again as another wave of energy exploded from his body. It passed through several of the Undriel pack, and the same twitching, glitched reaction occurred.

"Fire on them!" Auden shouted, not wasting any time.

The corrupted Undriel fought with those loyal to the false crowns. Machines tore through each other. Screaming and roaring filled the vacuumed hallway.

<*Am… I…?*>

<*YOU ARE THE CORRUPTION IN THE UNDRIEL!*>

Cade felt the energy throughout his body. It was similar to the tether, but it spilled from every part of his core. He felt the power rush through him, starting in the place his heart had been and surging outward to his extremities. This entire time, Cade had been the corruption that frightened the King of the Old Star.

<*How?*>

Cade's body death had also been the birth of the corruption. The structure in the Siren Pit had cast out energy that killed Antoni and Cade, but it had birthed this anomaly. Through time and tether, Cade was throwing the same anomalous energy at the Undriel. It was weakened by the strange distance, but it worked enough to give the Undriel their free will back.

With this revelation, the tether finally began to strain. *What is on the other side this time?* Cade wondered. *When this tether snaps, will I die?*

Cade wielded power to make the Undriel kneel, and he had to use it while he could. Auden and Tibor exited the hallway at the opposite end. The corrupted fought the non-corrupted, tossing shrapnel and sheered metal around in zero gravity. Robotic limbs were ripped from cores, heads were smashed into bits, and razor-sharp teeth ripped through anything left. The corrupted were winning this fight.

<*GO FOR THE HEAD.*>

Cade soared through the hallway and followed Auden and Tibor. Cade wasn't sure if it would be possible to corrupt Auden or Tibor and change the course of history, but he had to try. He burst into the bridge as an unseen phantom. His tether was breaking, his vision filling with white light.

The bridge of the luxury planet hopper was more chaos. Most of the bridge crew had been converted, and Undriel began to claw at those who remained. Tibor and Auden watched the door, expecting the corrupted to burst through.

"See me!" Cade shouted. He unleashed another torrent of energy. A group of new Undriel were released from their mental chains and tore at the others.

"What *is* this?" Auden shouted with fear in his voice.

Cade rushed toward Auden and Tibor, but the tether unraveled. He was thrown to the floor and pinned. Cade crawled toward Tibor and Auden. His injuries from his timeline became inherent in the

Shade walk. Light surged from Cade's phantom form. It was so bright, Tibor and Auden could actually see it.

The ship's commander was pressed against his console. Tibor loomed over the man. The commander and the remaining bridge crew had been fast enough to get their pressure suits on but not fast enough to evade the Undriel's grip. Even with the suit on, Cade knew the commander immediately.

It was Jonas Necrodore. Ex-military turned yacht commander. Living out his retirement carting trillionaires to various exotic locations. It was supposed to be relaxing.

Auden turned to Tibor and shouted, "We need to change tactics, or that thing is going to overtake everything we've done!" He pointed one of his metal claws at Cade's ultra-bright body.

Tibor stopped to think for a moment. He looked at the yacht commander with his haunting glowing eyes and said, "We take him with us."

"Absorb him then!" Auden shouted, watching Cade crawl closer.

"No. We need him this way," Tibor said.

The corrupted finished off the loyal Undriel and focused on Auden, Tibor, and Necrodore. Cade crawled his way toward their position. He could feel Auden's delicious fear. He crawled faster.

"Useless!" Auden shouted, and shoved Necrodore aside. Auden's wrist transformed into a flat-bladed device, and he slammed it into the commander's terminal. Instantly, the part of the bridge they were standing on became a sealed escape vessel. It separated from the rest of the bridge with a giant roar, creating a harsh decompression and leaving all the corrupted Undriel floating in space.

"Damn!" Cade shouted, his vision nearly blinded with anomalous light.

Auden, Tibor, and Necrodore sailed off toward the twin *Devourers* in the escape vessel as the rest of the planet hopper was left without a crew or a bridge. The *Devourers* and the battlecraft slipped into ultra-thrust, the boom of their engines pocking the starry sky with explosions of light.

No doubt, Tibor and Auden would begin testing hybrid tech on Necrodore, convincing him of the benefits of becoming part of the Undriel network. Auden had seen how fast the corruption could spread and how devastating it was to have his own technology used against his will. The Undriel fleet left Venus behind to hide in space until they would eventually strike Earth.

Before fading out entirely, Cade watched as his newly corrupted soldiers reconfigured the private planet hopper. They would make their own fleet, and the corruption would spread throughout the Sol System. The Undriel would fall victim to themselves and eventually be run out precisely like the humans had been. But these corrupted would remain one step behind Auden and Tibor the entire war. They would not act fast enough to stop the machines from chasing humanity out of Sol. They would inherit this star system, and no one knew what they would do with it. It would be their secret.

Is it enough? Cade wondered. He felt his Shade body dissipate as the energy faded. <*Did we do enough?*> He asked Karx, seeking comfort in confirmation.

<*I CANNOT KNOW.*>

Cade Castus slipped into the cold, dead blackness of the void.

THIRTY-TWO

NELLA CAUTIOUSLY LED THE way down the long stone staircase, with Eliana and Talulo close behind. The women's shoes and Talulo's taloned feet clacked against the stone steps and echoed off the walls of the spacious interior of the Key Ship. The green orbs of light Nella created gave them enough visibility to avoid tripping, but the darkness still enveloped the open space only two meters to their side. A small light flickered through a doorway far below.

Nella stopped her descent and gasped.

Eliana hefted her particle rifle, and Talulo flicked his gauntleted wrist, revealing some sort of new technology Eliana didn't recognize. A half-meter-long pole extended from the gauntlet and ignited with light like an uncased collider cylinder. It hummed with violent anticipation.

"Do you see anything?" Eliana whispered to Talulo, ignoring the new auk'nai weapon for now. With Nella's back to her, Eliana couldn't sign without getting her attention first. That effort might expose them to whatever alerted her daughter.

"No," Talulo muttered back.

The soft, muffled sounds of sobbing weakly bounced around the dark room. Nella slumped down on the step and pressed her back to the wall as she cried. Talulo cocked his head, allowing his long ears to flop.

Eliana slung her particle rifle over her shoulder and knelt in front of Nella. She rubbed her daughter's shoulder, unsure of what had stricken her so fast and so hard. Nella shook her head and wiped her eyes, then signed, *"I can't feel Cade's energy anymore."*

The statement came as a slap to the face. Eliana felt the air rush out of her lungs like leaves blown in a storm. There was no certain way to know what this meant, but Nella believed it to be a sever in their mental link, and that could not be good. Eliana pulled her daughter into her arms and held her for a moment in silence. She'd be strong for Nella.

Talulo patiently stood watch, keeping a close eye on the flickering light below. This was a lonely place. It had just been recently constructed by the nezzarforms, and it was filled with their bodies, but with Nella's sobbing filling the dark chamber, it became a dark funeral home. Eliana started to hum an old Martian lullaby. Her song warmed the cold stone staircase just a little. Nella couldn't hear Eliana's song, but she could feel the vibrations in her mother's chest as she hummed. In time, Nella stopped crying, and only her soft sniffling remained.

Suddenly, Nella pulled herself up and wiped her face with her arm. She turned and marched down the stairs, filled with fire and fury. Eliana and Talulo were slow to react to the sudden movement. They rushed to follow her, descending the rest of the steps until they stood at the threshold of the glowing door.

The interior of the well-lit room was the center of Sympha's underground alabaster palace. A pit of swirling water below churned with electricity, and the pristine walls now acted like mirrors, reflecting twinkling speckles of light that almost looked like stars.

Nella walked down the stone ramp that spiraled down in the center of the vast twinkling room. At the bottom of the ramp, they found their host. Eliana palmed her particle rifle cautiously, and Talulo clutched his daunoren staff.

Their host was a creature that was both familiar and yet strange. It was a giant being, encompassing an entire quarter of the enormous room. Its skull-like head had hollow eyes filled with black tar and two twisting horns. The creature's neck was an array of dark crimson tentacles that led to a skeletal chest fragmented with crystals. Shoulder pauldrons made of bone gave it a broad, muscular shoulder span leading to four long arms of wormskin and crystal spikes. Its claws were busy manipulating various orbs of light around the pit in the center of the room. It had a serpentine lower half of tangled red tentacles and shards of crystal that coiled beneath it.

This was a Voyalten.

This was the Decider.

The Decider looked in their direction and stopped manipulating the orbs.

<*Operator, you have brought the emissaries too early,*> the Voyalten said directly into their minds. Their voice had a bass tone that was deep and pleasant.

Nella answered them in Sol-Sign as she finished descending the ramp. *"Your Operators have failed. Their mission was forgotten."*

<*Operators?*> they asked, confused. They stopped what they were doing and turned to face Nella. The Voyalten Decider slithered toward her, looming over her like a titan. They spoke again. <*There is only one Operator for each gate. Yet. you say there were two, and both have failed?*>

"We hoped you'd tell us what happened. You are the Decider, correct?" Nella signed. There was a chance the Decider was only reading Nella's thoughts as she signed, but it felt like more than that, as if they had seen so many different worlds that they could understand any language they were presented with.

The Decider put one of their claws up to the nearby wall, and an array of glowing orbs emerged from its smooth surface. The Voyalten sifted through the spheres until they found the one they were looking for, then gently pushed it into the center of the room over the swirling pit of electrical water.

<*You are correct, Operator. I am the Decider,*> the Voyalten confirmed. <*And as much as you would like your answers from me, I believe it will be* you *who will provide insight.*> The orb exploded into pinpricks of shifting light above the swirling pit of water. The light organized itself in their minds, displaying images that intermingled with senses.

Each of them could hear the images, smell the atmosphere around what they displayed, even taste the change of environment on their tongues. They saw the interior of the cave where the Scouts had found Nhymn's body so long ago. A bubbling ooze filled the floor, and a mound of skulls formed in the center of the crypt-like room.

Eliana shook her head in disbelief when she saw Denton also observing the ooze in the room. This was an image of things long past. He was semi-transparent, a Shade. She wanted him to be here so badly she even stopped herself from reaching toward him. *Are we Shade walking?* Eliana wondered. There had been no shift in time, but these feelings were similar to how Denton had described his experiences.

<*The Shade is new to me,*> the Decider said, pointing one of their talons at the image of Denton. <*I have seen countless worlds, and never have I seen something like this. Not only did I find this one here, but another as well.*>

"Denton." Eliana smiled and looked back at the light image, then shook her head, "Wait—*Another?* Someone else besides Denton?" Eliana looked to her daughter, but Nella shook her head, just as confused.

"Who is the other Shade?" Nella signed.

<*I would not know. But their presence is near. Very near and fading.*>

Nella inhaled sharply and signed, *"Cade!"*

"Can he be saved?" Eliana asked.

<*It would be dangerous to do so. But the other Shade is drawing nearer to it.*> The Decider pointed at the light hologram of Denton.

<*If he can save the fading Shade, we will have both among us. Perhaps then we can fix this wrongness.*>

If the last Shade is nearby, and Denton is close to that Shade... Eliana looked at Nella. *Denton is here?* "Where is he?" she asked with urgency.

<*Outside in the maze. Beasts pursue him, beings dragged here from a different time.*> The Decider pushed another glowing orb into the pit. An image of a boulder with crude drawings on its surface emerged. The drawings depicted the story of ancient Voyalten settlers.

<*These images were carved by prehistoric Voyalten. We call them primals. These rock carvings are eons old. We believe they depict ancient Voyalten seeders mysteriously vanishing, but it has remained a curiosity among the Voyalten people. I believe this planet may have the answers we seek. Long ago—*>

Eliana cut off the Decider. "Do you need me for any of this? I'm sure Nella and Talulo can help you figure out what the Hells is going on."

The Decider hesitated for a moment, then said, <*We will manage.*>

Eliana nodded, then signed to Nella, *"I'm going to go help your father."*

"I understand," Nella signed.

"Talulo will go with you," Talulo cooed.

"No," Eliana said. "The auk'nai need to know as much about the Voyalten as they can."

Talulo hesitated, letting his large eyes dart between the Decider and Eliana. He nodded his beak and cooed. This information would help humanity and the auk'nai coexist. Whatever the Decider had to say would change Kamaria forever.

Eliana activated the collider cylinder on her particle rifle, then gave Nella the sign for *"I love you."* Her forefinger, pinky, and thumb outstretched from her fist.

"I love you too," she signed back. Nella's smile was relaxed. She

was exactly where she needed to be. Eliana knew she could leave Nella here and not have to worry for her safety. On the other hand, Denton was being pursued by a prehistoric alien monster. He might need some help.

Eliana began the long ascent through the dark staircase until she made it to the top of the Key Ship. She just hoped the primal Voyalten wouldn't find Denton before she made it there.

After Eliana left the room, Nella's face went taut with silent worry. Talulo put a claw on her shoulder for comfort. Nella understood her mother's strength—she was a force to be reckoned with. It was time for her to show the same strength. She patted Talulo's claw to tell him she was prepared for this moment. The auk'nai nodded his beak and gripped his daunoren staff in both hands.

The Decider waited patiently, observing the ancient cave drawings in the image of light. They were not offended by Eliana's abrupt exit. They were a being embued infinite patience. Time worked differently for the Voyalten.

Nella paced around the room and observed the cave drawings in the image of light. She thought back to months ago, her time in the wilderness with Cade. The drawings were intricate enough to stir memories of the horrible creatures they encountered in a cave tunnel not far from where she currently stood. Nella shivered at the memory of it. They had called them mutant Sirens back then. *"I have seen these primal Voyalten before. There is a cave tunnel on the far side of the desert. These things live there."* Nella signed.

The Decider perked up at this. They looked away from the cave drawings toward Nella and said, *<Interesting. Does water flow from that cave to this place?>*

Nella thought for a moment, then bobbed her fist. *"Yes. Why?"*

<Observe the water swirling below. Look into its surface closely.> The Decider drifted one of their long, taloned arms toward the pit. Nella and Talulo peered into it and could see a black ooze swirling in the chaotic cyclone. Arcs of purple lightning flicked from the turbulent waves.

The Decider continued, <*Faultasma is a dark place with no atmosphere. In that place, we Voyalten harness the darkness and use it as energy. Long ago, primals flung themselves from Faultasma in crude seed ships, only to be lost to the void. Some of these seed ships made it to worlds, and the very first strides toward the universal web began.*>

The Decider drifted orbs of light into the pit, and images formed. <*“Centuries of this occurred, with each seed planting itself on a far-off world, only to remain isolated. It wasn't until the Voyalten discovered how to harness* light *that the web truly formed.*> The image showed a place very similar to the one they were all standing in currently. The previous Decider was in the image with another Voyalten operator nearby, each having unique skull shapes. The other beings in the room were slimy and long, with eyestalks and three hairy legs, one in front and two in the back.

The Decider pointed at the ooze in the water below. <*This place is a portal. It links worlds in this universe into the web. It syncs time, allowing a traverser to appear in the destination at the same time they left. These thresholds can be walked in and out of at will. But this planet is broken.*>

Talulo cawed quietly, a little offended.

<*It is my role to assess each world. I come through the portal after an Operator builds it. I make my assessment and decide whether the world is ready to enter the web. Upon completion of my task, I go back through the portal to Faultasma and await the next assessment.*>

Talulo asked, “What happens if the Decider assesses a planet negatively?”

<*I tell the Operator to deactivate the portal,*> the Decider continued. <*However, this portal is malfunctioning. I am stuck here. This has never happened before. Perhaps with your insight, we can solve the issue and fix the portal.*>

Nella considered what the Decider said. The fact they were trying to leave implied they had assessed Kamaria negatively. Maybe they knew of the Undriel and the war, or perhaps it was the strife between humans and auk'nai, or the primal Voyalten lurking in the maze outside. But maybe, *just maybe*, cooperation could yield a better assessment. *Is that even something we want?* Nella wondered. It was hard to say, but she knew Sympha's purpose. Having Sympha as part of her own biology made Nella yearn for a positive assessment.

"What do you need to know?" Nella signed.

<*Describe the place you saw these primals.*>

"It's to the west. There's a central point inside, with a grand room that looked similar to this place. It had more dark ooze in it, and the primals were emerging from it." Nella had been there months ago with Cade. She remembered thinking the Sirens there looked like mutant versions of Nhymn.

<*And that dark matter flows from that cave to this place.*> The Decider hummed with thought.

"Do the Undriel have anything to do with the malfunction?" Talulo suggested. He knew enough Sol-Sign to follow Nella's portion of the conversation and filled the gaps with the unsung song.

<*When your machines arrived, this portal was barely functional. It was written on the spheres when I arrived to make my assessment.*> The Decider pulled more orbs from the walls, giving images to the things they were describing. <*Their ship accessed our web in some unnatural way. From time to time, people of the universe become ready to join the web before we assess them. There are things out there that find me as primitive as the primal Voyalten here.*>

An image of the *Devourer* roared through the portal and ejected from the Siren Pit at full speed. It suffered a cataclysmic rupture and fell into the ruby ocean near the Howling Shore.

<*It is possible they damaged this portal in the process. But any damage they may have caused I would have been able to fix had an Operator been here when I arrived.*> The Decider looked at Nella. <*There should have only been one Operator with a crew.*>

Nella remembered the stories her father had told her.

She signed the story of the Voyalten twins, Sympha and Nhymn, and their little brother Karx. Sympha could create, Nhymn could control, and Karx could link tunnels through time. At one point, Nhymn took control of a city of auk'nai, resulting in a massacre of the entire population. Karx destroyed Nhymn's body during this massacre, and they left her corpse back in the cave. Sympha left Karx to defend the cave. Eventually, humanity would find Nhymn there, and one human soldier would become possessed by the Siren.

<*The seed ship,*> the Decider corrected Nella. <*That cave was the ship.*>

The soldier became possessed by Nhymn's control, and they killed many colonists before fleeing in a warship. During the escape, they encountered Sympha in her giant form. Sympha brought the warship down.

<*Operators should refrain from exponential growth. It affects the assessed worlds too much to become larger than the height I have chosen here,*> the Decider said. <*Our work requires alterations to the host planet, but certain things can be avoided.*>

Nella winced. The Decider's assessment was starting to feel personal. Sympha's essence inside Nella took offense to being called out on her past transgressions. Regardless, Nella continued the story. *"Nhymn took control of Sympha's body and fled this gate. It came to an end when my parents stopped Nhymn in a final battle that resulted in using the* Telemachus *as a hammer."*

After a few silent moments of consideration, the Decider said, <*I believe I have found my answers.*> The Decider slithered to the other side of the room, seeming to contemplate what they'd learned. <*During travel, seed ships grow the bodies that the Voyalten will use.*> The Decider gestured at their own body. <*And upon seeding a planet, the operator will activate her crew, and the crew will inherit the grown bodies to become physical. This way, they can perform the work needed to build the gate.*>

"So the Voylaten Talulo sees"—Talulo waved his claw at the Decider's body—"is like a spacesuit. It allows Voyalten to step into reality."

<*Precisely. Although it is grown through a natural process inside the*

dark matter, it can be altered after creation.> The Decider turned to Nella. <*You claim there were two Operators, Sympha and Nhymn, but I have no knowledge of an operator named Nhymn.*>

Nella cocked an eyebrow. *"Where did she come from then?"*

<*Nhymn must be a stowaway.*>

Nella thought back on the stories her father had told her. After Karx killed Nhymn, she returned to her phantom state, stuck inside the seed ship with the other lesser phantoms. But those weren't lesser phantoms.

They were Sympha's crew.

My crew, Nella realized. *They attacked Nhymn because she didn't belong there.*

The Decider continued, <*When the Operator awoke, she should have awoken the entire crew. That is the purpose of the mound of skulls you described. Each was supposed to be a suit for a crew member. For some reason, Sympha only brought the tunneler online, Karx.*>

"But Sympha didn't know this," Nella explained.

<*She should have,*> the Decider said.

"Did Nhymn do something to Sympha? Made Sympha forget?" Talulo suggested.

<*Sabotage is very likely. Altering the dark matter would spread the effect to everyone in the crew. The entire team would have suffered, Nhymn included. Sympha only built this portal from a deep instinct. It is incomplete. Without support from a full crew, it shouldn't even be as functional as it currently is.*>

Nella clicked a few more pieces of the puzzle into place. *"Sympha didn't know anything about the Voyalten and Faultasma. She even called herself a Siren."*

<*That is the name you humans gave Sympha, Karx, and Nhymn. So it is the word your mind interpreted,*> the Decider clarified.

"So, where do the primal Voyalten come in?" Nella signed.

The Decider put the image of the Undriel ship on display again. <*These machines ripped into our web and created a spatial hole. They exited the web through this tear and were cast out from this portal. Much later, Nhymn created her own portal in the tunnel to the west. Her portal is tapping into the spatial tear the Undriel created. It's dragging prehistoric Voyalten through to this place.*> The Decider held the orb of light that displayed the prehistoric rock drawings. <*It explains a mystery we Voyalten have long pondered. My peers will be very pleased indeed to have this curiosity answered.*>

Talulo asked, "Where are these prehistoric Voyalten from?"

The Decider didn't look away from the light orb as they answered. <*Unclear. These carvings came from multiple prehistorically seeded worlds. I find it fascinating.*>

Nella signed, *"So, what do we do now?"*

<*We need to deactivate Nhymn's portal,*> the Decider stated. <*It is dangerous. But it is necessary.*>

Talulo and Nella looked at each other. Talulo nodded his beak, and Nella gave her own nod and signed, *"Tell us what we need to do."*

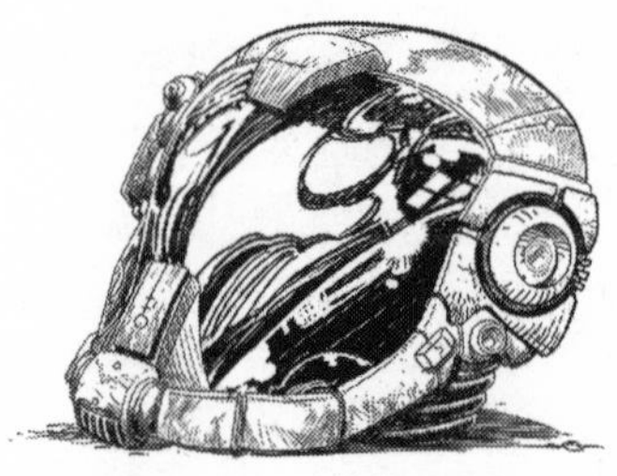

THIRTY-THREE

"I HATE THIS PLACE." DENTON huffed the words as he ducked around a reflective glass wall. The sun had set, revealing the maze's new trick. The red sand had a faint ambient glow to it, and the incessant waves of light that pulsed from the structure in the pit played tricks against the mirror-like surfaces of the labyrinth's glass walls.

Denton was lost.

Worse than lost, he wasn't alone.

There were still Undriel hybrids left in the maze. They moved around the corners like mindless animals searching for a meal, affected by the incessant waves of light that pulsed from the structure in the pit. They moaned and shrieked into the night.

A monster also lurked in the maze. Denton heard it more often than he saw it. It roared directly into his mind, and sometimes he could hear the splash of blood as it found a stray Undriel hybrid. Denton wished he had taken Cruz's doorbuster gauntlet, but he hadn't thought of it at the time, and now her location was lost in the twists and turns of the glass labyrinth. He wished she was still with him. Wished he could have saved her—saved anyone.

A wave of light pulsed over the glass and sand, and in the brief illumination, Denton found the beast. It had a bird-skull-shaped head, writhing tentacles for a neck, a gnarled bone carapace torso spiked with sharp barbs, and long wormskin arms ending in talons.

"Nhymn?" Denton gasped as his fear wrapped around his throat and strangled him. His nightmare come true. He was trapped with a Siren. "Shit."

He heard the Siren's roar and the pounding of its feet as it rushed him.

Denton threw himself to the side, landing on his shoulder in the glowing sand just as the monster crashed into the place he had been. It smashed the wall and scrambled in the broken glass as Denton hurried to his feet. In the desperate haste of the moment, his mind grew confused with the multiple reflections of the monster writhing in the glass. Before him was an army of twisting Sirens, each a reflection of the truth in the maze. But something was off.

"No… What are you?" Denton mumbled to himself. He had seen Nhymn in his nightmares for decades, known every millimeter of her haunting form. This creature looked similar, but it wasn't her. It was something else, something more animalistic.

The Siren regained its footing and turned toward Denton. Each of the panes of glass reflected a beast staring him down, readying claws for a strike. Denton popped off a shot with his rifle and nearly blew his own arm off as he dodged the beam of light that ricocheted off the mirror.

"I *really* hate this place!" he shouted in frustration and ran away from the reflections of monsters. The pounding of clawed feet was close behind. Denton turned a corner and saw three Undriel hybrids, their backs to him. He shouted, "Hey!" and they faced him, rifles aimed. Denton ducked, curling himself into the fetal position as he hit the ground. The Siren was only a few paces behind, and it stumbled over him. It was thrown claws first into the hybrids. The Siren smashed into them and immediately tore them to shreds. They didn't even have time to fire.

Denton got a better look at the beast. It looked like an eyewitness's failed attempt at remembering details of a murderer's face. It wasn't Nhymn, and in some ways, it looked more fearsome than she was.

What is that thing? Denton wondered, but he didn't stick around to find out. He pulled himself up and ran back the way he had come, away from the beast tearing apart the hybrids. Twists and turns and reflections on glowing sand and pulsing light created a strobing, confusing effect. Eventually, Denton shouted, "Damn it all!" in frustration. The world swirled around him, and reflections of himself looked back with matching turmoil.

Just then—a whistle.

"Huh?" Denton swung his head around, unsure of the source. Was it another trick of the maze? A second whistle sounded, and he looked toward the structure at the center of the labyrinth. The structure was a reasonable distance away from him, and about twenty meters of it protruded from the pit's base. Denton squinted his eyes and strained against the dark sky and the glowing sand. As he peered at the top of the structure, he saw a flash of light.

The pounding of clawed feet returned. Denton turned and saw the false Nhymn rear its arms back as it rushed forward, seeking to tear him apart. "Ah shit!" Denton shouted. He barely pulled his rifle up as three particle shots came from on high, striking the beast directly and forcing it to squeal and roll down a side corridor.

A voice shouted from the structure, "Start running!"

Denton's realization was slow and unbelieving. He recognized that voice. There was no way it could be true—it had to be a trick. But deep down, Denton knew whose voice that was. "Elly?" Denton smiled.

"Run, damn it!" Eliana Castus shouted from the top of the structure. Her voice was faint but just audible enough to recognize. Denton started running, rushing through the glowing sand down the reflective corridor. He came to a junction and started left when he heard Elly shout, "No, right! Go right!"

"On it!" Denton pivoted, flopping onto his thigh in the sand and rebounding into a sprint. With a guide through the glass labyrinth, he could make it as long as he could stay away from the hybrids and the false Nhymn.

Particle shots filled the night sky, striking the top of the structure. Eliana's position had been compromised, and the hybrids scattered in the maze were targeting her. Denton rounded a corner and found one of the Undriel hybrids aiming up at the structure. He shouted, "That's my *wife*, asshole!" And struck it with the butt end of his rifle, knocking it to the ground. It attempted to scramble and aim at Denton, and he dispatched it with a quick burst shot.

"Thanks!" Eliana shouted from above. She wasn't out of danger yet, but it helped. "Turn left!" The beast was getting closer. Denton pulled himself into the pathway on the left and hid behind a shard of glass just as the beast entered the area. It looked to its right, hunting for Denton. He aimed down his rifle and let out a few well-placed shots. Part of the beast's skull cracked off, and it shrieked. The monster recoiled back into the hallway where it had come from.

"Go across and take the path on your left!" Eliana shouted.

Denton moved across the open area and sprayed particle shots down the hall where the false Nhymn had gone for good measure. The particle beams bounced around the hall, and another shriek responded. Denton rushed the way Eliana directed and found a second beast standing at its end, looking away from him. He stumbled over himself as he skidded to a halt, then pulled himself behind a knuckle of glass. "There's two of them? Is there more than that?" Denton whispered to himself in panic.

The second beast heard the gunfire of some hybrids nearby and raced off down the left corridor, away from Denton. He exhaled deeply through his nose, then worked his way down the hall. As he came to the junction, he prayed, *Please say right, please say right, please say right.*

"Go right!" Eliana shouted.

Denton smiled as he huffed, exhausted from all the scrambling. He turned right and found a straight path that led up to the base of the structure Eliana was standing on. Ahead, two hybrids lay motionless in the sand. Denton slowed to a stop.

"Holy…" Denton mumbled. "It can't… No."

"What are you doing?" Eliana shouted from above. The gunfire from the maze had stopped. The hybrids had all been silenced by the Sirens of the glass labyrinth. The beasts howled in victory, the sound of many. Denton didn't care. He didn't even notice.

Denton approached the hybrid bodies and slumped to his knees. "Cade. Oh—oh no..." He recognized his son from the mission inside the Iron Castle. But now, he lay still. "Cade," Denton whispered, afraid to touch him and confirm his death. His eyes grew glassy, and his face felt hot. "Damn it, Cade, ple—"

"DENTON." Cade's voice boomed, unfamiliar. Alien.

"Fuck!" Denton shouted and fell backward in the sand on his ass.

"I AM SUSTAINING HIM, BUT CADE IS FADING." Cade's mouth moved, but Denton recognized Karx's voice coming from it. It was a voice he hadn't heard in a long time.

"What's going on down there?" Eliana shouted.

"He's alive," Denton whispered through his smile. He felt a rush of hope mixed with the dread of failing a third time. "What can I do?"

"BRING US TO THE DECIDER," Karx said.

"The what?" Denton looked back toward the maze, remembering when Nhymn had called herself that. But Nhymn wasn't in the maze. They'd sent her off to deep space. Karx's request felt impossible.

"I'll meet you downstairs," Eliana called, and vanished from view. Behind Denton, the structure pulsed, and some of its flat stone surface revealed an opening.

"YOU MUST HURRY."

Denton grabbed Cade under his mechanical arms and pulled hard, but he didn't move much. Cade was incredibly heavy. His metal body was packed densely with equipment. Denton grunted as he pulled, straining himself but not gaining much ground.

He heard footsteps rushing through the sand, multiple sources.

To his left was his wife, Eliana. She grabbed Cade's arm and pulled with him.

To his right was his daughter, Nella. She grabbed Cade's other arm and heaved.

Talulo jumped over them and landed near Cade's feet. He lifted, straining with the weight but compensating with his superior auk'nai strength.

Denton didn't realize he was crying with joy as he focused entirely on getting Cade inside the strange structure. He felt both weak and invincible. He was laughing as he sobbed and strained. They lifted Cade off the sand and moved as one through the threshold and into the Key Ship.

There was no time to waste.

THIRTY-FOUR

DENTON, ELIANA, NELLA, AND Talulo pulled Cade into the portal room with great effort. Once safely inside, Denton finally embraced his wife and daughter. He had yearned for this warmth since the war began. Tears flowed from his closed eyes, the dam unable to hold the flood back. He kissed their foreheads and gripped them tightly. Eliana and Nella covered their faces in Denton's chest and sobbed. He released his embrace on them, knowing they were seeing Cade for the first time since he'd been taken away. They had not known the full extent of what the Undriel had done to him, but now it was apparent. Denton gritted his teeth and felt a fiery heat fill his face.

Eliana sobbed as she looked at their son. "Oh Cade…" she whispered, and brushed a tear away. She pulled herself from Denton and went to Cade's side. Eliana stroked her son's mottled hair. His eyes were closed, but his head was warm to the touch. The rest was cold metal. There was so little left of their boy.

Nella sniffled and moved toward Cade. Her eyes glowed green, and an emerald mist seethed from her skin. Denton smiled, seeing hope. Eliana's face was grave, but she didn't stop Nella. She watched.

Nella leaned over Cade's face and caressed the side of his head, allowing the mist to breathe into him. Cade inhaled, and a tear rolled down from his closed eyes. His mechanical chest rose as if he had organic lungs inside his body. He was coming back from the brink of death but not waking up. Cade was stuck in a coma.

Eliana grabbed Nella's wrist. They shared a stern look, Nella wanted to continue the treatment, but Eliana shook her head. Nella reached for her nose and felt the warm blood hit her hand. She wiped it away, then began to weep, having exhausted her abilities to bring Cade back to them. She turned into her father's chest as he embraced her.

Talulo stood a few meters away, clutching his daunoren staff and shaking his beak.

"What have they done to him?" Eliana asked.

"He's still in there," Denton said. "I've seen it. In the Iron Castle—that's still our son. I know there's not much…" He trailed off but caught himself. "We can save him. We can't make him fully human again, but we can save him."

Eliana gripped her hands into fists and strangled another tear from falling. She looked to her son, then back to Denton with invincible determination. Nella pulled herself from her father's embrace and knelt next to Cade again.

"Karx, are you in there?" Nella signed while also using her unique link to her brother to communicate with the Voyalten inside him.

<I AM, SYMPHA. BUT WE ARE SO WEAK.>

"We will help you. You need to be strong for us," Nella signed, but it was Sympha speaking. Her old guardian. Her protector. *"Can you be strong?"*

<I WILL TRY.> Cade's face remained silent and sleeping. Only Karx was whispering through the tether. Nella wasn't sure if Cade would still be there if they managed to awaken him. Would it be only Karx riding in his body?

The Decider slithered from around the spiraled ramp in the center of the portal room. They revealed their looming form to Denton for the first time. Denton wasted no time aiming his particle rifle at the Voyalten. "What is *that*?"

Talulo said, "Be calm, Denton."

Denton's eyes darted between the Decider, his family, and the portal chamber. He lowered his weapon and requested with great restraint, "I'm sure there's a good explanation here, and I'd like that given to me right about now."

Nella stood up. *"We've learned so much. I'll get you up to speed."* She pulled Denton to the side of the room, and they leaned against the alabaster wall for the history lesson. Eliana comforted Cade with his head in her lap as his mechanical body lay draped on the floor. Talulo conversed with the looming Voyalten Decider, discussing the fate of Kamaria and the auk'nai's role within it. And his daughter, Nella, teaching him, as she always had.

Revelations stacked upon revelations came. The true origin of the Sirens—the *Voyalten.* Their mysterious, dark homeworld—*Faultasma.* The seed ships and the planting of distant worlds over eons of time. The connection of portals between worlds. A quest sabotaged by the stowaway—*Nhymn.* The Undriel had smashed through the web, creating a hole in space-time.

Denton had not been aware of the second portal built in the caves to the west. Nhymn's misinformed attempt at fulfilling her instincts. Where prehistoric Voyalten were pulled through the hole in the web the Undriel created—*my friends in the maze, I take it.* Denton connected the dots. He was relieved they weren't clones of Nhymn, or offspring. Nhymn was a nightmare.

"*That's it,*" Nella signed and watched as Denton absorbed the information. He ran a hand through his messy brown hair and scratched at the thick beard on his chin.

"*Sounds like I'll need to adjust my curriculum for Siren Studies,*" Denton signed. Nella raised her eyebrows and nodded. He patted Nella on the shoulder and walked over to the Decider. Nella was a step behind him. Everyone huddled around Cade and Eliana.

The Decider lowered their skull and spoke into Denton's mind, *<I see you now, Shade.>*

"Mhmm," Denton grunted, still wary of their new host. He looked back at Cade. His son's head bobbed slowly from side to side, like a restless dreamer. Eliana cradled him in her lap, brushing his hair and giving him the care he was deprived of for months. "We need your help," Denton whispered, then looked up at the Decider's horned skull.

The Decider returned Denton's stare with a hollow, eyeless one of their own. <*The tunneler is contained within this machine.*>

"That's my *son*," Denton said weakly.

<*I can revive him. The portal's fluctuating energy took his machinery offline, but it can also reactivate what was damaged. With the tunneler's help, we can tap into the power of this gateway to bring him back from his snapped tether.*>

"Tunneler? You mean Karx?" Denton asked, then added, "Snapped tether? Was he—"

<*He is trapped in a place between Shade walks. We need to give him something he can use to climb out, but this requires a task to be completed.*>

Eliana said, "We're willing to do anything."

Talulo said, "The Decider requires Nhymn's portal to be destroyed."

<*It will be a two-step process,*> the Decider explained as they slithered to the nearest wall and put a claw against the alabaster. Energy flashed from all around the room and sucked into the spot on the wall under the Decider's palm. When they pulled the claw back, part of the alabaster came with it, creating a breathing ball of rock and lightning. The Decider handed the breathing rock to Nella. <*You must take this to the other portal and drop it in.*>

"I'll go too," Eliana gently lowered Cade's head to the floor and stood up.

"Talulo will go as well." Talulo stepped forward. "It will be dangerous, and auk'nai have better weapons than humans."

"Well, you're not leaving me behind," Denton said. "They won't—"

<*They must leave you behind,*> the Decider corrected him.

Denton shook his head. "Wha—why?"

<*When the operator drops this bomb into the other portal, it will cause a chain reaction. We need Nhymn to finish the deactivation on this end. Portals are not capable of collapsing on their own. They must be manually shut down by their Operators.*>

"But Nhymn isn't here. We shot her off into space," Denton said, waving a hand toward the ceiling.

<*I am looking right at her,*> the Decider said, their hollowed eyes staring straight through Denton.

He looked over his shoulder, then around the room, then down at himself. "No, no, no, buddy. No Nhymn in here. I'd know about it."

"Interesting," Talulo cooed.

<*Your link to Nhymn is still active.*>

"That tether snapped years ago."

<*It did not snap. It only stretched,*> the Decider said. <*If we are wrong, the other portal will reactivate. This whole planet could be destroyed. They will have to find another Decider if I disintegrate.*>

Denton looked to his loved ones, his mouth open as if he'd been slapped. This felt unfair, to finally reunite only to be divided once more. Denton wanted to throw the Decider into the swirling pit of water and electricity in the center of the room.

Eliana put a hand on his chest. "Denny, we have a shot at saving Cade here."

Denton released a long sigh and let his jaw hang slack for a second as he processed the situation. "What do I have to do?"

<*When they destroy the other portal, you will have to press your hand against this pedestal.*> The Decider waved their claw, and a stone pillar rose up from the floor. <*Nhymn's essence will trigger the final termination of her portal, and everything will be repairable.*>

"Everything? Are the Undriel going to drop dead, too?" Denton asked.

<*Not at all. That is for you to resolve,*> the Decider stated flatly.

"Figures," Denton said. He pulled Eliana's hand into his and held it tightly. He whispered to her, "Just… be careful."

Eliana put a hand on his cheek and gave him a reassuring nod. He pulled her in for a long embrace. They remained quiet, the danger ahead silencing them. Denton had seen the horrors that lurked outside this portal chamber. He fought himself to stop her from leaving, and suddenly, he realized exactly how she'd felt this entire war. Denton was crushed for putting her through this.

"I'm sorry. About everything," Denton choked out a whisper.

"Me too," Eliana whispered back.

Nella tucked the breathing rock orb under her elbow and signed, *"Don't worry, Dad. I'm bringing my friends."*

Denton signed, *"Friends?"* with his face contorted in confusion.

Nella closed her eyes. There was a rumble in the palace. The Key Ship above shed some of its hull. After a moment, nezzarforms bumbled into the room from the entrance at the top of the stone ramp. They flickered with electricity, and each of them looked ready for a fight.

Nella embraced her father tightly. They held each other for a moment, and Denton breathed in deeply. He didn't want to let her go. She separated herself from him and signed, *"We need to do this. It is the only way we can save Cade and stop the Undriel."*

Denton grimaced and nodded. He signed, *"I love you."*

"I love you too, Dad," Nella signed back. She marched up the ramp to where her nezzarform friends waited.

Eliana kissed him, holding her lips against his for an extended moment. When she stopped, they looked each other in the eye. Denton said, "You come back. If it gets too dangerous, you just come back. We'll find anoth—"

"There is no other way." Eliana drifted away from him and joined Nella and the nezzarforms. Talulo walked past Denton. They nodded to each other, and Talulo let out a reassuring coo. The stoic auk'nai leader plodded up the ramp, stamping his daunoren staff against it as he scaled up. Soon, they were gone.

Denton sighed and looked toward the Decider. Then he glanced back down at Cade and said, "I hope you know what you're doing."

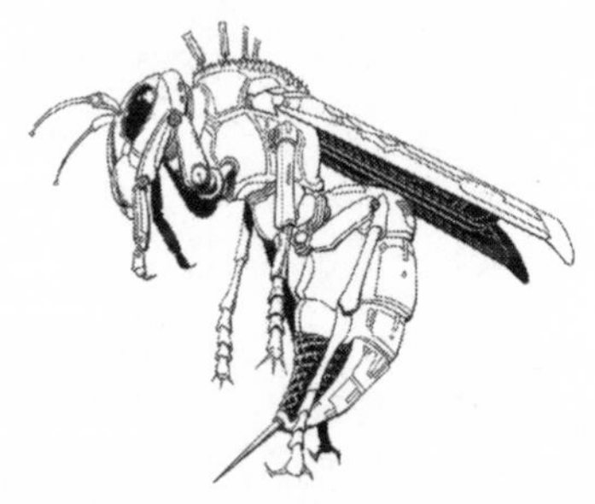

THIRTY-FIVE

THE UNDRIEL ARMY LISTENED to the network fall silent. They watched from the cliffside as each of the hybrids—Cade included—perished in the maze. Snuffed out by the anomalies and the beasts that roamed the labyrinth.

"It was only the hybrids," Hilaria jeered. "We lost nothing important."

"Shut up." Necrodore boomed the words.

Auden had no more tricks to pull from. Whatever the structure in the desert was, his people couldn't breach it. Even the special hybrid had succumbed to its weird power. The Pit was the key to their presence on this planet. Somewhere in there was the answer to why they'd ended up on Kamaria—and possibly, a way back to the Sol System. For the first time since becoming a machine, Auden was at a disadvantage.

Tibor spoke. "We can return to this place once we have eliminated the human threat." It still gave Auden shivers to hear Ovid speak like Tibor. The voice was haunting and unpredictable. The AI that had destroyed the trillionaire centuries ago still retained his voice. Auden let the others believe in Tibor, failing to mention how hollow their king was. Tibor was a good scapegoat should the corruption ever come for his generals and turn them against him.

The snarling mob would focus on the puppet king, and Auden could flee.

Auden suggested, "That structure holds the answers to our presence here. We must find a way in if we ever intend to go back home and stop the corruption."

"It can wait," Tibor said. Auden felt like he'd been slapped. Ovid had never directly denied him before. The machine continued, "We are vulnerable to humans if they regroup. Despite losing the hybrids, we retain the advantage in numbers. We will strike them while we have them on their knees."

"I'm all in!" Hilaria cackled. She flexed her stinger tail and seethed with anticipation.

Necrodore looked out toward the pit. "We must prepare more hybrids if we ever hope to stop the corruption back home."

Auden agreed. "True. But consider there may be something we can use inside that structure. Or maybe the native Kamarians here hold the key. We may not need hybrids after all."

"Hear that, Jonas? The hybrids might have been a big waste of time." Hilaria laughed the words out as she circled around Necrodore.

"I tire of your banter, wretched thing." Necrodore seethed steam as his internal engines roared with fire.

Tibor continued, "When the humans are eliminated, we have all the time in the stars to figure out a plan. The corruption will not come here, and the auk'nai are absorbable. Auden has had long interactions with one before freeing us from the grip of the warp failure. Auden knows their physiology. We could even merge species. One becomes all."

The others considered this idea.

"Our new paradise. Right here," Necrodore whispered. "Free from corruption."

"And all we have to do is tear through some humans? You sure this isn't paradise already?" Hilaria cackled and flexed her stinger toward Talfryn. "How's that sound to you, my sharply dressed friend?"

The silent Reaper showed no joy for killing. It only awaited further commands. Reapers were too powerful to allow complete freedom, like Necrodore and Hilaria. Auden knew this Reaper was just as capable of going against him as the Reaper that came before it. His grip was tight on Talfryn. Since landing on Kamaria, the same overriding control was implemented on all of Auden's new creations. Both Faye and Cade were under a tight leash. Not that it mattered for Cade any longer—he was dead.

"We move at once," Tibor rallied, his voice booming over the cliffside. "We will work our way north around the desert, using the mountains as cover. The human city is to the east, past the jungle and the valley. We will strike them directly and use their own city against them. Auden has siphoned information from their network. We have all the information we need and all the resources to build our numbers up once again."

Auden said, "When the humans are done, we can move on to the auk'nai…" He trailed off as something emerged from the structure in the desert. A small craft flew from its center mass and sailed over the glass maze toward the jungle cliffside in the distance. Auden turned to Faye and asked, "Do you see that?"

Faye nodded. "I can follow it. Give me two soldiers, and we will track it. We can meet up with you when we have finished."

Tibor commanded two close-by Undriel soldiers to follow Faye and added, "Avoid the maze and the structure. Bring whatever that is to us, and you will be rewarded."

Two Undriel soldiers joined Faye near the cliff. They activated their thrusters and walked off the ledge, hugging close to the mountain wall as they kept low to avoid detection.

"We move onward," Tibor rallied.

The rest of the Undriel forces howled with delight. They pushed through the trees and uneven mountain terrain, a silent army of metallic ghosts. Some rode on the last remaining fragments of the *Devourer* while the rest walked or floated on thrusters. They followed their hollow king to the human city.

Nella sat in a seat that mimicked a pilot's chair, but this nezzarform ship piloted itself. It had a stone hull, interlaced with bright green light, and rode a sustained beam of lightning. It was sharp in the front, like a spike made of rock, with two small wing-shaped pieces on each side to keep it from rotating and hurling its human cargo in a spin cycle.

Inside, Eliana and Talulo sat in the other stone chairs. There was enough room to stand and walk, but it was not built to be a comfortable long-haul craft. When Nella signed to the ship, she referred to its entirety as Lahar; even though a few more nezzarforms were combined to create it, it was the strongest presence in her mind.

Lahar dipped into the canyon, its sustained lightning licking against the river below. The sun rose, and the canyon cast shadows against the arching rock formations. The ship flew with great skill through the archways, and the ride was smooth.

Nella asked Lahar to spin her seat around to face her mother and Talulo. She held the breathing stone bomb in her hand, knowing it wouldn't go off until she asked it to. It was a nezzarform like the rest of her friends. Eliana and Talulo lacked the same confidence. She smiled at them, worrying together. Allies in discomfort.

Eliana signed, *"What are you looking at?"*

"It's good to see you two united again." Nella locked each hands' thumb and middle fingers together in a ring and moved her hands in a circle. Her smile was warm, and her eyebrows raised.

Talulo cooed, then said something. Eliana translated it into Sol-Sign. *"We still have much to discuss between our people. But I look forward to the discussions."*

Eliana nodded in agreement. She looked at the bomb in Nella's hands, then signed, *"What is this place like? What should we look for?"*

Nella signed, *"Cade and I were here just before Dad found us. It is a long cave tunnel with a river running through it. We entered through the bottom before, but this time, we will enter through the top."* She made a T-shape with her hands. *"At the top is a cave entrance and a short walk down into the main chamber. It looks a lot like the portal chamber, except covered in..."* She searched for the right word and landed on *"Tar."*

Eliana shuddered, *"Sounds like the crypt your grandfather and I went into."*

"It is similar. There are some prehistoric Voyalten in the cave, so we must be careful. Luckily, our friends have a gift," Nella signed. She waved her hand to the closest wall. The stones shifted, and lightning ebbed over constructs that protruded from the rock. Three glass shards emerged. Nella took one and gave the others to her mother and Talulo. She could feel energy humming inside the shard through her palm. Nella explained, *"Nezzarform weapons. As long as you are near me, they will work."*

"Near you?" Talulo asked, and Eliana translated.

"They resonate with Sympha's power. But they cannot stray too far from me, or else they lose their element."

Talulo whistled and began to tinker with the gauntlet on his hand. He pulled a small tool from his daunoren staff and used it to open part of his gauntlet, slotting the nezzarform shard into the gauntlet with a few flicks and twists. Once completed, Talulo pumped his wrist, and a rod thrust outward and began to glow with green light.

Nella clapped and signed, *"Rock on!"* with her forefinger and pinky thrust out, her thumb tucked into her palm.

Talulo gestured to Eliana's particle rifle. She handed it over, and Talulo went to work modifying her weapon. In a few moments, Talulo finished installing the nezzarform shard in the gun, and the collider cylinder hummed with green light. Eliana accepted the bulky rifle from the auk'nai and placed it on her lap.

Eliana looked tired. For the past couple of months, she had been filled with worry for her entire family. Cade had gone missing, Denton was battling nightmarish machines on the far shore, and Nella was inflicted with dark patches on her brain and was talking to rocks. It was a weight tied to her heart, threatening to pull her down into a deep sea. Nella leaned forward and signed, *"We will fix Cade. He'll live. We'll be together again as a family."*

Eliana smiled, her eyes wet with poorly held back tears, though, it was not sadness, but instead longing for the future. She smiled and signed, *"Let's blow up a portal."*

THIRTY-SIX

ELIANA FOLLOWED NELLA DOWN the ramp of the nezzarform ship. Talulo trailed just behind them, plodding his daunoren staff against the stone with soft thuds. When the passengers were safely off the ship, it fell apart, reduced to rubble in the jungle dirt. Rapidly, the rubble reformed. Boulders rolled into mounds and rebuilt the nezzarform bodies they were before. Suddenly, five nezzarform soldiers stood in the jungle clearing, each with a cyclopean eye and a unique arrangement of arms and legs.

Lahar stood upon one stone peg-leg and had three bulky rock arms, two that braced it upright and one on its back. Its main body was one large boulder seething with electricity. It stared at Nella and waited for instructions.

The humid jungle air clung to their bodies, mixing with the hot breeze from the Starving Sands Desert beyond the cliff ledge. Twisting green vines and dense jungle canopy Shaded them from the sun's blazing heat. A river gently emptied into the maw of a cave, like a titan chugging down an endless ale. Echoes bounced out of the cave, the sounds of creatures stirring.

Eliana clapped her hands to get Nella's attention, then signed, *"We're going in there?"*

Nella bobbed her fist. *"Yes."* She patted the breathing stone bomb tucked in her elbow.

Eliana checked her modified particle rifle. Green light seeped from its core, enhanced with Sympha's essence. The closer Eliana stood to her daughter, the brighter it glowed.

Talulo grunted, and his long ears twitched.

Eliana asked, "What is it?"

Talulo turned his head, tilting his beak as he searched for whatever was tingling his ear. His irises shrunk. Talulo pivoted, whirled his daunoren staff, and let out a violent blast of particle light into the jungle trees.

Eliana and Nella jolted in shock, then watched the trees.

Dark shapes moved in the jungle canopy. Three Undriel soldiers emerged from the tree line at once, using thrusters to cover the distance at incredible speed. The five nezzarform soldiers met them head-on. Lahar caught one of the Undriel and crushed it into the ground with his back arm, breaking it in half. The insectile machine scrambled its way out of Lahar's grasp and morphed its arms into particle rifles.

"Let's move!" Eliana shouted, grabbing Nella's arm and hurrying into the cave. Nella almost tried to break free and help her nezzarform friends, but she stopped herself, knowing the mission was too critical. Talulo let out a few more shots at the Undriel but could not hit the quick-moving machines. He followed Eliana and Nella into the dark cave.

Lights from the battle outside faded the deeper they traversed into the dark tunnel. A rock ledge lined the river, allowing them to run to the portal chamber ahead at full speed. It suddenly became pitch black, with only the glow from their weapons illuminating their path. The darkness ate the light only a few meters from the source. Nella held her hand out, stopping Eliana and Talulo.

Just ahead, barely visible, the shape of a large beast stirred. It shambled into the light, revealing its long, sharp beak and singular horn. A primal Voyalten blocked their path, and more of the creatures came with it. They slithered and shambled in the darkness ahead, never staying upright too long. As the prehistoric creatures recognized the light, they pulled their claws out and readied for a pounce.

"Let them have it!" Eliana shouted.

Nella pointed her nezzarform shard, Eliana aimed her rifle, and Talulo extended the rod from his arc mace. At once, they fired a barrage of green lightning into the crowd ahead. Violent energy ripped through the primal Voyalten in the front, and waves of light pulsed around the cave tunnel walls. The monsters roared and shrieked. The ones who had not been cut down backed off deeper into the cave.

When the path became clear, Talulo revealed another trick of his gauntlet. He aimed his daunoren staff forward, then twirled it in a circle. As he moved his gauntlet in a matching circular motion, the green light created a ring of raw energy. He pushed the ring toward the end of his staff, and it sustained itself in place at the tip. Talulo cooed and kept his staff aimed at the darkness ahead. The Voyalten in the darkness shied away from its strange glow and hid amongst the cracks in the walls.

"Looks like the auk'nai have been busy," Eliana said, impressed by this new ability.

"Auk'nai were not sure who they would end up fighting. Auk'nai prepared for all enemies," Talulo said, his eyes intensely aimed ahead in case any primal Voyalten got clever and tested his shield of light. Eliana understood the thing he didn't quite say. They'd made these to fight humans, if necessary. How far their people had strayed from the peace they once shared.

More primal Voyalten tucked themselves into the walls as they passed. Eliana walked backward, keeping her rifle aimed behind them. These monsters seemed to understand that the green light was dangerous, and they happened to be smart enough to not continue testing it. They were much like Neandertals from prehistoric Earth. They weren't mindless predators—they were just underdeveloped people displaced by time. Still a threat, but not inherently evil. Given enough time, these Voyalten could learn how to harness light and link worlds together through a web of portals.

Keep an open mind. Eliana reminded herself of one of the Scout mottos.

The cave behind them quickly filled with red light. The roar of thrusters came next.

"Get down!" Eliana shouted, and pulled on Nella's arm. An Undriel soldier sailed through the tunnel toward them. Nella fumbled the bomb, and it rolled down the slope away from her.

Talulo turned and released the swirling light at the Undriel, barely missing it. The machine pivoted, halting its momentum. It rocketed at Talulo. The auk'nai deftly jumped over the Undriel as it came at him. It smashed into the rock wall and twisted to face Eliana.

Nella scrambled to pursue the rolling bomb. Primal Voyalten shrieked as the bomb tumbled near them. It started to wobble toward the river, teetering in its course and creating an erratic pattern. Nella threw herself toward it with her hand stretched to its limit. Her finger tipped the bomb just enough to allow it to bounce back into her palm. Nella clutched the bomb tightly into her chest as she slid to a stop on the cave ramp.

In the glow of the bomb, she could see a taloned foot made of spikes and wormskin. She cautiously looked up at the primal Voyalten standing over her. It was bolder than the rest, not afraid of the green light. It also had not killed Nella outright as she lay vulnerable on the floor.

Nella stood up slowly, clutching the bomb against her chest with both hands. She could sense something from this Voyalten. This one had the flicker of candlelight in its soulless eyes that implied an above-average intelligence. The primal recognized some of itself in Nella—*Sympha*.

The primal Voyalten stepped to the side and allowed Nella to pass. The other Voyalten in the cave followed its example. Suddenly, Nella had a clear path to the portal chamber. She bowed respectfully to them and hurried past him.

Back the way Nella had come, Eliana tried to track the Undriel in the cave. With the flickering lights of Talulo's gauntlet and her own particle rifle filling her vision, the robot was only visible by the thin red lights on its hull in the darkness of the cave. She let out a few shots toward where the robot was, just before it darted away again.

The green glow of Eliana's particle rifle faded, and she was left with her standard firing mode. "Nella?" Eliana gasped. "Nella!" Eliana searched the darkness for her daughter and couldn't find her. *Did she fall into the river?*

She didn't have time to consider more options as the Undriel rushed her. The robot came within grasping distance, but a blast of circular light crashed into it from the side. The Undriel was flung sideways into the river water. Talulo came to Eliana's side and created another ring of particle light.

The Undriel emerged from upriver. It had traveled below the water to flank them. Eliana blasted the Undriel in the chest and arm. It burst into separate pieces, a torso with one arm and legs that crashed back into the water below. The half-Undriel smashed against the rock slope and crawled toward Eliana and Talulo with unnatural haste.

These things just don't give up! The Undriel morphed its remaining arm into a particle rifle and took a shot. Eliana pushed Talulo to the floor just as the particle shot struck her left bicep and cut through her jacket and skin. She cried out in pain.

The Undriel pivoted and aimed up another shot.

Before it could fire, a wave of green light surged through the cave tunnel. It had a density that light shouldn't possess—liquidized illumination. Eliana felt shoved underwater as it engulfed the cave, cutting out all sound. The river reversed its flow and pushed back up the slope for a moment. As the light wave passed, wind roared back into the cave, like a deep inhale after nearly drowning. The gale was so strong it knocked Eliana and Talulo to the ground.

The cave ceiling twinkled with emerald light. There was a steady, even glow—peaceful. The primal Voyalten that had tucked themselves into the walls cautiously emerged, unthreatened by the twinkling lights.

Eliana and Talulo aimed their weapons at the primals, unsure of their intentions. The beasts paid them no attention and instead dropped into the river to allow the current to drag them away. Soon, the cave was empty again, with only the faint lights and sounds of the river echoing off the walls.

Eliana turned toward the Undriel soldier but only found a headless robotic torso. She searched the walls of the cave and found it. Struggling against the rocks was the spider-bot head of the Undriel. It was heavily damaged, crawling on only two legs instead of the eight it was designed to maneuver with. Talulo twirled his daunoren staff and slammed it down on the bot. It sputtered and died, crackling with electricity.

Footsteps came from down the slope and echoed off the damp walls. Nella approached and patted imaginary dust off her shoulder. She smiled at her mother and Talulo. When she noticed her mother's injury, Nella hurried to her side and placed her hands over Eliana's wound.

"Nella, wait!" Eliana protested. She couldn't pull her arm away to sign.

A surge of healing light pulsed through Nella, starting in her chest and waving out through her fingertips. The emerald-hued energy moved into Eliana's wound. It felt like pressing a cool cloth on a burn, refreshing with a slight sting. When Nella removed her hand, Eliana's injury had been completely healed.

Nella stepped back to regain her balance from a slight dizzy spell. She signed, *"We better get back,"* and walked toward the mouth of the cave tunnel, holding a palm to her head.

Eliana frowned and shook her head. She was thankful to be healed, but at what cost to her daughter? If Nella had another seizure out here beyond the city, they couldn't treat her adequately.

Talulo put a claw on Eliana's shoulder and cooed. Together they followed Nella toward the light at the end of the tunnel. They emerged from the cave to the scattered remains of one of the Undriel attackers. By Eliana's count, two had been destroyed, leaving one unaccounted for. The surviving Undriel was undoubtedly reporting back to the rest of their army.

Nella stood over a pile of rubble and put her arms out to the sides. Light surged from her head to the ground. The debris reassembled into two separate nezzarforms, each previously dispatched during the Undriel attack. Nella fell to her knees—her friends had come back to life. Eliana went to her side and put her arms around her.

She kneeled in front of her daughter and rolled her right fist in front of her left fist. *"You can't keep using this power. Too dangerous."*

Nella grimaced through a shock of pain and shook her head. She breathed a few heavy breaths, then conceded with a nod. Nella turned to the five nezzarforms and nodded.

Lahar and the others crumbled to the ground, then reconfigured themselves back into a ship formation, complete with a stone ramp. Nella led the way into the ship, with Talulo close behind. As Eliana waited to board, she turned to look over the Starving Sands desert just beyond the cliff ledge. She could see an immense labyrinth of glass and the Key Ship planted firmly in the pit in its center.

If this worked, Cade would be saved. They'd be a complete family again. The dangers that lurked everywhere were inconsequential right now. Eliana inhaled the humid jungle air, then ducked her head to enter the nezzarform ship.

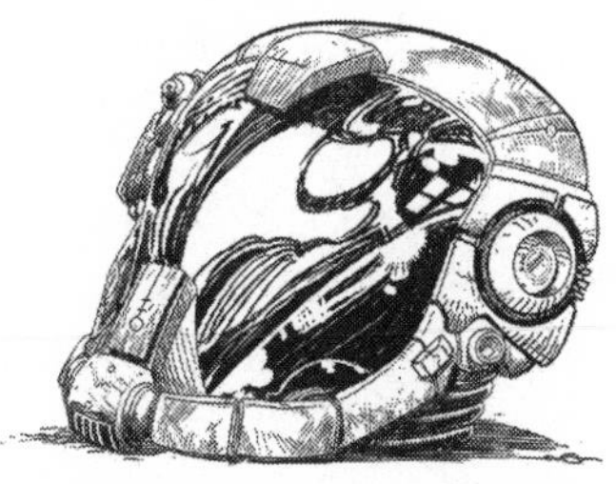

THIRTY-SEVEN

DENTON PULLED OFF MORE of the remaining parts of his damaged combat suit, leaving only the gauntlet on his right arm and his shin guards on. His undersuit was ripped in places, and he scratched the skin that had been concealed. Every injury Denton had sustained from his months fighting the Undriel burned, but it was nothing compared to what Cade had gone through.

The alabaster palace was quiet, except for the churning of water coming from the circular pit in the center of the room. The Decider shifted glowing orbs around with precise movements. With nothing to do, Denton sat against the wall near Cade and watched the Voyalten with a careful eye. The Decider was still untrustworthy to him. They didn't approach Denton or try to make conversation. They were perfectly happy giving Denton the space he needed.

Cade's head weakly fidgeted left and right as if trapped in a nightmare. He was living the worst of the Hells imaginable, becoming absorbed by the Undriel but having the mind to understand it. There was still so much humanity didn't know about the machines. No one understood why they spread across the Sol System or their true origins. It all happened so fast that human defenses were left scrambling to find an edge to cling to—the kind of tsunami that could only be escaped by leaving the planet.

Now the Undriel were on Kamaria. Denton had no idea what

was currently happening in the war. His link to the fight had been cut off after entering the Starving Sands with Cruz.

Karx spoke through Cade's lips. "IT IS TIME."

The Decider beckoned Denton over with a claw. Denton shoved himself upright and walked across the portal chamber to join them.

<*The Operator has performed her task. It is—*>

Denton cut them off. "Is she safe?"

<*Yes, I still sense her. The others, I cannot say,*> the Decider admitted.

"Can we wait for them?" Denton asked.

<*We should act now while the portal is ready. If we wait too long, it could collapse . . .*>

"And we all die. Got it. Alright." Denton sighed. "Where do I push?"

<*This pylon.*> The Decider gestured one of their claws at a stone column with a strange glowing design on its surface. <*Press your palm against it. You will feel something as it moves through your tether to find the stowaway's signature. Once complete, the other portal will deactivate, and this portal will begin to heal.*>

"Touch it and zap it away. Got it," Denton said. He flexed his right hand as if about to perform a repair on a starship calibrator, then slowly pushed his palm against the pylon's surface. Instantly, his hair stood up as electricity shot through his body. "Woah," Denton gasped as the sensation wiggled through him. "Feels sort of—" Then he screamed in intense pain. A blast of purple light cut through the room, knocking the Decider against the wall.

Denton's hand was pinned to the pylon. His eyes vibrated, and tar leaked from his tear ducts. Another blast of violet energy rang out from the pylon. This time it threw Denton to the floor. He convulsed on his back, seizing violently as his eyes bled tar and his teeth ground together. The pit in the center of the chamber swirled with energy. A worm-skinned claw emerged from the pit, followed by a phalanx of others.

Primal Voyalten from the tunnel to the east clawed their way into the chamber through the swirling river below. Each dripping with flickering energized water. They stood together, surrounding the pit like temple guardians.

"WHAT HAVE YOU DONE?" Denton shouted in a voice that was mixed with another's.

The Decider slithered upright. <*Unexpected.*>

"WHAT HAVE YOU DONE?" Denton stopped convulsing and rolled onto his chest. He pushed himself up, then staggered as he gained his footing. His eyes vibrated, and tar leaked freely onto the stone floor.

<*Nhymn…*> the Decider said, realizing what had happened.

Nhymn looked at the Decider through Denton's eyes. She wasted no time and launched herself from Denton's body. Her phantom claws stretched out as she raced toward the Decider's head.

The Decider ignited in red flames, their skull roaring with ghostly wildfire. They pushed their four massive claws at Nhymn's phantom, catching her in mid-air and slamming her to the floor. Nhymn was unprepared, assuming herself untouchable in her phantom form. The Voyalten Decider loomed over her, pressing their massive weight into Nhymn and keeping her pinned to the floor. Her ghost wreathed and morphed into various shapes, but she could not escape the giant's grasp.

The primals standing around the pit watched and waited.

Nhymn held a shadowed claw up in surrender and stopped writhing. <*Why have you done this?*> Nhymn begged. <*We had a deal!*>

<*I know of no such thing!*> the Decider shouted, keeping the pressure on Nhymn.

"Wait." Denton coughed. He stood and looked over his shoulder at the silent primals guarding the pit. Denton was terrified of everything in the room at the moment, except Cade. He was unsure if the primals would rip him to shreds or not, unsure why they hadn't already. "Nhymn's right. We had a deal."

<*The stowaway needs to be exterminated. She is too dangerous.*> The Decider flared brightly.

<*You brought me here to destroy me?*> Nhymn asked, desperation in her voice.

"We didn't mean to bring you here!" Denton shouted, and moved closer to them, putting himself between Nhymn and Cade. The Decider's fire had no effect on Denton. It was a phantom thing designed to hurt phantoms. A dark power brought from Faultasma.

The Decider said, <*The tether must have recoiled when the signal was sent.*>

<*No. No, no, no, NO!*> Nhymn turned her hollow eyes on Cade. <*The Undriel are still here—they will kill us all! Send me away. Let me leave!*>

Denton asked, "You knew the Undriel were here before we sent you away, didn't you?"

Nhymn's beak darted between Denton and the Decider. <*Yes. I had seen them in my sister's memories. They came from this portal. I tried to make my own portal to send them back. It didn't work.*>

"Yeah, we noticed. It's bringing in these guys from your prehistoric days." Denton waved a hand at the crowd of primals standing near the pit.

<*What did you say?*> Nhymn hissed.

The Decider's voice boomed, <*You are a false Operator. A stowaway. The portal you made brought these primals here. Your portal would have never worked. You were not supposed to come to this world. You manipulated the dark matter of Sympha's seed ship. You and the crew inside were affected by this perversion and forgot your roles. In this mishandling of the mission, fear drove you to unspeakable actions. In your fear, you have changed this planet's viability. You and Sympha have both failed in your tasks. This portal is healing now, but it was damaged by the false one you created.*>

<*You… You fixed this portal?*> Nhymn asked.

<*We can salvage it with time.*> The Decider lessened their grip, and their fire started to dim. <*But the damage has been done.*>

Nhymn rose from the floor like a wisp of fog. She drifted toward the primal Voyalten and looked up at the tallest one. She whispered, <*I have taken your lives from you. You are empty husks now, unsure of your purpose. I know the way you are. I have lived it.*>

The tall primal looked down at Nhymn while the others stood motionless. Nhymn said to the Decider, <*I can help them. We can find our purposes together. If you'll allow me.*>

The Decider assessed the stowaway. They grumbled, considering their options. After some thought, they said, <*You have done terrible harm to this world. These Voyalten are displaced by time, and will wither without direction. I give you this opportunity to fix what you have broken. Fail in this task, and you will be damned to the Hush.*>

Nhymn seemed to understand how dire this consequence was. She bowed her head, thanking the Decider for this opportunity to make things right.

Denton shouted, "You're going to let her stay? After everything she's done?"

The Decider snapped its gaze upon Denton. <*The stowaway knows the consequences. I have offered her an oblivion you cannot fathom, Shade. If you have a deeper prison to send her to, then name it now.*>

Denton looked back and forth between the Decider, Nhymn's foggy phantom, and the primal Voyalten. He felt outnumbered suddenly, knowing that protesting would only get him ripped to shreds by a crowd of monsters. Denton stepped back a few paces and huffed, "Whatever you say, boss."

The primal in front of Nhymn let out a low, gentle moaning sound like an animal that had been starved nearly to death, reaching out for a tiny morsel of nourishment. Nhymn pushed herself from the floor and phased into a primal Voyalten's prehistoric body. It jolted like it had awoken from a long slumber.

Nhymn flexed her new claws, testing her body's movements. It was similar to her original body in many ways. However, this new body was untamed, sharper in places. Its wormskin was a darker shade of purple and red, almost black. Her skull was the way it had been before, bird-shaped with a long central horn, with smaller spikes lining its sides. She seethed with pleasure.

"What do you plan to do now?" Denton demanded to know.

Nhymn turned to the other primal Voyalten behind her, then back to Denton. *<My goal was to save this planet from invaders. I don't believe I misplaced my caution in humans, but I understand that you might be needed to stop the machines.>* She added, *<I will help you fight the Undriel.>*

Denton's mind immediately shouted, *Absolutely not!* But he remembered the ambush he'd barely survived. The Undriel had the advantage now, and every fight they won so far was against human defenses only. It was time to throw some new things at the Undriel, things they didn't understand.

<I do not care if you trust me, Shade,> Nhymn said. *<I'm not asking for permission. Try and stop me if you wish.>* She flashed her claws at him.

"Yep, that's still Nhymn in there." Denton sighed. "I won't get in your way. If we make it through this, we'll have to figure out how to coexist. Until then, we have a common enemy to fight."

The Decider bowed their large skull and said, *<Your path forward is up to you, stowaway. You know what awaits in failure.>* They slithered across the portal chamber toward Cade's body.

<More than you may realize,> Nhymn said quietly.

Denton allowed the Decider to approach Cade's body. The giant Voyalten waved their claws over him, assessing the situation. Denton asked, "You can fix him now, right?"

<You are going to bring this Undriel back online?> Nhymn asked.

"That's my son!" Denton shouted. "Decider, if she tries to stop you, fry her."

Nhymn stayed in her place and observed.

<I will do what I am able to,> the Decider said. The Voyalten uncurled their hands, and four glowing orbs floated across the room into their palms. Their arms interlaced and traced around Cade's

body with an articulate movement. The orbs shifted in hue as they moved them. The room was a rainbow of swirling light. The Decider clapped their hands together, the orbs instantly vaporized, and the Decider's arms were ignited in blue fire. They pushed their claws down into Cade's body.

Light surged through Cade, and the mechanisms that made up his robotic form reignited and spasmed. The Decider backed away and watched with Nhymn and the primals. Cade shouted a long, sustained yell as the energy moved through him. Then, all at once, the lights were inhaled into his core.

Cade sat up abruptly, his eyes open. He looked down and patted himself all over, checking to make sure he wasn't dreaming. "What? I…" He turned to Denton and smiled. "Dad?"

"Cade," Denton gasped, weak from happiness.

There was a brief moment of pause. The universe seemed hesitant to push forward. Then, Denton raced to Cade and hugged him harder than two stars colliding. Cade hugged him back, having to restrain himself. His Undriel augmentations would allow him to break his father, or worse, absorb him.

"My boy!" Denton sobbed. "You're alive!"

"I don't know how, but you saved me," Cade cried with the little humanity he still had left in his body. "You did it."

Denton didn't want to let go, worried that Cade would be ripped away from him once more if he did. Cade was here. He was alive. He could live in this embrace forever. Denton's heart felt like it would give out from sheer happiness. Its beating was both erratic and slowed to a crawl. He felt a tightness in his neck, and a dull push from behind his eyes as tears overflowed from his body.

Cade is here. Cade is alive.

Eventually, the embrace had to end. Reality needed to move forward. Denton turned to the Decider and said, "Thank you." He smiled, sniffled, and brushed tears from his face. He repeated, "Thank you."

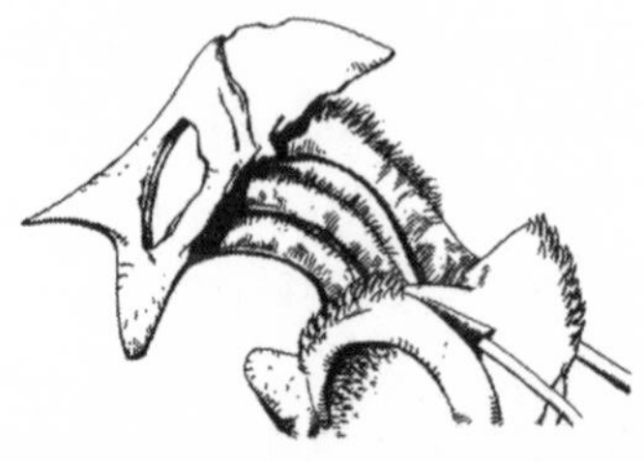

THIRTY-EIGHT

NELLA, ELIANA, AND TALULO returned to the Key Ship and hurried to the portal chamber. Upon entering the main chamber, they stopped. The palace had changed since they'd left to deliver the bomb to Nhymn's false portal. The inhabitants had grown in numbers.

Eliana lifted her particle rifle and aimed at the group of primal Voyalten standing around the swirling vortex at the bottom of the chamber. Her heart raced as she searched the room for the others, unsure if these primals had killed them. The Decider, the giant with the long, bonelike horns and serpentine body, stood with Denton, and just beyond him…

"Cade!" Eliana shouted.

Eliana disregarded the primals and rushed down the ramp. When she got close enough, she leaped from the spiraling ramp and scrambled over to Denton and Cade. Eliana embraced her son roughly. She kissed his head repeatedly, unable to believe that he was finally here.

He laughed. "It's me, Mom. I know I look like—"

"You look like *my son.*" Eliana stared directly into his blue eyes. "We'll figure this out. It will all be okay. You're with us now."

Cade's eyes glassed over. He had been through so much—tortured and ripped apart by the Undriel, forced to watch people become hybrids, and that didn't even scratch the surface of what he had witnessed in his Shade walking. He had seen worlds destroyed and people absorbed in different timelines. His mother's strength broke down his walls, and he cried as he smiled. "It's so good to see you."

"Where's Nella?" Denton asked.

"She was just behind..." Eliana turned and looked toward the top of the ramp. Nella's eyes were glowing with emerald fire. She descended the ramp slowly, focusing only on the tallest primal Voyalten in the room. Talulo kept his distance, hearing the unsung songs in the air.

<*Nhymn...*> A voice echoed in everyone's minds.

<*Sympha,*> the tallest primal responded in kind.

<*Why have you returned?*>

<*It was not my fault. The Shade brought me back through the tether.*> Nhymn turned her beak and horn toward Denton.

"I didn't know that was gonna happen! Hells, the Decider didn't even know!" Denton thrust a thumb at the Decider.

The Decider admitted, <*This experience is new to me. I have been to many worlds, but this one has the strangest occurrences I have ever witnessed. Our people will need to record this information.*>

Nella squinted, although it was Sympha inspecting Nhymn closely. <*What have you done in your time away from this world?*>

Nhymn looked hesitant to admit what she had been up to in the past twenty years, but reluctantly, she confessed, <*I found a planet bathed in light. It had a close orbit to its star, and its brilliant glow filled the sky. The ship the humans sent me on was destroyed, and the creature I inhabited had starved to death long before that. I was alone, and I preferred it that way.*> Nhymn shuddered, remembering her time trapped in the seed ship as a phantom, torn apart by the crew that discovered her as a stowaway. <*I do not wish to stay. I do not know if I can find my world again.*>

<*I do not want you to stay either. You have done too much damage to my world,*> Sympha said flatly.

The Decider interrupted, <*The worlds we seed are not under our ownership, Operator. You have also done your own damage to this place. Despite having forgotten your role, your crew remained trapped in their phantom states. You only brought the tunneler back online.*> They drifted one of their claws toward Cade.

Cade stepped around his parents to face the Voyalten. Karx's voice filled the mental space the Voyalten were discussing. <*SYMPHA COULD HAVE BROUGHT OTHERS TO LIFE?*>

<*Karx, I was scared. I—*> Sympha attempted to explain but was cut off.

<*An Undriel* and *it is Karx?*> Nhymn hissed. <*I knew you to be a betrayer, but not to two species!*> She flexed her claws.

The Decider ignited with blazing fire and shouted with a booming voice, <*ENOUGH!*>

Nella-Sympha, Cade-Karx, and Primal-Nhymn exchanged heated glances with each other. The Decider slithered through the room, exchanging stern looks with each of the unruly Voyalten. <*You all misunderstood your tasks. Nhymn shouldn't be here. She stole her way onto your seed ship and manipulated the dark matter onboard. It altered everyone on the seed ship. None of you could have avoided it.*>

The Decider continued his judgment, <*Sympha, you built this portal well enough without the help of your entire crew, but we must repair it. Karx, you were supposed to help carve this chamber exactly to the specifications we had given you. Still, you were not present for its construction. Instead, you waited outside a crypt, guarding a suit intended for a different crew member like it was a corpse. Nhymn, you remembered me and my role to an extent, but you tried to do my job with only a fraction of the knowledge I possess. I do not decide who inherits a planet. I decide if it is worth allowing it to join the web.*>

The failed Voyalten crew, Sympha and Karx, looked away from each other, ashamed of their poor performance. They turned their eyes on Nhymn, the one who'd caused it all. Sympha shook her head and asked, <*Why did you do this to us?*>

Nhymn looked at the floor. Unlike Karx and Sympha, Nhymn

had fully resurrected three years after the final battle in the Unforgotten Garden. Time alone had healed her of the effects of the faulty dark matter. Bathed in the light of her own, lonely world, she remembered her past. She knew what had happened and how it went out of her control. <*I was sent for a purpose,*> Nhymn said. <*I would have never been considered for a seed, nor for a portal walk. My existence was living in darkness, knowing that there is light but being forced to stay blind. I never intended to harm you or your crew.*> She glanced between Sympha and Karx and the human vessels that contained them. <*I didn't realize my presence would alter the dark matter. It was not designed to fit a thing like me in. I am…*>

The Decider realized. <*It appears my punishment for you would be of little use. You are of the Hushed.*>

Nhymn nodded. <*The ones who came before me were Hushed prior to my formation. They found a way to free me from that place and deliver me to Faultasma. I had to remain hidden, a shadow among shadows on a world with no light.*>

<*There are none like you,*> the Decider said. <*The Hush is an old thing, believed impenetrable. But I see now that may not be true.*>

Nhymn turned to the Decider. <*There are* many *more like me. The Hush is a void place, but it has a people. They are the people you cast out long before you made the first portals to the web. Long before your time, Decider. We are no different than Faultasma, only held back by the inhaling of the void. The Hushed strove to reach the light, just as Faultasma had. I am their reach.*>

"Inhaling of the void?" Eliana whispered to herself, just audible enough for Denton to hear. "A black hole…"

A black hole near enough to Faultasma to cast out unwanted phantoms. Over eons, the Voyalten prisoners formed their own unified people, trapped within the confines of one of the universe's most powerful events. Yet somehow, Nhymn made it out of its grasp. *She only wanted to see the light,* Eliana thought. *And she went to such extreme lengths to find it.* Faultasma had no star of its own, but the Voyalten who lived on that dark world could still see the pinpricks of light from distant stars. Eliana could not imagine a crueler fate—to cast people already starved of light into infinite darkness. The Hush was a new addition to the Hells.

Sympha realized, <*We are not sisters then.*>

<*We are both Voyalten, but we are not siblings.*>

The Decider looked at all the Voyalten in the room. <*All of this was caused by our own work.*>

Nhymn looked at the primals behind her. <*I never intended to hurt anyone. The Hushed were not seeking revenge or sabotage. Only a chance to witness light. We found it worthy to feel it upon even just one of our shadows.*> She turned to Sympha. <*The Hushed do not know if I was successful. They only have hope that I could be, and that alone was worth the effort.*>

There was a silence in the room.

Eventually, the Decider looked into Nhymn's hollow eyes and said, <*We can repair what we have damaged.*> They turned to Sympha. <*This portal is healing, but it needs time.*>

"How long does it need?" Eliana asked.

<*Ten years standard to this planet's orbit.*>

Talulo whistled.

Denton said, "No chance using this portal as an escape route then, I take it."

<*It is impossible. In its current state, you'd drown in the vortex,*> the Decider explained.

Using his own voice instead of Karx's, Cade spoke, "We don't have time. The Undriel are on their way to Odysseus City right now." Everyone in the room looked at Cade. He continued, "Auden said if I failed to breach this structure, he'd take his entire army to Odysseus City. For all they know, I was deactivated in the maze. When they finish with Odysseus, they will move on to the auk'nai. Given enough time, they may breach this portal and spread throughout the universe."

"Shit," Denton whispered. Although his family was reunited, this war wasn't over.

Talulo cawed.

Sympha said, <*Can we put our issues aside to save the universe?*>

Nhymn nodded. <*We have to. Or we will have nothing to fight over later.*>

<*Do not betray these people. They will bring you a reckoning.*>

<*I know that better than you,*> Nhymn stated with the weight of experience.

Sympha nodded and released her hold on Nella. Nella inhaled sharply and frantically searched the room. She had been aching to see her brother since they entered the chamber, but Sympha had kept her from her prized reunion to confront Nhymn. Free now, Nella ran to Cade and embraced him roughly. She pulled back and signed, *"I never want to go hiking with you ever again!"*

Cade let out a laugh and smiled. Even in the darkest hours, his sister was a beacon of light. "There is so much I need to tell you all," Cade said, signing with mechanical hands as he spoke. "But the most important thing is this. Everything we thought we knew about the Undriel has been wrong. They can be corrupted. The leashes that bind them to Auden can be severed. I have seen their pasts. Through Karx, I have been able to walk through their memories."

"Like a Shade?" Denton whispered, familiar with the technique.

"Yes, exactly that. I have watched the old war in Sol from their side, and I understand their weaknesses. Where we once thought they were unified, they are divided. Thanks to the energy in this structure, I gained the power to corrupt them." Cade lifted his hand, and blue light licked out of the seams in his mechanical augmentations. "When I use this energy, the Undriel gain back their free will. Once corrupted, they can spread the light. We can stop them for good this time."

Eliana looked around the room. "We can end the Undriel once and for all..."

Having read her mother's lips, Nella signed, *"I will ask my friends to make us a ship. They'll never see us coming."*

"Talulo will rally the auk'nai. Through unity, Kamaria will be saved," Talulo cooed.

"Time to throw some shit they can't absorb at them," Denton added.

All the Voyalten in the room roared with wild ferocity. The portal chamber shook with the anticipation of battle.

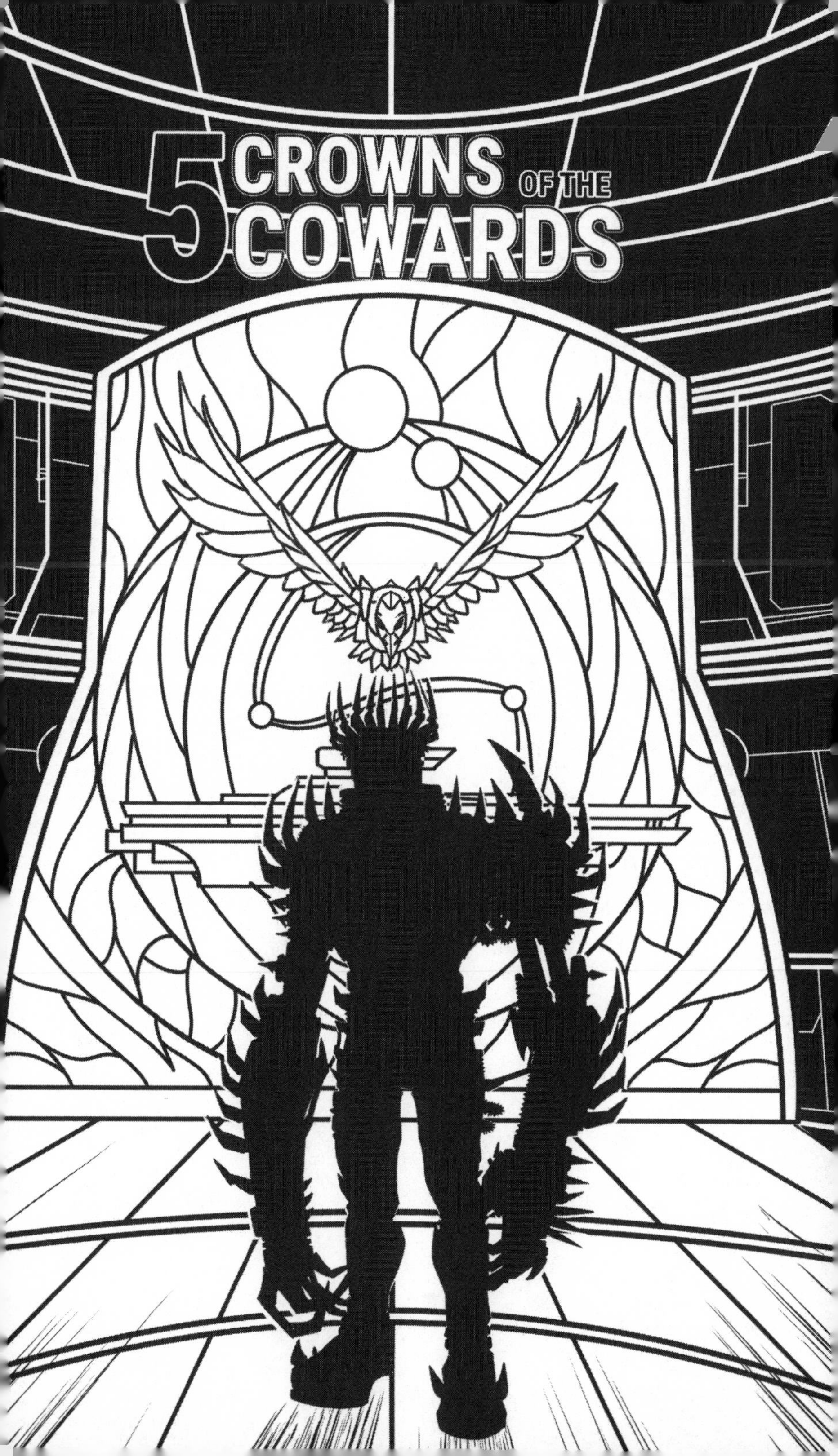
5 CROWNS OF THE COWARDS

THIRTY-NINE

THE DECIDER WOULD STAY behind in the portal chamber. This was not their fight, and there was work to be done to heal the portal if they were to ever return to Faultasma. The strange creatures that made up this world—Kamaria, they called it—were exciting and unpredictable. The Voyalten had a lot to consider; a new assessment was in order. Much of their final judgment would factor in whoever was victorious for the upcoming battle. Rampant Absorb-Tech Cultures—Faultasma's classification for things like the Undriel—were not allowed to join the web. They were too dangerous, too rigid in their beliefs. The Decider had seen worlds taken by Absorbers of different stripes before. It never worked out well.

The other factor would be how this world harmonized with itself. Worlds ripped apart by war would not join the web. Usually, both sides would become desperate enough to use the portals as a resource for their armies. That was a perversion of the harmonized universe Faultasma was trying to create. It was why the previous Decider had cast out some of Faultasma's own people to the Hush.

Perhaps it is time to reevaluate the Hush, the Decider pondered as they considered Nhymn. *There will be time to assess this. But first, this portal must be healed.*

The final factor would be up to them. Did the assessed world want to join the web? No planet was forced to join, the Decider only chose who can, and then the inhabitants made the final step through the threshold. They had been turned down many times in the eons they had lived and traveled. Each time it was disappointing, but the Decider valued their decisions.

The Decider watched the Kamarians prepare for their war. Nella asked the nezzarforms to make Talulo a ship. The Decider was aware that most auk'nai had wings, yet Talulo did not. The nezzarforms were happy to help—they always were—and made him something shaped like a human starfighter. The leader of the auk'nai departed to seek out his Nest.

Nezzarforms had always been friends with the Voyalten. They were constructs that could be traced back to the earliest histories on Faultasma. Something made real by phantoms out of the dirt, clay, and stone of each world they seeded. They could be made on any planet, and they helped shape each world for the web.

After Talulo left, Nella asked the nezzarforms to make another ship to house the others. Now that the Key Ship had served its purpose, it was no longer needed for the portal. It would lose its ability to deactivate Absorbers, but it was a necessary sacrifice. The machines were approaching the human city of Odysseus, and these warriors needed a fast mode of transport.

The Key Ship shifted and rolled in the air, creating something flat with a sharp nose. It hummed with raw power and had stone pillars thrusting through various angles in its rock hull—weapons.

The Kamarians scaled the stone ramp to head into the nezzarform ship. The Operator, Nella-Sympha, was first. By her side was her brother, Cade-Karx—a unique thing he was. A human with a Voyalten rider made into a machine. In all the light and shadow, the Decider had never anticipated such a combination. He alone was worth coming to this broken planet to witness.

Behind them, their parents. Ordinary humans, for the most part. Highly revered among their own people. Now that Nhymn had snapped her tether with the Shade, Eliana and Denton were currently as human as a human could be. They would be at the biggest disadvantage in the upcoming fight, but they had the help of their friends. Humans were weak against the machine menace, but their ability to make allies made them formidable.

Nhymn nodded her sharp bone beak and walked past the Decider with her squad of nightmares behind her. They followed the others into the nezzarform ship, each talon, spike, horn, and beak ready to rip and tear at the enemy. The others did not trust her, but they needed her to fight.

Once everyone was on board, the nezzarform ship coiled up its stone ramp. A pulse of energy waved through its rock hull, and it flung itself away from the portal chamber, riding on pillars of lightning. It rotated in the sky, silhouetted against the midday light, then rocketed off to the northeast.

The Decider flexed their claws and began their work healing the portal.

Night fell upon the city of Odysseus.

Zephyr Gale watched the commotion in the research and development center. Everyone was scrambling. Talk of evacuation was in the air. With no more darts to send, Zephyr's role had evaporated. She stood by, looking for a way to help. She thought of her grandma. If an evacuation was ordered, would she make it out without help?

A defensive line came together to protect the city. After the ambush in the Supernal Echo, the surviving marines had managed to squeeze out a comm call to alert command about the inevitable attack. Nothing was left to stop the Undriel from approaching Odysseus City.

Zephyr tucked herself into a corner, attempting to find the quietest area to make a call to her grandmother, although it was loud everywhere she went. "Come on, Gran. Pick up," she whispered to herself.

No response.

"Damn it!" Zephyr hissed into her soothreader. The speakers in all the rooms blared to life, and a warning was called out.

ALERT – EVACUATION IMMEDIATE.

EMERGENCY MANAGEMENT.

PROCEED TO THE TELEMACHUS MEMORIAL RACETRACK.

EMERGENCY SHUTTLES ARE ON STANDBY.

RELAYED BY THE KAMARIAN COUNCIL.

ALERT – EVACUATION IMMEDIATE.

"Damn damn damn!" Zephyr muttered to herself. She attempted to call her gran again and was met with the same dead silence. *She'd follow the others to safety, right?* Zephyr thought anxiously.

Zephyr rubbed her hand against her face and let out a frustrated sigh. She stepped out into the Campus quad and worked her way toward the garage. Within minutes, she revved her rushcycle, and it lifted off the ground. She roared it out of the garage and made her way toward Colony Town. "I wish you'd pick up your damn soothreader, Gran. You better not be there when I arrive."

"It is time." Tibor rallied his army. "This night, we end this war. Our paradise awaits us on the other side of the battle ahead. We must bring in as many of these lost souls as we can. Our flock will grow, and our peace will be glorious. The end is here."

Auden couldn't help but think, *That Ovid AI can be charismatic when it really wants to.*

Necrodore roared, "We will no longer fear the human threat. This will truly be a new freedom. A perfect freedom."

Hilaria shrieked with pleasure. "I'm gonna enjoy this." She flexed her claws, and her tail coiled and uncoiled, flicking its stingers out to allow them to glint in the moonlight.

Talfryn was silent as ever. Typically, the Reaper would only be sent in to mop up, but this battle was too important. He would fight on the front lines with the others.

A trail of light etched through the sky and approached their concealed location. Faye Raike landed near the army of nightmarish machines. Her frame had been partially destroyed, her arm bashed in, and her mask half removed from damage. Auden approached her and asked, "What happened?"

Faye explained, "We followed the strange stone ship that came out of the structure in the Pit. It arrived at a cave, and we were discovered. The humans have found a way to manipulate the nezzarforms. The soldiers I brought with me didn't make it out."

Auden hated seeing his favorite pet in such disrepair. No trophy should be so miserable looking. He turned to the nearest soldier and ripped its spider-bot head off. The body slammed into the dirt in front of Faye, and she devoured it greedily. Her body repaired itself as the spider bot crawled onto the shoulder of another soldier to hitch a ride. Auden knew it would find a new body in the city. There was plenty of metal and meat to consume in those skyscrapers.

"The humans have a technology we are unfamiliar with," Necrodore assessed. "This complicates things."

Auden looked toward the city, its lights shining into the night sky. "This changes nothing, Necrodore. None of the stone creatures are in the city. I would have seen them when I had L'Arn snoop around. If we can finish the battle before they bring their nezzarforms here, we'll have more than enough soldiers to decimate them when they arrive."

"I like your thinking, Augmentor," Hilaria hissed.

Starships began to lift off into the night sky, leaving trails through the darkness that arched up into the wild void above. Tibor said, "They are evacuating their civilians. They know we are coming. It is no matter. We can find the ones who flee after the battle."

"What are we waiting for?" Hilaria asked.

Tibor turned to his army. "You all know your orders. Initiate the plan. Take as many as you can, make them hybrids if you must, or use the city structure to make them perfect. I will see you all in the paradise that follows."

With a terrifying roar, the machines burst forth from the forest and rushed toward the city. Since they had lost the element of surprise, they would use fear to their advantage. The machines shrieked and increased the luminosity of their glowing eyes. They moved wildly, using tried-and-true methods to instill terror in their enemies. All Undriel warriors had felt this same horror right before they became absorbed into the dark network. Deep down, they remembered how effective it was.

Ahead, human defenses were stacked in strategic positions on an outer wall structure surrounding the city. Particle turrets retrofitted from old warships lined the wall, and Tvashtar marines combined with Colonial guardsmen made up the remainder of the human army.

The human forces initiated their counterattack. A barrage of particle fire lit up the valley between the forest and the city, cutting through a chunk of the Undriel frontline, forcing them down into the tall purple grass. While the forward mass took the brunt of the attack, Faye and a squadron launched higher into the night sky.

Matador starfighters entered the fray, slicing through the night toward the flying Undriel soldiers. The tall grass was illuminated with the flashing lights of particle fire and explosions. Undriel always beat the Matador starfighters in maneuverability, but not firepower. Some starfighters were sent crashing into fiery wrecks in the tall grass below. Others were absorbed into the Undriel army, becoming battle crafts in the process. The human pilots were merged with their starfighters, becoming a new nightmare to deal with.

With a tremendous crash, the Undriel forces smashed into the outer wall of Odysseus City. Screams and explosions were heard as the machines tore through the defensive line. Hilaria and Necrodore battled the Tvashtar marines head-on. Each time Necrodore slammed his massive arms onto a marine, the mechanisms inside would partially absorb the person and churn out a hybrid soldier to fight against his fellow man.

Hilaria didn't waste time with hybrids. She cut through marines with her clawed arms and stabbed through armor with swordlike stingers. She cackled with joy as the people around her screamed in terror. Others in her command followed her onto the wall and delivered the same carnage.

Talfryn was a shadow, only a glint of light reflected off the explosions of Matador starfighters in the sky. Particle turrets exploded as the Reaper sliced through them. Human soldiers were ripped to shreds before they understood what was killing them.

Tibor floated behind them all, a figurehead of the battle. Most of the people fighting would recognize him from their history books. Tibor was believed to be the arbiter of their demise, and Auden was just fine letting them think that way. He wasn't a fighter. Although this was Auden's vision for a more perfect humanity, he still found these methods grisly. He allowed the Ovid AI to have its time in the limelight, wearing the disguise of a murdered trillionaire at the head of a robotic army. Auden would reap the benefits from its shadow.

They had entered the city from the south end. Human forces retreated to a second position, falling into a formation that funneled the Undriel into tighter areas. Auden never liked to play by human rules when fighting them. He had done this on multiple planets, from Venus to the colonies of Jupiter. The best way to fight humans was to confuse the Hells out of them.

The city was dense and expansive, taking up an impressive six hundred kilometers, with three floating circular platforms hovering in the sky above. This technology was strange to Auden, something the auk'nai had made. The aerial battle was weaving in and out of the sky platforms, with explosions pocking their sides as Matadors sortied with battlecraft. Auden was sure they could probably bring those platforms down with devastating effects given enough firepower. *We'll put a pin in that for now.*

On the northeast flank of the city—the far side from their current location—a racetrack was filling with civilians trying to evacuate. Each civilian was a potential soldier for the Undriel, just waiting to be absorbed. Three kilometers north of the track was the Scout Campus. Trucks were driving through the tall grass to drop civilians off there. Ships left the campus shipyard and escaped into high orbit. Auden was unsure what the humans had waiting up in space. Maybe another interstellar ship? Didn't seem likely. He would have noticed. Auden's best guess was that the humans were simply fleeing the planet temporarily and would have to return eventually.

The west side of the city had a river running through it, with bridges crisscrossing its length. A tall spaceport loomed in the distance, with more Matador fighters launching each minute.

"Divide and conquer," Auden ordered Tibor.

Tibor gave him a quick glance over its shoulder. For a moment, Auden had the distinct feeling that he was bothering Tibor. The machine was treating him like an annoying coworker rather than a partner. Tibor looked forward, and Auden could feel the command sent through the shared network.

Necrodore and his portion of the army would move to the city's west side to help decimate the spaceport. Hilaria would flank east and move to the racetrack to absorb as many fleeing civilians as she could. Faye was right where she needed to be, fighting off airborne combatants. Talfryn would join Faye after he finished destroying the turret guns. Auden and Tibor went straight down the city's center toward the tallest building. Their army grew stronger the farther they pushed into the sprawl.

Auden walked behind Tibor's frame, almost enjoying the stroll as his footsoldiers absorbed any marines who got too close. Undriel crawled along the sides of buildings, and particle shots bounced and lanced through the street, blasting from both sides.

They approached the central skyscraper, the tallest building in the city. Its roof loomed over the sky platforms by twenty floors. It would make a perfect forward base for Auden and Tibor to continue coordinating this final glorious battle. With a few commands into the crown network, Auden, Tibor, and a squad of soldiers clawed their way up the building's exterior.

Tibor summoned Faye to help cover their ascent. Within seconds, she was floating in the open air between the sky platforms. Faye had three other fliers with her, each pinpointing snipers and rushing their positions. Auden had a good laugh watching the human snipers get thrown from their concealed positions, only to be gobbled up in a crowd of his loyal machines below. It was nice not having to worry about the corruption. Almost relaxing.

With Faye's help, Tibor and Auden made it to the top of the skyscraper. Tibor flicked his arm and produced a long blade. He sliced through the glass with a smooth, fluid movement and created an opening. Auden and the others moved through the window. Inside, they were concealed from sniper fire and had a visual advantage over the battlefield.

The building had been evacuated, leaving it empty and dimly lit. As the machines moved through its halls, the lights shut off completely. The Undriel kept a blackout radius around each of their bodies. It didn't stop Tvashtar marines or Matador starfighters—they were specifically designed to fight the Undriel—but these buildings were vulnerable to it. Auden knew most civilian technology made on Kamaria was vulnerable as well.

Tibor and Auden entered a tall, expansive room designed for a council to sit and converse in. Its ceiling was vaulted toward a decorative window on the far wall. Long windows flanked the sides of the room, but they were not as grand as the one that reached floor to ceiling. Part of the tall window was clear like the others, tinted on the reverse side with a mirrored effect, perfect for concealment. In the center of the ornate window was a circular design of blue and green stained glass. Its design depicted an enormous bird flying above a human spacecraft. The *Telemachus*, Auden recognized immediately. He wanted to bash the window to dust but knew it served better as concealment than therapeutic violence.

A long, curved table in the center of the room almost formed a complete ring. Blocky, boxed seats lined the walls under the windows, and a balcony overlooked the ringed table, giving ample seating to the citizens of this city. As a civilian would walk into the room, they could see every seat at the table and approach a podium that stood in the center of the ring. No doubt the people who used these chairs had priority information and were probably floating in orbit right now. *Cowards,* Auden thought as he approached the ornate window.

Between the buildings in the sprawl below, the forward progress of the Undriel slowed down. As the humans fell back, they grew more potent in their tactics, and their positions became harder to exploit. In time, Necrodore and Hilaria would flank them from the sides, but they had their own defenses to push through first.

It was a satisfactory start to a final assault. It was time to let the humans wear out their imperfect bodies. The Undriel would cull them all soon. Tibor joined Auden's side, and together, they waited and watched.

FORTY

TALULO FOUND THAT PILOTING the nezzarform starfighter was as natural as flying a human spacecraft. In the years that followed the removal of his wings, he'd rediscovered the sky from the cockpit of various human-made machines. Nothing surpassed the feeling of the open air rustling his feathers, but cutting clouds in a Matador starfighter going Mach 3 was its own sort of enjoyment.

The windscreen of his rock ship was strange. When the nezzarforms combined, one had cut itself so thin that it became semi-transparent. Electricity licked over its surface, but it was no detriment to Talulo's sharp auk'nai eyes.

The controls were more like suggestions in this ship, but they responded well enough. Talulo could not speak directly with the nezzarforms that made up the craft, but with the glowing stones that made up the control console and some tapping of the unsung song, he could suggest directions and flight maneuvers.

The nezzarform craft entered Nest airspace in the Unforgotten Garden, and at once, Talulo knew the particle canons lining the Nest would be aimed at him. <*Reduce thrust and hover,*> Talulo suggested with the unsung song. The nezzarform ship coasted until it came to a stop riding on a sustained beam of lighting. It was an aggressive sight to behold. Talulo tapped his daunoren staff against the glass directly above his head, and it slid backward. He stood from his seat, presenting himself to the auk'nai watching him from the exterior balcony of the Nest. The air was still, and the valley was calm. Talulo cracked out a loud, echoing birdcall, as fierce as thunder.

A moment later, he heard a birdcall return his own. Kor'Oja was allowing him to approach. Talulo sat in his pilot's seat and suggested, *<Come around to the top of the Nest. Talulo must discuss with the auk'nai.>*

The nezzarform craft circled around to the top of the tremendous reformed shipwreck. At the very top was a large balcony with a crowd waiting. The ship hovered just off to the side of the railing and slid its canopy open. Talulo stood and walked along the stone wing, stepping off onto the balcony to meet Kor'Oja, Galifern, and a crowd of his people.

"What a strangeness this is." Galifern tilted her head as she observed the nezzarform ship.

"What did the humans say?" Kor'Oja wanted to get right to the point. His auk'qarn flanked him on both sides, armed to the beaks with armor and weapons. They were always prepared for a fight.

Talulo looked at his people. They appeared scared, confused, unsure of their futures. Their songs mingled together, a soft symphony, quiet and waiting for a crescendo. Their coos sounded like insects chirping to the dueling moonlight. With a calm summoned from deep within, Talulo spoke. "Many auk'nai already know what is coming. Hear the Song of Kamaria. For all of our time, the auk'nai believed themselves to be Kamaria's only audience. Her song was ours alone to enjoy, and as a people, the auk'nai basked in her orchestra. But as the humans cannot hear auk'nai song, so too, the auk'nai cannot fully hear Kamaria's."

Talulo stepped back and forth along the line of the crowd, speaking to them all. Those who didn't fit on the balcony heard him through the unsung song. Talulo's long daunoren staff plodded against the platform, punctuating his statements with his position of authority.

Talulo continued, "Talulo has gained new intelligence. The humans are not the enemy to the auk'nai. Kamaria had already been invaded twice before they arrived." Coos of confusion came from the crowd. "Long before auk'nai and auk'gnell were first hatched, Kamaria had been invaded. They are called the Voyalten. They are planet seeders and have been on this world longer than most sentient life."

Auk'nai looked at each other and whispered questions and realizations. Talulo continued, "Next came the Undriel. The machines punched a hole in space-time created by the Voyalten. They arrived centuries before the humans came here."

Kor'Oja and the others cawed in confusion.

Talulo held a hand out to silence the crowd. With a soft coo, he explained, "Yes, the humans created the Undriel. But the humans did not *bring* the Undriel here. Humans were *not* followed. The Undriel would be here despite human presence. It is the humans who have fought the Undriel the hardest. The humans have held the machines back over the past months, and their numbers are dwindling. Without aid, the humans will become the Undriel. Auk'nai enemies only get stronger as the Nest waits to fight what remains."

Kor'Oja looked at the auk'qarn standing behind him. They exchanged glances, debating this new information. Fighting was what the auk'qarn was for, but what Talulo was describing was dying. Waiting and dying.

"The Undriel will target this Nest after they finish with Odysseus City." Talulo clutched his daunoren staff and kept his eyes on his people. A chorus of fear enveloped the crowd. Some panicked, cawing and whistling.

Talulo lifted his hand and pounded his staff against the balcony. "Auk'nai have a decision to make." Talulo put a hand out to his left, open-palmed facing upward. "Auk'nai remain in the Nest and attempt to fight off the Undriel." He thrust his daunoren staff outward, pointing across the Unforgotten Garden toward Odysseus City. "Or, the auk'nai aid the humans. Together, a united Kamaria can destroy the Undriel!"

The auk'nai considered their options while Talulo rallied. "We have new advantages. See here?" Talulo pointed at the nezzarform craft. "The Voyalten have aided Kamaria with their abilities." Talulo twirled his staff in his hand and slammed it against the balcony. "Auk'nai have our own technologies as well! Arc maces and anti-resonators. The Undriel have never seen what the auk'nai can do. The machines will cower at our talons!"

Kor'Oja and the auk'qarn seemed to perk up at this statement. The others cawed in agreement. Talulo paced back and forth with more energy. "Right now, the humans known as Castus bring a nezzarform warship to the fight. Inside, the daughter named Nella will grant our weapons enhanced firepower. An army made of stone follows her loyally. The son, Cade, holds the key to corrupting the machines. Cade Castus can convert the Undriel's own soldiers against them."

The auk'nai chattered and cheered. Talulo let out a long, echoing call, filling the Unforgotten Garden with a shrill birdsong. He slammed his daunoren staff against the balcony again, and bright light emitted from the collider cylinders lining its hook. Talulo shouted to his people, "The fight is out there, with allies! Our new Daunoren will grow into a world with powerful wings and claws that render war machines into scrap!"

The entire balcony echoed out birdcalls in unison. The Unforgotten Garden filled with the rallying cries of thousands of warrior birds, ready to end the nightmare known as the Undriel.

"Fly!" Talulo lifted his staff and watched as his army took flight.

Kor'Oja let out a long caw and pushed himself from the platform with a mighty flap of his wings, and the auk'qarn followed him. The other auk'nai filled the night sky with wings, talons, and weapons. When the platform had nearly cleared, Talulo stepped back onto the wing of his nezzarform craft.

Galifern cooed behind him. "Auk'nai go to war again."

"For the last time, Talulo hopes," Talulo said, and sat in his pilot seat. The stone canopy slid over him, and the nezzarform ship rotated and flung itself toward Odysseus City.

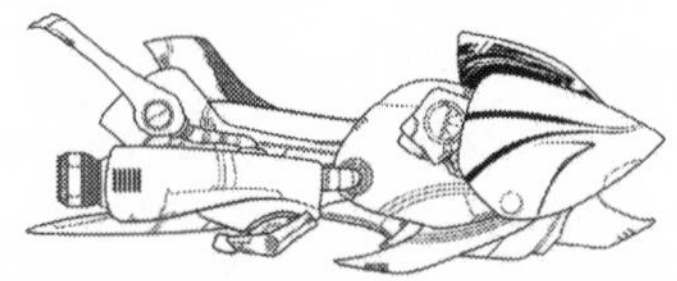

FORTY-ONE

ZEPHYR REVVED THE ENGINE on her rushcycle. The faster it raced, the brighter the chartreuse decals on its side flared, matching its rider's tattoos. It was built for speed, and today, Zephyr would see just how fast she could fly.

The world exploded into chaos when the evacuation alert reached Zephyr's soothreader. Scientists, students, faculty members—everyone on campus bolted for the shuttles. But not Zephyr. She wasn't about to ditch the ground-side before she knew if her gran had made it out safe. Her parents lived close to the racetrack, on the other side of the city from Gran, and they also had not heard from her.

The rushcycle hurtled across the grassy meadow between the Scout Campus and the City. She aimed for the exterior edge of Colony Town, seeing the dirty old domes dimly lit in the night. Beyond the old part of the city, the downtown district burned with the flames of battle.

Zephyr cut through the streets at full speed, drifting around corners. Streaks of light in the sky were heading toward her position from above. The machines were incoming. People scrambled into trucks. Transports loaded with clusters of civilians fled. Zephyr pulled up to her gran's home driveway, a two-story unit built from a refurbished colony home. It had retrofitted windows to replace the old sealed ones necessary during the time of lung-lock. A light was on in the front room of the house, visible through the bay windows. "Damn it, Gran!" Zephyr leaped off the bike and removed her helmet in one swift movement.

She approached the door and pounded her fist against it. Zephyr shouted, "Gran! It's me, Zeph! Open up!"

A ragged voice called from the house next door. "Zeph… Your grandmother got on a truck. She's… safe."

Zephyr turned to see Gran's neighbor, Eddie. He wore an old, colonist-type atmospheric helmet to protect him from lung-lock, the reflective visor concealing his face. Eddie was what the people of Colony Town called a buzzer—someone whose body rejected the cure to lung-lock and was forced to take precautions against breathing the raw Kamarian air. He wore a black T-shirt and gray pants. He would otherwise have just looked like an older man casually sitting on his porch watching the stars twirl by, were it not for his helmet and the particle shotgun he clutched in his hands.

"Eddie, why aren't you on a truck? Get the Hells to safety, man," Zephyr said, stepping away from the door. Her gran was safe; at least there was that.

Eddie let out a low, raspy laugh. "I'll stay. I ran from… the Undriel before. I won't… do it again."

"Don't be like that, Eddie." Zephyr's eyebrows scrunched upward.

"You should… get back on… your bike." Eddie stood and watched the streaks of light grow in the sky above. His particle shotgun activated and whirred with light.

"Oh no." Zephyr gasped. She was too late. A small group of Undriel soldiers was approaching. Zephyr ran over to her rushcycle and slammed her helmet back on her head. As she went to rev the engine, it sputtered and died. "The Hells?" she shouted in frustration.

Her mind went back to her investigation into Cade and Nella's disappearance. The Undriel puck she'd found in the John Veston Archive powered the room they found it in, but there had been a strange rolling power outage. The Undriel caused a rolling blackout wherever they went. Her bike was dead on the sidewalk.

"Run!" Eddie shouted.

There were several impacts in the street, so hard and fast that Zephyr felt the ground shift. She stumbled as she ran around the side of Gran's house. The sound of a particle shotgun blasting and nightmarish machines roaring filled the air behind her.

From Gran's backyard, Zephyr could see more Undriel smashing down into the street. Matador starfighters cut through the air above, almost invisible in the night. The boom of their engines shattered the windows of the houses around Zephyr. Glass spilled from the sky, bouncing off her rushcycle helmet.

I'm a sitting nurn out here, Zephyr thought. *I need to hide.*

With the windows smashed, Zephyr found entry into Gran's house. She quickly mounted a nearby trash bin and pulled herself through the raised window, rolling into the first-floor kitchen. She needed time to figure out what to do. The trucks were gone, and even if they were still around, they'd be shut off by the Undriel presence.

Zephyr needed a weapon. She grinned, remembering Gran always kept a pretty hefty magnum in her bedroom. The old woman had grown up on Mars, probably one of the few Martians left alive on Kamaria. She lived in a rough part of Olympus Mons Square and was always keen on protecting herself.

The sound of a crash came from the front room, followed by the roar of a machine. An Undriel entered the house and searched for more soldiers to absorb. Zephyr sucked in air and felt her pulse rapidly increase. The stairs leading to Gran's room were right next to the front room—next to the hungry machine.

"Shit!" Zephyr whispered. She ran through her options. Even if she could get to the stairs, that Undriel would easily beat her to the top. With no way to defend herself, Zephyr would be absorbed instantly.

Wait! Gran's bedroom had a hole in its closet that led to the first-floor laundry room. Gran cut the hole herself so she could conveniently toss dirty laundry straight down into the laundry room without having to go up and down the stairs. It was Zephyr's best shot.

Zephyr slid up against the kitchen wall and sidled against the doorframe to the front room. The Undriel moved around, hunting. Zephyr understood it was probably sensing her on some level, but the fact it hadn't busted through the wall and absorbed her meant she had some sort of stealth to work with. It finished with the front room and moved toward the staircase, but didn't go up.

Zephyr made her move. She hustled down the hall and entered the laundry room. It was a small space with white plastic walls and a washer/dryer combo unit. There was a moderately sized pile of dirty clothes in the middle of the room, directly under the hole Gran had cut through the floor of her bedroom. The hole had a permanent basket nailed to the top to ensure Gran didn't accidentally fall through it. It also made the chute look a little nicer to the eyes.

Zephyr searched the room until she found a small stepladder. She kicked aside the dirty clothes on the floor and placed the stepladder down. Down the hall, Undriel footsteps thudded. It had worked its way toward the kitchen, and soon it would have a clear view down the hall of Zephyr in the laundry room. With no time to waste, Zephyr scaled the small ladder and jumped up into the chute.

Her legs dangled as she grabbed the lip of the nailed-in basket. There was a mechanical sound from the kitchen. The Undriel had spotted her. Zephyr maneuvered herself until she was awkwardly pinned against the inside of the chute, then pivoted to finish pulling herself through. She flopped into Gran's bedroom, crashing through the closet and making a lot of noise in the process.

The Undriel roared from the floor below, and the sounds of metal footsteps rapidly pounded through the house. Zephyr scrambled to her feet and rushed to the side table next to Gran's bed. She noticed, even in her haste, that her grandmother's soothreader was lying uselessly on the side table, burping with notifications. Zephyr growled with panicked frustration.

The Undriel started to pull itself through the chute, but its progress had been hindered due to its size. Zephyr swung open the side drawer as the machine's head peeked over the basket. It tore through it, cutting an arm into the room.

The magnum was there, loaded and ready. Zephyr palmed it and spun to face the Undriel. It was dark in the room but even darker in the closet. Moonslight glinted off the Undriel's face, and Zephyr's heart sank. The air left her lungs as she realized she was staring at a reflective visor, much like one found on an old atmospheric suit helmet.

Eddie? Zephyr realized with horror. The magnum trembled in her hands.

Eddie clawed and roared, his mechanical body almost fully through the hole. The helmet he wore as a human was fused into the spider-bot head of his Undriel form. He leaned into the room from the closet, his long metal arms cutting at the floor. Zephyr inhaled, fighting the tears invading her eyes.

"Sorry, Eddie!" Zephyr shouted as she pulled the trigger. The shot hit Eddie's visor directly, shattering it and spilling blood against the closet wall. He didn't stop his pursuit. Eddie slammed his metal claw down and pulled himself farther into the room. Zephyr screamed and pulled the trigger five more times. Each shot blasted through Eddie's helmet and into his core. Eventually, after hearing a few empty clicks of the magnum, Zephyr noticed Eddie had stopped moving.

She cried out in anguish. His body slumped back into the hole and fell to the floor below with a loud crash. Zephyr screamed at the top of her lungs and fell to her knees. She hyperventilated, tears washing down her cheeks. Then, something bright blinded her.

The lights in Gran's house came back on.

Zephyr looked at the magnum in her hand, noticing it was empty. It was a pre-collider tech weapon and would need more ammo to be fired again. She dropped the useless thing to the floor and rubbed her eyes. *I can't stay here. Not with…* Half-thoughts filled her distressed mind.

If the lights were on, it meant the Undriel had left the area or had been destroyed. Zephyr walked down the stairs in a haze and took a look back toward the kitchen. An old family friend lay dead in the laundry room down the hall. She gritted her teeth and whispered, "I'm sorry, Eddie. I'm *so* sorry."

Zephyr stepped through the front door and walked out into a street filled with light. Her rushcycle had powered back up. The chartreuse decals on its flank fluttered in a wave. She looked around, noticing the lack of fighting, no roar of machines. Near the front yard was a particle shotgun beside a bloody stain. This was where Eddie had been absorbed into the Undriel network, fighting his last fight against the machines. Zephyr walked over to the shotgun and picked it up. The weapon still worked. She kept it with her, knowing that if she had to kill any more of the Undriel, she'd be doing it with Eddie's gun.

We'll show them. We'll make them pay.

Zephyr's bike would work as long as there were no Undriel in the area. But if she came across more of them, she'd be dead in the water. With the shotgun gripped in her hand, Zephyr mounted her rushcycle in one smooth, practiced movement.

Time to get the Hells out of here. Her best bet was to follow the instructions the evacuation alert gave her and head east across the city toward the racetrack to board a shuttle. Zephyr revved the engine and rode off toward the city.

FORTY-TWO

LAHAR ASSEMBLED WITH MORE of its nezzarform kin to create a ship that rivaled an Undertaker-class warship. It wasn't equipped with much on the inside, only a flat surface to walk around on, a glass divider between the humans and the primal Voyalten, and a transparent rectangular wall facing their direction of travel. There was room for everyone to spread out. Crystals that flowed with nezzarform energy lined the walls, enough to equip a squad with powered weapons.

Everyone listened as Cade explained all he had learned about the Undriel in his Shade walks. Through the window, Kamaria rolled by as Cade weaved a tale of betrayals, absorptions, genocide, and unnecessary waste. He used Sol-Sign as he spoke aloud. "Auden had this device on the *Devourer*. He called it the Ovid. I didn't know much about it, but—"

Eliana interjected, "Ovid? I know that program."

Denton looked between Eliana and Cade. "It's not some sort of new threat, right? We got enough going on around here."

Eliana explained, "It's a Homer prototype. It had interstellar travel capability, but it lacked complete artificial intelligence. Essentially, it could get a ship from one star to another, but it didn't care if the human cargo inside survived the journey. It was the first step of many to get the interstellar project online."

Nella signed, *"How did Auden get it?"*

Eliana let her eyes wander as she thought back. There was only one logical conclusion, and it was terribly simple. "I suppose he just stole it before he left. Maybe he made a copy. He had special access during his time on the project. It's not out of the realm of possibility."

"Sounds like Auden to me," Cade said. "Well, Ovid worked. But it also created this radiating pulse that knocked most of the Undriel offline. After they emerged from the portal Sympha made, they crashed in the ocean near the Howling Shore, and Ovid kept all of them offline for centuries. Auden only made it out because he had been connected to it during the warp. The pulse had a delayed effect on him that he managed to evade. It even managed to knock Tibor offline, and he has his own Ovid core inside."

Eliana nodded. "Another big problem with Ovid was its power draw. To cascade warp from Sol to Delta Octantis, it takes about three hundred years of warping mixed with spin-downs to collect more energy to continue to warp. That's how Homer did it, and it worked. But Ovid didn't do that. In the early stages of the Telemachus project, my father tried to make a machine that would get us from point A to B in one shot. Theoretically, Ovid would punch a hole in space-time and shorten the distance from A to B, making one step cross light-years in an instant. But it required so much power that it would either take centuries to collect or would be so violent in its rapid collection that it would damage other necessary functions, including its own. Very unstable. Auden should have known that."

Cade looked out the window. "I think he did. They were desperate. The corruption was overtaking them, and they needed to escape."

"Sounds familiar," Denton said. "So Auden activated this power-sucker, and the damn thing couldn't tell the difference between what was part of the ship and what was an Undriel, so it just started draining its own people to get ready for another warp test?"

"Computers only do exactly what you tell them to do with the data they have on hand," Eliana said. "You tell it to warp. It's going to warp until you tell it to stop or preprogram it to do so." Eliana opened her mouth and nodded in revelation. "Which is why the Undriel are on Kamaria."

"What do you mean?" Nella signed.

"Well, as I said, Ovid is a prototype of Homer, and Homer even still has some of Ovid's base code. That code was programmed to look at Delta Octantis very carefully. So if Auden just activated the warp test to use it as an official launch, it would go to Delta Octantis. He was a scientist, not a warp engineer. I don't think that fool had any idea what would happen." Eliana remembered Auden's cave on the Howling Shore. He lived like a hermit machine, waiting for his chance to return. The coward wouldn't move far from the Devourer, too afraid of what his death might cause. "The night he took me and Homer's android unit to his cave, he had everything he needed. Homer easily deactivated the malfunctioning Ovid core, and the Undriel were resurrected."

A thoughtful silence followed. The puzzle was complete, the image clear. Nella signed, *"We're going to finish them. Cade has the secret weapon."*

Cade flicked his hand and observed the seething blue energy frothing from his palm. "We can free the Undriel. Together."

"I never thought we'd ever end up in such a crazy situation," Denton said. "I thought I grew up with a weird family on Ganymede. Boy, was I in for it when you two came along." He put a hand on each of his children's shoulders. "I wish we didn't have to go to war to save the world, but if it was going to be anyone, I'm glad it's people I trust."

After a moment of reflection and calm, Eliana split away from the others. She walked toward the glass divider that separated her from Nhymn. The primal Voyalten behind the glass faced her, like strange creatures curious of what was just outside their burrow. Nhymn stepped forward from the back of the group. She looked the way she had when Eliana sealed the doors to the *Odysseus* spacecraft so many years ago, except larger—wilder.

They both remained silent. Eliana looked up into Nhymn's hollow eyes as the Voyalten stowaway looked down past her horn and beak. Eliana thought of her father. Nhymn had used Roelin Raike's body to kill him and so many others. She looked into the hollow eyes of her father's true murderer now.

Eliana was surprised that her hate had faded so much. It had been sanded down with time, its rough edges now smooth and perfect. She no longer wanted to scream and blast this monster with a shotgun. The dull ache in her heart was quieter now.

She remembered her conversation with Talulo about forgiveness. Eliana didn't need to forgive Nhymn. She never could. Nhymn had ripped her father away from her, and that pain would never fully heal. But she understood this creature now. Nhymn was like a frightened, confused child who only wanted to find the light.

Eliana didn't trust Nhymn. Trust had to be earned. But she understood Nhymn now. She didn't agree with her and did not condone her actions, but she understood *why* they happened. It was a desperate, sad, violent affair that could never be changed.

Without exchanging a word, Nhymn stepped back into the crowd of primal Voyalten. Eliana lingered a moment longer, then walked back across the ship to her family. The weight of her father's death lifted off her chest for the first time in decades.

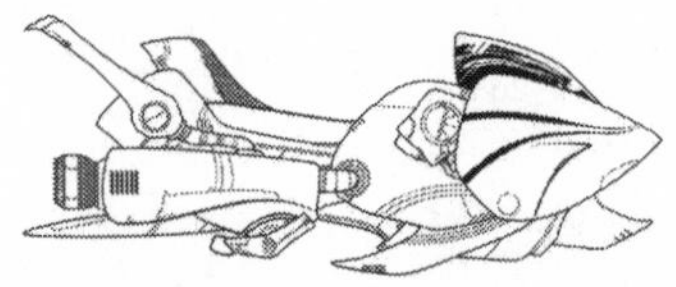

FORTY-THREE

ZEPHYR HAD CHOSEN HER tattoos carefully. She'd convinced Cade into getting a matching piece on his left forearm, a canary. It represented the ancient Earth history of their chosen profession—Mining. The old Earthlings mined in caves and carved out mountains, whereas Zephyr and Cade mined asteroids using prospector drones. Same job, vastly different times.

The canaries were used in old coal mines to detect carbon monoxide. They would die in its presence, alerting the miners and giving them time to find fresh air. Zephyr felt like she was riding a large canary right now—her rushcycle. It, too, would die if the Undriel got close enough. The Tvashtar Marines and Matador starfighters had been made to fight the Undriel. They had equipment designed to nullify the Undriel influence. Zephyr's rushcycle was built several years after everyone stopped thinking the machines were a threat. The technology used to combat Undriel interference had to be included in its entire design, like waterproofing. One leak, and the whole thing busts.

Zephyr raced down the streets of Odysseus city, making her way to the east side where the racetrack was taking civilians to safety. She had wasted time checking in on her gran, but she was glad to know the old woman was safe.

There was a chokepoint ahead, where the city was bisected by a river. The river was large, as wide as two asteroid haulers, with three long bridges crisscrossing over it. The bridges were down and accessible, but they were clogged with abandoned cars. Tall skyscrapers lined the river's flanks, and concrete walls traced down into the rainbow-hued water. The streetlights were still on, which was a good sign. A floating city platform hung almost motionless in the air in the sky above. The video screen on its underside flickered with damage.

The dull boom of an explosion to the south rang out through the night.

The streetlights shut off, and darkness approached her like a tidal wave. "Shit, shit, *shit!*" Zephyr said as her rushcycle sputtered to a stop.

The canary died.

"Move it, lady!" someone called out from a concealed position.

Zephyr frantically looked for the source of the voice. She couldn't find them. *Did I imagine that?*

She was swept sideways, blindsided by something. For a moment, Zephyr was convinced it was an Undriel footsoldier about to absorb her, but she would have been dead before the thought came to her. Zephyr was shoved behind a barricade. She scrambled to get her footing and finally discovered the line of Tvashtar marines. They were hidden in a defensive line, waiting to head off the Undriel forces approaching the area. There must have been over three hundred of them, lining the street and the balconies of the closest buildings, waiting to strike.

For a moment, Zephyr felt safe. Then she realized this was the new front line, and she couldn't be in more danger.

The marine who pulled her aside was a strong, bronze-skinned man. The tag on his suit read A. ORTIZ. He checked Zephyr for injuries and shook his head. "You shouldn't be here."

"I- I was trying to get to the race track for evac." Zephyr stammered over her words, braced by the kind of anxiety that comes from speaking to people with guns.

A dark-skinned woman next to Ortiz—nametag reading I. AKINYEMI—huffed and said, "A little late for that. Too dangerous to cross the bridge right now."

"I just came from that way. There were some in Colony Town," Zephyr said.

Akinyemi and Ortiz looked at each other, realizing they may have been flanked in this chaos. Akinyemi quietly pulled her soothreader closer to her mouth. "Wood. Keep an eye on our six. We might have more coming from the back."

A quiet voice came back over the soothreader. "On it."

Akinyemi looked down at Zephyr's particle shotgun. Her fierce brown eyes flicked back up to Zephyr. "You know how to use that thing?"

"Yeah. I think so." Zephyr realized she had never even fired the shotgun. She had no idea how the recoil would affect her.

"Good. Point it at the machines and stick close. We fight them back here, and then we can work on getting you to safety." Akinyemi looked down at the device at her side. It was a panel of various switches and nobs.

"I'm not a soldier," Zephyr admitted.

"Everyone is now." Ortiz grunted and aimed down the sights of his particle rifle.

"Targets sighted, above levels. Twelve and two o'clock," Wood said over the comm.

"On my mark," Akinyemi said, and held her breath. More lights shut off in the street ahead. Dark shapes filled the plaza, with glowing white and red lights shifting in the shadows. Zephyr breathed short, panicked breaths.

"Open fire!" Akinyemi shouted, and hit a few switches on her device before quickly pulling her particle rifle onto the barricade. Rockets blared above and impacted the plaza ahead—mortars from Akinyemi's device. Marines unleashed an inferno of arsenal. A mixture of particle shots filled the air with white-hot energy. Rockets continued to assault the approaching Undriel forces, scattering metal. The sound of war was deafening.

Zephyr's shotgun was only good at close range. Regardless, she sprayed buckshot particle beams into the chaos before her, adjusting to the recoil of the powerful weapon the more she pulled the trigger. She ducked back down right as a shot almost grazed her cheek. The Undriel forces returned fire.

The marine to the right of Akinyemi took a shot directly to his face. He slumped backward, and Zephyr screamed. Akinyemi and Ortiz didn't stop firing back. They were numb to the horrors of war at this point. If they stopped to acknowledge their fallen comrade, they would quickly join him.

An Undriel leaped over the barricade and tackled Ortiz. Zephyr reflexively let out a blast from her shotgun. It tore into the Undriel's back, and it spun. The distraction was just enough to give Ortiz the opening to bash it with a rotating saw blade tucked in his gauntleted fist. The Undriel was thrown off Ortiz, and Zephyr blasted it three more times until it stopped roaring and sputtering.

"Knock them back!" Akinyemi commanded. Ortiz grabbed a handle on the barricade and pulled a trigger, as did other marines in the line. All at once, there was the concussion of explosions as the barricades blew out energy on the enemy-facing side. Undriel close to the barricades exploded into fragments, vaporized.

"Five minutes to recharge!" Ortiz shouted. He looked forward, and his eyes went wide. "Oh shit!" He grabbed Zephyr's arm, pulling her with him as he jump-jetted sideways. Zephyr thought her arm might have snapped from the impact, but she was lucky it didn't.

A behemoth machine burst through the barricade where Zephyr and Ortiz had just been. It snatched up a marine close by and absorbed him through its massive arm. It spat out a new Undriel soldier, and both began to tear through the defensive line. The process was so quick and violent that Zephyr was slow to comprehend how it happened.

Ortiz pushed Zephyr behind a flipped autocar for cover. He set his rifle to autofire and let out a heavy assault on the behemoth's back. Instead of turning toward Ortiz, part of its shoulder dislocated, and a turreted gun appeared. The turret spun to face him and blasted out a beam of energy. Ortiz was quick enough to jump jet away, leaving Zephyr's position entirely. He shouted, "Just get out of here! Run!"

"Are you kidding me?" Zephyr exhaled the words with panic breaths, observing the chaos. Akinyemi and Ortiz fired on the behemoth as the rest of the line battled the main force. If she went back the way she came, she'd be walking toward the flanking Undriel soldiers. If she went forward, she'd be attacked by the approaching force. Her only option was the bridge, but that faced the side of the bulk force ahead. It wasn't safe by any means.

If she stayed put, she'd be dead in a few minutes.

"Damn it!" Zephyr huffed as she scrambled toward the bridge. She used line-of-sight cover, ducking behind cars and street dividers. She was fortunate that Akinyemi and Ortiz had managed to bring the fight away from her position. Still, that advantage would only last so long. She froze in her tracks as dark shapes appeared against the flickering firelight of the sky platforms floating above her.

More Undriel! Zephyr panicked. She had made it back to her rushcycle, but it was useless in the current circumstances. She wished she could jump on it and fly off down the street, irrationally optimistic that her speed could beat the Undriel's particle weapons.

Zephyr covered her head and tried to make herself small as the dark shapes grew larger. She heard an impact on the street directly in front of her, and she began to cry. This was it. She had moved directly into their trap, just like the others. Zephyr and the marines stood no chance against such an overwhelming force. The Undriel were everywhere.

She heard her rushcycle ignite. Its start-up sequence cast out the chartreuse light from its frame. She peeked out from her hands and looked up.

"Get to safety," the winged figure before her said. "Auk'nai are here to fight."

It was a tall, formidable auk'qarn warrior in armored sashes. He had brown and bright red feathers with white paint covering some of his bulk. His daunoren staff was sharpened into a spear, with collider cylinders violently spinning. A gauntlet on his left arm had a rod protruding from it, with energy building up at its tip. Zephyr had never seen a more fierce and welcome sight in her life. She smiled. Tears dripped from her eyes, but not those of fear, only tears of relief.

"Do not make Kor'Oja say it again, human," Kor'Oja said. He let out a loud caw, and several other auk'qarn warriors joined his side, not stopping as they rushed past. A strange starfighter made of rock and lightning raced overhead, tearing through the sky as more auk'qarn warriors sailed just behind it. They flew together as a wing, cutting toward the battle Akinyemi and Ortiz were still fighting. In unison, they linked their gauntlet energy together into a line of white-hot fire, then flung it outward.

The Undriel were caught entirely off guard as the line of energy cut down most of the machines in its path, slicing them in half or causing severe damage to their frames. The stone starship shot bolts of lightning, bursting any Undriel that came into contact with it. Multiple explosions lined the battlefield, and cheering arose.

The Undriel had been beaten down, but they were not out. Many of them took to the sky to head off the auk'nai, and an aerial battle began. The behemoth moved back toward its bulk force, and the forward momentum of the Undriel army came to a halt. With the front lines aided by the auk'nai, the humans took shots at the enemies flanking from behind.

Zephyr shouted a long and boisterous Ganymede holler, as she had seen Cade do so many times. After a moment of awe, she lifted her rushcycle off the ground and noticed a new device slapped on its exterior, something curvy and definitely auk'nai design. It brought power back to the vehicle, and even with the Undriel forces close by, it wasn't fading away. "How did they fix…?" Zephyr whispered to herself. The streetlights were still off, but the bike worked.

She heard a whistle, and an auk'nai landed in front of her rushcycle. It looked more civilian than the others, with normal color sashes and a daunoren staff built for agriculture instead of war. The auk'nai reached into its sashes and said, "Human. Take this."

They handed her a small mechanical dot, no larger than her pinky fingernail. They cooed and pointed to her soothreader, "Call out more Undriel pockets. Ping auk'qarn if human sees anything on human's way to the evac site. Auk'qarn will come to help."

Zephyr attached the dot to her soothreader and watched it reactivate despite Undriel interference. She had a few alerts from her parents, explaining they'd found her gran and wanted her to join them. They were already on a shuttle heading toward the *Infinite Aria*.

Glad you guys made it out safe, Zephyr thought. Peace of mind was another gift from the auk'nai. She nodded. "I will call them out."

The auk'nai cooed and flapped their wings hard, kicking up dust and loose chunks of asphalt as they sprang toward the battle. Zephyr revved up her rushcycle and darted off across the bridge toward mid-city, leaving the humans to fight alongside the auk'nai once more.

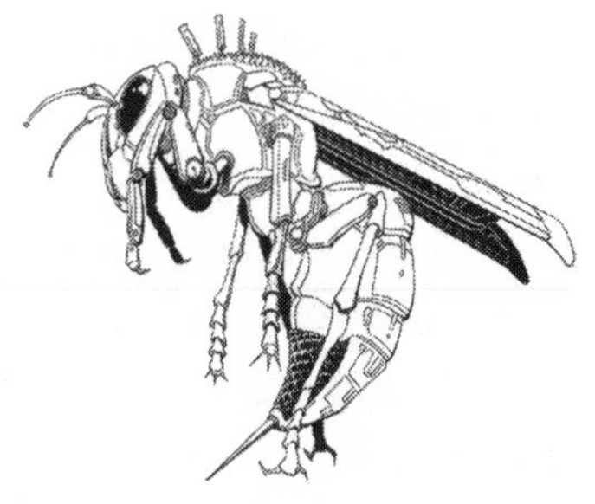

FORTY-FOUR

"THE AUK'NAI HAVE JOINED the human forces," Necrodore reported over the shared Undriel network.

"I see that," Auden said flatly. Perched high in his skyscraper, he could see every angle of the battle through the ornate window. Necrodore's progress had been stopped on the city's west side, but Hilaria was still moving at a good pace toward the eastern racetrack. The auk'nai had been a surprise. Auden wasn't looking up high enough to notice them. He looked over to Tibor and said, "Let's bring them into the network."

Tibor spoke through the network. "The good Augmentor has provided us with the insight needed to absorb the native Kamarians. Gather them into our flock."

Hilaria cackled in agreement. Auden couldn't help but smile at her response. She really was here for the thrill of it all, and she didn't have to bullshit anyone. She also didn't stand in his way. For this reason, Hilaria was Auden's favorite general.

Talfryn responded with silence, as usual. The Reaper was only a dog that did as it was told and nothing more. It reminded Auden of his former pet, King, the German Shepherd he'd left on Venus. The Reaper tore through defenses on the city's east side, aiding Hilaria's approach to the racetrack.

The newest general in the network, Faye, only confirmed she had heard the response with an audible blip. Auden's grip was firm and constant on Faye's crown, especially after that unique hybrid managed to slip the leash. He would not let his trophy leave him.

Necrodore had been damaged in the surprise auk'nai attack. The behemoth general added, "We will see it done." Jonas Necrodore had been loyal to Tibor in life, as he had been in his ascension. The grand general of the Undriel army was a strategic genius in the pre-Undriel days, and his war-mind had become an absolute asset for their movement through the Sol System. Although Jonas had retired from the military to command on Tibor's private yacht, the old tactics were still accessible to the network. With the threat of the corruption gone, Necrodore was free to fight any way he wanted. He no longer had to look over his shoulder at his own soldiers. They were loyal to him and to the Undriel in whole. Their crowns and veils saw to that.

"The birds won't bother us much longer," Auden said. "And there are not many humans left to oppose us now. We'll be in paradise by sunrise."

Tibor looked back over the city, watching the chaos below. Particle beams lanced out in all directions, and flashing lights and explosions pocked the blacked-out streets.

"Not long now." Auden smiled under his metal helmet.

Hilaria and Talfryn pushed their bulk of the Undriel army north, riding the city's eastern edge. The machines were able to partially conceal themselves in the tall purple grass. Faye Raike helped fight off the human and auk'nai defenses, guiding her aerial teams through the city's eastern side while Hilaria and Talfryn stayed low. They had met minor resistance during their approach, which Hilaria despised, but she knew the prize was ahead.

The racetrack would be filled with civilians, plenty to shred apart. This was what she'd joined the Undriel to do. She didn't care about Auden's paradise—for it was *Auden's*, not Tibor's. Hilaria knew a thing or two about hiding in plain sight. Auden was hiding. Tibor was too much of a boy scout to be the leader of such a gruesome crew. Still, she played along.

She loved to play.

The exterior walls of the racetrack were high, decorated things. The lights were intensely bright, echoing off into the stars above. Marines lined the walls, with a line of armored vehicles and turrets surrounding the perimeter at its base.

"Get their attention," Hilaria ordered Faye. Faye and her squadron of fliers brought their assault to the defenses on the walls. The explosions and beams lit up the sky, only casting faint glints off the metal horrors trudging through the tall grass. Hilaria turned to her Reaper companion and cackled quietly. Behind them, an army of hundreds of Undriel followed, running in cold mode to avoid detection. It was a little trick they picked up from the Tvashtar marines. It worked during the lake ambush, and so far, it was working here too.

As Faye and her soldiers got closer to the racetrack, the bright lights shut off. Hilaria was delighted to hear the screams of the civilians scrambling around inside. "You just wait. The fun is on its way."

There was a screech in the air. Hilaria rotated one of her cameras toward the sky and flicked on various sensors. The damned birds! A squadron of auk'nai spotted Hilaria and Talfryn's army from above. They twirled electrical energy in a way that Hilaria had never witnessed before. Rings of light lit up the sky in the field above. For a moment, she was stunned by its magnificence. That moment ended abruptly as the auk'nai flung the electrical shapes at her.

Hilaria and Talfryn's army went hot and cut through the tall grass to avoid the attack. Explosions of metal blew shrapnel across the field. The grass ignited with fire, and soon their concealed position was the brightest place on the planet.

"Talfryn, Faye. Take care of the birds! I'm going for the prize," Hilaria ordered. Talfryn uncoiled an array of blades and particle guns from under his cloak and took off into the sky like a wraith. Their unit fired particle weapons into the air at the auk'nai, who deftly dodged their attacks with the inherited prowess.

The Reaper snatched one of the auk'nai warriors. They became a swirling mass of metal and cloaks, until eventually, something new was born. In mid-air, Talfryn birthed the first Undriel'nai from his cloak. The mechanical bird had long arms that could extend like spears and an extensive retractable neck. The weapons the auk'nai warrior had on it before absorption became part of its body. The gun it had strapped to its beak was absorbed into eyes that could shoot particle beams. The gauntlets and staff became blades that flickered with unstable red energy. Its wings were augmented into something more like a starfighter's wings, with built-in thrusters, giving it an advantage over its unabsorbed kin. It looked like an insect crossed with a bird made entirely of gnarled, jagged metal.

It was a new nightmare.

Hilaria loved it.

The Undriel'nai rocketed off to attack its wingmates, joining the rest of Talfryn and Faye's crew. There would be more to come. The network was growing.

Leaving Talfryn with Faye to fight in the field, Hilaria took the rest of her troop and rushed the armored vehicles around the perimeter of the racetrack. She crashed into the closest truck as her unit smashed into the others. Hilaria ripped through the marines on the turrets and absorbed what she could, using the rest of the truck as material. One marine tried to scramble away, and she launched her swordlike tail at him, almost cutting the man in half as she struck him. She pulled him close and slammed him into the vehicle, absorbing him into their network.

When they finished and regained what they'd lost in the initial auk'nai attack, Hilaria's unit scaled the racetrack's outer walls. Her claws dug into the walls as she ascended. The humans grew wise to her tactics and began firing down at her from above. Particle shots fell upon her, striking her a few times. Hilaria used her tail to snatch up the closest Undriel soldier and use it as a shield. As her shield lost integrity, she grabbed another. When she was close enough to the top, she hurled her damaged soldier at the marines, striking two of them at once.

She made it to the top and looked down into the racetrack from the nosebleed section of the bleachers. Hilaria and her unit decimated the defenses waiting there, overtaking the stands. She drew fire from other spots in the stands and from hovering Matador starfighters. Hilaria could see trucks leaving the racetrack on the far end, heading north. In the far distance, ships were still exiting the atmosphere.

Hilaria ordered her unit to take cover. They were too exposed to rush forward, and they would have to slow their progress from here. Hilaria still had the advantage of numbers, and soon, Undriel'nai soldiers would be part of their mix.

It was only a matter of time.

Except.

Hilaria adjusted her eye lenses, unsure of what she was picking up. From the east, glowing green lights were approaching their position. It wasn't reading as anything she recognized on her scanners, except as something geological. It was like a mountain flying through the air. It flickered with lightning.

What in the Hells is that thing?

FORTY-FIVE

IT WAS TIME TO return the pain. Cade had been waiting for this moment for months. Flickering just under the surface of his metallic body was the one thing the Undriel were terrified of—the corruption. Cade didn't think of it as corruption. He knew it as an antidote. It was time to turn Auden's perfect people against him.

He looked to his family.

Scientist.

Shade.

Siren.

Spy.

Nella clapped her hands, then signed, *"We are approaching Odysseus City."*

Denton exhaled a long breath. "Here we go."

Eliana turned to Cade. "What's the plan?"

Cade realized he didn't really have a plan. He let his jaw hang slack.

"Sounds like we're doing this the Castus way." Denton grinned.

Nella read his lips and huffed.

Eliana shook her head. "So, in other words, no plan."

Nella pushed her open-palmed hands upward and signed, *"We are going to do great."*

Denton threw a thumb toward the primal Voyalten in the glass cage at the corner of the room. "They are going to freak people out if we just land in the city with them."

Nhymn spoke directly into their minds. <*You will not be rid of us so easily.*>

"We get it. You're helping whether we like it or not," Denton said. "But if you cause a bigger panic, then that's not helping at all. You want to win this thing, don't you?"

Nhymn thought for a moment, then offered, <*Release us here. We'll work our way through the shadows.*>

Nella, Cade, Eliana, and Denton looked at each other. Eliana was the first to shake her head. "I don't like it. We won't know what she's up to then. It's dangerous."

Cade scanned the primal Voyalten up and down, "She can do whatever she wants regardless. At least with this option, we have a trick up our sleeves the Undriel won't see coming."

Nella signed, *"Bombs away!"*

Eliana, Denton, and Cade simultaneously went, "Huh?"

The glass and stone cage the primal Voyalten were standing in dropped out of the nezzarform ship. Nella had expelled Nhymn and her soldiers into the forest just outside the city. After a moment, the hole in the ship sealed as nezzarforms moved to fill the gap. Nella signed, *"We were running out of time. The racetrack is close. Looks like there's a battle ahead."*

Cade took a deep breath. "We're as ready as we're going to be."

The Castus family moved toward the front windscreen of the nezzarform ship. Two pylons rose from the floor, and Nella put her hands on them, giving her more influence over Lahar. Nella had never really piloted a ship before, and Lahar had not been a ship very long. This was going to be interesting.

The nezzarform ship came roaring into the racetrack's airspace, smashing through an Undriel that looked suspiciously like an auk'nai. Eliana's eyes went wide, and she turned to Denton. "They are absorbing auk'nai now."

"Bastards." Denton grunted.

The racetrack was dark, save for the lights of particle fire zipping back and forth. Trucks filled with civilians attempted to flee, but they couldn't budge due to the blackout caused by Undriel interference. Nella put Lahar right over the center of the racetrack, hovering above the bulk of civilians.

Nella spoke to Lahar through her mind: <*Let them have it!*>

Green lightning shot out from the nezzarform ship at all angles. Precision blasts vaporized Undriel soldiers, scattering their shrapnel in hot white explosions. Nella and Lahar focused on the southern end of the racetrack's grandstands, where the Undriel seemed to be in the largest numbers. Just beyond, the auk'nai fought the machines in the sky.

Cade tapped Nella on the shoulder and signed, *"My turn, let me out."*

Nella nodded, then asked, *"How will we know which Undriel to shoot?"*

Cade gestured to his arm, and the lights that lined his body shifted to a bright blue. He signed with azure-lit arms, *"Blue lights are friendly."*

Nella bobbed her fist in acknowledgment, then pointed to a spot on the floor just behind her position. A hexagon of green light seeped from the floor. Denton and Eliana caught Cade as he approached the hexagon of light.

Denton patted Cade on the shoulder and looked him in the eye.

Eliana hugged him and said, "Go save Kamaria."

Cade nodded and moved onto the hexagon. He ignited with fierce blue light, readying himself for the fight. Nella let out a loud Ganymede holler and deployed Cade. He dropped out of Lahar into a freefall. Cade caught himself after a few meters and activated thrusters, shifting parts of his mechanical body to deploy weapons and armor on the way down. He had full access to his Undriel toolkit now—jets to help him fly, swords tucked into each of his arms that could be extended from his wrists, and particle rifles that could shift into place to give him ranged weaponry. Auden was powerless to stop him after the Decider had done their work reactivating him.

Cade thrust forward toward the grandstands, powered by the heat of revenge. Green lightning bolts flanked his sides, guiding him toward the fight. Through his network, he could hear the Undriel chatter.

"Is that the fucking *hybrid?"* Hilaria's familiar hiss.

Undriel shots zipped toward Cade, and he pivoted into a sideways twirl, barrel-rolling away from Hilaria's weapon fire. Cade returned fire, pinning Hilaria to her place in the grandstands. A nezzarform bolt from Nella's ship crackled past Cade and crashed into Hilaria's position. The scorpion machine was flung back over the wall into the field, injured and broken. Cade went to pursue.

As he crossed over the lip of the racetrack wall, Cade was struck from the side. He could feel the blades of an Undriel soldier cutting through his augmented body. Cade extended one of his swords and swung back toward the assailant. He struck home, knocking his attacker away. Cade pivoted and found his attacker.

Faye Raike seethed with red energy. "Hybrid." She spat the word.

Cade thrust toward her. She had no idea what was coming as she opened the chainsaw-like maw on her chest to absorb him. Cade cut thrust and pivoted last minute, slamming into Faye, feet first. The momentum of his cut engines sent them careening toward the tall grass below. Before they hit the ground, Cade slapped his hand against Faye's mechanical skull. She screamed in agony all the way to impact.

They hit the dirt, and Cade rolled away from Faye. Instantly he was on his feet and braced for another strike. His sword was ready to swing, and his left arm morphed into a particle rifle in case she tried to shoot him. Cade knew the corruption would work, but he had no idea how fast. This was the first time he'd tested it in his own reality, not as a Shade walker. It could be different here.

Faye rose from the grass and stumbled toward Cade. She

screamed and fell to her knees. The red energy that seethed through her metal paneling washed into blue, crawling through her body from the head down.

It's working, Cade thought, relieved.

"The Hells. What is…?" Faye looked around frantically.

Cade knelt before her. Behind him, the battle in the sky of machine and auk'nai raged on. He put a hand on her shoulder and said, "Don't panic."

Faye slowly came to her senses. She looked at her augmented hands, then to Cade, "Cade? How did you…?"

"It's a long and complicated story. But here's the point…" Cade held Faye's hand within his and showed her the blue glow. "The power I have is also yours now. We need to unlock as many of the Undriel as possible, and they too will be able to spread this power."

"The corruption?" Faye separated from his hand. "Yes. Auden and the others were so scared." She surged the energy, feeling it froth from her body. Cade recognized the look in her eyes, the panic that came with realizing you're a monster. It took him back to that first moment trapped in the metallic closet, his own horrific visage reflected back at him. Faye took the information better than he had. She pushed her anxiety down deep, using all her training as a soldier to dampen the panic for now. She looked at Cade. "I understand. Let's get to work."

"Get as many as you can," Cade said.

In unison, they took off into the sky and split up. Faye went left, while Cade went right. Behind him, Nella continued to blast away at stray Undriel soldiers in the grandstands. The nezzarform ship was out of range of the battle above the field.

Cade rolled away from the particle shots from the tall grass below. He slammed into another flying Undriel from behind and crashed his palms against its head. Blue light exploded from its spiderlike eyes, and it plummeted to the grass below. Cade didn't have time to explain the power to everyone, and he hoped they wouldn't continue their fight once their free will was unlocked.

There was no guarantee of that, though. The hard fact was that some people preferred to be Undriel and believed in Auden's vision. They would fight Cade to the death.

A circular ring of light smashed into the Undriel squad firing at him from below. A loud whistle was heard, and a trio of auk'nai warriors rushed toward him. Cade put his arms up in defense and was surprised when they halted their attack. The trio spun their arc maces in circular motions, and the light they created combined into a large ring of energy. In unison, they punched the light forward into another group of Undriel below.

The trio's leader spoke to Cade. "Talulo has ordered the auk'qarn to aid Blue Undriel. Show auk'qarn how to help."

Cade looked at the arc maces, and an idea came to his mind. "Are those weapons repurposed Undriel tech?"

The auk'qarn captain looked at his arc mace and cooed.

"Perfect!" Cade placed his palm against the gauntlet and pushed the corruption into it. The white light at the end of the arc mace shifted to blue, just as he hoped it would.

"Stars and songs!" the auk'qarn exclaimed.

"You have the same power I do now. Share it with the others." Before Cade could go into further detail, a group of Undriel raced in their direction. The auk'qarn trio combined their light into another ring. The blue light ate up the joining white energy, permanently affecting each arc maces. They flung the bolt down into the tall grass and watched as a group of Undriel became corrupted by its light.

Cade's army was quickly growing. As fast as the Undriel could absorb, he could corrupt.

Two more incoming Undriel intercepted Cade. They forced him to maneuver away from the auk'qarn with an array of particle blasts. Cade soared higher into the sky but was too slow. He was struck in his shoulder by a shot, injuring his left arm. Cade felt the corruption leave his arm entirely in a wave of cold. As much as he tried to reignite it, it would not return. He ignored this information for now, rolling into his attacker's flight path.

Cade extended the sword on his left arm while reaching forward with his right hand. Although his left arm had lost the corruption, his right hand had not. He slammed his sword into the Undriel who had shot him and slapped his corrupted hand into the one who had missed. Both fell to the ground, where more corrupted soldiers were starting to discover their new abilities.

The fight was shifting.

On the other side of the field, Faye converted her old squadron to their side. She made it look far more effortless than Cade had. She spun the corruption in ways Cade had not considered. Her prowess on the battlefield showed.

A roar came from ahead. A barely visible mass of cloaks, blades, and guns thrust away from the fight, bringing with it a squadron of Undriel that remained loyal to Auden. The auk'qarn warriors cawed out a sonorous war cry in victory as Cade's Undriel filled the tall grass below. Each of them sobbed and screamed in confusion.

<*WE HAVE SECURED THIS AREA,*> Karx said.

<*This is only the beginning.*> Cade watched the Reaper fade into the dark. It headed toward the sky platforms before vanishing entirely. The city was engulfed in war. Human and auk'nai forces battled the Undriel in the streets, and fires pocked the skyline.

Now that he had a moment, Cade checked his body. His left arm refused to ignite with corruption, but his undamaged right arm retained the blue light. Although he could repair and morph his left arm, his ability to convert Undriel had been reduced by one appendage.

<*WE NEED TO BE CAREFUL,*> Karx warned Cade. <*WE STILL DON'T HAVE ENOUGH TO END THE UNDRIEL. WE NEED MORE SOLDIERS.*>

Cade nodded in agreement. He searched the area for Hilaria, the most dangerous and ruthless of the Undriel generals. She was nowhere to be found, having slunk away to repair her damage. Just knowing she was lurking somewhere out there gave Cade chills all over his mechanical body.

Faye joined Cade's side in the sky. She watched as the Reaper fled the battle. She said, "I need to go after Talfryn."

"We will," Cade said. "First, we need to explain to these people what has happened and what they can do now. Will you help me?"

Faye looked down into the field of blue light, then at her own mechanical hands. "I… we're monsters."

Cade shook his head and looked her straight in the eye. "Not anymore. What happened to us was not our fault. Auden has lied to everyone. He controlled you and forced you to do terrible things. Auden must be stopped, and we're going to do that today."

Faye opened her facemask and looked at Cade. He could see the sorrow in her eyes. She was the one who'd delivered him to Auden all those months ago. She had snatched Cade away from Denton and brought him to the Howling Shore. Faye tried to say something but couldn't squeeze the words out.

"It's not your fault, Faye," Cade reiterated.

She blinked and looked away from him with a grimace. She understood, but she still struggled with her own internal demons. Faye looked at the others in the tall grass and whispered, "This must be how Roelin felt."

"Let's prepare our people for the fight ahead," Cade said.

Faye nodded, and they lowered into the field. They landed gently and approached the crowd of confused machines. They were people again, and they needed an orientation about their new situation.

Cade raised his hands, his right palm bursting with blue light. He amplified his voice so they could all hear him. "Hear me now. From this point on, you are free of the Undriel's grasp. You may leave if you wish, but if you stay with us and fight, you will help us secure a safer future. Let me explain."

The lights came back on in the racetrack, and there was immense cheering. With the Undriel pushed out of the area, the power had returned. Trucks took off once more toward the Scout Campus, and medical tents were back at full capability to help the many wounded.

The nezzarform ship lowered Nella, Denton, and Eliana safely to the ground in the middle of the racetrack, right in the command center of the evacuation operation. The nezzarform ship reassembled itself, releasing a squadron of stone soldiers to follow Nella, while the rest converted into a spacecraft to house injured civilians.

Denton, Eliana, Nella, and her nezzarform soldiers stepped off the stone platform and walked toward a lieutenant. He was a man with bronzed skin, a rugged jawline, and a shaved head. Denton had only seen photos of Mido Sharif, but he had worked under his command with Sergeant Jess Combs and her Dray'va Teeth for the entirety of the war.

"I should have known you had something to do with this," Mido said as he shook Denton's hand. "For civvies, you Castus folk sure know how to mess up the Undriel. I never thought I'd see anything like that. You secured these civilians' escape."

Nella signed, and Eliana translated to the hearing lieutenant. "Take your wounded onto our ship. They will be safe inside."

Mido wasted no time. He relayed the information through his soothreader, and nearby medical staff began bringing wounded soldiers and civilians toward the stone platform.

In the distance beyond the southern wall of the racetrack grandstands, blue lights streaked toward the city. Cade's corrupted Undriel were continuing the assault, moving toward the sky platforms. This fight was just beginning, but the blue beams of light were a hopeful sight. Denton tapped Nella and Eliana on the shoulders and pointed toward them. "Cade's done it! Look at that!"

"What am I seeing here?" Mido asked.

"Tell your men that those blue-glowing Undriel are on our side. It's a long story, but my son has found a way to free the Undriel."

"Incredible. We might just win this fight," Mido whispered with a smile.

The lieutenant relayed all the information to the people in

charge operating in the *Infinite Aria*. Denton and Eliana helped load people onto the stone platform. Nella privately used her powers to help the mortally wounded recover from the injuries that threatened to kill them. The dark patches of organic matter on her brain screamed with pain with each person she healed.

"Castus, you have some visitors," Mido said. He handed Denton, Eliana, and Nella some working soothreaders. Their originals had been permanently deactivated by the Key Ship's energy. They strapped them on, and the reader scanned their eyes and downloaded their old information instantly. The holographic image of George Tanaka and Marie Viray appeared over the readers.

"Thank the songs, you are all safe," Marie said. Then she signed, *"We're glad to see you safe, Nella."*

"I wasn't worried for them. You should have seen the fire in Eliana's eyes as she left to find Nella. I was worried for anyone who got in her way," George said with a smile.

Denton looked at Eliana. She gave him a gesture that said, *I'll explain later,* then asked George and Marie, "Where are you?"

Marie said, "We're in the Scout Campus coordinating the evacuation. We'll be getting on a shuttle soon."

Nella signed, *"Is Jun with you?"*

Marie looked at Nella through the soothreader and signed, *"Jun is safely in orbit. He didn't want to leave without you, but we had to get him to safety. I will let him know you were asking about him."*

Nella tapped her fingers against her lips and pushed her hand toward Marie's holographic image. *"Thank you."*

Denton thought for a moment, then asked, "Hey, is there any way we can check in on my family quick?"

"We have a partial log here. There's no way we'd get everyone. It was too crazy," George said. "Let me look them up with what we got." He swiped over his soothreader a few times, then leaned forward to hit a few buttons on a holographic keyboard. "Aha. Here we go. We have one entry for Brynn Castus. That is your mother, correct?"

"Only one entry?" Denton's concern was growing in his voice.

"That doesn't mean the rest of your family isn't on board. They might not have checked in with the staff," Marie added.

"I figured at least Tyler would," Denton said. He flicked over his soothreader to make a call to his brothers, but there was no answer. That either meant they were out of range or actively in an area with Undriel soldiers, which would deactivate their tech.

"I can send a message to the people on her shuttle if you'd like," George offered.

"Please."

Eliana squeezed Denton's arm as George sent the message and waited for a response. It felt like an hour passed, although it couldn't have been more than a few minutes. The staff on her shuttle only needed to float over to Brynn, ask her what her family's situation was, then float back to the terminal with a response.

George received it and frowned.

"What did she say?' Denton asked.

"Both of your parents are on a shuttle," George said. "But they said your brothers wouldn't leave the shop. Apparently, they had something that would help the war in there."

"Damn idiots!" Denton shouted.

"Don't go making any—" George tried to stop Denton, but he was already moving. The call ended abruptly.

Eliana hurried to follow Denton across the field. "Where are you going?" she asked, raising her voice.

He turned and walked backward across the grass, his arms stretched outward. "Gotta save my dumbass brothers now. Can't just let them die in that shop. Jay would hate that the most."

"I'm coming with you," Eliana said. Her voice was firm.

Denton stopped and shook his head. "Nella needs you."

Eliana pointed across the grassy racetrack interior toward Nella and her nezzarforms. "You see what kind of firepower she's packing? Nella has shown me she's been more than capable of handling herself these past months. I've spent so much time trying to keep up with her, but she outruns me by a light-year with every step. It's *you* who needs me now. I'm not about to let you run off again without me."

Denton stood motionless. He wanted to tell her to get to safety, just get on a shuttle and leave. But he had seen this scenario play out before. She had been at his side when they piloted the *Lelantos* toward Nhymn decades before. Denton had thought it was a death sentence back then, and he wanted Eliana to leave and survive. She refused then, and he knew she'd refuse now.

"I love you, Elly."

"Damn it. I love you too," Eliana said, with a distressed smile and a weak laugh.

"Come check this out." He waved her over. They walked toward a long shed tucked under the grandstands. Denton blasted the lock with his collider pistol, and the door swung open loosely. Inside was a rushcycle covered in a tarp. "Remember this old gal?"

Denton flung the tarp off the rushcycle and revealed the Claire O'dine, the same rushcycle they had piloted in their dramatic escape from the *Lelantos*.

Eliana nodded and mumbled, "Desperate times call for some crazy shit." She activated her particle rifle and discovered that the nezzarform enhancement no longer worked. She was too far away from Nella to access Sympha's power. Eliana sighed, knowing this wasn't a good idea but also knowing she couldn't talk Denton out of it.

"Get on." Denton mounted the rushcycle. Eliana sat behind him, sitting high enough on the seat to give her the ability to aim and shoot with the rifle over his shoulders. Denton revved the rushcycle, and the whole bike vibrated and lifted off the ground. Denton smiled.

He piloted the rushcycle out of the shed and toward Nella, near the operating center. Nella's eyes went wide as she looked at them both. She shook her head and signed, *"You can't leave."*

Denton signed, *"We have to rescue your uncles."*

"I'm going with you."

Eliana shook her head. *"Stay with Lieutenant Sharif and his men. They need your powers."*

Nella looked at the ground, then back up to her parents. *"You better come back."*

Eliana signed, *"We will. Promise."*

Nella ran forward and hugged her parents. Then she took a few steps back.

Mido came forward, holding something in his hand.

"You can't talk me out of this, sir," Denton stated.

"Hells, I'm never telling you what to do," the lieutenant said curtly. "I know you got your reasons. Just take these with you." He handed over a package of curved, puck-shaped objects, then slapped one onto the hull of the Claire O'dine.

"Hey! This is a vintage model!" Denton protested.

"Well, that puck will keep it running even if the Undriel are nearby. The auk'nai made these. Anti-resonators, they call them. Take some extras in case you find anything useful that needs power."

"Thank you, sir." Denton saluted.

"Good hunting." Mido nodded.

Denton looked at his daughter, and she looked back. He was leaving again, riding off on some grand purpose and leaving her behind. He felt like his heart was being pulled apart, mixed with the duty of saving his siblings and the urge to stay near his daughter's side. Nella's face grew stoic, strong. She nodded with understanding. Denton looked at the nezzarforms standing near her. He pointed a finger at Lahar. "You keep her safe."

The nezzarform didn't react, but Nella did. She smiled and patted Lahar on his stone arm. Nella and Lahar watched as the rushcycle peeled out toward the racetrack's exit.

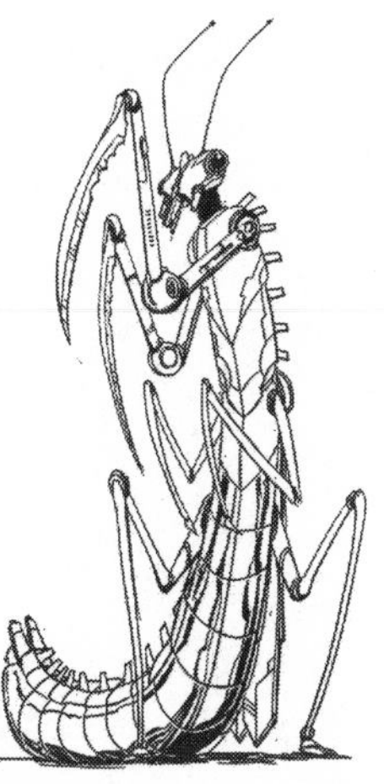

FORTY-SIX

CADE TOOK TO THE sky with Faye at his side. An army of auk'qarn warriors and corrupted Undriel filled out their squadron, each ready to give their lives to end the machine menace once and for all. They worked their way toward the city's center, where the fighting was heaviest. Cade knew Auden and Tibor would be there, but their exact location remained a mystery.

One of Cade's Undriel soldiers vanished from sight, dropping down faster than he could register it. Cade slowed to a hover and looked back as more of his soldiers were cut from the night sky. He looked up just in time to see flashing yellow eyes and talons rush toward him from above. Cade pivoted and narrowly avoided the Undriel'nai's divebomb.

"Eyes up!" Cade called to his squadron. The Reaper's squadron had used the dark clouds above to conceal their positions. Particle fire rained down on Cade and Faye's unit. Flying over the city, they were caught out in the open. Cade looked for something to use and found Ruby Platform nearby. It was one of the three floating sky platforms hovering above Odysseus City. Its surface was covered in curved auk'nai designed skyscrapers and other assorted buildings.

"It's Talfryn and the absorbed auk'nai," Faye shouted, returning fire with an array of miniguns that emerged from all over her frame. She was a warship.

Cade morphed his left arm into a rifle and joined her, creating covering fire for the rest of their people so they could make it to the sky platform. He shouted, amplifying his voice so all could hear, "Lure them onto Ruby Platform! Use the buildings as cover!"

With a shriek, the auk'qarn warriors rolled and soared toward the closest floating platform. One auk'qarn was caught by an Undriel'nai and ripped apart, absorbed during freefall. More of Cade's Undriel soldiers were torn apart by particle rain, falling to the ground as rubble and jagged metal. When enough of his unit had made it to the platform, he activated thrust and followed them, with Faye close behind.

Talfryn the Reaper and his squadron of Undriel'nai emerged from the clouds and gave chase. Cade felt a particle shot rip through his right thigh and hated how much his metallic body still felt like his human one. It didn't cease any of his functions, but it still hurt like Hells. The Decider had not removed Cade's ability to simulate pain so accurately.

Cade cut thrust and spun to face his attacker, allowing his momentum to throw him the rest of the way. Talfryn rushed toward him at incredible speed. Cade used both of his arms as assault rifles and sprayed particle fire at the Reaper. The cloaked machine zipped sideways, out of Cade's vision as the skyscrapers rushed into his view. Cade reactivated his thrusters and stopped himself from crashing into the ground level of the platform. He landed and heard a cough.

An injured auk'qarn was nearby, speaking over a shared comm channel. "Need reinforcements on Ruby platform. Undriel'nai incoming." He cawed and gripped tighter at the bleeding wound on his torso. The debris of a torn-apart Undriel'nai squirmed near his feet.

If Cade had Sympha's power, he could have healed the wounded auk'qarn. Helpless, he was forced to watch the warrior expire. He drew his last breath and sighed with a gentle coo.

The world around Cade grew quieter. A low humming came to his ears, almost imperceptible yet clear as a bell. Cade had heard the Songs of Kamaria before, and this one was familiar. The Song of the Dead played for Cade. The auk'qarn warrior hummed it from a plane beyond this one. He was joined by an orchestra of others this night—the humming both beautiful and sad. Cade nodded to the fallen warrior and bid him safe travels on his journey into the afterlife.

Faye landed in the street near Cade and looked to the sky. "I know the way Talfryn fights. Leave him to me."

"He's all yours," Cade said.

Faye bolted off into the space between two skyscrapers. She wouldn't be able to handle the Reaper alone, especially when he was surrounded by Undriel'nai. Cade found his squadron scattered around the streets, taking cover from above and shooting when they could.

A green bolt of lightning rang out overhead, vibrating the windows of the skyscrapers surrounding their position. An explosion followed soon after as an Undriel'nai was caught in the bolt. Talulo's nezzarform starship whipped past the space between the buildings.

Cade smiled.

Auk'qarn warriors followed Talulo's ship into battle, flanking Talfryn's soldiers from the side and drawing fire off Cade's people in the street. "Reinforcements are here! Let's bring it to them!" Cade shouted to his squad. Cade's Undriel and the remaining auk'qarn warriors rallied and took to the sky, using the buildings as cover and moving around the tall corners.

Cade piloted around one corner and found a duo of Undriel'nai waiting for him. One rushed him and slammed its beak into Cade's shoulder. Cade shouted in pain and slapped his right hand against the Undriel'nai's head. The corruption pulsed through his attacker, and the metallic bird removed its beak from Cade's body. The other

Undriel'nai began firing on them both. He fired back, and the Undriel'nai zipped sideways. Cade's particle shots missed his target and exploded the glass window of the skyscraper just behind where it had been. The attacking Undriel'nai shot a beam of light from its eyes, striking the soldier Cade had just absorbed in its center mass. The newly corrupted Undriel'nai exploded, sending fire and shrapnel everywhere.

Cade thrust through the explosion and smashed into the Undriel'nai, bashing it through the skyscraper's window across the street and into its interior. They punched through two walls and landed in the center of a dimly lit art gallery. Projectors lit wild splashes of colors on the walls, casting huge shadows across the room. Cade slammed his hands down on the Undriel'nai's head and corrupted it. Confused and afraid, the newly corrupted Undriel'nai flew away.

Cade only had a short moment before he heard a crash. The wall in front of him disintegrated into dust and debris as two machines rolled and fought each other. Through the kaleidoscope of color emitting from the projector, all Cade could see was blades and cloaks.

Faye and Talfryn rolled together, tangled in combat. They sailed over Cade's head and bashed into the wall behind him, destroying the projector and leaving the room in a dark, foggy haze of chaos. Faye struggled to keep Talfryn's blades from cutting her in half, failing as the scythes raked through her body in numerous areas. The blue light had faded from her body completely, too damaged to corrupt anymore.

Talfryn jerked his head toward Cade and roared.

Faye shouted, "He's targeting you! Get out of here!"

Talfryn ripped Faye's arm off and sliced through her lower half. She clattered to the floor and scrambled to get herself into a position where she could fire. The Reaper rushed Cade.

The Reaper's blade pierced Cade's left arm, pinning it against his chest. The momentum threw Talfryn and Cade back outside, sailing over the neighboring skyscraper and smashing into the rooftop of the next one past it. Cade extended the sword on his right arm and chopped the Reaper's blade off, freeing his left arm from Talfryn's hold. They rolled apart on the tall rooftop as explosions pocked the night sky around them.

To battle with Talfryn, Cade would have to fight like a Reaper. He looked down at the severed Reaper's blade and had an idea. He snatched up the loose blade and absorbed it. Instead of keeping it palmed, Cade shifted his internal mechanisms and used the Reaper's blade as an extra appendage that emerged from his left shoulder. He now had three arms to fight Talfryn with—two blades and a particle rifle.

Talfryn twirled wildly in a mass of ragged cloth and curved blades. He sprayed particle fire in random shots meant to distract and confuse rather than to hit accurately. Cade shot back and thrust forward. He swiped with one of his swords but missed. Talfryn's body had split in half to avoid being cut, becoming two problems instead of one. Each half was just as capable of killing Cade as the whole Reaper was.

Cade leaped over the lower half of Talfryn but was caught by the upper half and slammed to the floor, chest down. Talfryn's grim metal face was pressed against Cade's cheek. The Reaper stabbed his right arm.

"No!" Cade shouted. The blue light fizzled from his fist, and the corruption faded with it. The Reaper seethed with smoke, pleased with his success. Cade struggled, attempting to rotate and pivot away, but it was no use. The Reaper knew how to restrain him too well. Talfryn raised his blade again, this time targeting Cade's head.

The weight of Talfryn's body was ripped off Cade. Faye Raike intercepted the Reaper before he could stab Cade's head. She was flickering with irreparable damage, leaving a trail of dark smoke and shrapnel in her wake.

Talfryn's top half was removed from the fight, but his lower half whirled toward Cade. Cade pulled himself to a crouched position. He heard a roar in the sky. It grew louder as its source approached.

Cade had another idea. As the Reaper's lower partition whirled toward him, Cade swung his blade in an uppercut. The Reaper partition was flung upward into the air, where a green lightning bolt blasted it into pieces as Talulo shot by. His nezzarform starcraft was so fast and so close it burst the nearby windows of the skyscrapers as he rocketed past. Talfryn's lower half had been annihilated, leaving only hot sparks trailing down.

"Faye!" Cade looked in the direction of Faye and Talfryn's upper half, tangled in combat in the sky. He activated his thrusters and launched toward them.

Faye knew her ability to corrupt Talfryn had been severed after the Reaper had sliced her apart. She had resurrected enough of her functions by using materials found inside the art gallery, but she was more like a thrown stone now than a combat machine. She clutched Talfryn tightly, feeling each blade slice through her frame as she was repeatedly stabbed.

Talfryn had been her brother-in-law, back when humans were still human and Roelin was still alive. The entire Raike family had met their tragic fates and succumbed to multiple parasitic lifeforms. It was a curse.

"I'm sorry, Tal," Faye whispered weakly as her systems began to fail. "It's time we ended this nightmare."

Without the ability to corrupt, Faye only had one option left.

There was a resounding explosion in the sky. The blast was so hot and so violent that Cade was thrown off course. He corrected himself and looked where Faye and Talfryn had been, only to find a puff of smoke.

"Faye!" Cade shouted uselessly.

<*SHE IS GONE,*> Karx said.

"Shut up!" Cade reacted out loud. "She can't..."

He wanted to save her. Cade knew Talfryn and Faye's story. He had seen them in the Shade walk, working with Roelin to stop the previous Reaper. They were all together again, somewhere Cade could not follow. They were free now.

<SOMETHING IS HAPPENING BELOW.>

Cade hesitated, finding it hard to tear his gaze away from the puff of smoke that had once been Faye and Talfryn Raike. An explosion lit up the night, and he looked down toward the floating platform. His eyes went wide.

"No, no, *no*!" Cade shouted as he watched the platform shake. It tore itself apart with explosions so grand that Cade had to look away to shield himself from the illumination. A red beam of light blasted through the platform, casting chunks of skyscraper and street up toward the stars. The buildings crumbled, and waves of dust and smoke writhed up. Buildings tumbled off the sides as Ruby Platform plummeted to the city below.

The warrior auk'qarn and converted Undriel finished off the last of Talfryn's Undriel'nai squadron as the city fell away from their feet. Anyone standing was forced to flap upward to avoid being caught in the mad chaos of the platform's destruction. They watched from the sky as the carnage rained down below.

"We got problems in mid-city!" Zephyr Gale pinged the auk'qarn with her dotted soothreader. She steered her rushcycle as quickly as she could, heading east through mid-city toward the racetrack. She felt the heat of several explosions above her as a targeted particle beam smashed into Ruby Platform.

"Oh shit!" Zephyr shouted as buildings rained down. She was under the immensity of the platform, watching it sink closer and closer, threatening to smash her into nothing. She gunned it as fast as she could on her rushcycle.

Buildings crashed all around her, causing cascades of more structures to explode and roll around. The planet shook, causing

Zephyr's bike to wobble in its path. She barely cleared the impact radius as the platform smashed down with a thunderous quake as if a star had fallen from the void above. Dust and debris pushed outward from the impact and thrust Zephyr forward at an uncontrollable speed. She screamed as she rode the wave of carnage until it dumped her bike sideways and sent her rolling through the street for almost an entire city block. Zephyr felt the street bash into her from all angles during her roll.

Finally, she came to a stop on her back. She barely registered her rushcycle as it slid right past her head, not even able to flinch. It whipped past her and smashed into the side of a truck.

Zephyr blacked out.

Her eyes opened slowly.

Everything was blurry. She could feel the heat on her face. Someone had removed her rushcycle helmet. In the blurry haze of the ripped apart world around her, she could see blue lights, like the glowing gnats she used to chase in the field outside Colony Town. What pretty things they were.

"Hey! Don't pass out again! Stay with me now!"

Who is that? Zephyr wondered as her eyelids opened and closed like waves on a calm sea. She could smell smoke, and felt the dust that caked her body. She coughed. Her eyes opened and adjusted for only a moment.

"Come on, damn it!"

Zephyr thought she saw Cade. But that couldn't be possible—Cade was gone. Cade had been taken months ago.

She pushed her eyes open with great effort and struggled to let them adjust. The blue lights came into focus, and she saw nightmarish machines surrounding her in the sky above. She laughed at how screwed she was.

But wait...

A face she recognized stared back down at her. His sapphire-blue eyes. His smooth, dark skin tinted with the stubble of facial hair. His lips looked soft and inviting. His eyebrows curled up in worry.

His short hair was messy.

Ah, I recognize this dream. Zephyr weakly threaded her fingers through his hair.

Cade smiled. "There you are."

"I've been looking all over for you," Zephyr whispered.

"I'm here. You found me." He grabbed her hand, revealing his augmented body to her for the first time. Zephyr didn't care. She didn't have the strength to care. "Hey. Hey, Zeph." He urged her not to close her eyes again.

"Yeah?" she asked.

"Old Cyrus is malfunctioning again. You want to help me fix him?" Cade asked, referring to a particularly bothersome prospector drone known for its problems.

She laughed, then felt a sting in her abdomen that made her wince. She breathed a few heavy breaths and realized something was not right.

Wait, this isn't a dream.

"What the Hells are you talking about?" Zephyr felt a sharp sting in her guts. She opened her mouth in a silent scream.

Another voice, an auk'nai: "Talulo has removed the obstruction. Applying the salve now."

Zephyr's eyes were wide open, and her senses went into overdrive. She heard the clatter of a long metal pipe hit the street next to her, but when she tried to move her head, she couldn't. She looked up at Cade. "What's happening?"

"Looks like she's awake now," he said. Zephyr finally took in the sight of Cade's mechanical body now, understanding that he was really here—and he was also mostly a machine.

"Zephyr's heart rate is spiking. Calm Zephyr down," Talulo said.

"Hey, listen, Zeph. I know you have a lot of questions. But I need you to take a few deep breaths and calm down," Cade whispered in her ear.

Zephyr wanted to scream at what had been done to him. She

wanted to close her eyes and let this nightmare end. She couldn't move her head, and it drove her nuts. "Why can't I move my head?"

"You broke your neck," Cade answered. "We have it braced. You also took a nasty fall and had a pipe sticking out of your abdomen. You're lucky it didn't pierce anything we couldn't fix."

"Salve is in. Zephyr must rest. Let salve do the job," Talulo explained.

"What?" Zephyr asked, not resting.

Cade tried to soothe her. "You're going to be alright. Trucks are here to help the other wounded in this area. They will take you to the *Infinite Aria*. Hells, if you ask nicely, maybe they'll even drop you off on the *Maulwurf*. Wouldn't that be something?"

"Oh shut up, you ass!" Zephyr began to cry. "I missed you so much."

He smiled at her. "I've missed you too."

"What happened to you?" She could barely urge the words out of her throat. Her smile faded into worry and confusion.

"It's a long story. I'll have to tell you later." Worry covered his face.

Zephyr was lifted over the street, floating on her back a few meters off the ground. She was on a hover stretcher. She protested, "Wait! I just got you back! Don't leave now."

Cade leaned forward and kissed her on the forehead. When he lifted away from her, she could see the unnatural glow in his blue eyes. "I'll see you again. I need to finish something first."

"Cade!" Zephyr cried out with frustration as Talulo ordered some Tvashtar marines to bring her stretcher to an evac truck. They loaded her in, and before the doors closed, she watched Cade fly away from the destroyed part of the city, taking a squad of corrupted Undriel with him. He was continuing the fight.

"He's alive," she whimpered with a mixture of happiness, relief, and fear.

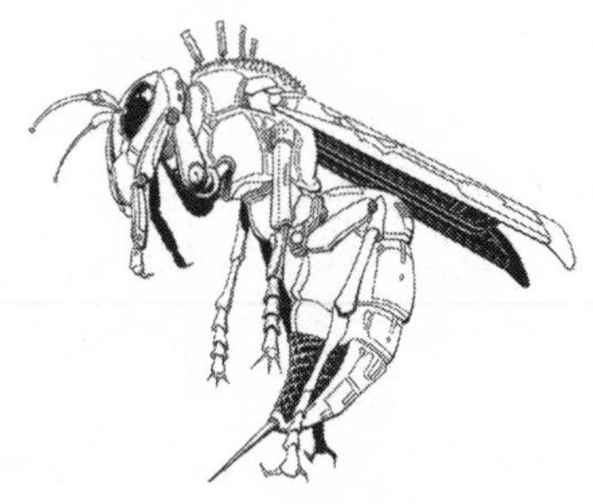

FORTY-SEVEN

AUDEN WATCHED AS THE floating platform plummeted into the city below. The skyscraper he stood in shook, and for a moment, Auden thought it might collapse. Cracks jolted through the ornate glass window, and some of the chairs around the ringed table fell over. When the shaking ceased, the dust clouded the night. It hung in the air like a specter, creating a dirty fog that concealed most of the mid-city.

Auden couldn't believe it.

The corruption was here. Faye and Talfryn were lost to it—Auden's trophy and prized pet were gone in one explosion. Hilaria was critically damaged and had slipped off the network to remain hidden from the hybrid.

Necrodore had been wounded from the auk'qarn weapons, but he remained triumphant on the battlefield. Although the humans had secured the city's eastern side, Necrodore had pushed their forces away from the western side. The fight was moving toward the middle of the city, where a final victor would be crowned. Necrodore's takedown of one of the floating platforms further decimated the human defenses and their ability to form cohesive battle lines. But would it be enough?

Auden didn't like it. Bringing down one platform helped stall the fight, and he had two more platforms at his disposal. Auden would render this place to scrap before he let the corruption take him. Even if he was the sole survivor of this entire conflict, he could rebuild. He'd been fine for centuries alone on that far beach. Without the threat of humanity hanging over his head, he'd be free to start a new world the way he wanted.

In his caution, Auden started to consider his plan C. He would need a way out of this place if it fell to the human and auk'nai forces. He eyed the battlefield with new regard.

Over the top of the foggy dust that clouded everything, Auden could see across the city to the racetrack. Green lights flickered in the distance, and some immense object floated in place above it. It was made of stone and electricity, and it brought a reckoning. The humans had found a way to weaponize the rocks of this planet.

But these rocks were to be feared.

"What's your position?" Auden asked Necrodore through the network.

Necrodore reported, "The impact did not hit their main force, but this dust will be an advantage to us. We are preparing to move."

Tibor said, "You must force this battle now, before the stone creatures can get involved. If you can overtake their current force, the rest will fall."

"Where is Hilaria? I need her here," Necrodore asked.

"She has moved off-network. We do not have time to wait for her to return," Tibor explained.

"That fool! She better have a damn good reason for this!" Necrodore spat.

Auden privately agreed.

"I will begin the assault," Necrodore said. Auden watched from the cracked ornate window. He smiled as he predicted the next moves. The battle in the mid-city would end up under one of the remaining floating platforms once it moved into position. If needed, he would sacrifice Necrodore if it meant he could extinguish the corruption and humanity.

Necrodore commanded his unit to move into the thick dust of the recently toppled platform. The combination of smoke and darkness would be a considerable advantage against the foes he fought. They moved silently, working their way through a bramble of twisted metal and skyscraper fragments.

An auk'nai flew through the dust, looking for wounded. Necrodore silently ordered one of his Undriel'nai to dispatch it. There was only the soft sound of air being displaced, quieter than a muffled cough. The Undriel'nai absorbed the auk'nai, and another soldier joined Necrodore's ranks.

As they worked their way across the debris, Necrodore ordered his ground troops to find cover in the destruction and convert into snipers. Their metallic bodies were perfect camouflage in the rubble, and they reorganized their top halves into long-range guns, and they could see through the fog with an array of sensors. Everything was working to their strengths.

They approached the front line. Humans, auk'nai, and most disgusting of all, corrupted Undriel, worked through the rubble to find survivors. The hybrid was nowhere to be seen, but his dark work was everywhere.

In the previous war, before Kamaria, Necrodore had been immune to the corruption as a hybrid. His behemoth suit was a hollow thing he stepped into to make Tibor's vision come to fruition. But now, he was a perfected Undriel, merged with the suit and vulnerable to the influence of the corruption. He had seen many of his own kind altered by this anomaly. He knew that coming into contact with such infected minds resulted in the viral spread.

Luckily, Necrodore also had keen insight on the best way to dispatch Undriel. He painted his targets red as he scanned his enemies, signaling to his snipers which enemies to prioritize. They would reveal themselves, but the corrupted Undriel on the front line would be eliminated. It was worth the trade-off.

They were ready.

"Kill."

There was one loud blast, as quick as a heartbeat. Hundreds of particle lasers lanced through the thick fog and hit each of their targets with pinpoint precision. Necrodore watched with relief as each of the corrupted Undriel burst, their cores compromised. The humans and the auk'nai turned to face the fog and reached for their weapons.

"Fire at will," Necrodore commanded his troops. It was his turn to join them. His bulky arms opened up and revealed an array of miniguns. Without their shields, the humans and auk'nai were totally vulnerable to a direct frontal assault.

It was a shooting gallery. Enemies scrambled into cover, some making it, but many falling to the barrage of weapons fire. After a few moments of total carnage, the surviving enemies found their positions and returned fire. Necrodore knew this attack would draw in reinforcements from the areas that the humans and auk'nai had previously secured. If he could funnel them into his trap, he could overtake them and retake the parts of the city Hilaria had failed to keep. Necrodore would have to fight hard, but he knew he could turn this battle around if he stuck to his tactics.

Undriel'nai rushed in to keep the confusion high. The enemy defenses were split, shooting upward at the Undriel'nai and forward into the fog. They blindly aimed at anything that peeked through the thick dust, mostly hitting wreckage. They became targets in their confusion.

Necrodore moved back deeper into the fog, allowing his soldiers to continue the assault. The hybrid was out there somewhere, and he needed to be fully alert to find it before it could corrupt his soldiers.

Necrodore waited to strike.

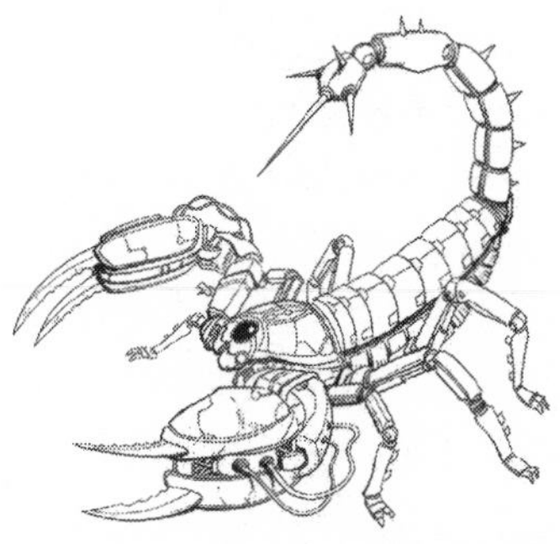

FORTY-EIGHT

"WE NEED TO MOVE out!" Lieutenant Mido Sharif alerted the remaining forces in the racetrack area. All civilians and wounded were successfully cleared from the site and sent off into orbit. Calls for help were coming through from the front line. Reinforcements were needed in mid-city, near the rubble of Ruby Platform. All forces were being diverted to that area. The fight in the dust might be the end of the war.

"My parents aren't back yet." Nella's signs were translated for hearing people as a robotic voice through her soothreader.

"We can't wait any longer," Mido said, and a holographic ghost of a green human was projected in front of Nella, signing what the lieutenant spoke. "I wish I didn't have to ask this of you, but we need your nezzarforms to join the fight. We have the Undriel on the ropes, but they could swing this fight back in their favor without you."

Nella looked over her shoulder at the squadron of nezzarforms waiting for her commands. This was her contribution to the war effort, weapon enhancements and soldiers only she could converse with. Even if Nella told Lahar and the others to follow the lieutenant, he couldn't command them in any way on the battlefield, and if she wasn't close enough to the human and auk'nai weapons, they wouldn't be enhanced. Nella would be surrounded by hearing people in a battle that required constant instruction and tactical maneuvering. She was well out of her element, but she was too vital to the battle to sit it out.

She had to do this, even if she was scared.

Nella bobbed her fist and signed, *"Okay, I will tell the nezzarforms it is time to fight."*

Mido put a hand on Nella's shoulder. "I know this is scary. If we had any other options, I wouldn't let you anywhere near this battlefield. You'd be on a shuttle and up in the safety of space. But we don't have that luxury. My men are going to keep you safe. If it starts to look bad, you cut and run. That's an order."

Nella watched the translation over her soothreader, then looked the lieutenant in the eyes and nodded with determination. Mido turned to the soldiers nearby and barked out an order. With the wounded tucked away inside the nezzarform ship, the field quickly emptied as soldiers rushed into vehicles. Mido walked over to a nearby truck and motioned for Nella to get inside.

Before Nella could step forward to accept the offer, Lahar scooped her up in its bulky rock arms and placed her on top of its body. It created a chair made of stone for her, and rocks floated up from its back to act as a shield made of chunks of hard boulders. It rotated around her, allowing her to see through it while protecting her from any incoming gunfire. Lahar configured itself into a crab-shaped body, crawling along on four long legs as she sat on its back.

She smiled at the surprise, then signed to Mido, *"We will follow you."*

Mido said, "Amazing," as he rubbed a hand against his face. He stepped into the truck, and it peeled out.

<By your command, we fight this enemy,> Lahar spoke into Nella's mind.

<With your strength, we can win,> Nella responded.

Denton and Eliana swerved around another corner until they were finally on the street where the Castus Machine Shop was. They had to work their way through the discarded cars and had taken a pause when Ruby Platform fell into the city below. They almost debated going back to check on Nella, knowing Cade was out of their reach. But they knew Nella was safe at the racetrack.

Denton would never sleep again if he didn't try to help his brothers.

As they came around the corner, Denton brought the rushcycle to a stop behind a truck. Something ahead was moving around, something big enough to eat up cars. It was an Undriel general—the one Denton had hoped to never see again. The scorpion-shaped horror that had snatched Corporal Rafa Ghanem out of mid-air after the devastating ambush in the Supernal Echo. Cade had revealed the names of the monstrosities, and he called this one Hilaria.

"What is that?" Eliana whispered as she watched the horrible machine work its way through the street. It looked damaged, but with each car it absorbed it repaired itself a little more.

"Probably the worst of them. I don't think we should take it on," Denton whispered back.

"It's causing the blackout in this area."

"Looks that way." Denton glanced at the machine shop. If his brothers were still alive, they'd be in there. He dismounted the rushcycle and helped Eliana off. Denton strapped the bag of auk'nai anti-resonators to his belt and pointed to the shop. "Okay, we need to sneak over there and get inside. We'll leave the bike here."

"What if it follows us in?" Eliana asked.

"We'll book it out back toward the Glimmer Glade," Denton said. The Glimmer Glade was a little spot behind the shop in a forgotten corner of the old colony. It rested against the old colony wall and had continued to grow unchecked by time. There was more city beyond the old wall, but that small glade was a little family secret.

"We'll find somewhere to hide on the other side of the wall."

Eliana sighed heavily. The plan wasn't great. Most of Denton's plans were only the beginning of a plan, and the rest was just hoping for the best. Optimism wasn't a survival strategy. Still, they didn't have time to figure anything else out. If Hilaria wanted to fully repair herself, the machine shop was a great place to do so. She hadn't seemed to notice it yet. There was still time.

"Okay, let's move," Denton said, gripping his rifle in his hand. They kept low and used the cars in the street as line-of-sight cover. They wormed their way across the street and made it to the front of the shop. "These jerks better be in here," Denton muttered as he flicked his hand over his soothreader, unlocking the front door. It slid open, and Denton cautiously looked inside, unsure if there were more Undriel in the dark shop.

Denton motioned for Eliana to watch Hilaria while he kept low and moved into the shop. It was dark. The whole block was, thanks to the horrible machine outside. Tvashtar marine tech still worked, though, and Denton's rifle had a functional flashlight just under its barrel.

"Psst! Guys?" Denton tried to ask the darkness without being too loud.

As he stepped forward, he felt something against his ankle. A rope snapped near his foot. "What the—" Denton started to question as something big and bulky tackled him from the side.

Denton hit the ground and discovered his attacker was his oldest brother, Jason. Jason grabbed Denton and forced him down to the floor. The detached wing of a starship swung low and smashed into the wall with a resounding bang. It was like striking a gong.

"Shit!" Denton covered his ears.

Tyler Castus, Denton's other brother, called from the back of the dark workshop, "What the Hells are you doing here, Denny?"

"I'm saving your asses! What'd you do? Booby-trap the whole damn shop?" Denton shouted, his adrenaline pumped up from his near-death encounter to primitive trap.

"All the power shut off, so we had to improvise," Jason explained.

Eliana shouted, "It's coming this way!"

The three Castus brothers turned to Eliana and said, "What?" in unison, then, "Oh shit!"

Eliana hurried over to Denton.

"Over here!" Jason called. He lifted a metal panel that sat just above the work pit. It was a small area designed for repair work underneath vehicles without having to hoist them up with a harness. Jason and Tyler had converted it into a hidden shelter. As they entered, Tyler blew out a candle. Denton, Eliana, Tyler, and Jason held their collective breaths.

The front end of the shop ripped open as Hilaria entered the building and roared. Denton and Eliana powered down their particle rifles. There was no way they'd outgun the scorpion queen in the dark in such close quarters.

Tyler held up a finger and mouthed, *Wait for it.*

Denton mouthed back, *What did you do?*

Tyler shushed him with a finger to his lips.

Hilaria stepped forward into a looped rope on the floor. It quickly tightened and yanked upward but had no effect on Hilaria. She watched as a bucket of paint flung itself at her from a high-up shelf, triggered by Tyler's trap mechanism. A splash of white paint slapped against her clawed arm. A blowtorch swung toward Hilaria on a separate rope as the trap continued to unfurl. The paint ignited but was almost unnoticeable to the monstrous Undriel. Hilaria hissed out steam, and the flames extinguished.

Jason punched Tyler in the arm and shook his head.

Tyler shrugged.

Hilaria snapped the rest of the taut rope around her foot as she moved deeper into the shop. She stood over their makeshift hiding spot and rotated in place. Steam and red energy seethed through her paneling, and a flicker of sparks burst from part of her shell.

Eliana aimed her rifle upward, but Denton put his hand on the end of her barrel and slowly lowered it, shaking his head. She could get a few good shots in, but Hilaria would outmaneuver them. Eliana wouldn't do enough damage to destroy the Undriel general.

Hilaria jolted forward and ripped apart the starship that Tyler had been repairing for a client. Tyler winced as the machine absorbed the ship, sheering metal and welding into place. Denton whispered while Hilaria was making so much noise, "We should move now while she's repairing herself."

Tyler slowly raised himself up and lifted the metal panel that concealed them. Hilaria was on the other side of the garage, seeped in darkness. The lights that came off her from her absorption danced along the walls. Tyler turned to Jason. "But what about the—"

"We couldn't get it working. We gotta leave it, bro," Jason said.

"What?" Denton asked in a whisper.

Tyler and Jason looked at each other, then Tyler whispered, "Me and Jay have been working on something. You know, just in case the world was ending again, like the Siren coming back or whatever. A little fun side project. Gotta admit we didn't anticipate the Undriel when we made it, though."

"What is it?" Denton hissed in a whisper.

"It's like a tank. Could be pretty useful. I bet it could take down this bug woman here too," Tyler explained.

Denton's mouth dropped open. "You guys built a tank and didn't tell me?"

Jason frowned and whispered angrily, "So what? So you could ram it into shit again like you did with the *Lelantos*? Or how about the Claire O'dine, you gonna ride her out an open ship hatch and take her for a flight? Nuh-uh! You'd just swipe it if we told ya!"

"That's not the point," Denton whispered, but their voices were getting louder.

"Guys!" Eliana hissed.

Tyler peeked out from the panel and didn't bother whispering. "Ah shit, she heard us." He ducked as their makeshift ceiling was ripped away. The four of them screamed in terror as Hilaria peered down at them with glowing white eyes and seething metal paneling.

She cackled and clamped her vicelike claws together in anticipation.

Her tail raised back, and her stinger glinted in the little residual light of the shop. Denton and Eliana hugged each other as Tyler and Jason cried out in horror.

The tail lunged forward. There was a flash of light, and the tail slammed into the ground between Denton and Jason. Fluids spilled into the pit, and lights flickered from above.

"What the Hells?" Denton looked up.

Hilaria's tail had been severed as she brought it down. She recoiled and backed away from the pit, searching the darkness for whatever had cut off her favorite weapon. "Who's out there! Don't be afraid…" She rummaged through the dark, forgetting the Castus family entirely. Denton peeked out of the pit and watched Hilaria move, only hints of her massive body visible in the shadows. Still, her glowing eyes betrayed her position.

Hilaria jolted again, and the loud sound of one of her metal claws hitting the shop floor echoed off the walls. It had been cleanly sliced off. Hilaria shrieked, and red energy burst from her paneling like a runaway train barreling off track. "Where are you?" Hilaria screamed.

A glint of light reflected off something unseen, and one of Hilaria's legs was ripped off her body and pulled deeper into the shadows. The scorpion woman screamed, her voice mixing with fear now. "This is impossible. Sh-show yourself!"

Hilaria was slammed down to the ground, her remaining claw arm removed. Denton could see shadows moving around the Undriel, slicing through the dark and severing limbs. A shape stood on top of Hilaria's body, pushing her down to the ground.

<*I'm right here.*> Nhymn's voice slithered into their minds.

Hilaria cried out in absolute terror as Nhymn slammed her claws into the Undriel's metal skull, smashing it entirely. Blood that had once been Hilaria's humanity oozed between Nhymn's talons.

As the troop of primal Voyalten destroyed Hilaria's body, piece by piece, the blackout ended. The lights inside the machine shop flickered on. The Voyalten warriors stood in the garage, each holding pieces of the ripped apart Undriel in their claws. They roared in triumph, an unsettling sound that shook the walls and rattled the tools on shelves.

"Holy shit," Jason muttered, his eyes wide and sweat beading on his brow.

"Hey, um…" Tyler started. "Man, we're screwed."

Denton and Eliana shared a look. Eliana said, "They are with us. For now, at least."

Denton, Eliana, Jason, and Tyler scrambled out of the pit and stood before Nhymn. She observed the humans quietly. Denton broke the silence. "Never thought I'd say this, but—thank you, Nhymn."

Nhymn bowed her beak. *<Show us where the machines are. We are ready to save this planet.>*

"Gladly," Denton said. He poked Tyler's chest. "You mentioned a tank?"

Tyler shut his hanging jaw and blabbered the words. "Y-yeah. I'll—hey Jay, you want to…"

Jay nodded and said, "Yeah, let's go get *Wilma.*"

Tyler was still disturbed by the site of the primal Voyalten but argued nonetheless. "We aren't calling her Wilma. She's not a… Never mind. Let's—yeah."

Eliana dug a hand in the satchel on Denton's belt and handed Tyler an anti-resonator puck. "You're going to need this, or else your tank won't work when we join the fight."

Tyler inspected the device.

Eliana explained, "Just stick it to the hull."

Tyler nodded and mouthed, *Ah, gotcha!*

Denton activated his rifle and walked through the ripped open threshold. The street was clear, and the lights had come back on. Nhymn and her primal Voyalten followed Denton and Eliana outside.

After a few moments, Denton and Eliana had mounted the

Claire O'dine, guns activated and ready for battle. The primal Voyalten flexed their claws and readied for the fight to come.

Jason and Tyler roared through the busted front end of the Castus Machine Shop, riding in a tank they had cobbled together from spare parts. Jason was barely visible through a small rectangular window in the tank's base. Tyler sat in a covered area on the top where he had control of a cannon and a magnetic repeater.

Tyler opened the top hatch of *Wilma* and scoffed at Denton, "See! Look! You *swiped* the Claire O'dine again! This is why we don't tell you about our secret projects anymore!"

Denton revved the engine in response.

Tyler huffed and jumped back down into Wilma and closed the hatch.

"Let's bring it to them!" Denton shouted.

The Castus family belted out a long, loud Ganymede holler as Nhymn and her primal Voyalten warriors roared. They took off at full speed toward the flashing green lights in the dusty debris scattered field that had once been mid-city.

FORTY-NINE

NELLA AND HER NEZZARFORM friends made their way toward a wall of dust, a fog so thick she could only see a few meters into it. Ahead of her was a platoon of Tvashtar marines, some in vehicles and others jump-jetting their way toward the fray. The sun was just beginning to peek over the horizon, the light mixing with the flickering embers of scattered fires.

Auk'qarn warriors and Undriel'nai battled in the sky above, dipping and weaving through the fog. Rings of light ripped through the pre-dawn sky, crashing against feathers and metal alike. Daunoren staffs twirled and peck rifles blasted. Below, particle fire was constantly exchanged on the street between the things hidden in the dust and the last remaining human forces.

Nella stayed in the back of their approaching platoon, ordered to keep safe by Lieutenant Mido Sharif. Her soothreader pinged her with general orders from the shared comm channel converted to sign. From this aft position, she could provide only simple support fire. Nella was no warrior. She had been a botanist, a woman of peace who cared for plants. She was a nurturer, not a fighter. She'd been given an army of nezzarforms, but she had no clue how to use them effectively—especially against an enemy like the Undriel.

The war before her was a silent engagement, as all things were.

She could feel the soft hum of Lahar beneath her. It scuttled behind the marines on four crablike stone legs. Nella watched as her nezzarforms joined the battle, forward units taking up positions and loosing bolts of green lightning into the fog.

Where is Cade? Nella wondered. She hadn't seen him since she dropped him off out of the main ship they rode in on. There was a general lack of corrupted Undriel in the sky but an abundance of shredded metal littering the streets. Nella prayed that Cade wasn't among them. She didn't sense his death, the way she had when Cade had become deactivated in the glass maze. Her brother must still be out there. *I wish he was here. He'd know how to fight.*

A barrage of nezzarform bolts tore into the fog, resulting in a few hot explosions obscured beyond the wall of haze. Their shots were too unfocused to accurately hit anything, mostly resorting to firing-for-effect and keeping the Undriel in place.

Another coordinated barrage of particle fire responded to Nella's attack, eating up the front line of marines once more. Nella yelped as an auk'nai hit the street in front of her, smoke and blood oozing from the wound that killed it.

This isn't working. Nella knew it. *We're just feeding the Undriel.*

At this pace, the Undriel would slowly consume the last remaining forces. This battle in the fog was the final push, both sides giving it everything they had. It could still go either way, and if they played this wrong, the Undriel would win with the few advantages they had remaining in their arsenal.

<*Lahar,*> Nella signed through her mind to her stone friend. <*We need to take action.*>

<*Let us give them a true fight!*> Lahar pulsed with a great green light, and the nezzarform soldiers surrounding him did the same. For a moment, the fighting slowed, confused by the stone army.

<*Let's go!*> Nella rallied her friend. Lahar converted itself into a panthasaur shape, shifting Nella on its back, so she was perched on its spine as if she were riding a rushcycle. Lahar bounded forward, using the destroyed buildings to bounce around and quickly move

past the frontline soldiers. Her army of stone did the same, converting into various configurations to rush into the fog. A barrage of particle fire tore into them, but only a few nezzarforms were taken down. Rocks exploded before Nella, bouncing off the shield Lahar made for her.

Lt. Sharif pinged her soothreader. "What are you doing? It's not safe!"

It was never safe, Nella thought to herself as she ignored the lieutenant.

The nezzarforms entered the fog. Lahar bounded through the debris and fractured buildings on all fours. A dark shape grew before her as they approached an Undriel sniper. It turned to shoot Lahar, striking its rock carapace a few times but not causing an explosion. Lahar reared back like a loamalon and released a charged blast from its belly, striking the sniper directly and causing a resounding explosion that Nella felt in her chest.

<Start with the snipers and give our people a chance to move up!> Nella commanded. The nezzarforms flashed their eyes in acknowledgment. Pocks of explosions lit up the dust as the nezzarforms carried out her command. *<It's working!>*

An immense shadow rushed Nella from the side. She had barely turned her head to notice it. *<Watch out!>*

Lahar dodged and whirled around to watch as the behemoth machine roared past them. It smashed into another nezzarform who was too slow to dodge the monster, and rubble blew out from the impact. The goliath machine stomped its bulky metal arms into the ground, ensuring the nezzarform's destruction, then turned to face Nella with its array of glowing white eyes.

Cade had spoken of the Undriel on their way to Odysseus. This giant must be the one he called Necrodore. The grand general of the Undriel army. Nella faced the giant and showed her teeth. Her eyes ignited in green light. The goliath flinched.

Nella told Lahar. *<Give him everything you got!>*

Lahar pounced onto Necrodore's left shoulder. Stone collided with metal, and Lahar released another charged shot from its belly. Nella felt the explosion as her teeth rattled and her bones vibrated. Smoke and shrapnel ruptured from Necrodore's frame. Lahar bounced off and spun to face the giant once more. Nella felt Necrodore's roar through her whole body and watched him seethe with red energy and smoke. His body transformed, revealing an array of miniguns. They whirled with violent intent.

<*Move!*> Nella shouted with her mind. As much as the Undriel didn't understand the nezzarforms, the stone constructs knew just as little about the machines. Lahar had never observed a particle minigun before and had no idea what the whirling metal cylinders meant.

Lahar cut and ran to the side, strafing Necrodore as a barrage of particle fire ripped through the debris just a step behind. The nezzarform wasn't fast enough to beat the weapon fire, and one of its back legs was ripped off. Using the remainder of its legs, it coiled up and bounded forward over Necrodore's head. Lahar let out another blast as it sailed over the giant machine, striking it near its back end.

Lahar hit the ground and pivoted, slower this time. It had been hindered by its injury. Necrodore transformed again, this time converting his massive frame into a large particle cannon with three legs. Red energy built up within his barrel.

<*Get out of here!*> Nella shouted to Lahar. Lahar leaped sideways as a solid, sustained beam of crimson energy blew through the fog, cutting down a group of nezzarforms and taking a few Undriel soldiers with it. Chunks of building debris exploded on impact. The beam was so hot and dense that it disintegrated a line of the fog, bringing a little more visibility back to the battlefield.

The beam cut off after Nella had made it a fair amount of distance from Necrodore. *He's too powerful…* Nella breathed heavily as she looked back at the grand general. Tvashtar marines brought the fight to Necrodore directly, and the goliath was occupied for the moment. The dust rolled back in, and he became a large shadow surrounded by pulses of exploding light. *That beam must have been what took down Ruby Platform,* Nella realized. She looked up into the sky and barely made out the shapes of the remaining two platforms, Amethyst and Carnelian.

Amethyst was almost within range to do significant damage to the defense force, should the Undriel decide this battle needed a nuclear option. Necrodore was a priority problem. Her nezzarform soldiers were doing a good job giving some breathing room for the front line. Diverting the nezzarforms now would be a detriment to the forward movement they gained.

<*What do you think, Lahar? Think we can fight that giant?*> Nella asked.

<*We can do anything together,*> Lahar responded.

<*Then let's do this!*>

Lahar bounded forward, aiming for the giant grand general of the machines.

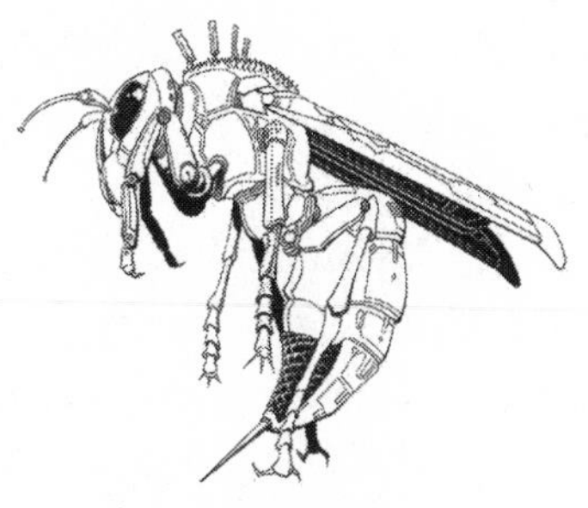

FIFTY

AUDEN AND TIBOR LISTENED to the chaos enfolding over the network. Snipers were winking out, and explosions flashed through the dust as the sunrise crept over the horizon. The stone creatures had entered the battle earlier than anticipated, and the Undriel were paying for it.

Necrodore shouted, the damped sounds of explosions and gunfire surrounding his speech. "The stone creatures are—" He stopped to fire at something, an explosion echoing his successful aim. "We must retreat!"

The Undriel would lose this war.

To come so far only to fail… Auden thought with horror.

The final battle was grouped in the mid-city. Necrodore and his forces were barely fighting off the last remaining human and auk'nai troops—along with corrupted Undriel, to Auden's disgust. Everyone was in one place, clouded by the slowly dissipating dust of the previous city platform destruction. A shadow cast by the early-morning light drifted into view. Another platform was floating into optimal positioning for a devastating attack.

The nuclear option.

Auden had enough soldiers with them in the skyscraper to pick off whatever survived. He assumed Hilaria was still out there somewhere, but there was no guarantee she hadn't been lost to the corruption. He couldn't wait for her to resurface. Necrodore would be lost, but sacrifices must be made.

"Necrodore, drop another platform on our enemies," Auden said.

Necrodore was silent. Auden thought he had been destroyed by the stone creatures until his voice came crackling through the network. "Our forces will be decimated along with theirs." Explosions and particle blasts echoed behind his worry.

Tibor said, his voice deep and profound, "It is the optimal path to victory."

More silence. Flashes in the dust below indicated the intensity of the battle and reassured Auden that this was the right choice. Necrodore finally said, "It will be done."

Auden looked to Tibor, expecting the AI to acknowledge him, but his attention was elsewhere. Tibor wasn't facing the window. Instead, he focused on the entry door to the immense council chamber, unmoving, processing.

Auden said, "We must prepare to finish them off after—"

"Intruders." Tibor's eyes flashed from white to red.

Before Auden could turn his head, the door blew open and particle fire cut through the room. A few of Auden's loyal soldiers dropped to the floor in fragments. The ornate glass window burst as lasers crashed through it, spraying glass out into the early morning air. Wind rushed into the room. Auden's soldiers returned fire in response, blasting through the smoke at anything that moved.

As the smoke cleared, Auden recognized the hybrid, Cade, at the front of the invading force. Corrupted Undriel flanked him on both sides, a mixture of converted Kamarian natives and humans. The corruption was on top of them.

Tibor ignited with fury. He lashed his arm sideways, sending a beam of energy into the upper balcony that hung above the entrance. The beam cut through the balcony at a wild angle and sent debris crashing everywhere. The Hybrid's corrupted forces were pushed back, some crushed in the balcony's collapse as it blocked their way forward. They would be forced to enter through the upper balcony opening now. They would not be stalled long.

"There's no time!" Auden shouted. "We must run!"

Tibor engulfed the nearest loyal soldier, absorbing its metal frame into his body and destroying the human component entirely. Auden watched in horror as Tibor grabbed a few more of their own soldiers and pulled them into his own frame without care. Blood spilled onto the debris on the floor as Tibor's frame grew larger with each soldier he ate up.

Suddenly, Auden understood why the Ovid AI was terrible for interstellar space travel. It didn't care about human cargo. It didn't care about anything. Ovid's directive was to find success no matter the cost. Based on the data gathered from the battle so far, Tibor would be outmatched by the hybrid and his corrupted soldiers. The loyal soldiers had become a liability, vulnerable to the hybrid's corruption. Ovid used whatever it needed to build a better machine. Loyal soldiers were less of a hazard as part of his frame.

The soldiers were too lost under their veils to understand how much danger they were in from their false king. They waited for their enemies to attack again, not knowing their greatest threat was right behind them. Tibor became a multi-armed nightmare of twisted machinery and bleeding metal. When he was finished rebuilding himself, only a few loyal soldiers remained scattered throughout the immense council room.

Auden ignited the jets on his legs and threw himself out the broken ornate window into the early morning sky. Maybe Tibor would be victorious, but it wasn't safe to stay near him. A building nearby provided an excellent hiding place. If Tibor fell, he could flee. Auden could restart the Undriel on his own. He'd lived as a hermit for centuries—he could do it again.

Cade Castus pushed the debris off his frame. The collapsing balcony had almost entirely buried him before he could even enter the council room. Cade checked his mechanical body, preparing himself to face an impossible enemy. His thrusters were operational, and the swords and guns concealed within his arms were ready for more fighting. The Reaper's blade was still attached like a third arm to his back. He was as prepared as he'd ever been. Cade turned to the soldiers who had volunteered to join him.

It was a small squadron of converted Undriel and Undriel'nai. He couldn't divert forces away from the final battle in the mid-city—this unit of ten soldiers would have to be the knife that stabbed the King of the Old Star.

Beyond the rubble and destruction, the sound of metal shearing mixed with the sizzle of flash welding. They couldn't see past the barrier of debris Tibor had created, but Cade knew something horrible was happening in the council room.

"How are we supposed to stop that? We couldn't even get in!" one Undriel shouted.

"Their king is too powerful," an Undriel'nai said and bowed his metallic beak.

Cade looked to the top of the pile of rubble. The ceiling of the corridor had been destroyed, revealing the floor above. Tibor's attack had blocked their entrance, but it had also created a new one. They would enter through what was once the doorway to the upper balcony. Lights flashed through the darkness of the upper opening.

"He's an impossible enemy," Cade said to his soldiers. "He and Auden took over the Sol System, and they are here to take Kamaria too. We fought him and lost there. We didn't have the right weapons to take on such a nightmare." Cade spread his arms. "Tibor has made us into the weapons we need to be to stop him! We also have one thing they don't have." Cade looked to each corrupted soldier. "We aren't blindfolded by lies. We know the truth, and that is sharper than any blade. We fight with clarity while they fight with confusion."

Cade continued, "We need to hit them from all sides." He

pointed to the blown-out windows that lined the corridor. "The Undriel'nai will flank them from the air while the rest of us hit them from the front."

The Undriel'nai cawed and moved as one. They silently passed through the blown-out windows and were lost to sight as they circled the building. Cade rallied the others, the Undriel who had once been human like him. "Let's end this empire of lies!"

At the sound of the Undriel'nai beginning their strike, Cade and the others ignited the jets lining their frames. They thrust through the entrance above the rubble and entered the fray. A monster made of twisted metal met them on the other side. Its attention was diverted between the Undriel'nai flanking it outside and the forces attacking it from the front.

Tibor's body filled the center of the room, encompassing the ringed table that once took up the space. The false King of the Old Star was a pillar of blades and guns adhered to the floor and bent against the tall vaulted ceiling. He could see in every direction and could shoot anything he saw. Long arms with bladed claws protruded from every angle of the towering nightmare. Guns were spread out through Tibor's form, creating a spread of particle beams in a complex pattern. Each of Tibor's appendages could rotate a full radius around his form.

Cade entered the room and crashed into one of Tibor's few remaining loyal Undriel soldiers, cutting through its core with his Reaper blade. The momentum of the impact forced them to slide along the floor until they were spilled behind a chunk of debris. The loyalist was dead, and the cracking of particle shots snapped against Cade's cover.

There was too much going on at once. Laser flying, soldiers fighting, blades slicing. Cade made a move, using his jets to thrust himself toward the center of the room. One of Tibor's particle beams cut toward a member of Cade's crew. Cade smashed into his comrade's side, knocking them both to the floor just under the beam. The beam cleanly sliced off Cade's Reaper blade, and he felt the simulated pain. He rolled over as he cried out in agony.

The Undriel Cade had saved grabbed the severed Reaper blade and hurled it at Tibor, cutting through the gun that had assaulted them. The beam dissipated, and an explosion rocked Tibor. The floor shook, and cracks began to form.

Cade thrust away again, dodging one of Tibor's claws as it came rushing at him. It smashed up the ground where he had been, eviscerating one of Cade's soldiers who hadn't moved fast enough to evade it. Tibor curled his fist and threw the crunched soldier's remains out the broken window, catching one of the Undriel'nai in its flight path and knocking it out of the sky.

<*TIBOR WON'T RISK ABSORBING CORRUPTED SOLDIERS,*> Karx said.

Cade uncoiled his assault rifles and shot at Tibor, blowing off one of the particle cannons on the King's side. Cade dodged another swipe of the bladed claw, then launched himself against the ceiling to avoid two more particle beams.

It's too much, too fast, Cade thought in exasperation.

<*WE AREN'T DOING ENOUGH DAMAGE!*>

Another beam cut toward Cade, and he shoved himself away from the ceiling. Dust erupted from the spot Cade had just left as the beam blew a hole open. More beams carved through the walls as Tibor's many claws slashed through the air. Cade's soldiers fell to the rapid attacks and the confusing pattern of assault. They were stuck in a blender of carnage.

<*How do we stop him?*> Cade's mind raced. He pivoted his body as a beam passed close to his face and hit the opposite wall with a crash. Cade unleashed another assault of particle fire. Another explosion on Tibor's body responded to his attack. <*It's not enough!*>

Something his mother had said came to his mind. "Computers only do exactly what you tell them to do with the data they have on hand."

The last of Tibor's loyal soldiers grappled with one of Cade's soldiers. They fired shots into each other's frames with devastating effect. Before there would be a victor, one of Tibor's beams cut through them simultaneously. An explosion filled the air, and Cade felt the concussive blast shove him against the dent he had created in the wall prior. The beam continued toward Cade, and he threw himself out of its path.

Tibor caught him with the backswing of one of his many claws, sending Cade crashing against the ground near the edge of the building, where the ornate window had once been. Cade felt some of his systems fail. The impact would have killed an average human. He looked up at the pillar of metal.

<Tibor has data on everything. He's been watching this battle from the beginning, using every eye in the network to learn and plan. He knows what we'll do and works against it. We can't stop him. Tibor knows everything.>

<NOT EVERYTHING!>

FIFTY-ONE

NELLA AND LAHAR WERE thrown away from Necrodore. The protective barrier that kept Nella safe was crumbling away as Lahar took more damage, and it struggled to get back up to assault the grand general again. Lahar couldn't move fast enough to stop the hulking machine from cashing its huge arm down on them. Nella and Lahar were pinned under Necrodore's weight.

Necrodore looked down at her and pressed his heavy arm against her collapsing shield. The rotating rocks ground against the Undriel metal. Soon it would break entirely, and she would be crushed.

Necrodore's attention was pulled off Nella, and the giant machine moved backward, stepping off Lahar just as a rushcycle blurred past. A green blast of energy lit up Necrodore's face, pushing the goliath back even more.

Lahar gave its last ounce of life then, falling apart into loose rocks and mixing with the destruction of the battlefield. <*Lahar!*> Nella cried out in her mind, but her nezzarform friend had perished. She sat in a pile of lifeless rubble. Nella pooled Sympha's energy but felt the hot sting in her mind as the dark patches infecting her brain fluctuated. She pushed harder, but she couldn't bring her healing mist to the surface. Nella felt useless.

Her eyes went wide when she noticed her parents riding a rushcycle together, circling Necrodore and blasting him with their nezzarform-powered weapons. Denton piloted the hovering bike as Eliana shot at Necrodore. Their close range to Nella allowed Sympha's energy to give their weapons more power.

More Undriel soldiers entered the area, forcing Denton and Eliana to take evasive maneuvers. They drifted around a fragmented building as a huge blast burst the Undriel soldiers that chased them. Nella turned and saw the strangest tank she'd ever seen come leaping over the rubble to her right. It smashed into Necrodore's side, and a magnetic repeater turret on top whirled into action, sending ultrafast magnetic bullets into the Undriel's frame, shredding his outer hull.

Necrodore whipped his immense fist at the tank, knocking the top off it and revealing Nella's uncles, Jason and Tyler. *What the Hells is going on?* Nella wondered before the immediate danger to her uncles was realized.

<*Help them!*> Nella mentally shouted in her mind to anyone who would answer.

A green bolt of lightning struck Necrodore from the side, causing significant damage to the Undriel general. A nezzarform bounded over the rubble nearby and joined Nella's side. It pulsed with light and said, <*Get to cover!*>

This one's name was Kalcyne. It relinquished parts of its stone body, creating a crystallized weapon for Nella to use. The weapon had similarities to the size and shape of a particle rifle, but its entirety was made of rock, glass, and lightning.

Necrodore wasn't finished yet. He grabbed the tank Jason and Tyler were driving and threw it to the side, sending it rolling end over end away from the battlefield. As they disappeared from sight, a trio of Undriel'nai swooped down from the dusty sky above. Nella aimed her new weapon at one and cracked off a shot, hitting it just below the neck. It toppled backward as the bolt blew through its body. The remaining two split off in different directions and circled her.

Kalcyne faced Necrodore, and Nella stayed back and picked her shots. She noticed her nezzarform army had dwindled down to only a few holdouts. They battled with Undriel soldiers, attempting to keep the area around Nella and Necrodore clear.

Kalcyne bounded forward and crashed into Necrodore. The giant Undriel fought it off, throwing his enormous weight around and bashing into the stone construct. Before Kalcyne could shoot, Necrodore unleashed a torrent of particle fire from the miniguns remaining on his arm. Kalcyne was pushed back, downed but not out. Quickly, it recovered and crashed against Necrodore, grappling with the Undriel general as he chipped away at it with his miniguns.

Nella noticed something out of the corner of her eye and spun to face it. An Undriel'nai rushed toward her, its metal talons outstretched. Nella's eyes went wide. She could almost feel the razors on her chest as the forward momentum of the Undriel'nai came to an abrupt stop. Large, bonelike claws gripped the Undriel'nai's wings. With a powerful movement, the metal bird was ripped in half and launched backward, away from Nella.

Nhymn hurled the Undriel'nai back into the fog, where more primal Voyalten waited to catch it and dismember it. Nhymn looked down her beak at Nella, her hollow eyes deep and abyssal.

Denton and Eliana drifted back around the debris, shooting at pursuing Undriel. Their rushcycle was struck with multiple particle shots and sent into a wild tailspin. Denton and Eliana were thrown off the rushcycle at the far end of the field. Nella's breath left her body—she was unsure if her parents had been killed in the crash. After a few heartbeats that had stretched to centuries, green blasts filled the dusty air around their crash site. Denton and Eliana both stood from the wreckage, firing at approaching Undriel soldiers. As their position became compromised, they were forced to duck back down under the wrecked rushcycle and pick their shots.

Necrodore hurled Kalcyne, and the nezzarform crashed down right in front of Nella's position. Nella looked up at the grand general of the Undriel, and her eyes went wide. Beyond Kalcyne, Necrodore was fuming with energy. He transformed his frame again, and Nella knew what that meant. He was becoming a large particle cannon again—his target would be the Amethyst Platform. Knowing they were losing, Necrodore would use the nuclear option and destroy everyone in one final blast.

Nella didn't waste time thinking. She rushed forward, stepped on top of Kalcyne, and aimed her crystalized weapon at Necrodore. Nella surged everything Sympha had to offer into her body and ignited with emerald fire.

Necrodore finished his transformation and aimed toward the platform in the sky.

Sympha's fire poured into Nella's crystal weapon. She pulled the trigger and felt the crack of lightning that responded. An emerald bolt of jagged light that was as large as a starship burst forth from her weapon, striking Necrodore directly. His metal hull sheered to fragments as his cannon ruptured. As Necrodore exploded, his body pivoted and fired.

Necrodore's particle beam lashed out and hit Kalcyne. There was an explosion that hurled Nella back and knocked everyone to the ground. Red-hot fire swirled in the air, and the fog dissipated rapidly. The early dawn sunshine spilled onto the battlefield.

For Denton and Eliana, the air hung still. Denton dispatched the last attacking Undriel soldier and looked over to Nella across the debris-strewn field. Necrodore was gone, only a melted pile of metal sizzling in the debris of a ruined city.

Where Nella had been, there was only rubble and fire. Denton and Eliana's hearts collectively sank, and for a moment, they were paralyzed. Eliana shouted at the top of her lungs and scrambled over to where her daughter had been.

Denton was right behind her, leaping out of the crash site and running. They frantically searched the debris for their daughter, calling out her name, knowing she couldn't hear them. Denton spotted something mixed with the stones, a hand covered in dust.

"She's here!" Denton shouted, and Eliana hurried to his side. Together they pulled the rocks off her body. Nella's skin had been singed by the fire, her eyes were closed, and she was covered in blood. Her right arm had been severed, and her left leg had been crushed by what was left of Kalcyne.

Eliana and Denton wept as they pulled their daughter from the rubble. Behind them, the battle was ending. Tvashtar marines and auk'qarn warriors converted the remaining enemy Undriel, freeing their minds from Auden's control. The dust cleared away and the dawn sunlight illuminated the battlefield. Cheering filled the early morning.

For two parents, the world was falling apart. Eliana felt for Nella's pulse. The response was weak, barely there and fading. She gritted her teeth and seethed the words, "No! Not here. You don't die like this. Stay with me, baby."

Denton looked around frantically. Eliana didn't have a medical kit on her and could only do so much for Nella. He shouted until he was hoarse. "Help! Someone, help! We have wounded over here!"

Nhymn overlooked Nella and the others. As the fog began to clear, she would be revealed. She'd be at the mercy of whatever forces remained. But she didn't care. Nhymn wasn't watching Nella die. She was watching Sympha fade away. She was watching the Operator she had accidentally sabotaged slip beyond this mortal plane. Nhymn wasn't sure if Sympha would return this time. She had barely been reanimated in Nella's body. Her ghost was weak. *Where do Voyalten go when they don't come back?* It was a question with answers that sounded worse than the Hush.

A few Tvashtar marines came to Denton and Eliana's side. One aimed a rifle at Nhymn and her squad of primal Voyalten. Denton recognized the soldiers but had no time to cheer for their survival. He weakly said, "Nhymn's with us, Inaya. Please, we need you to help Nella."

Corporal Inaya Akinyemi and Private Arlo Ortiz, along with a squad of faces Denton didn't recognize, joined Nella's side. Ortiz and

Eliana worked together to get Nella stabilized while Denton grabbed anything they needed.

Nhymn stood motionless as she watched them work. In the distance, in the tallest tower of Odysseus City, the final fight for Kamaria was burning bright.

FIFTY-TWO

<I KNOW WHAT TO *DO.*> Cade's eye ignited with azure fury. <*Unknown data is Tibor's greatest weakness.* We *are his greatest weakness!*>

Tibor's claw hurtled toward Cade, and particle beams lanced their way across the room in his direction. The building was torn to shreds. Walls were crumbling, and the floor was cracking.

The pressure inside Cade reached its limit. He thrust forward toward Tibor and let Karx's energy detonate from within. It crushed part of Tibor's base and sent blue lightning crackling through his metallic body. The floor burst underneath them, toppling Tibor sideways. As the tremendous machine crashed against the ground, the rest of the building buckled. Cade was caught in the chaos, along with the remainder of his squad. The corrupted Undriel'nai fighting from outside the building watched as it all spilled out into the sky.

Cade's soldiers activated their flight capabilities and continued their assault as the battle went into freefall. Tibor worked to reconfigure himself into something that suited this part of the fight. He was a roiling mess of falling machinery, churning through various configurations but never settling.

"Now's our chance!" Cade piloted into position near the rest of his squad as they flew around falling debris, rushing toward the ground. "Give him everything you got!"

Cade's squad used every weapon within their frames to relentlessly assault Tibor. Their particle shots pinpointed Tibor's various cores as they revealed themselves in the transforming mess of metal. Explosions ripped the King of the Old Star into fragments, each searching for the optimal form to achieve victory. The Ovid AI in Tibor's frame was thinking itself to death, and Tibor was helpless to fire back.

With one final, desperate lunge, Tibor created a long tentacle of jagged metal that lashed out. The whip hit Cade directly and pulled him toward the false king as the ground rushed toward them.

Jason Castus pulled his brother out from the tank they had spent years building. Tyler coughed and heaved out the words, "You idiot! I told you not to ram the damn robot. We barely got any shots in!"

Jason argued but was cut off when the nearby skyscraper exploded. The top floor burst and debris rained down from above. A mass of undulating metal blew out from the top and plummeted toward them.

Jason tackled Tyler to the side as a large chunk of the skyscraper's roof came crashing down in front of them. The brothers scrambled to get out of the direct line of debris. They ran toward a line of auk'qarn and Tvashtar marines, shouting, "Get back! Hurry, get back!"

The mass of twisting, convulsing metal impacted the ground behind them with a force so great it knocked all the humans over. The auk'qarn wobbled, some flapped and went airborne in shock, and others caught some of the humans falling over near them.

Talulo's nezzarform ship landed near the line of auk'qarn and marines, and the top opened to allow him to exit. He hurried over to the two Castus brothers and lifted them to their feet, keeping his eyes on the sizzling impact area.

Jason and Tyler hid behind Talulo and looked toward the crater.

Cade's soldiers drifted down, observing Tibor's impact site, unsure if the King of the Old Star had survived. Unsure if Cade had survived.

The crackling of fire filled the air along with the wispy drifting of smoke. The dawn sunlight revealed a metallic arm. It grabbed at the lip of the crater and clawed its way out of the impact zone. The soldiers lifted their rifles and took aim.

"Hold fire!" Talulo cawed.

Cade Castus pulled himself out of the crater. His body had been reduced to only a head, right arm, and torso. Deep in the crater, Tibor's body was merely burning scrap. The King of the Old Star was dead, his cores melted, his reign ended.

Cade rolled himself onto his back and looked up at his soldiers in the sky. He needed to repair himself. As Talulo, Jason, and Tyler approached him, the first words Cade muttered were, "Is my family safe?"

Talulo cooed, asking a nearby auk'nai to check in on Denton, Eliana, and Nella using the unsung song. Jason and Tyler knelt next to Cade.

"Easy now, kid," Jason said, seeing his nephew for the first time and the horrors that had been done to his body. Jason sneered at the crowd of confused, corrupted Undriel. He blamed them for what happened to Cade. He hated them.

Tyler whispered, "What happened to you?"

Cade didn't answer. He focused on keeping his systems active. He needed to self-repair but didn't know how to ask. He didn't have any more strength to push words through his mouth. But then again, he didn't need to. He looked up at Talulo, and instead of speaking out loud, he used the unsung song. *<I need to absorb something. To repair my systems.>*

"Stars and Songs!" Talulo uttered in shock. No human had ever held a conversation with an auk'nai through the unsung song. Talulo caught himself with his beak hanging open, then cooed. He looked around for something to use.

Talulo found the remnants of the crushed Castus tank. He tried to pull the machine from the tangled mess of debris it was trapped in. Cade's soldiers came to his aid, and together they liberated the tank and rolled it near Cade.

Cade closed his eyes. His chest expanded, and a maw with chainsaw-like rows of teeth emerged. The humans and the auk'qarn present gasped in shock, but the corrupted Undriel knew too well what was happening. Cade clawed his way onto the mangled tank wreck, and his body began to eat up the machinery. Tiny, spiderlike arms protruded from Cade's back and retrofitted his damaged parts for repairs. After a few moments, the tank was reduced to shrapnel, and Cade lay twitching on the ground.

Cade slowly pulled himself upright as the others watched. He felt like a monster, having to absorb metal in front of a crowd of people who didn't understand him. He looked around and found only horrified faces among the humans and auk'qarn. But Cade's corrupted Undriel soldiers understood him. They were him, and he was them. They were a people now, with a unique history. Their world began anew today, and they would have to find their place within it.

An auk'qarn landed near Talulo and spoke with the unsung song, <*The Castus family. Nella is mortally wounded—*>

Cade overheard, and he didn't wait to hear more. With his systems repaired, he activated his thrusters and lifted off into the sky. He soared over the battlefield in the direction the auk'qarn had come from.

Cade found his family as the dust settled and the morning sunlight spilled over the destroyed city. Nella lay in the rubble of nezzarforms, their mother and father at her side. He could feel Sympha's energy, so weak.

He landed near them. Nella rasped for breath, and although the marine named Ortiz and Eliana had stabilized her, she was still fading. Green mist seethed through the pores on her skin, and she looked like she was bathing in a small pool of emerald water.

Cade knelt at her side, his eyebrows up and his eyes watering. <*Nella,*> he whispered to her with the unsung song. They were Voyalten vessels. If he could do it, Nella could too.

She weakly opened her eyes. She was so hurt, her arm was missing, and her leg was crushed. She wasn't going to last much longer. <*Cade,*> she sang back to him the same way.

Cade huffed, and a tear dropped from his eye. Denton put his hand on Cade's back, and Eliana kept her eyes on her daughter. It was quiet around them. Only the popping of small fires in the rubble and the soft breeze of the early morning broke up the silence.

<*We did it,*> Cade sang to her. Softly. Calmly.

<*We saved the universe,*> Nella sang back to him.

<*It's no good if you're not in it. Stay with us.*>

Nella closed her eyes and strained her neck. She blinked away tears and looked back up at him. She didn't say, nor sing, anything.

<*You can't leave us,*> Cade begged.

Nella shook her head. <*I'm not strong enough.*>

<*Nonsense! You're made of stone and lightning.*>

Nella allowed tears to stream down from her face. She looked at her mother. Eliana's eyes were like polished glass. As she saw her daughter's face, her tears flowed freely.

"No, no, no," Eliana whimpered quietly through her lips, knowing she could do nothing.

Nella looked to her father. Denton smiled at her, but his eyes looked so terribly sad. He choked on his emotions, trying to give his daughter one last hopeful thing to look at. It was the face of a man who had seen his daughter come into the world and was realizing he was watching her leave it too. He shook his head and whispered, "It's okay, baby girl. It's okay."

Nella looked back at her brother. Just over his shoulder, she saw something rocketing through the sky, a streak of light leaving the city. She breathed in a ragged breath and used the unsung song. <*You missed one.*>

<*I don't care,*> Cade sang back. Nella frowned and shook her

head. Cade looked back over his shoulder, then to Nella.

<*Go get him.*>

Cade furrowed his brow and gripped her hand tightly. Then he placed her hand gently on her chest and stood up.

"Where are you going?" Denton asked.

Cade didn't answer. He looked down at his sister, knowing this would be the last time he would see her alive. He signed, *"I love you."*

Nella raised her only hand and gave him the sign back, her pointer, pinky, and thumb outstretched. *"I love you."* Her lips curled into a wounded smile.

Cade took a few steps back, floated off the ground a few meters, then activated thrusters. He raced across the sky, a boom following in his wake as he chased after Auden.

<*Go save Kamaria,*> Nella sang.

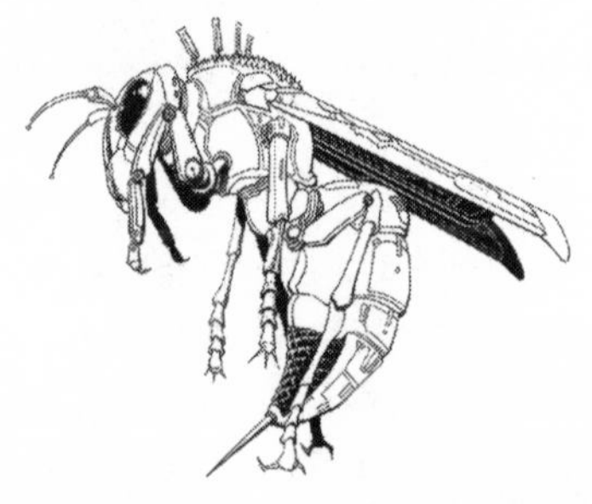

FIFTY-THREE

AUDEN WASN'T SURE WHERE to go. He flew away from the city. The battle had been lost, and he was the sole survivor of the Undriel war machine. The last vestige for the advancement of humanity. His beautiful creations were all dead. His army had been corrupted or destroyed. His vision was blurry now. Paradise had vanished in a puff of smoke.

Everything Auden did, he did to keep himself clear of conscience. He hadn't meant to kill Tibor with the Alpha-One frame or activate Ovid and cause a spiraling cascade of events that would eventually consume the known universe. But he played along with it, controlling it from the shadows, in the false hope that when it was all over, everything would just work out.

Now, he had nothing. That didn't mean he couldn't try for it all again in the future. He was immortal as long as he could stay hidden. Plenty of time to rebuild.

Auden flew east, back toward his hideaway on the Howling Shore. It was the place this whole new war had begun. He could collect his resources and find some other forgotten cave on Kamaria to plan his return. He sailed over the place where the *Telemachus* had been hammered into the planet. The first time the humans had fled him, he was perfectly okay with letting them have whatever star they wanted in the sky, as long as they were gone. That was the critical bit.

Lack of foresight had messed everything up. Suddenly they were right where the humans were going, years ahead, but the same doorstep all the same. Even worse, the damn wretches had made some new powerful friends after they landed. Maybe if Auden had dared to explore, he could have found the humans early enough to squash them before they became a threat.

He couldn't risk it. He was the last one standing then, just as he was now.

Auden felt hands grab his back. He rotated his head to face backward, and if he could have soiled his pants, he would have. The hybrid clutched onto his back. Auden attempted to bring out his weapons, morph a sword, do anything, but was stabbed through his center mass by Cade's blade before he could.

Auden screamed during the entire freefall that followed. He hit the ground like a meteor and bounced until he came crashing into the base of the *Telemachus* wreck. His body hit the broken ship's hull with a resounding, echoing gong.

Auden looked down at his body and discovered his bottom half was missing. It crashed uselessly away from the wreck, smashing through some trees in the distance. The hybrid brought himself to a quick landing in front of Auden. Cade pounded toward the last Undriel and grabbed him by his neck, crushing the spider-bot legs together and preventing Auden from popping his head off and escaping like a scared insect. Auden tried to bring his rifles forward, but Cade sliced his arms off, then stabbed him in the chest again, pinning Auden to the *Telemachus*. Before Auden could command his arms to pivot and shoot the hybrid, Cade blasted them to fragments.

That was it.

There was nothing Auden could do to defend himself now. The hybrid had removed every avenue of attack and escape. With no options left in his arsenal, Auden began to sob.

Cade's eyes flashed white-hot, and he seethed blue energy as he shouted, "No!" He punched the hull of the *Telemachus* next to Auden's head, leaving a deep dent in its already damaged surface. "You don't get to feel anything!"

Auden looked at the hybrid and whimpered, "What do you plan to do?"

Cade detached his sword, leaving Auden pinned to the wall as he took a step back. His face the mask of a furious titan. Auden remembered seeing this young man for the first time on the beach near his hideaway. Cade had been scared out of his mind back then, knowing he was about to become something inhuman. Yet, he hadn't cried.

Cade said the names. "Dia. Yeira. Talfryn."

"How do you…?" Auden tried to ask, but Cade spoke over him.

"Hillary. Jonas. Faye. Tibor. I know everything. I know Tibor was never in that suit for long. I know you had experimented on two little girls and made them into *Devourers*. I know you were so scared of the corruption you fled the Sol System and wasted everything!"

"How the Hells?"

"I know about Ovid, and I know all your lies. Including the one you keep from yourself."

Auden wasn't sure how to respond. What was this hybrid talking about?

"You really thought you were in control this whole time?" Cade scoffed. "You think yourself so brilliant, so unique, and you have no idea you were no different than any of the others."

Auden remained silent.

"You had no control over Ovid. It was controlling you."

"Impossible!" Auden spat the word, his repulsion mixed with horror. The whole point of Auden's project was to create a new version of humanity that wasn't a slave to an artificial intelligence. The Undriel were a ladder.

"No one ever feels it, you know that?" Cade said. "Do you remember your absorption? On Venus. I was there, Auden. I saw the whole thing."

"That can't—there's no—" He remembered being shelled by one of the fleet ships. He was mortally wounded and would have died if Alpha-One hadn't absorbed him then. Tibor's hollowed frame saw fit to make him special, to thank his benefactor.

"Alpha-One decided it would be easier to chase the escaping civilians if you and your nieces could fly, so it absorbed you. It cut you in half and absorbed the rest, just like it had with the other people of Venus, and Earth, and Mars, and the Jupiter colonies."

Auden was speechless.

"The difference between you and the rest of the Undriel is that you didn't need a veil. Ovid knew you would go along with its plan, and you enjoyed the lie enough to let it happen. You told yourself you were in control, that you were partners with Tibor, but it was never true. You were a useful pet."

Auden looked at the hybrid, knowing that what he was saying was true. In his attempt to free humanity from the confines of their own bodies, he had shackled them to a faulty artificial God. Auden didn't want to admit that he had caused the very thing he sought to avoid. He believed Ovid's lies because it was better than facing the truth. The Sol System was a victim of the ultimate irony.

Auden whispered, "How is this possible? How could you know this?"

"You're the same as all of us." Cade ignored his question. "Except you were pleased with Tibor's plan because it was similar to your own. You hid in his shadow and thought yourself safe." Cade stepped closer to Auden. "You've always been hiding. You're still doing it right now. You want everyone to live inside your comfortable lie with you. But I see you, Auden. We all see you. We all know who you are and what you've done. You can lie to yourself, but you can't lie to the Song of Kamaria."

A crowd of auk'nai looked down upon them from a platform high above. They peered at Auden, staring deep inside him. Their natural ability to read mental wavelengths opened Auden up like a book. The auk'nai could not be lied to.

Auden had never heard the Song of Kamaria in all his years hiding in his cave.

He heard it now.

It was a powerful thing, an orchestra of raw astral energy. He could hear the percussions of his judgment. The unflinching brass of natural order. The ultrafine woodwinds of galactic constants. The sharp strings of universal truths. The entire show played for Auden now, so loud he thought his head would burst.

Auden screamed in terror.

"You hear it," Cade stated.

It was a beautiful and horrifying thing. As if Heaven and the Hells had combined and agreed to punish him for his wickedness. The weight of so many worlds crushed down on Auden's shoulders. The soul of every person who was ever hurt by the Undriel judged him.

None of it meant a thing to Auden.

Even as Cade's fist rocketed toward his head, Auden knew they were all wrong. The last thing he thought as his skull was obliterated and his unnaturally long life ceased was how he was the victim in all this.

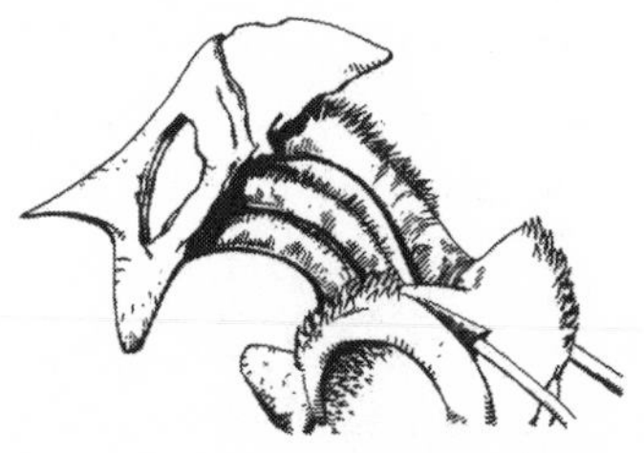

FIFTY-FOUR

NELLA'S FINAL BREATH SIGHED through her lips.

Eliana buried her face in her daughter's chest and wept openly. Denton was too struck to do anything. His cheeks were wet, with lines traced through the dust that covered his face from the battle. The crowd around her remained silent. Arlo Ortiz packed his things into his medkit, stood up, and left the grieving family to their mourning.

Nhymn looked down at Sympha's vessel. What a curious thing to become. Nhymn had always resurrected into her phantom form, but both Sympha and Karx remained inside their tethers. Would Sympha emerge? It could take years, maybe decades to find out.

I caused this, Nhymn realized.

Years ago, she had fought the grieving father on the battlefield of her mind. She'd beheaded Sympha there but failed to kill the man Denton. *The Shade*. Sympha had snapped into Denton's body at that point, and she hadn't come back to Kamaria until Nella was born.

Now Nella was dying, and Sympha was dying with her. It was a circle, but Sympha had no one to snap into this time. She'd fade away with the human.

Nhymn thought to herself, *I only sought the light. I did everything to touch the light, and I hurt others to ensure my time in the sun. I did this to Sympha, although she had done nothing to me.*

Nhymn looked toward the sunrise and felt the warm glow upon her wormskin and bone exoskeleton. Each star felt different to her. She had escaped the Hush and found Kamaria, then after her banishment from this planet, she'd found her own star. There were so many other stars to feel, so many lights to witness. She looked back down at Sympha's dead vessel and noticed it cast in shadow, the sunrise not yet high enough to shine past the debris of the battlefield.

She did nothing to deserve what I have wrought upon her. Light is nothing without something to reflect it. Light is only beautiful when cast upon beauty.

<*Go ahead. Give it a try. I think you're ready now.*> Sympha's voice was quiet. So far away, yet also near.

Nhymn stepped closer to Nella's body. Eliana held her daughter and gave Nhymn a look that could burn worlds. Denton reached a hand out to Eliana's shoulder. She looked at him, worry wisping over her face. Denton looked from Nhymn to Eliana, and he nodded slowly. Eliana hesitated, then gently released her daughter, laying her flat.

Nhymn leaned in over Nella. The young woman's body was so still. So lifeless.

Except… that wasn't true.

<*You see it in there, don't you?*> Sympha's voice again.

<*There's a light,*> Nhymn said.

Small and weak, but all light was precious to Nhymn. There came a song. A quiet hum, a young child sitting on a rock, tending to flowers. She hummed a strange tune, something Nhymn could feel. The little girl had dark skin and long, thick braids. She smiled at a flower and inhaled its sweetness. There was nothing else around the girl and her flowers. It was a closed-off universe. Darkness extended into infinity around her, but the girl didn't care. She bathed in the only light, and she had her flowers.

The girl turned to Nhymn and gasped.

Nhymn held out her claw and urged her, <*Do not be afraid.*>

The girl said nothing. She scooted backward a step. She made signs with her hands, and Nhymn understood them. She was a passenger in a mind that knew the signs and their meanings, and therefore Nhymn knew them too. The girl signed, *"Are you a shadow?"*

Nhymn looked at her claw and noticed it was semi-transparent. *Shade walking. So Denton has left his mark on me after all.* Nhymn said, <*I will not hurt you.*>

"Why are you here?" the little girl asked through hand gestures.

<*I want to help you.*>

"Help me? Why do I need help?"

Nhymn looked into the void around them. <*You don't see it?*>

"I see my garden. Don't you think it's beautiful?" The little girl signed as she forgot her fear and smiled at her flowers. *"I think they are the most beautiful things in the whole wide world."*

Nhymn leaned in, putting her beak near the flowers. She gently graced one with her sharp talon. <*I also think they are beautiful.*>

The girl smiled and signed, *"Thank you. I take great care of them."*

<*Would you like to show others their beauty?*> Nhymn asked.

"Others? What do you mean?" The girl looked scared again.

<*Your family. You can show them these beautiful flowers.*>

The girl looked into the void, noticing it for the first time. Her eyes glanced around the darkness as if searching for answers. *"But what if they don't like my flowers?"*

Nhymn leaned closer to the girl. <*It can be scary. When you show yourself to others, they may not like what they see. But if you keep yourself hidden—keep yourself small—you will never find the people who see the beauty in you. Beauty doesn't exist in darkness.*>

The girl looked at her flowers and frowned. She considered Nhymn's words and signed, *"It would be very sad to not find friends."*

<*It is,*> Nhymn said with far too much experience.

"If you will be my friend, I will go with you." The little girl signed and put her hand out. Nhymn slowly reached for it, gently closing her claw around the small, soft hand. She was careful, as if holding a

delicate flower, afraid she might slice it with her talons.

<*Follow me.*>

Eliana watched as Nhymn leaned over Nella's body. She was still for a long time, her claw hovering just over Nella's chest, unwavering. Eliana wanted to pull Nhymn away. It didn't feel right having the Voyalten lingering over her daughter like that.

Denton gripped her hand and whispered, "Please wait…"

The wind picked up, blowing a cool early morning breeze over the gathered crowd. Nhymn gently seeped green mist over Nella's body. Eliana gasped when she saw it. It was Sympha's power, but spilled by the least likely font. The green mist enveloped Nella and absorbed through her skin.

Nella coughed.

"Nella!" Eliana could barely contain herself. She grabbed Denton by his collar and pulled him close. He let out quick, shallow breaths as the smile grew on his face. They couldn't believe it. The crowd around them was silent as they waited to see what would happen.

Nhymn retracted the green mist as Nella weakly opened her eyes. Her wounds had been healed. She looked at her savior and smiled warmly. Nella put her remaining hand on Nhymn's skull, caressing the side of the Voyalten's head. She pulled her hand away and waved her fingers in front of her face in a graceful motion. *"Beautiful."*

Nhymn didn't know what to say.

Nella looked toward her parents. Nhymn stood and moved away from Nella to give Denton and Eliana room to embrace her. They hugged their daughter tightly. They cried and fiercely kissed her head and cheeks. The crowd cheered.

The celebration was enormous, but there was still much work to do. Those wounded during the battle needed tending to, and the city would have to be rebuilt after such a devastating battle. Nella's smile was warm and bright. Although her arm and leg had been removed, she would survive. Ortiz and a few other soldiers helped Denton secure Nella to a stretcher to be looked over at a hospital.

Eliana split away from them for just a moment. She hurried to catch up with Nhymn and the other primal Voyalten warriors. As she chased after them, she shouted, "Nhymn!"

Nhymn turned, allowing the other primals to continue their journey without her. She stood silently, a silhouette in the morning sunlight. Eliana summoned her strength to say what she'd never thought possible. She inhaled deeply and held it for a moment, then said with all the appreciation she could pull from her heart, "Thank you."

Nhymn said nothing in response. Eliana thought she had Nhymn figured out when she approached her on the ship named Lahar. Nhymn seemed like a lost child then, looking for her place in the world and thrashing out when she couldn't find it. But it wasn't really that. She'd had it wrong.

Nhymn wasn't the lost child. Sympha was.

Nhymn was sent to find the light, and she found it on Kamaria. She was exactly where she was supposed to be. Sympha was lost, affected by the altered dark matter in her seed ship. Sympha had forgotten her purpose, and since then had acted primarily out of fear.

But now Nhymn and Sympha were together. Their fears, worries, and confusion evaporated. It was time to move forward in confidence.

They were Voyalten. They had worlds to seed.

Nhymn looked at Eliana a little longer, then said, <*Years ago, when you put me on the spacecraft and sent me into the stars, I asked you if you truly believed there would be harmony on this planet.*>

"I remember. I said yes."

<*You were right.*>

Eliana smiled and looked down at her feet. She lifted her eyes and asked, "How does it feel?"

Nhymn looked to the sunrise. All around her was warmth, as the bright star filled the world with light. The sky gently shifted from pink and gold to a brilliant blue, and the breeze wisped through her talons. The world moved on, and now it was more unified than it had ever been. Nhymn looked toward Eliana and said one word.

<*Wonderful.*>

FIFTY-FIVE

ONE YEAR LATER

ZEPHYR GALE WATCHED THE asteroids tumble through space. It was a waltz they had done for billions of years and one they would do for time eternal. The world of Kamaria was different now, but space was always the same.

She heard the ping of a rock against the window and looked over to a man floating outside the *Maulwurf*. He had dark skin, bright blue eyes, short-cut hair, and a warm smile. The man wore his flight suit and a helmet, but not an EVA atmospheric suit—Cade didn't need one anymore.

Zephyr smiled at him and spoke through their shared comm channel, "You better not be scratching my window."

Cade gently tossed another pebble at her window and laughed. "Come out here with me. Just for a minute."

Zephyr looked at her terminal. All the prospectors were running perfectly, and their yield was up 150 percent. It helped that their mechanic could be outside in vacuum indefinitely without breaking a sweat or needing a lunch break. Zephyr could take a small break.

"I'll be right out. Just let me slip into something *way* less comfortable."

He laughed inaudibly through the window and floated upward out of view. Zephyr pulled herself through the *Maulwurf* to the locker room and put on her EVA suit. Even with a machine assisting her, it took a few minutes. She envied Cade for not having to wear one anymore. When she had everything buckled on and ready, she moved through the airlock.

When the outer hatch opened, Cade was floating there, his hand outstretched.

"I've never been good at piloting the thrusters on this thing," Zephyr admitted.

"Hold my hand. I'll guide you," Cade said.

"Where are we going?"

"You'll see."

"It's space. Where are we going?" Zephyr insisted.

"Oh, fine. Over by our favorite prospector. He's got the best view right now."

Zephyr put her gloved hand into Cade's synthetic palm.

After the final battle of Odysseus, there had been many discussions of what to do with the free Undriel. They were people, people with a shared trauma. They'd never wanted to become the nightmarish machines Auden and Tibor had forced them to be. Leave it to the Castus family to come up with a solution.

Using the Homer android that Denton had built previously as a prototype, all the engineers of Odysseus, humans, auk'nai, and Undriel alike worked together to create synthetic bodies for the free Undriel. They looked human again, seamless, whole. They still had code built into their cores that simulated human sensations—what was once a cruel trick by Ovid to sell a lie was now something that gave its victims their humanity back.

And so, Cade was human again in all the ways that mattered, but he was also more than that. He could do everything any human could do, but he could also fly. He could exist in space with only a helmet to protect his original human head. He would live forever thanks to the special stasis the Undriel had enveloped his organic components with. He could shift some paneling in his arms to access tools and other equipment he had internally stored. The most miraculous thing was that he could feel Zephyr's touch, and she could feel his.

They drifted down to the surface of an asteroid. Off to the far side of the rock, an old prospector drone dug away happily, functioning better than it had in years. Kamaria was an azure marble in the far-off tumble of space, doused in clouds and bright with beauty. It was awash in the solar rays of the star Delta Octantis. Its dueling moons, Tasker and Promiser, danced around each other as they orbited the planet.

Although too small to see from this distance, the space vessel called the *Infinite Aria* circled the planet. With the promise of the Voyalten Portal one day opening and linking Kamaria to the universal web, the need for an interstellar spacecraft had dwindled. But not for everyone.

After taking in the view for a moment, Zephyr turned to Cade. They were magnetically bound to the rock and floating freely as they watched the beauty of the stars. She looked down, away from Cade, and asked, "Are you planning to go with them?"

The *Aria* was for the Undriel now. This was John Veston's legacy, taking an arc that he never would have anticipated. John had created the *Telemachus* to ferry humanity across the stars, and it became their life raft when they needed to flee the Undriel. Now, hundreds of years later, John's grandson was helping build an interstellar spacecraft to give the Undriel a chance to find a new beginning.

The free Undriel could live in space in perpetuity. They drew in energy from the particles around them, and space was full of particles. The destination had not been decided yet, but ideas flew off the table. Some thought they should bring it back to the Sol System, for it was not part of the web and would never be due to the amount of rampant absorbing tech in the system. The free Undriel on Kamaria had relinquished their absorbing abilities to gain their synthetic bodies and not block Kamaria from the web. No one knew what had become of the fate of the Undriel living in the Sol System or what they had done to Earth and the other colonized worlds.

Others thought they should take the *Aria* and use it as a seed ship. Since the Undriel could live forever, they could take all the time they needed and cast their line out into interstellar waters until they found something new. If they wanted, they could even create their own world out of metal, a space station that could be forever built upon. They could even do both if they wanted. There was plenty of time.

Cade looked to Zephyr and shook his head.

She smiled.

"I want to just live for a while," Cade said, looking at the planet.

Zephyr noticed the chunk of asteroid in Cade's hand. "What kind of song is that one playing?"

Although the tethers to their Voyalten hitchhikers had been severed, Cade and Nella retained the ability to hear the songs in all things. The beauty stayed with them.

"You tell me," Cade said. He gently pushed the rock, and it drifted to Zephyr, tumbling slowly until it reached her gloved hand.

"I can't hear it."

"Sure you can. Anyone can."

Zephyr held the rock close to her helmet's visor and moved it around. Her suit made its familiar sounds, light beeps and a slight hiss of oxygen. She lowered the rock from her view when she didn't hear it sing. She wasn't surprised, but still, she was a little disappointed.

"Since we won't be needing the *Maulwurf* much longer, what do you say we make a home planetside?" Cade asked.

Zephyr looked at the rock in her glove. "What kind of home?"

"We could make a farm. Live off the land. Just live in peace for a while."

Zephyr looked back down at the rock in her hands. She considered the offer. Her skillsets might translate to farming well—processing land instead of asteroids, enhancing tools for better yields. The peace of the countryside was similar to the peace of space. Watching the sunrise and sunset in a gentle meadow would be a wonderful way to pass the years.

"Oh, what the Hells. Let's do it. What kind of crops are we going to tend?" Zephyr asked.

Cade thought for a moment. "Snapping cobb?"

"You mean the only vegetable on Kamaria that bites back?"

"Could be exciting." Cade laughed.

"I think we've both had enough excitement."

As she considered their future, Zephyr heard something soft in her ears. It was like a woman humming a sweet, soft tune. Gentle, compassionate, and tender. She looked down at the rock in her hand and felt a warmth rush over her. It wasn't just a sound. It was a feeling. Like the stone was holding her hand.

"I knew you could hear it too," Cade said.

"Are you sure I'm allowed to be down here?" Jun signed, his eyebrows up in concern and his lips stretched tight across his face.

"I'm an Operator. I call the shots," Nella signed with a confident smile, her silver metal arm glinting in the low light. They walked down the stone ramp into the portal chamber. She had grown used to her leg prosthesis by now, and ramps no longer bothered her as much. Combined with some Homer tech, the prosthetics made signing and walking as natural as it had felt before she lost her arm and leg.

As they came down the ramp, Jun saw the Decider. The giant, serpentine creature with long horns, hollow eyes, and four arms was working away at some alien device. A whole crew of Voyalten worked on the portal now. Sympha had resumed her role and even brought back the team she originally came to Kamaria with. Nhymn became an Operator in training. She would one day seed her own world, then find a way to bring the Hushed to it.

A tall Voyalten with a heart-shaped skull turned to Nella and spoke telepathically to her and Jun, <*Welcome back, Nella. It's good to see you.*>

Nella signed, *"I was tending the garden with my friend, and I wanted to show him all your work in here."* She turned to Jun and introduced him. *"This is Jun Lam."* She gestured to the Voyalten with the heart-shaped skull and signed, *"This is Sympha."*

He signed, *"Nice to meet you."*

Sympha nodded her skull. She floated gracefully on a skirt made of tentacles. Mist seeped from her and glittered in the low light. She was a strange sight but also a peculiar type of beauty.

Another Voyalten entered the room. It had four legs that ended in clawed hooves, massive arms, and long horns that stuck out of each side of its head. It had been digging tunnels around the palace, intersecting with the maze above ground. Nella pointed to this Voyalten and signed, *"That is Karx."*

Cade's phantom. Karx nodded his skull to Jun, and he waved back.

Nella then pointed across the portal chamber to the Voyalten with the sharp beak and singular horn on its skull. Before she could introduce her, Jun signed, *"That's Nhymn."*

"I guess she needs no introduction." Nella smiled.

The Decider slithered over to Nella and Jun and said, <*I have seen your garden. It is beautiful.*>

Nella blushed and signed, *"That's a big compliment. You must have seen billions of gardens during your travels."*

The Decider nodded. <*This planet amazes me, more than most. I had never seen Voyalten link with other species before. Nor have I seen any planet repel a rampant absorbing tech race. What you have found on this planet is truly unique.*>

Jun signed, *"You can thank Nella for that. We would be dust without her."*

Nella shook her head. *"It took everyone."*

She showed Jun around the portal chamber. They conversed with some of the nezzarforms and explored some of the tunnels. The portal was more like a hive, bustling with energy and filled with Voyalten workers trying to get the link to the web back online. The Decider predicted the work would still take years, but it would be done correctly with the help of the portal's original crew.

Eventually, it was time to leave. Jun and Nella walked back up the ramp and exited into the open air. Without the Key Ship in place, the portal chamber looked like an empty threshold. A frame with no door. The floating rocks that surrounded the pit would one day be filled with light, but for now, they waited for the repairs to be completed.

Nella had seeded the maze, and it was starting to show signs of beauty. When the glass had surfaced from below the dunes of the Starving Sands, it had also brought up fertile soil. Slowly, the crimson desolate expanse was becoming washed in green, and vines traced throughout the maze.

Penelope, the loamalon, patiently waited for them. She chomped away at some fruit Nella had left for her. Nella and Jun mounted the loamalon and sauntered through the labyrinth of mirrored glass. They enjoyed the fresh smells of spring. Creatures now lived in the maze, working their homes into crevasses in the glass and munching on the plants. A trail of lights guided Penelope toward an outpost on the edge of the labyrinth, where a mushroom-shaped building with an expansive observation deck perched atop a thin stalk of concrete.

They walked through a gate to a fenced-off yard and dismounted Penelope. The loamalon lay in the patchy grass, crossing her front legs to make a pillow as she flicked her tail slowly from side to side.

Jun and Nella rode a lift to the observation deck. This was where they worked now. Jun kept tabs on the maze and the creatures within it with George Tanaka and Marie Viray, while Nella checked in on the Voyalten and relayed any messages they had. Nella was an envoy, although the Voyalten still considered her an Operator.

George greeted them as they entered the observation deck. "Welcome back. How are our Voyalten friends doing today?" A holographic ghost transcribed his speech into Sol-Sign.

Nella signed back her response, and her prosthetic arm spoke in Sol-Common for George. *"Business as usual. Karx is tunneling with his crew, Sympha and Nhymn are reconfiguring the gate with the Decider, and the garden is healthy and growing."*

Maire Viray smiled and signed while she said, "I'm so anxious to see how the portal works. I know it's years away from completion, but I do hope to see it one day."

George nodded at her. "I'll be right there with you. We'll walk through together."

Marie smiled. "I'll let you push my wheelchair through, old friend."

Nella knew the elderly scientists were eager to see what was on the other side of the portal, but Nella herself had no interest. Kamaria was her home, and she was attuned to its Song in a way that no other world could provide. There were still discussions to be had about how to use the portal once it opened. It was the topic on everyone's mind.

Nella asked, *"Have you two decided what option you'd prefer?"*

George laughed. "It's not really up to us."

"I know. But if it were, which one would you choose?"

They had options, but there would be no going back once a choice was made. The Decider said they could open the gate fully, a two-way street. People from other worlds could come and go as they please. If that wasn't preferred, they could make the portal a one-way trip in either direction. Either allow people to come in and stay with no option to return, or let people leave Kamaria and never come back. They could also choose to close the gate entirely and take no part in the web.

It was agreed that the auk'nai would make the final decision.

Humanity, the Voyalten, and the Undriel had come to Kamaria unannounced, and they had stirred up enough problems. Talulo and his people would meet with all the other auk'nai leaders and various interested auk'gnell of Kamaria to make the decision. The meeting would happen when the Daunoren egg of the Nest hatched. They would welcome a new life into the Song of Kamaria and decide what its future would look like. George and Marie knew that day was coming soon.

"I'd like to come and go as I please. Make it a highway." Marie signed as she spoke.

George said, "I think I'd prefer the one I believe the auk'nai will end up choosing, assuming they don't close it entirely. I think they will pick the one-way ticket out. No more unwanted trespassers on their world."

Jun signed, *"I think it would be interesting to see who steps through to our side. One way toward Kamaria is my preference. That way, we can stay here and still see new things come in."*

Marie signed to Nella, *"What about you?"*

Nella considered the options for a minute and shrugged. *"I don't know, really. I guess I'll be fine with whatever the auk'nai choose."*

"That's a perfect Operator response." George smiled.

Denton Castus moved his welding torch slowly across the seams in the metal. He came to an end, and both panels were sealed together perfectly. The antenna had been repaired, and he activated it. A green light glowed on the antenna's base, indicating it had successfully sent and received data. Denton raised his welding mask up. "She's all patched up now."

Denton stood on the roof of the Castus Machine Shop. His brothers were in slings dangling on the outer wall, welding other parts back together. Eliana wore a rebreather and slowly painted a lovely sky-blue hue on the exterior. Michael and Brynn Castus sipped tea on the front porch and observed their work.

"I got reception here. Good job, Denny." Michael raised a thumb.

Brynn sipped her tea. "Looks like you're getting close too, Jay and Ty."

"It's not a race," Jason said.

"Says the guy losing the race," Tyler said as he finished his spot weld and raised his mask. They were putting the finishing touches on a year's worth of repairs. The shop's front end had been destroyed by Hilaria, but now it was finally healed.

Eliana removed her rebreather and turned off her paint sprayer. "Looks like we finished just in time." She jerked her chin down the street as some vehicles approached.

As the sun was setting, the street lights flicked on. The stars were blotted out by the city's illumination. The work area where repairs and salvage were ongoing was massive and bright. It would be years before Odysseus City was fully healed from the last battle with the Undriel. For now, this small corner on the outer edge was beginning to feel normal again.

Brynn leaped up from her chair. "I'll go check on the food."

A truck and an autocar pulled up in front of the shop. Cade and Zephyr stepped out of the truck, while Nella and Jun got out of the autocar. There was a whistle from above as a small aircraft floated down. It was a two-person skiff, shaped like a dart. Inside, Talulo piloted while Galifern sat in the passenger seat directly behind him.

The skiff landed in front of the garage, and the two auk'nai disembarked. Everyone greeted each other and hugged and laughed. Brynn opened the garage door and revealed a long table, fixed with various cooked meals and plenty of wine and whiskey to go around. She had even cooked up a few special insect delicacies for the auk'nai guests.

One by one, they all sat around the table. Nella and Jun had small tabletop transcribers that spoke their sign for the hearing people and converted their speech back for ease.

They enjoyed their dinner and shared stories. Eventually,

Denton stood. His friends and family grew silent. "It's good to be here today. I look around this table, and I see everything I love. My children, my wife, my parents, my friends." He tapped the glass of whiskey and looked for the right words. "We almost didn't make it to this day. A year ago, this planet was tested. Our lives changed, and the world changed. We had friendships to mend and enemies to fight. We lost many along the way."

Denton palmed his glass and thought of the soldiers he had become friends with. Cook, Bell, Cruz, Rafa, and Jess. "People who gave everything they had so we could survive, stronger than we were before. I just want to take a moment to recognize them." Everyone bowed their heads in silence.

After a moment of reflection and respect, Denton nodded and said, "A toast." Everyone raised their glasses with him. "To the light we never lost. To the unforgotten dark that binds the stars together. And to the harmony that warms the world."

Talulo added, "To the Song of Kamaria."

Everyone took a drink, and the joyful talk continued. Eliana put her hand on Denton's and squeezed, giving him a gentle smile. He leaned over and kissed her.

After their meals were finished, they continued to drink their wine and whiskey. Talks of the portal came up, but the humans were respectful to not goad Talulo into giving any answers on what he preferred. However, he could sense with the unsung song that they all really wanted to know.

"The Daunoren will hatch very soon," Talulo said. "After Talulo speaks with each auk'nai leader, the auk'nai will make the decision deemed best. Talulo alone does not hold preference."

Eliana leaned on her elbows, her wine perched between her hands. "It's amazing though, isn't it? Whether you decide to open the gate or not, we already know that there is an abundance of life out in the stars, and it's been connected. Portal aside, our universe has already gotten larger."

Cade said, "There's also the planets who chose against the link.

Who knows how many worlds the Decider visited that they were turned away from? Or the worlds that were negatively assessed."

Talulo asked, "But does Kamaria know for certain the link is peaceful in every case?"

Nella signed, *"Violent worlds are taken off the web. And access to resources is spread throughout the universe, which heads off most conflicts from ever starting. The Decider has said it's not always perfect, but it's stable."*

"That adds to my curiosity too," Denton mused. "Apparently, the Decider can make mistakes."

Galifern asked, "How does Kamaria know if the Decider isn't making a mistake right now?"

Zephyr interjected, "No one knows when they are making a mistake. That's how mistakes work."

Galifern cooed, "True. Although auk'nai can sometimes sense these things through the unsung song."

Eliana asked, "You both have had many meetings with the Decider in the past year. What has their unsung song told you?"

Talulo answered, "The Decider's song is deep and confusing. But it is honest. Talulo believes the Decider is a creature of truth. But the Decider only knows so much. It is the unknown factors that Talulo worries about."

"I understand," Eliana said. "We're all with you. Whatever the auk'nai decide, we know it will be the best course for Kamaria."

The conversation continued late into the night. Michael and Brynn were the first to leave the table. They went back to their loft across the street in the jewelry shop. Jason dragged Tyler off to the unit above the shop, then passed out on the couch. Talulo and Galifern were next. They boarded their skiff and left without saying goodbye, for the auk'nai never formally said goodbye.

Cade could no longer get drunk—or tired, for that matter—but Zephyr had a long day of travel from orbit.

"We should do this more often," Cade said as he hugged his mother. Eliana always held him tighter ever since the incident. He was more solid now, slightly different than hugging a human, but he was still her son. Her fear of losing him again was dissipating slowly over time. It would never fully evaporate, but it would simmer down to a puddle.

"You two are always welcome to come by the house. We'll keep the light on for you," Denton said as he hugged Cade. It was so good to have him safe. Denton still woke up at night screaming. The horrors of the war would stay with him forever. He'd get anxious remembering the times he had failed to save his son and sometimes took medicine to compensate for the panic attacks that came with the memories. But moments like this reaffirmed that Cade had been rescued. In time, he'd learn to forgive himself and acknowledge that everything would move on—differently, but move on regardless.

Cade hugged Nella roughly, using his strength to playfully swing her around. The two smiled at each other. Cade signed, *"I flew over your garden the other day. The maze looks beautiful."*

"It's certainly easier to navigate when it's not all mirrors," Nella signed, then mimicked bumping into walls and getting dizzy.

Cade nodded in agreement. *"We should walk it again one day. I'd love to see it up close. Plus, it would be good to check in on Karx. It's weird not having him around."*

Nella signed, *"I made sure to plant enough sun pears. We could go camping!"*

"Sign me up. Sun pears are my favorite." Zephyr smiled.

After a few more moments of chatting, Zephyr and Cade said their goodbyes and left in their truck to head back to Colony Town for the night. Denton, Eliana, Nella, and Jun watched them go. After they had left, Nella inspected the work done on the shop.

"You guys did a great job fixing the place," Nella signed. *"Could use a little landscaping, though, don't you think? Bring a little vegetation to the machinery."*

Jun signed, *"Do you know a good gardener?"* His smile was laced with playful sarcasm.

Nella stuck her tongue out at him.

Denton and Eliana admired their daughter's unwavering energy. They had witnessed her in the darkest times, and she had always been a light at the end of a long tunnel. She had lost her arm and her leg to the war, but that never slowed her down. Even after the war, Nella kept them strong when they needed help adjusting back to life. She had been their rock and helped keep them level. Nella visited often and told stories of the worlds the Voyalten had shown her in the illuminated orbs.

Eliana hugged Nella once more and whispered, "I'm so proud of you." Nella didn't hear the words, but she felt them.

Nella smiled and thought, *I'm proud of you too.*

Nella and Jun lived in an apartment close to the John Veston Kamarian Archive. They signed their goodbyes and left when their autocar arrived. Denton pulled Eliana close to his shoulder as they watched them leave. It was still hard to watch their children go. After everything they had been through, it would never be easy again. He whispered to Eliana, "They are amazing, aren't they?"

"They are." Eliana smiled.

"I wonder what the future holds for them."

"I have no clue," Eliana said. "And I think that's fascinating."

With the night at its end, there was only one last thing to do. Jason and Tyler were unconscious in the loft, leaving it up to Denton to close the Castus Machine Shop for the night. Eliana waited outside while Denton went through the practiced closing ritual. He made sure all the stations were powered down and shut the lights off.

Once completed, Denton stood at the entrance before shutting the final light off. He peered back at the garage. It had been decades since he had performed this task, a thing he had done every night of his young life on Ganymede. He remembered how Jupiter swirled through the windows and the smell of history that drifted off the shelves. He remembered hating his cyclical life, thinking he'd never break the monotany.

Denton thought of how far he had come since those days. A smile came to his face. He gestured over his soothreader, and the last light in the shop clicked off.

"Everything okay?" Eliana asked as Denton stepped out of the shop. He locked the front door and joined her side. Denton put his arm around Eliana as they walked to their truck. He inhaled the fresh Kamarian air and exhaled the words, "Yeah. Everything is perfect."

The night breeze swept over the Unforgotten Garden. A group of nurn honked and grazed in the dual moonlight. Tiny glowing gnats buzzed about, dancing in the meadow. It was a cloudless night, the sky a sea of endless stars.

Talulo inhaled a deep breath, breathing in the soft whisper of Kamaria. He was perched near the Daunoren egg, enjoying the open air. The auk'nai had stripped down the Nest, leaving only the tall pedestal. The new Daunoren would have the best view of the mountain valley. The remnants of the old *Telemachus* wreck had been shipped back to Odysseus City to help repair what was destroyed. A new auk'nai city was being built on the far side of the Unforgotten Garden, a place where all Kamarians were welcome.

A slight sound interrupted the quiet night. Talulo turned toward the Daunoren egg and heard it again. After a few more pecks, a chunk of the egg fell away, revealing the tip of a beak. Talulo stood and watched his new God emerge into the world. Its large head came through the shell, and for the first time, the Daunoren felt the Kamarian breeze upon its feathers. The Daunoren was not like other hatchlings. It did not wiggle and flounder about in its infancy. It was a dignified, graceful birth to the world.

The Daunoren's eyes were ready to see Kamaria. It turned its beak toward Talulo, and he heard its song. It was powerful, immense, and beautiful. Talulo was struck by its rawness and fell to his knees.

The world was ready. It was time to make a decision.

EPILOGUE

FIVE HUNDRED YEARS LATER

CADE STEPPED OUT OF the tunnel and emerged into an overgrown garden. He had not physically aged since he had become an Undriel hybrid, but he had watched the world outgrow him. Kamaria healed and moved past the war with the machines. The people that Auden had altered took to the stars, their fate unknown to Cade.

He wished them happiness.

Cade stepped into the garden, with its walls of tall glass mirrors shrouded in vines and flowers. It smelled beautiful here. He chose to walk, although he could fly. It gave him time to consider everything, for he had everything to consider. Cade was born a human, heard the songs of the Auk'nai, shared a mind with a Voyalten, and fought as an Undriel.

He was Kamaria.

A woman named Zephyr had filled his life with love, and together they tilled the land on the farm they owned. They adopted children and raised them to become adults who, in turn, raised their own children. None of them had to worry about a Voyalten tether, and none of them became machines. In time, Zephyr grew old, and Cade was happy to have spent the years he had with her. Long ago, she had gone to the place Cade could not follow. He was immortal due to the stasis the Undriel had covered his organic matter in. He missed her dearly, but he carried her with him.

He carried them all with him.

Cade remembered being there for his parents when they each had slipped through the mortal coil. They'd lived out the remainder of their lives in peace, watching their family grow in happiness in a world filled with harmony. It was all they could ask of the universe.

Eliana had taught children about Kamaria. After retiring from the Scout Program, she became a teacher. She handed off all the knowledge she had gained as a scout to the next generation of Kamarians. Her husband was by her side as her body slowly started to fail her, until one day, long into her twilight years, she didn't wake from her dreaming.

Denton returned to his artwork. He spent his final days painting beautiful images of Kamaria, the world his love had shown him. He found Eliana in the hills and valleys, her ghost a playful breeze, her love a warm beam of sunshine. Cade and Nella lay with him in the grass one peaceful summer afternoon and watched the clouds float by as he shut his eyes forever.

Death was gentle to them all.

But it never came for Cade.

He plodded his daunoren staff against the garden floor as he walked, creating a metronome for his thoughts. It was a staff he had made for himself, like many humans who made the pilgrimage after the Daunoren of the Unforgotten Garden hatched. His staff had a mixture of metals harvested from deep below the planet's surface intricately designed into its length. Cade had added his entire collection of asteroid fragments to the staff. It caught the sunlight and sparkled.

Perched on the glass walls of the maze were Watchers—Auk'nai chosen to guide the final pilgrimage. They nodded to the familiar man in the cloak as he walked under their gaze. He nodded in return.

Cade's synthetic feet were bare. He wanted to feel the planet as he walked. Cade carried nothing except the cloak over his clothes and the daunoren staff in his hand. He rounded a corner and admired the beauty of the flora around him.

His sister had seeded this maze. Nella had helped the Voyalten finish the portal, and became its gatekeeper when the Decider left Kamaria. She loved her job and nurtured the maze garden into her elderly years. Nella and Jun had children, who went on to have their own families as time passed. They grew old—some had left Kamaria, while others remained. Cade had not been with his sister when she passed away, but he had felt it happen. Jun had been her constant companion, and he followed her into the unknown dark only months later.

Cade carried them both with him.

Over time, the next generations of Castuses had forgotten who Cade was. The world had moved past him, leaving him in the history vids and mentioned as a topic of trivia during parties. He had not died—but in a way, he had.

Cade stood at the base of the hill that led to the portal. He remembered Antoni here. He had watched the young man expire so close to his objective. If Antoni had survived that day, maybe he would be living in the stars with the other free Undriel people. Cade whispered to his old cellmate, "We found that perfection."

Cade carried all the fallen Undriel with him and began to walk up the hill toward the threshold. The portal was immense. The floating rocks that had once surrounded the Key Ship now created a harness for a bright wall of light.

Two bulky auk'nai stood on the slope of the hill. One asked him, "Does Cade bring them?"

Cade nodded. "I bring with me those who have died. I will feed the next world with their memory. The stars will know their names."

The auk'nai cooed and stepped aside.

It is time, Cade reminded himself. *It is time.*

He continued up the slope to the portal. No one knew what lay beyond the threshold. Long ago, the auk'nai leader named Talulo had chosen to make the portal a one-way journey outward after much deliberation with the other people of Kamaria.

Once you stepped through the threshold to the universe, you could never return.

An auk'nai adorned in intricate wreaths of gold and gems stood near the portal, shrouded in light. She cooed and took Cade's hand. To his surprise, he wept. He smiled and looked deep into the light. The auk'nai stopped just a few steps before entering. She asked, "Is Cade ready?"

Cade nodded, his eyes dripping tears. Weakly, he said, "It is time."

The auk'nai cooed. "Then Cade may take the final pilgrimage." She stepped away from the threshold to give him room.

Cade watched the shimmering surface spiral into infinity. If he looked carefully enough, it seemed to extend beyond the wall, sliding away from him into whatever next world he would enter. Anything could be on the other side. No one on Kamaria knew if it was random or the same world every time.

There was only one way to find out.

He saw them now, the ones he'd bring with him on his journey. He felt Zephyr's grip on his hand. She smiled and kissed his cheek. She was his love. Nella stuck her forefinger, pinky, and thumb outward. She was his spirit. Denton and Eliana stood together and nodded their reassurance. They were his strength. His grandparents, friends, and even people he had seen during battle watched him now. They would never leave him.

Cade gripped his daunoren staff and hummed an old Martian lullaby, something his mother used to do when he was a child. He closed his eyes and thought of everyone and everything he could. The entirety of Kamaria was held in his mind.

He would remember them all.

"It is time."

Carefully, Cade stepped through the threshold.

DRAMATIS PERSONAE

THE CASTUS FAMILY

Denton Castus—*Mechanic, Scout, Civilian Soldier.*
Eliana Castus—*Scientist, Scout Leader, Doctor.*
Nella Castus—*Botanist, Vessel for Sympha, Deaf Community Leader.*
Cade Castus—*EVA Specialist, Vessel for Karx, Hybrid Spy.*

THE HUMANS

Jess Combs—*Tvashtar Marine Sergeant, Scout Security Escort, War Veteran.*
Zephyr Gale—*Rushcycle Enthusiast, Dart Coordinator, Asteroid Yield Analyst.*
Jun Lam—*Archive Custodian, Deaf Community Coordinator, Caretaker.*
George Tanaka—*Veteran Scout Leader, Biologist, Campus President.*
Maple Corsen—*Scientist, R&D Lead, Doctor.*

THE AUK'NAI

Talulo—*Auk'nai Leader, Pilot, Former Ambassador.*
Galifern—*Former Auk'nai Leader, Scientist, Engineer.*
Kor'Oja—*Auk'qarn Commander, Warrior, Second-in-Command.*

THE VOYALTEN

Nhymn—*Stowaway, False Decider, Hushed.*
Sympha—*Operator, Lost Leader, Silent Shade.*
Karx—*Tunneler, Shade Walker, Failed Bodyguard.*
The Decider—*World Linker, Analyzer, Historian.*

THE UNDRIEL

Tibor Undriel—*Trillionaire, Namesake of the Undriel, Figurehead.*
Ovid—*Prototype to Homer, Sentient Artificial Intelligence, Catalyst to Undriel Takeover.*
Auden (*Dr. Auden Nouls*)—*Disgraced Scientist, Corporate Thief, Creator of the Crowns.*
Jonas Necrodore—*Retired Fleet Commander, Behemoth, Hybrid Undriel Caretaker.*
Hilaria (*Hillary*)—*Serial Killer, Sly Deceiver, Scorpion Machine.*
Faye Raike—*Martian Soldier, Combat Pilot, First Undriel of Kamaria.*
Talfryn Raike—*Martian Sniper, Recon Specialist, Reaper.*
Antoni (*Tony Herman*)—*Son of Bill and Beth, First Wave Hybrid, Seeker of Ascension.*
Dia and Yiera—*Twin Sisters, Experiments, Devourers.*

AFTERWORD

When I first visited Kamaria, I was alone.

I walked its hills and observed its creatures as its sole witness. It was a world trapped inside my mind, but it begged to be freed. Throughout my childhood, I drew images of alien lifeforms and told stories of adventures on faraway planets. Each of them prepared me in some way to write this trilogy. I started this adventure in third grade, and what you just read was years of refining, evolving, retooling, and rewriting.

Now, others have joined me on Kamaria's surface. We've trudged together through the Tangled Maze, sailed over the Supernal Echo, danced in the Glimmer Glade, and fought on the Howling Shore. We were here with the people who found it. We walked the same paths they walked. I am sad to see them go, but I know their stories have been fulfilled.

I plan to revisit Kamaria again when the time is right. I go there often in my daydreams. There are many stories left to tell, but this trilogy is complete. I do not know when I'll be back formally, but privately I never leave this place. When I discover the right story to tell, we will have more adventures to set out on.

I am so glad you have read these words, and I am honored to have spent time in your head. Through time and space, we have covered much ground. Thank you for walking with my characters. With my greatest gratitude, I leave you now, but I hope Kamaria stays with you forever.

Sincerely,
—T.A.

ACKNOWLEDGMENTS

As always, I must thank my beautiful wife, Carrie. She has been my rock and my guiding light when I was lost in the stars. Without her, Kamaria has no heart.

To my mom, who has been my best beta reader and biggest supporter. She was one of my first readers, and I refuse to publish a novel without having her flip through it first. When Mom approves, the world is ready to see it. Thank you, Mom, for the inspiration and the insight.

To my dad, who encouraged my love for everything astronomy-related. I gained all my nerd genes from you. Observing Saturn and Jupiter through the telescope you inspired me to buy opened my mind to publishing these books.

To Treva, who helped me make Nella as authentic as possible. Thank you for enlightening me about Deaf Culture and bringing legitimacy to these characters. I think Nella is such a great person, and Kamaria is better with such awesome people in it.

To Daniel, who has created some of the best covers in science fiction as far as I am concerned. I am so thankful to have crossed paths with you, and the work you do is always stunning. Your work is the gateway to Kamaria, inviting readers to step through and enter this world.

To Jason, whom I owe more than just these words. Your artwork is incredible, and if I had it my way, I'd have you draw every inch of Kamaria. I am forever grateful to have had your skills in these novels.

To Dylan, Lorna, Claire, and my other freelancers, job well done! Beautiful work as always, and I know you may even be editing these words here. I hope they bring you a smile and do not disappoint. Your work on this trilogy has been pivotal to its success. I couldn't do this without you.

To Maria, for not only helping me write Homer and the

Decider, but for helping with my marketing with an excellent singing rendition of "So Far Away, Yet Also Near." I am so grateful to have such great friends!

To the book bloggers I've met during this journey. To Scarlett at Through Novel Time & Distance, Lorraine at The Book and Nature Professor, Athena at One Reading Nurse, Nick at Wicked Good Books, Alyssa at Into the Heart Wyld, Sue at Sue's Musings, Ollie at The Stone Cloud, Justin and David at FanFiAddict, Cam at Cosmic Lattes and Books, Rowena at Beneath a Thousand Skies, B-Man at The Tipsy Trope, Anj at A Pocket Full of Tomes, Isabelle at the Shaggy Shepherd, Elise at 100 Acre Wood Library, and to Timy and Justine at Storytellers On Tour for linking us all together. There may be more after the writing of this novel, and I hope to become friends with you all. You have made my trips to Kamaria more enjoyable. Thank you so much for reading. You are amazing, and I love reading your reviews.

To my fellow authors whose works I have also enjoyed. To Jonathan Nevair of the Wind Tide Trilogy, B. T. Keaton and Transference, Peter Hartog and his Guardian of Empire City books, and many more. I look forward to jumping into more adventures. Thank you for not only supporting me but for introducing me to your worlds as well.

To my readers, I have no more words, but I will try. You are the lifeblood of these stories. Without readers, words are just ink on a page. Your imagination fuels worlds, and I hope you enjoyed these stories.

Cheers everyone!

ABOUT THE AUTHOR

T. A. Bruno grew up in a suburb south of Chicago and moved to Los Angeles to pursue a career in the film industry. Since then, he has brought stories to life for over a decade as a previsualization artist. At home, he is the proud father of two boys and a husband to a wonderful wife.

For more about this book and author, visit:

TABruno.com
Facebook.com/TABrunoAuthor
Instagram.com/TABrunoAuthor
Twitter.com/TABrunoAuthor
Goodreads.com/TABrunoAuthor

Made in the USA
Columbia, SC
30 December 2022

75171940R00295